THE LAST TRUE GENTLEMAN

THE TRUE GENTLEMEN — BOOK 12

GRACE BURROWES

GRACE BURROWES PUBLISHING

The Last True Gentleman

DEDICATION

To all the true gentlemen

CHAPTER ONE

"Mr. Dorning, I come to offer you a proposition."

Sycamore Dorning was frequently propositioned by ladies who'd played too deeply at The Coventry Club.

By gentlemen in the same unfortunate circumstances.

By gentlemen who'd gambled to excess and thought to offer Sycamore a wife or mistress's favors in exchange for forgiveness of a debt.

Jeanette, Marchioness of Tavistock, owed the club not one penny, alas.

"My lady, do come in."

She had no escort. Her coach was plain to the point of shabbiness. Neither coachy nor groom wore livery, and her cattle were stolid bays, not a hair of white between them. Moreover, she'd waited until well after dark to pay this call.

All quite intriguing.

"Walk 'em," Sycamore called out to the coachy.

John Coachman merely looked askance at the marchioness.

"Will you see me home, Mr. Dorning?" her ladyship asked.

"Of course." Given the chance, Sycamore would have seen his guest safely returned from the underworld.

Lady Tavistock wasn't conventionally pretty. She had auburn hair, forest-green eyes, a nose shading toward well defined, and swooping brows that added an air of imperiousness. Sycamore had never heard her laugh, never seen her touch another in anything but strictest propriety. He did not want to merely escort this woman home, he wanted to *matter* to her.

She exuded such an air of self-contained calm that Sycamore also wanted to make her giggle, to hear her curse, to see her in high dudgeon and in casual deshabille. He was ever the dreamer, in the opinion of his family.

"Mr. Dorning will see me home, Angus," her ladyship called.

Angus spared Sycamore a glower, then moved the horses on at the walk. "Scottish?" Sycamore asked, closing the door.

"Scottish and former military, the confluence of all that is stubborn and loyal."

"May I take your cloak?" A conspicuously drab article, given how fashionably attired the marchioness usually was.

She removed her plain straw bonnet, stashed her gloves in the crown, and passed it to Sycamore. He hung the bonnet on a hook and drew the cloak from her ladyship's shoulders. She watched him from the corner of her eye when he stepped behind her, as if expecting him to commence a seduction in the very foyer.

With other women, he had done exactly that on many an occasion. Nothing ventured, nothing gained, after all.

"You arrive on my doorstep alone," he said, "late at night, in a disgracefully ancient conveyance, and you speak to me of propositions. Are you hoping I will make amorous advances, or fearing I won't?"

Her cloak bore a faint scent of jasmine, a light fragrance for a woman of such... such... presence? Such consequence?

Sycamore did not know exactly how to describe her ladyship, which was characteristic of her appeal. Her smiles were rare and startlingly warm. She was ferociously protective of her step-son, and at the card table, she was a shrewd and disciplined gambler. One of few in Sycamore's experience smart enough to walk away from both winning streaks and losing streaks.

"I assumed you would flirt," she said, "and you are welcome to make whatever overtures will flatter your male vanity, but I came to talk rather than dally."

"As it happens, I command equally vast stores of talent for both conversation and dallying, not that the two activities are mutually exclusive." Sycamore offered the lady his arm. His long-suffering butler had gone to bed an hour ago, and the premises employed no night porter.

"You would rather dally," her ladyship said, wrapping her fingers lightly around his sleeve. "You are an unattached, increasingly wealthy young man from a titled family. Dallying for such a one is almost a civic duty."

Unattached, like a boot discarded by the side of the road, a weathered wagon wheel left leaning against the wall of the garden shed.

"What I prefer might surprise you," Sycamore said, ushering her into his personal parlor. The fire was lit in here, as were the candles, but he'd chosen to entertain her in this room because this was his private place to idle about when at home. He wanted her ladyship to see his bound collections of satirical prints, the French novels any schoolgirl could translate at sight, the botanical sketches every self-respecting Dorning considered necessary to a domestic decorative scheme.

"Deadly nightshade?" her ladyship murmured, studying the frame to the left of the dartboard. She moved to the frame on the right. "Night-blooming jasmine?"

"My father was a passionate amateur botanist. We all take an interest in plants, my own talent being the growing of potted ferns."

Her ladyship eyed the massive specimen situated in the bow window. "We all?"

"We Dornings, of the Dorsetshire Dornings. I am one of nine."

She likely knew that, because her late husband had been a marquess, and Sycamore's oldest brother was the Earl of Casriel. Polite society kept track of its own.

"While I have only the one brother," her ladyship said, applying a finger to the fern's soil.

"You borrowed your brother's coach tonight because you didn't want anybody to know of this call, and yet, you haven't told me exactly why you're here. Will you join me in a nightcap?"

She dusted her hands together. "Armagnac, if you have it. Early spring nights are both chilly and damp."

Early spring nights were lonely. Sycamore poured two servings of a lovely year and passed one to his guest. "To interesting propositions."

Lady Tavistock eyed Sycamore over the rim of her glass as she sipped. "This is delightful." Her second taste was less cautious. "You have something I want."

Were Sycamore not tired, were he not missing the most recently married of his many recently married siblings, he might have replied with a reference to passionate kisses, a comfortable bed, or talented hands.

But he was tired *and lonely,* and no longer the randy boy her ladyship would dismiss at a glance.

"I have something you want." He gestured to a pair of reading chairs near the hearth. "Or do I have something you need?"

Her ladyship settled gracefully into a chair, glass in hand. "Want assuredly, need possibly. I don't know as I've ever seen a collection of knives decorating an informal parlor before."

Sycamore took the other reading chair. "My brother claimed displaying them elsewhere was in poor taste." And why had she saved remarking on the blades fanned into a gleaming half circle on the wall for after her polite notice of ferns and botanical prints?

"You are reported to be quite handy with a knife, Mr. Dorning."

By firelight, her hair was a palette of myriad colors. Gold, russet, garnet... If asked, Sycamore would have said her hair was the color of a midsummer night bonfire, while her hands wrapped around the crystal glass put him in mind of purring cats and sleepy cuddles.

"I am skilled with a blade," Sycamore said, imbuing that statement with not even a hint of prurience.

"Will you teach me how to throw a knife?"

Of all the things she might have asked of him, that request hadn't been even remotely near the list.

"Why, my lady?" Women took up the bow and arrow for diversion. They might on rare occasion participate in a shoot, particularly on their own family's land. A few women rode to hounds, usually in the second or third flight.

But knife throwing?

"You ask me why." She set her drink aside. "Because a knife doesn't have to be kept dry at all times and loaded with powder and shot prior to each use. Because a knife can be carried in a reticule or pocket or sheathed against the body. A knife is silent and can be used again if the first throw misses—or if it doesn't."

Sycamore had only two sisters, and neither of them had much use for their Dorning menfolk. His mother had been a perpetually disappointed and disappointing virago, and by his choice, his lovers were more interested in pleasure than the man providing it.

He did not, in other words, have much experience fathoming the labyrinth of the adult female mind to any useful depth.

"I understand the allure of knives," he said, "but why do *you* want to acquire skill with them?"

She picked up her drink and took another visual inventory of Sycamore's private parlor. "I am not in the habit of explaining myself. Will you teach me or not?"

Her ladyship was very good at the subtle set-down, but not quite good enough. "You are asking not only for instruction, but for my utmost discretion."

"I am."

She was a widowed marchioness of substantial means and considerable self-possession, and she wanted to learn—in secret—how to make a knife throw count.

"You can't acquire the skill in a night," Sycamore said. "Not in a week of nights." Though practice would result in progress, a lot of practice would be difficult for her to manage if she was bent on secrecy.

"Then we'd best get started, hadn't we, Mr. Dorning?"

Would she be all business in bed too? No kissing, no touching her hair, God forbid anybody broke a sweat? For her sake, he hoped not.

"If I spend thankless hours teaching you the basics of how to handle a blade, what do you offer me in return?"

She turned a frankly curious gaze on him. "What do you want, Mr. Dorning?"

Sycamore wanted his brother Ash to take the same interest in The Coventry Club that he had before matrimony had turned Ash into a doting dimwit.

He wanted Casriel to get his lordly arse—and wife and offspring —up to Town to vote his damned seat like a good little earl.

He wanted brother Oak to extricate himself from the embrace of rural Hampshire—and the embrace of marital bliss—and come to London to do some lecturing at the Royal Academy.

Of course, a romp or twenty with the marchioness would have been lovely, too, but romping undertaken in return for services rendered wasn't romping at all.

"Can you buy out Jonathan Tresham's interest in the Coventry?" Sycamore asked.

"One wondered what the arrangement was. Yes, I can, but no, I will not. I am not a quick study, Mr. Dorning, but I am determined to acquire skill with a knife."

She was also very good at keeping her emotions to herself, as any successful gambler must be.

Sycamore crossed an ankle over a knee. "You are doubtless a paragon in many regards, my lady. I am not a paragon, though I am a gentleman. I will show you the rudiments of the art of knife-throwing as a favor between friends."

She wrinkled her nose, probably because Sycamore had referred to himself as her friend. "How good are you?"

Sycamore smiled and sat forward as if to impart a confidence. In the next instant, the blade he carried in his left boot was silently quivering in the middle of the cork target across the room.

"I am that good."

Her ladyship studied the blade until it was still. "You didn't even look." The marchioness, however, swiveled her gaze to Sycamore. She inspected him, no longer visually dismissing him, evading his eyes, or turning a wary regard on him.

"My dear marchioness, *looking* rather destroys the element of surprise, which is half the beauty of a well-thrown knife."

She crossed the room and withdrew the blade. "Teach me to do this, and you can demand almost anything of me in return."

Almost. A prudent woman. "You hate to be in anybody's debt, don't you?" Sycamore had made her a loan once before, at a rural house party, and she had repaid him to the penny within days of the house party's conclusion. The sum had covered her step-son's gambling debts, and what consideration she had extracted from the hapless lad was a secret between her and his young lordship.

She passed Sycamore his knife and watched as he returned it to the sheath in his boot. "I loathe being in debt to anybody," she said, resuming her seat, "particularly a man. Women have little enough power, and a woman in debt is a woman all but asking to be exploited."

Sycamore understood an independent nature, but not the bitterness behind her ladyship's words. He also understood pride, however, and to become her ladyship's instructor, he would have to surrender some scintilla of his own pride.

He had a bit to spare, after all. "Here is the favor I will accept in return for teaching you what you seek to know: Once a week, we will meet at the Coventry to practice throwing, and then you will dine with me on the premises."

"Supper?" With a single word, she conjured a reference to all manner of hedonistic excesses.

"Food, wine, conversation. I can inflict some of my laughable French on you. You can tell me who is walking out with whom."

The wariness had returned to her gaze, muted by curiosity. "You are serious?"

"I do not dissemble, even when my family dearly wishes I would." Her ladyship still looked doubtful, so Sycamore resigned himself to *explaining* his situation to her.

"My brother Ash is my business partner, or he used to be. Now he's too besotted with the wedded state to do more than keep an impatient eye on me at the club—not an eye on the club, mind you, an eye *on me*. When we talk, it's 'Della says,' 'Della hopes,' and 'my dear Della tells me.' I love my sister by marriage—I love the entire herd of them—but Della has entirely made off with my dearest brother."

Sycamore rose to pace rather than sit passively before her ladyship's scrutiny. "I cannot gossip with anybody about club business, or with nobody but Tresham, and with him, it's 'Theodosia believes,' 'my darling Theo would say,' and more of same. Casriel is the worst of the lot. He has daughters, which adds entire rhapsodic chapters to his litany."

Sycamore paused before the corkboard, which would soon have to be replaced because the center was too pitted from multiple throws hitting the same mark.

"I spend almost every night," he said, "amid the witty and wealthy, and while I can flirt, make small talk, and flatter until my eyelashes fall off, that's not the same as a good meal with a pleasant companion."

Her ladyship rose. She was tallish, but more than that, she carried herself regally. "I am rarely pleasant."

"One of your many fine attributes." Also one of Sycamore's. "You are intelligent, well-read, honest, and knowledgeable about polite society. Let's give it a month, shall we? The Coventry is closed on Sundays. We'll have privacy there and some room to practice."

She had come to make him a proposition, but he'd purposely put himself in the position of one making an offer.

"Four lessons and four suppers?"

"Or I can simply teach you to throw." And thus put her subtly in his debt.

She stuck out a hand. "We have a bargain, Mr. Dorning. I will meet you at the side entrance to the Coventry at five on Sunday."

Sycamore shook, pugilist fashion, then bowed over her hand, gentleman fashion. "I will look forward to it. Shall I call for my coach, or would you rather I walk you home?" He was several inches over six feet, though those inches had taken forever to show up. He also fenced, rode, and boxed and considered himself a match for any footpad, even without his knives.

"I prefer to walk, please."

The faster option, given that a groom and coachman would have to be roused and the horses put to. Also the less conspicuous choice.

Sycamore contented himself with the role of gallant escort and parted from the lady at her front door. He made sure the night porter did not see him lurking at the foot of the terrace steps, and when her ladyship was safely behind a locked door, Sycamore returned to his own address by wandering several streets out of his way.

Two conclusions made his midnight stroll a thoughtful undertaking. First, in her determination to learn the art of the knife, her ladyship revealed a fear for her safety. Because she was neither fanciful nor stupid, Sycamore thus feared for her safety as well.

Second, whoever had followed her ladyship from Sycamore's rooms had felt it unnecessary to follow Sycamore on his journey home.

~

SYCAMORE DORNING WAS like the knives he wielded—a

dangerous ally. Jeanette had listed for him the advantages of the knife as a weapon, but she'd not mentioned the primary disadvantage: A knife had no loyalty and could become the weapon of anybody with the speed and skill to throw it. Guns, once fired, were of little use, particularly if cast into a handy patch of mud.

Jeanette had thought long and hard about paying a call on Mr. Dorning, and in the cold light of a spring morning, she was glad she had. Maybe even a little proud of herself for taking that much initiative.

"Good morning, Step-mama." Trevor, Marquess of Tavistock, strode into the breakfast parlor looking like the embodiment of young English manhood at its finest. He had his father's blond hair, height, and blue eyes, but he lacked the late titleholder's cold heart. Trevor had been a good boy thanks mostly to his tutors and to Jeanette's ingenuity.

He was well on his way to becoming a good man. "Good morning, Tavistock. How was your ride?"

"Splendid. I met Jerome in the park." His lordship piled half his plate full of eggs, the other half full of crispy strips of bacon. "He invited me to his club for supper."

The less said about Trevor's sole male cousin, the better. "Have you given any more thought to returning to your studies?" Supper at Jerome's club would turn into a few hands of cards, which would turn into Trevor owing money to Jerome or to one of Jerome's dodgy friends.

Trevor set his plate at the head of the table. Jeanette had abdicated that position when Trevor had turned eighteen, though when she was eating alone—which she did most evenings at home—she sometimes moved her place setting to its former location.

Widows were permitted a few eccentricities, after all.

"I don't know as I shall return to my studies," Trevor said, setting a full rack of toast by his plate. "Butter?"

Jeanette passed him the dish, knowing it would be empty before Trevor finished eating. He was an active young man, and his appetite was bottomless. His father, by contrast, had been a sybarite, preferring a few elegant pleasures indulged with exquisite focus. Havana cheroots, silk shirts, specific French vintages, and half-wild bloodstock.

"You have never said exactly why you left university, Trevor." And Jeanette hadn't until now asked him directly.

"Boredom," he said, scraping butter over his toast. "Two years of Latin, Greek, natural philosophy, mathematics, and great literature after years of same from my tutors and public school were enough to impart a general flavor. Might I have the tea?"

Trevor was such a dear, and such a bad liar. "You are scholarly by nature, sir. You did not leave out of boredom."

He made himself a sandwich of scrambled eggs, bacon, and buttered toast—university-boy fare. "I did, actually. One can study anywhere, and our library here in Town is ample enough that I will always find something interesting to read, but the company at school..." He munched thoughtfully. "How many times am I to laugh at the same fart jokes? How often should I flirt pointlessly with the same harried tavern maids who smile at me because they would rather earn coin with a smile than through more intimate means? How many references to male anatomy or female anatomy is one conversation supposed to hold? I found it all pointless."

That, Jeanette could believe. Trevor's calling lay, if anywhere, in the Church. He was an earnest soul who cared for others. He had a wide streak of decency and was generally liked. He had not, however, referred to making any good friends in his two years among the philistines.

And alas for him, he was a marquess and fated to sit in the Lords.

"Is the company at Jerome's club so much more sophisticated?" she asked, passing over the teapot.

"A hit, Step-mama, but that lot does occasionally discuss politics. What is the point of passing labor reforms if Parliament won't tuck along any money for enforcing the new rules? Factory hours can be reduced, but then somebody needs to drop 'round and make sure the place is actually closing when it is supposed to."

Great Jehovah's hoary beard. Jeanette mentally chided herself for underestimating Jerome's choice of companions, a potentially dangerous mistake.

"That's what you'll discuss with Jerome?"

"Well, no." Trevor's smile was bashful. "Jerome is smitten with the Chalfont heiress. I will have to hear about her ankles and her ears, I'm sure. Noble brows might earn a mention as well, along with a discreet reference to her settlements."

How different that lament was from Sycamore Dorning's bewildered late-night confession. He loved his sisters-in-law, clearly, and he resented them to a lady.

"Has your fancy been taken by any particular ears or ankles?"

The Tavistock succession hung by a pair of slender threads, namely, Trevor and Jerome, though Jerome's father was still extant. Lord Beardsley Vincent was loyally, if not exactly happily, married, and his lady wife was no longer of an age to bear children.

"Allow me some privacy, Step-mama," Trevor said. "You cannot shoo me back to school one moment and shoo me into parson's mousetrap the next."

From Trevor, that was a rebuke, albeit a gentle one. Jeanette was torn between a need to protect Trevor from the heartaches adulthood inevitably brought and resentment of her role as his sole parent, counselor, and authority figure.

"I want you to be happy," she said, sipping tepid tea and searching for honesty. "I ask about the young ladies because I suspect Uncle Beardsley lectures you endlessly to take a wife and secure the succession. There's time for that Trevor, time later."

"Uncle Beardsley's letters to me at university were... I sometimes think Aunt Viola wrote them. They sound very like the letters she sends to Jerome. She has his allowance all budgeted, right down to which chop shop should have his patronage even though it's five streets away from his rooms. If he can save tuppence by walking the distance and eating cold hash, then walk the distance he must."

The Vincent family had profited enormously over the past century from Britain's preoccupation with conquest and war. Soldiers had to be clothed, fed, armed, and shod, and every phase of that undertaking meant profit for a few and expense for the ratepayers. Six marquesses ago, when the Dutch were still hostile to English shipping, the Vincents had figured out how to stay on the profitable side of the equation.

Two marquesses ago, with the loss to the Americans, the situation had shifted, and not in favor of the marquesses. Jeanette was very comfortably well-off, and Trevor would be considered wealthy, but he'd not have the fabulous fortune his grandfather had enjoyed.

And Lord Beardsley's situation had honestly become a trifle straitened. "Aunt Viola has two more daughters to marry off," Jeanette said, "and she is quite particular about whom she will accept as a son-in-law. Jerome would do well to heed his mama's advice."

Trevor paused to construct a second sandwich. "Jere says Auntie has me in mind for Cousin Hera. You must not abet that scheme, Step-mama. Promise, and don't let her throw me at Cousin Diana either."

In Trevor's earnest smile, Jeanette caught a glimpse of the slender, curious, soft-spoken boy he'd once been.

"I promise. You and Hera or Diana might suit, but that should be entirely a decision for you and your intended, and a decision for some point in the future."

Trevor went about the important work of cleaning his plate, while Jeanette contemplated a jaunt out to Surrey to call upon Viola. Was it meddling to warn off a meddler? Would antagonizing Viola make the situation worse, or turn that lady's active mind to the more productive challenge of seeing her two unmarried daughters fired off? Jerome had five sisters, and the first three had married respectably but not impressively.

The next in line—Diana—was making a belated come out. In the spring of her eighteenth year, her next oldest sister had yet to marry, and thus Viola had decided that Diana's presentation could wait. Diana had broken an ankle in the spring of her nineteenth year. Her maternal grandfather had died in the spring of her twentieth year, and last year, her dear grandmama's death had once again prevented a court presentation.

Viola was understandably determined to see her daughters well launched. Jeanette was equally determined that Trevor should make his own decisions regarding the eventual taking of a wife.

"What will you do with yourself today, Step-mama?" he asked, refilling his tea cup.

"No social calls. I was out a bit later than I'd planned last night." Though the excursion had been successful.

"You ask me about ankles, and I must return fire by inquiring about handsome cavaliers. Has any fellow caught your fancy?"

And there was proof that the sweet boy was gone forever. "I have no wish to remarry, Trevor, you know that." He did not know why Jeanette held marriage in such low regard, but Trevor was a perceptive fellow. He had grasped early in life what his father expected of him and had met those expectations with every appearance of good cheer.

If Trevor ever did decide to kick over the traces of propriety, his rebellion would be well earned.

"I'm not suggesting you remarry, my lady, but neither must you take holy orders. You are deuced pretty, and more than a few of my friends... Well, suffice it to say a good opinion of your looks is frequently expressed."

A year ago, Trevor would have blushed to offer that compliment. Now he simply returned to the sideboard for another round of sustenance.

"I am content," Jeanette said, and she was also wise enough to treasure her contentment. That somebody sought to disrupt her hard-won peace provoked as much anger as it did fear.

"Do you seek for me to be merely content, my lady?"

"I seek for you to be happy."

"Well, then." He grinned as he returned to the table, his syllogism complete according to his lopsided male logic. If a bride was the sure guarantee for his happiness, then a husband must be the sine qua non of Jeanette's. "Let the right fellow waltz you onto a few moonlit terraces and strive for more than mere contentment."

I am done striving for anything where moonlit terraces and waltzing partners are concerned. "You ask about my plans for the day. I will be off to the soldiers' home for much of the morning, and I am meeting with the solicitors this afternoon. If you are available, I hope you'll come with me to call upon the lawyers."

Trevor consumed this plateful directly without bothering to build himself any sandwiches. "What is the agenda for the meeting?"

Putting the fear of waste, fraud, and chicanery into a law office that had never earned Jeanette's trust.

"The usual quarterly review of the investments. If your allowance is inadequate, I will direct Smithers to increase it."

Trevor took an inordinate interest in the bottom of his tea cup. "A bit more blunt would be appreciated. Town life puts a few demands on the exchequer."

Trevor's bills were sent to Jeanette, who paid them out of the fund set up for his direct maintenance. She had insisted he have his own money besides, enough to hold his head up among his chums, not enough to get into trouble.

Again. "Another twenty percent?" she suggested.

Trevor's relief was disturbingly obvious. "My thanks, and no, I am not gambling it away. Jerome has mentioned dropping around to The Coventry Club for a few hands, but I told him I'd go along strictly as an observer."

Jeanette had offered to show Trevor around at the Coventry, but apparently her company on such a sortie paled, as it should.

"I haven't been on the Coventry's premises since last autumn," she said. "The Dorning brothers were very helpful at the Wentwhistle house party. If you see them, please give them my regards."

She would warn the footmen of Trevor's plans, for they were as close as she could come to assigning him bodyguards. Her own footmen were loyal to the Vincent family, and she could not rely on them to safeguard her wellbeing if somebody—say, Uncle Beardsley or dear Auntie Viola—was intriguing against her.

"I thought I detected a bit of liking on your part for Mr. Sycamore Dorning," Trevor said, refilling his tea cup.

"Both Dorning brothers comported themselves honorably." Sycamore's honor had surprised her and pleased her, hence her recent request of him. He was not a sweet boy making a calm transition into young adulthood. He had likely never been a sweet boy.

Sycamore Dorning was shrewd, self-interested, and quietly ruthless—also tall, dark-haired, and charming, as well as possessed of exotic, amethyst eyes that saw much and gave away little.

Jeanette would pretend the suppers he'd asked for were a bit of a penance, but the truth was, she liked him. She also trusted him to keep his word to her, and that was far more than she'd trusted any other man since speaking her misbegotten marriage vows nearly ten years ago.

CHAPTER TWO

In his first two years overseeing the Coventry, Sycamore had anticipated the spring Season with delirious glee. The controlled pandemonium in the kitchen, the tumble of the dice against felt-covered tables, the whirr of the roulette wheel... Those had been his odes to joy, and the scent of beeswax and signature perfumes had been the fragrance of the life he'd been meant to live.

His enthusiasm this year was tempered by a hint of resignation to drudgery, perhaps because Ash was preoccupied with wedded bliss. Surely that reasoning explained why a session of knife throwing with Lady Tavistock held inordinate appeal and had taken eons to arrive?

Sycamore watched for her at the staff entrance, appalled when she arrived on foot and without an escort.

"You walked?" he asked, drawing her into the Coventry's back hall.

"My brother's coach dropped me off at the corner," she replied, untying the ribbons of her plain bonnet. "I trust you will see me home?"

"Of course."

"Are we alone, Mr. Dorning?"

Did she want to be alone with him? Her expression suggested she was dreading the prospect. "The undercook and her assistants will remain in the kitchen until we dine, and we will have the rest of the premises to ourselves."

"Then let's get started." The marchioness stalked off down the corridor, removing her bonnet as she went.

"My lady?"

She turned, her cloak swishing as she smoothed her hair with one hand and held her bonnet by its ribbons with the other.

"We'll be in the cellars for this lesson. Stone walls mean wild throws have less chance of doing any damage."

Her return journey was slower. "Wild throws?"

"You are here to learn to wield a knife, are you not?"

"Well, yes, but I thought we'd start with how to stab a footpad."

Sycamore held the cellar door for her. "You are bloodthirsty, my lady."

"I am determined to remain safe." She processed down the steps with more dignity than a duchess at a state funeral. Sycamore had lit every sconce on the stairway and in the main cellar passage, and still, the space had the feel of a private lair.

"The wine cellar runs the length and breadth of the street," Sycamore said, "and this passage becomes a tunnel connected to the kitchens beneath my private rooms. Shall I take your cloak?"

She peered up at the shadows dancing on the stone ceiling, then at the racks and cabinets of bottles. "I had no idea this was down here. You must have a fortune in wine."

"The club consumes a fortune in wine, and our inventory is high now in anticipation of our busiest season. I've suggested to Tresham that he invest in a champagne vineyard, but he does not listen to me." If Mrs. Theodosia Tresham had made that suggestion, the vineyard would have been purchased within the fortnight.

"This doesn't smell like a cellar," her ladyship said, wrinkling her nose. "The scent is more that of a lumberyard, oak rather than pine."

"We have a few barrels of Scottish whisky for the stout of heart, and a small ocean of ale. You will want to remove your cloak."

"I'm chilly."

No, she wasn't. Not in any sense. Uncertain and mistrustful, but in no wise chilly. "You'll warm up fast enough once we're throwing, and you need the ease of movement that fewer clothes provide." Sycamore shrugged out of his coat and slipped his sleeve buttons free of his cuffs, then draped his coat over an upright barrel at the foot of the steps.

"What are you doing?"

Marshaling my patience. "If you cannot see how I achieve the results I do, you will have a harder time emulating my success. I, too, need ease of movement to throw at my best. You were married. A man in undress should not shock you."

"A husband in undress is one thing. You, however..." She still had not taken off her cloak, and now Sycamore understood why. The marchioness was ambivalent about this venture that she'd so boldly embarked upon earlier in the week.

Her courage, in other words, was flagging.

"I am much the same as any other man," Sycamore said, unbuttoning his waistcoat. "Arms, legs, hands, ribs. The design varies little from one specimen to the next. The more clearly you can see what I'm doing, the faster you'll be able to pick it up yourself."

"And do you expect me to peel down to my shift?"

"Not unless you'd like to." Sycamore set the target in the center of the passage. For this occasion, he'd selected an eighteen-inch-thick disk of spruce trunk measuring a good two-and-a-half feet in diameter. "We'll start with the target on the ground," he said, undoing his neckcloth, "standing right next to it. Then we prop it against the wall, still on the floor, then we gradually raise it to chest height. Your cloak, my lady?"

She passed him her bonnet, which he set atop his clothes on the barrel. She was again watching him as she undid the frogs at her throat.

She laid her cloak over his coat and remained standing by the barrel. "Now what?" Her gaze went to the steps, as if she visually assessed whether she could beat Sycamore out of the cellar.

This wealthy, attractive, self-possessed woman was afraid of him —not merely reserved or cautious in an awkward situation—and that made Sycamore incandescent with... frustration? Ire? He wasn't sure what, but the emotion was powerful and angry.

He stepped closer, and she held her ground, though he had the sense it was a near thing. "If I should in any way menace or insult you, you drive your knee into my cods, hard. No mercy, your ladyship. Jab your fingers into my eyes, stomp your heel for all you're worth onto my instep. Fight as if you mean it, not as if we're having a polite disagreement over afternoon tea, then leave the scene at a dead run."

"Your... cods?"

"My stones. Testicles are the Creator's joke on male hubris. Funny looking, delicate, and ever so vulnerable. A single well-placed kick, and I will be retching on the floor."

She brushed a glance south of Sycamore's waist. "Why are you telling me this?"

Because I want your trust, and I want to kill whoever abused it. "You seek to learn to throw a knife, so I gather personal defense generally is of interest to you. Knives are lovely, but not always practical. You never know when a few back-alley tactics might come in handy."

She studied his eyes, then assayed an inspection of his boots. "Back-alley tactics. I like that."

"Delightful. Might I remove my shirt?" He was careful to inject more impatience into the question than he felt. For her permission to disrobe, he would wait eons.

"You may remove your shirt."

Sycamore hung his shirt on the cork of a wine bottle protruding from the nearest rack. While he bleated on about the characteristics of good throwing knives—not to be mistaken for daggers, kitchen knives, or skinning blades—he realized that he and the lady had just made substantial progress, though he could not have said toward what specific goal.

SYCAMORE DORNING DID NOT PREEN, and his physique was spectacularly preen-worthy. The late marquess, by contrast, had strutted about the bedroom in his silk dressing gowns as if reasonably fit forty-year-olds—complete with thinning, graying hair, knobby knees, and slightly protruding ears—were the secret dream of every young bride.

Mr. Dorning discoursed about balance points, weight distribution, stance, and spin, all without any apparent awareness of his own state of undress.

Jeanette was aware of him. The ever-present caution afflicted her, because she was alone with an adult male, but so, too, did reluctant appreciation. The marquess had ridden frequently and fenced on occasion, but Sycamore Dorning's body seethed with muscle as an ocean seethed with energy.

From broad shoulders that rippled when he shoved barrels around like so many ninepins, to biceps that flexed and bunched with power, to hands... Jeanette was supposed to study his hand, to attend how he seated the hilt of the knife right against the base of his thumb, but in those hands, she saw competence and skill.

An alarming degree of competence and skill.

"Your turn," he said, passing her a knife, hilt first. "Don't think too much. Just let fly and start getting a feel for the blade."

Knives for throwing had smooth hilts so that nothing impeded the hand's release of the blade. They were weighted more toward the blade and less toward the handle, and they were sharpest at the point. The feel of the knife in Jeanette's hand was warm from Mr. Dorning's grip, heavy, and exotic.

"This is a weapon," she said, "not a tool. I can feel the difference."

Sycamore moved behind her. "Much like conversation can be a tool or a weapon. Try to get the knife stuck in the target, your ladyship. Don't be concerned if it bounces off the first few times."

The target lay on the floor, a circular surface about a foot and a half thick. Jeanette was two steps away, and she knew she would somehow contrive to miss the target. She was not a quick study, as her late husband had frequently informed her.

"I don't like you lurking back there, Mr. Dorning."

"Would you like me better with a blade protruding from my handsome foot?"

"No."

"Focus is an important part of success with a knife, your ladyship. You have a goal: Get the knife to stick in the target. Ignore me, as dazzling as I am. Pretend my magnificent form is somewhere in the Peak District. My sparkling wit and joie de vivre have removed to Paris. My towering intellect and visionary instinct for—"

Jeanette let fly with the knife, which embedded itself in the wood with a satisfying thump. "I hit it!"

"Dead center." He removed the knife and passed it to her. "Take a step back and try again."

Another half-dozen throws all sank into the wood, though, granted, Jeanette was standing nearly on top of her target. Mr. Dorning propped the target against the wall, still resting on the floor, and two of her next six knives bounced off.

She had *hit the target* most of the time. Her joy was eclipsed only by her surprise.

"Your aim is good," Mr. Dorning said, "and the knife bouncing off has to do with your release, not with your accuracy. Watch me, watch my hand in particular, and the index finger that rests on the balance point. I will try for a slower throw."

Even with him moderating his speed, Jeanette found it difficult to discern when in the downward arc of his arm the knife left his hand.

"You put your body into it," Jeanette said. When armed, that body was a lean curve of lethal male.

"You can throw from the wrist, the elbow, or the shoulder, but we all have a natural throw. I do best over longer distances, with more of my body behind the motion, but the most powerful knife strikes are usually in close quarters. Give it another try."

As they moved gradually farther and farther from the target, he demonstrated, he corrected, he watched and commented, and slowly, Jeanette's awareness of him as a man faded into her determination to master the knife.

Which, apparently, was not an impossible objective.

"Your shoulders, being female, are designed differently from mine," he said, passing her the knife yet again. "But that doesn't affect how accurately you can throw. Your throw will simply look different from a man's."

Imagine that. The female version was simply *different*, not weaker or worse. Jeanette threw again and buried her blade a few inches off-center in the target, which was now sitting on a chair several yards away. She and Mr. Dorning had a rhythm now. He passed her a half-dozen knives, one at a time, and then retrieved them for her.

"I can see why you enjoy this," she said as he ambled forward to pick up the one knife that had bounced off the target and pulled the other five free. "It's entrancing, like an intricate passage at the pianoforte. You work your way through it slowly, over and over, until you can add a touch of speed, but only a touch. You can feel the music, but you can't produce it, not until you've paid the price in patience."

Though, according to Jeanette's late husband, she'd never demonstrated any feeling for the music, no matter how perfect the notes.

Mr. Dorning resumed his place behind her. "My lady is a philosopher. This is your last set—win, lose, or draw."

"But we've barely started."

"Enjoying yourself?"

She glowered at him over her shoulder and accepted a knife. "I am, and I am making progress." Already. Immediately. How she wished she'd embarked on this activity years ago.

"You are off to a good start," Mr. Dorning said, "thanks to the superb quality of your instruction."

She hit dead center, a result that so pleased her that she then missed twice in succession. "I want to do another set after this."

He passed her the fourth knife. "Throwing requires a gambler's discipline, my lady. You quit before your senses grow dull, because to practice poorly only ingrains the bad throws that much more deeply in your mind. You toss sixty knives, then stop, or ninety and then stop. Exercise restraint. Besides, you will be sore tomorrow if we keep at this all evening."

Nothing in his tone made the comment naughty, and neither did anything in his expression. "I cannot believe a few more minutes of practice would overtax me." Jeanette had tasted unanticipated success, a rare and heady treat, and she did not want the session to end.

"We've been down here for an hour and a half. Dinner will soon be ready, and I keep the kitchen waiting at my peril. Three more throws, and we finish for this week. Make them count."

The time had flown, along with the blades, and Jeanette had enjoyed every minute. Her shoulder was in truth protesting mildly, but every time the knife sank into the target, her heart rejoiced. *Take that, and that, and that.*

She mentally toed her mark, relaxed on an exhale, and let the knife fly on the silent count of three. Mr. Dorning slapped the hilt of the next blade into her hand, and she repeated the throw in the same rhythm, then finished with a third throw.

A triangle of blades protruded from the center of the target, the knives several inches apart.

"That," said Mr. Dorning, "is exactly how you want to conclude a session. Well done, my lady. Very, very well done."

Jeanette stared at the circle of wood, at the blades so snugly biting into the grain, and wanted to twirl and clap and laugh—and also to cry. For years, her life had been consumed with not offending her husband and trying to exorcise the memory of the many times the blade of his judgment had embedded itself in her soul.

Today, she'd done something different, taken a new path, and applied her mind to a puzzle other than pleasing his lordship, avoiding his lordship, and enduring or recovering from his lordship's nasty remarks. The man had been dead for three years, and she'd yet to truly put him to rest.

"Thank you," Jeanette said, and that felt good, to thank a man sincerely. Not for a stupid courtesy like handing her down from a coach, but for making her a more confident and formidable person. "I wasn't sure I could do it."

She had been convinced, in fact, that the task would be all but hopeless, another skill—like polite conversation or a graceful quadrille—that she would acquire only by grueling, protracted effort.

Mr. Dorning wrapped an arm around her shoulders and squeezed her in a casual half hug, as Orion might have offered such affection to his little sister in his younger, better years.

"With me for a teacher, my lady, your success is assured."

Jeanette elbowed her instructor in the ribs—good-naturedly—and met a solid wall of muscle. "You are awful."

"No need to be jealous of my talent," he said, letting her go. "You will soon be throwing like Astley's finest marksman, or markswoman. I do advise some liniment for your shoulder, arm, and wrist tonight. Eventually, you can become proficient with both hands, but that's a challenge for another time."

He pulled his shirt over his head and began doing up the buttons.

"Why did you become so skilled with knives?" Jeanette asked, passing him his waistcoat.

"Because I am the youngest of thousands of siblings, and I wanted a means of besting brothers who were all taller, stronger, and smarter than I. I thought I was the runt, but I could at least be the runt with a blade in my hand. As it is, the passing skill I acquired only made me that much more different from the brothers I longed to emulate."

Jeanette considered one of the most purely attractive men she'd ever encountered. That he'd at any time suffered a sense of inadequacy intrigued her.

"You do realize you are no longer the runt?"

"The Creator saved the best for last," he said, his smile dazzling. "Might you help me with my sleeve buttons?"

Jeanette complied. His sleeve buttons were plain gold, though his cuffs were edged in blond lace. "Your neckcloth." She passed him linen also edged in lace.

He tied the knot himself, a complicated series of twists and folds that resulted in the lace cascading just so. "Where did I put my—?"

Jeanette held up a cravat pin topped with a small amethyst very nearly the color of Mr. Dorning's eyes. "Allow me."

She positioned the pin amid the lace and linen and held Mr. Dorning's coat for him. The tailoring was exquisite—and free of padding across the shoulders.

"Will I do?" he asked, buttoning the coat and taking up Jeanette's hat and cloak.

"Passably." He was stunning, of course, but then, he'd been stunning without his shirt too. "Thank you for an informative lesson, Mr. Dorning."

"You are welcome, and now you must pay the piper, my lady. Dinner awaits." He swept her a bow, gesturing with his arm, and she preceded him up the stairs. When they arrived at a private dining room on the first floor, Jeanette found a table set, the food warming in trays on the sideboard, and the wine breathing beside a bouquet of daffodils.

"I hope you are hungry," Mr. Dorning said, closing the door and holding a seat for Jeanette near the hearth. "I enjoy hearty appetites and make no apology for that."

The room was well lit, considering that darkness had fallen. The aromas of roasted beef, buttery potatoes, and subtler scents—tarragon? oregano?—had Jeanette's stomach growling.

Mr. Dorning's comment—about his hearty appetites—might have been another attempt at naughty innuendo, but Jeanette sensed he was simply being honest.

"I am famished," she said as Mr. Dorning took the place at her elbow. "I had not considered that knife throwing is a particularly athletic activity."

"You didn't think it would be so enjoyable, did you?" He poured them both a glass of claret. "You can be honest with me, my lady. Your secrets are safe here."

Jeanette had bet her reputation on that assumption. "Knives are serious business," she replied, "and no, I did not think I would enjoy my lesson half so much as I did."

He touched his glass to hers. "To enjoyable lessons. Shall we start with the soup?"

As her host prattled on about temperamental kitchen personalities and the upset caused when the sovereign spent an evening at the Coventry's tables, Jeanette reflected that she had indeed enjoyed her lesson. She had enjoyed Sycamore Dorning's instruction, even as she'd been puzzled by his combination of jocular arrogance and sexual indifference.

She thought of her last three throws, an equilateral triangle of success, and of how much that pleased her. To her consternation, she was even more pleased to have spent nearly two hours in the company of a handsome, half-clad man and felt no threat or impropriety from him. She had no use for men, generally, and particularly not for the half-clad, handsome variety.

That Sycamore Dorning could be a perfect gentleman when naked from the waist up and alone with a lady was a pleasant surprise, and one which, oddly, made Jeanette curious about their next encounter. Mildly curious, but curious nonetheless.

~

DINNER WITH LADY TAVISTOCK did not go as planned.

Sycamore had intended to continue drawing upon previously untapped stores of acting talent to lull her ladyship into viewing him as a charming raconteur, gracious host, and an all-around harmless—albeit handsome—fellow.

He was not particularly handsome. His eyes were an off color, shading lavender rather than Nordic blue or dark and dreamy. His hair was merely brown and prone to wave rather than fashionably curl. Whereas the older Dornings, including Jacaranda, made height look majestic, Sycamore felt gangly. After years of longing for his siblings' stature, he still occasionally forgot to duck when wearing a top hat that brushed the lintel of a doorway.

He had inherited Grandpapa's *stately* nose and Grandmama's *imposing* eyebrows, meaning his features were less than refined.

But the Coventry had taught Sycamore many lessons, the first being that handsome was more a matter of presentation than looks. He was scrupulous about his toilette, he observed the courtesies, he paid his tithes to Bond Street, and he carried himself as if he should turn heads.

And thus heads turned.

Lady Tavistock had learned the feminine version of the same lesson, apparently, for she ate with exquisite manners, consumed only half a glass of wine with each course, and generally exuded the air of a proper widow.

How Sycamore hoped that was at least partly presentation rather than substance.

Somewhere between the soup and the roast, Sycamore forgot to be charming and instead turned up contemplative. How this had happened, he did not know, but he suspected his guest was to blame. She had a habit of putting a question to him, then regarding him gravely, as if she would be disappointed in him for replying with a superficial witticism.

"I disliked university," Sycamore said after she asked how he'd come into managing the club. "I had no meaningful role at Dorning Hall, and thus I was at loose ends."

She dabbed butter on a slice of bread. "You did not take to the curriculum of wine, women, and song?"

"One need not go to university to enjoy those subjects, but because my family is titled, that seemed to be all that was expected of me. That and wagering, cards, and whining about allowances that never stretched far enough. I suspect the true purpose of university is to establish places where young men can act like jackasses without embarrassing their families."

The marchioness tore off a bite of bread and considered it. "Why do young ladies have no such freedom? We are watched over and guided from infancy right up until we speak our wedding vows, and then a husband decides exactly how foolish we are permitted to be."

Interesting question. "Because when a young man makes an ass of himself, the worst that can happen is that the world is short one foolish young man. Tragic, but the consequences land mostly on the person being reckless. If a young lady is foolish, babies can result, and the ruin spreads to her family and offspring."

Lady Tavistock put down her bread. "Why do you assume that a young lady's version of foolishness must include partaking of what young men—and old men, too, for that matter—are ever so eager to impose on her? Why can't she ride astride in a moonlit steeplechase? Make wagers involving hot air balloons and the coast of Normandy? Why can't she stay up late with her friends, drinking and singing lewd songs? Why must everything a lady does be fashioned to ensure some man gets a piece of her joy?"

This diatribe raised all sorts of possibilities, regarding the lady and the men who'd stolen pieces of her joy. Rather than speculate, Sycamore focused on her questions, because she deserved his answers.

"My sense of why I, and most of my associates at university, were reckless is because we sought to test ourselves against the greatest possible risk, while pretending our courage made the undertaking a mere lark. The drunken steeplechases, the abuse of spirits, the ridiculous wagers are all tests of courage." As had been, come to think of it, the duels and brawls.

"Bravado," her ladyship retorted. "Courage displayed for effect, not courage in its truest, quiet form."

"A boy's courage," Sycamore said. "Courage that needs the reinforcement of admiration, perhaps."

Lady Tavistock glowered at her wineglass. "To show the world how foolishly brave she is, a woman marries, Mr. Dorning. She becomes the property of a rutting fool who can get children on her until his lust kills her. She puts herself under the dominion of a man who can raise his hand to her because the Bible exhorts him to such tender guidance where his wife and children are concerned. Women have no need for any greater display of bravado than that exercised when we speak our wedding vows, but we could surely use opportunities to enjoy the freedom you found so tedious at university."

Such magnificent, articulate anger. "I suppose some women come to the Coventry to exercise freedom, albeit a limited, polite version of it. If you were to undertake one daring indulgence in freedom, my lady, what would it be?"

Her ladyship's expression lost the guarded, poised quality that she'd worn since sitting down to eat. For a moment, she looked perplexed, then wistful.

"How is a woman to know how to have a reckless adventure when her entire life is spent doing as she's told, thinking as she's instructed, and focusing on the needs and happiness of others?"

"Have you met my sister Jacaranda?" Sycamore asked, taking the lid off the fruit compote. "She's not much of one for socializing, though she and her spouse bide in Town much of the year. When my mother abdicated all roles at Dorning Hall, save that of chief victim of cruel fate, Jacaranda was impressed into the job of de facto housekeeper. Would you like some fruit?"

"A small serving."

Sycamore took a modest portion for himself, knowing the kitchen staff would gobble up any leftovers.

"Jacaranda revolted," he said. "She went into service—scandalous, I know—and she had to do so without admitting her family connections. She became a housekeeper in truth. She said if she was to drudge for a pack of louts, she'd at least be paid for it. I gather she was ferociously competent at her post. Some cheese to go with your fruit?"

"One slice. What became of your sister?"

Sycamore pared off two slices of a pale Swiss cheese and laid a strip across her ladyship's bowl of fruit. He had no earthly idea now why he'd brought up his older sister, whom he'd missed bitterly when she'd decamped for a paying post, but then, the entire conversation with Lady Tavistock bore no resemblance whatsoever to the witty banter Sycamore had intended to offer her.

"We thought Jacaranda would be home in a fortnight," he said. "Several years later, we had to beg her to come back to Dorning Hall. Had her employer raised the slightest objection, she would not have taken pity on us even then. As matters unfolded..."

He fell silent while her ladyship took a bit of compote.

"What *is* this?" she asked, peering at the bowl.

"Mostly pineapple, with a few slices of orange for color."

"You *eat* pineapple, Mr. Dorning? Most people rent them to display, not to consume. I've never in my life... This is very good."

"My sister's husband has a head for business and hatched a notion to grow pineapples for profit. I bought some shares in that venture and accept the occasional dividend in kind. What is the point of displaying a fruit that will only spoil if not consumed?"

"This is marvelous," she said, taking another taste and closing her eyes. "Succulent, tart, sweet. Sunshine should taste like this."

"Have as much as you like." The kitchen would revolt, but the kitchen revolted regularly, as did the dealers, the waiters, the footmen, and the stable lads.

"When I die, there had best be pineapple served in heaven," her ladyship said, taking another spoonful. "Even the juice... nectar of the goddesses."

Goddesses, indeed. "You never did answer my question, your ladyship. What would your grand, reckless adventure be?"

"I am busy now, Mr. Dorning. I will ponder that puzzle later." She leavened her scold with a startlingly impish smile, then took another bite.

That smile gave away volumes. Somewhere behind her poise, her asperity, and her ruthless self-sufficiency lay a woman who had once been mischievous and sweet, too intelligent for fashion, and far too tenderhearted for the fate that had befallen her.

Sycamore wanted to learn the delights of that woman, much as Lady Tavistock was learning to savor her pineapple.

"Finish your tale regarding your sister's rebellion, Mr. Dorning."

What sister? "Jacaranda's rebellion led to wedded bliss when she married the man for whom she'd kept house. The pair of them are obnoxiously happy. All of my siblings are."

Lady Tavistock dredged her spoon through the fruit juice in her bowl. "Tell me more about your family. Lord Casriel is the eldest?"

Sycamore did not want to discuss his legion of busy, impressive, blissfully married siblings. "If we are to embark on that recitation, you should have seconds. Have you only the one brother?"

"Orion. I call him Rye, though he and I are not close. The war did not go well for him."

War, a tiny word to refer to twenty years of armed mayhem courtesy of the French, though to be fair, the Austrians had played an inciting role, and to be even more fair, England had been at war more or less for a century. The most recent wars with the Corsican hadn't gone well for much of anybody, save the British mercantile community.

"We Dornings did not serve," Sycamore said. "I ought to be ashamed of that, but Papa was furious that hostilities interfered with his botanizing. Napoleon, at least, put science above warfare where various expeditions or Josephine's roses were concerned, but England did not. Then too, Papa operated from a general sense of equity toward his children. What he did for one son, he felt he should do for all of us, and thus one commission could have turned into five or six."

Not seven, because Casriel, as the heir, would of course been required to bide safely at Dorning Hall.

Her ladyship set her empty bowl aside. "Did you want to go to war?"

Sycamore passed her his untouched serving. "I did not, though I am to say yes in that tradition of reckless boys full of false courage. Perhaps we're brought up to put on such displays because they make sending boys into battle easier?"

She turned the bowl of fruit as if choosing where to dip her spoon. "My brother might agree with you. He came to hate war and everything it stood for."

Not a popular position when so much profit was to be made supporting the military. Wrap profit up in patriotism, and John Bull would make endless, uncomplaining sacrifices. A great lot of complaining, rioting, and repression had gone on since Waterloo, however.

"I might like your brother."

"I originally came to the Coventry hoping to find him among the patrons. We meet by chance from time to time, but never by design. Do you suppose I might join your brother-in-law's pineapple venture?"

"I will ask him. Kettering frequently handles funds on behalf of women and finds the ladies have generally sounder investment instincts than men do. Maybe that false courage makes men stupid in commerce as well as war."

Her ladyship considered him over a spoonful of fruit. "You are not the strutting fribble you would have everybody believe you are."

"I cannot tell if you're pleased or disappointed by that conclusion. Don't tell my family of your discovery. In the Dorning lexicon, 'Sycamore' and 'scapegrace' are synonyms."

She tucked into his serving. "Because in your large and illustrious tribe, the job of scapegrace was the only one remaining by the time you came along, so you were determined to do it well. I was the good girl, the dutiful daughter. My mother died in childbirth trying for a spare—her third try, though none of the babies lived—and my brother became the little hero. I am determined that Trevor have a few years to indulge in reckless wagers and bawdy song before he takes on the full burden of the title."

Trevor would be her step-son, the youthful Marquess of Tavistock. "But you have no respect for that sort of behavior."

"I understand its purpose, Mr. Dorning. Wild oats, youthful high spirits, like a green horse has to gallop off the fidgets before tolerating a quiet hack. My objection is to the fact that young women risk ruin if they indulge in the same freedoms, though young women deserve those freedoms far more than young men do."

Sycamore ought to have paid more attention to her ladyship's words and less attention to the silver spoon sliding between her lips.

"Women need the freedom more than men because...?"

"Because for a woman, marriage can be tantamount to death, and it certainly curtails what little freedom she had. For a titled man, marriage simply means enjoying the favors of both a wife and a mistress, and little else changes for him. That is the nature of the institution."

Sycamore stuffed his slice of cheese into his mouth rather than point out the obvious: Clearly, the marchioness had been married to the wrong man, but neither could he argue her point. At law, a wife wasn't a person.

She was a thing, not quite even livestock, subsumed into her husband's identity, chattel that among the lower orders was yet a salable commodity. His Grace of Chandos had, in Sycamore's father's time, purchased his second duchess at a wife sale.

Sycamore had been raised with that legal definition of the married woman's status and hadn't once questioned its ramifications for the ladies, though he questioned it as the meal concluded, and he held her ladyship's cloak for her.

He escorted the marchioness home in his carriage, the hours in her company having given him much to think about. When he assisted her from the coach in the alley behind her home, he passed her a covered crock.

"The leftover fruit. Please don't refuse it, or it will just go to waste." A patent falsehood, his first of the evening, but offered in good cause.

"My thanks for a lovely supper, Mr. Dorning." She took the dish and bobbed a curtsey. "Until next week?"

He bowed. "I will look very much forward to it."

She walked off a few paces, then turned to regard him. "You mean that. I am difficult company, opinionated, and I do not suffer fools, but we did manage a pleasant meal."

"We kept our bargain."

Her impish, fleeting grin came again, this time tinged with something that might have been surprise. "We did, didn't we? Until next Sunday, Mr. Dorning."

He waited until she'd disappeared through the garden gate, then sent his coachman on without him. The coach had not been followed that Sycamore could tell, but he needed the brisk night air to clear his head, and to put from his mind the image of her ladyship savoring succulent fruit while she held forth about death, marriage, and dreams.

A year ago, he would have flirted his way around to presenting himself as a candidate for Lady Tavistock's next—or possibly her first—reckless adventure.

A year ago, he'd been delighted to face another Season of late nights, feuding staff, and heirs overspending their allowances.

A year ago, neither Ash, nor Hawthorne, nor Valerian had succumbed to the lure of matrimony.

That was then. Now, Sycamore wanted Lady Tavistock to regard him with the same rapt, pleasure-stricken expression she'd turned on her first bite of pineapple.

CHAPTER THREE

Jeanette's first lesson in knife throwing had gone well. Her first supper with Sycamore Dorning had gone wonderfully.

And that was a problem. As she savored the last of the fruit at breakfast Monday morning, she tried to parse where exactly the difficulty lay. Gentian eyes that missed nothing, a physique the Apollo Belvedere would envy, a mind both analytical and playful… These were all faintly troublesome because they meant Mr. Dorning would be hard to manage.

Jeanette had encountered perceptive men, well-built men, and men of impressive intellect, but Sycamore Dorning was more than the sum of those parts. Perhaps the conundrum was that he was so inherently attractive he didn't need to flirt or flatter to secure a lady's notice.

But no, that didn't feel quite right, because he was also bashful, occasionally unsure of himself, and he demanded attention.

Again, not quite right. Jeanette had been married to a man who'd demanded attention with the insistence of a baby who'd soiled his nappies. Sycamore Dorning did not *demand* attention, he *commanded* attention.

"Good morning, Step-mama." Trevor strode into the breakfast parlor and offered her his usual smile, though he was not attired for riding.

"Good morning, sir. We're to enjoy a beautiful spring day, it appears."

Trevor adjusted the drapes so the breakfast parlor wasn't quite so bright. "The manager at Jerome's club says we're in for a bad turn of weather later this week. His elbow is paining him, and Monsieur's elbow is a sure prognosticator of foul weather."

Trevor, usually a tea drinker, poured himself a cup of coffee. His fair complexion was shading sallow, and his eyes were tired and bloodshot.

"The coffee will help," Jeanette said, "but you should also drink several glasses of water and try a pot of willow bark tea."

Trevor took his place at the head of the table. "I don't believe willow bark tea would set very well just now."

Jeanette passed him the toast rack. "Your father woke many a time with a sore head." And with breath more foul than hell's jakes, and a temper to match.

"I don't recall him ever being anything less than in full possession of himself. The jam, if you please."

Jeanette set the jam pot at Trevor's elbow. Honey would have been a better choice, with only a smidgeon of butter, but she'd vowed two years ago not to nanny Trevor into manhood.

"Your father was fond of his brandy." Also of his horses, but not at all fond of his second wife. Jeanette had failed to produce sons and had thus been as useless as an unmatched glove and nearly as vexing, according to her late husband.

Trevor gulped an entire cup of coffee and poured another. "Papa was fond of his brandy, yes, but never to excess, that I recall."

Jeanette dredged up a spoonful of pineapple juice. Not for the world would she tell Trevor that his father had been frequently drunk and often intent on drunkenly exercising his marital privileges, which in a state of advanced inebriation had been an impossibility.

Many a time, Jeanette had endured half the night with the marquess snoring atop her. She'd been too fearful of waking him to move, and in the morning, he would have forgotten everything except his own imagined prowess.

"How is your cousin?" she asked.

"Jerome is a man beset," Trevor said, scraping jam onto his toast. "Aunt Viola never lets him forget that for nearly three years, he was the marquessate's spare, in line behind only his father, and one unfortunate day, the title might still be his."

"Therefore, Jerome must marry?"

Trevor's smile was sad. "Aunt is nothing if not consistent. Jerome will soon attain his majority, and even Uncle Beardsley has started lecturing him about the responsibilities of young manhood. Jerome was quite morose about the whole business."

And getting drunk was a sure cure for low spirits?

"What is Jerome's objection to marriage?" Between pineapple dreams, Jeanette had also revisited her conversation with Sycamore Dorning. She'd characterized marriage as a death sentence for women and the acquisition of a live-in mistress-cum-hostess for men. That description fit her parents' marriage and the marquess's two marriages, but not all marriages.

And yet, Mr. Dorning had not argued with her. She had wanted him to protest that *his* marriage wouldn't be like that.

"Jerome hasn't any property," Trevor said. "How is he to support a wife on his allowance? Auntie is all in favor of Jerome setting up his nursery, but she's rather short on ideas for how the operation is to be funded. Knowing Jerome, the nursery would be full to bursting in no time."

Not if Jerome took after his uncle, it wouldn't. "You want to make Jerome's situation better, don't you?"

Trevor studied his coffee. "I am the marquess. That makes me the head of the family in one sense, despite my eternal youth and endless inexperience. Jerome is a good sort, my only male cousin, and he spends most of his time escorting his sisters to every boring entertainment in Mayfair, unless I can be impressed into performing that office. I don't like to see him so miserable."

Miserable... to while away his days lounging about Piccadilly, calling upon one bachelor friend after another. For entertainment, Jerome would accompany another fellow to a fitting at the tailor's, then hang about the print shops to gawk at the latest satires. In the afternoon, he'd drop by a favorite tavern for some drunken singing, call upon a *chère amie* to grab a nap and indulge his manly humors until supper, then nip off to the theater, dancing, cards, or—for a variety—the cockpits, Jackson's, or Angelo's for a pleasing hour of gratuitous violence.

Rye had as much contempt for the average lordling-about-Town as he did for arrogant generals and stupid captains, and he was quite articulate on the details when provoked. The late Marquess of Tavistock hadn't had much taste for cockfights—too many low sorts in attendance—but the rest of the litany had still fit him twenty years after he'd finished at university.

Where on that continuum, between contempt for and mindless pursuit of masculine pleasures, would Sycamore Dorning fall?

"Your compassion for your cousin does you credit, my lord," Jeanette said, choosing her words carefully, "but what, exactly, is Jerome's problem?"

"Lack of blunt."

No, not quite. "And if you passed him a sum of money, would that solve the problem?"

Trevor scrubbed a hand over pale, unshaven cheeks. Because he was fair, and eighteen, he looked only slightly rakish for having come to the table without benefit of a razor.

"Unless I passed over a substantial sum—say, ten thousand pounds—I would not be solving the problem. Jerome wants an income."

"Does he?"

Trevor peered at her owlishly. "You think if he had an income, Auntie would only dun him all the harder?"

"He has an income adequate to keep himself independently in London." An income provided by a spinster great-auntie, according to the solicitors, not by Jerome's parents. "If he had a larger income, then his mother could march him up the aisle with the first available female. As long as Jerome must marry with a view toward the settlements, Viola's choices are limited."

"That is... that is true." Trevor pursed his lips and stared at plaster Cupids cavorting along the corners of the room's molding. "Jerome doesn't see limited funds as a check on Aunt's schemes."

"You can explain it to him when next you share a meal, and there's something else to bear in mind, my lord."

"You are 'my lording' me so early in the day, and me with a bad head."

And you, already eighteen. Only last week, so it seemed to Jeanette, a small boy had been bellowing for her to watch how high his kite could fly.

"Jerome has his own funds," Jeanette said, "modest though they are. He has two parents heavily invested in his wellbeing, and Viola, at least, has brothers and cousins and one fairly well-off uncle. If Aunt Viola knows you will open the Tavistock coffers for Jerome now, before there's any real need, she won't hesitate to importune you on behalf of your female cousins."

Or on behalf of her legion of grandchildren, nieces, godchildren, and Lord knew who else. Viola was a meddler by nature, and her husband, Lord Beardsley, had learned to leave her to it, lest she meddle with her husband instead. The Tavistock coffers would be opened to assist with settlements for Trevor's unmarried cousins—Jeanette would ensure that much—but they would not be used to lure bachelors to the altar.

"You make Auntie sound a bit ruthless."

Only a bit? "Beardsley abets her, and I have reason to know his means are not as lavish as a marquess's son might wish." Something Trevor would grasp if he once accompanied Jeanette to meet with the solicitors. "If Cousin Maribelle had made a spectacular match, matters would have gone better for Cousin Harriet or Cousin Lucinda, but none of them made a priority of money when choosing a spouse."

Maribelle's firstborn had arrived not quite seven months after the wedding, which had prompted the late marquess to direct endless snide observations toward his own wife's *laggardly performance.*

"Is Uncle Beardsley pockets to let?" Trevor asked, taking a bite of toast.

"Uncle has two more daughters to fire off, Trevor. He is probably hoping Jerome marries well and thus improves his sisters' prospects, but he's letting Aunt manage the situation. Is that a bruise over your eye?"

Only now did Jeanette realize that Trevor had remained slightly turned away from her. She'd sensed he was avoiding the light, but then, drawing the drapes closed had also made his bruise less apparent.

"Got into a bit of a dustup walking home from the club. Some of the other fellows were walking not far behind me, and between us, we routed the blackguards. A stout walking stick proves useful on occasion."

This is why you should take the coach and footmen. This is why I worry. If one of those blackguards had had a knife...

"Common pickpockets?" Jeanette asked, choosing a currant bun from the basket in the center of the table.

Trevor drained his coffee cup. "Rather large for pickpockets, but they scampered off quickly enough when Fisher and Durante joined the affray. Durante considers himself a pugilist, and Fisher loves a good scrap."

The streets of London were notoriously unsafe, particularly after dark. Drunken swells were a favorite target of the bolder thieves, and Trevor had doubtless been the worse for drink by the time he'd left Jerome.

"Where was Jerome?"

"Stayed behind at the club for another few hands. He was

winning, while I was ready to leave. What are your plans for the day?"

Jeanette longed to ask how much Trevor had lost. She'd arranged for the increase in his allowance to become effective immediately, and that would have to suffice.

"I have some research to do regarding a few investments." Research that would start with chatting up Cook regarding pineapples.

Trevor shuddered. "Investments?"

Jeanette was essentially managing the marquessate with an occasional nod in Beardsley's direction. Beardsley was Trevor's nominal guardian, though Trevor had made it plain upon his father's death that he considered his place to be with Jeanette. Beardsley, awash in children at the time, had conceded the point with apparent relief.

"Investments, which is where most of your wealth comes from, my lord. The cent-per-cents are fine for slow, steady growth, but we have the means to diversify, and that is only prudent when the price of corn fluctuates so wildly. You really ought to accompany me to my next meeting with the solicitors, Trevor. They must know you can catch them out in mistakes and dissembling, or they will grow lax."

Or worse, ambitious.

"Uncle Beardsley can explain matters to me when the time comes."

Uncle Beardsley did not understand *matters* well enough to offer that explanation. The late marquess, for all his myriad faults, had taken management of his wealth seriously and had ensured that Jeanette was educated regarding the family's means. That Tavistock had trusted her rather than his own brother to safeguard Trevor's holdings was probably the only compliment his late lordship had paid her.

Ever.

"Uncle Beardsley takes little interest in the marquessate, Trevor. Your father had nothing but contempt for Beardsley in that regard."

"Not contempt, Step-mama. Papa was simply somewhat colorful

in his language sometimes. I do believe a bit of sustenance has had a salubrious effect on my outlook. Perhaps I'll change into riding attire and brave the park after all."

Trevor rose, bowed, and took himself off without coming closer to Jeanette than four feet. She knew why: She'd smell the drink on him, even now, for he'd had far too much, lost badly at cards, nearly come to grief at the hands of footpads, and could not clearly remember the details of his evening.

Perhaps Trevor was more like his father than Jeanette was willing to admit.

THAT SYCAMORE WAS REDUCED to calling on Worth Kettering, Lord Trysting, was one of life's many injustices. Kettering was a mere brother-by-marriage to Sycamore, a chiseling-in sort of relation who swanned into Dorning family functions like the long-lost prodigal, Jacaranda on one arm, a smiling baby in the other.

Kettering was, if anything, more effective at annoying Sycamore's brothers than Sycamore was, and that was a worse betrayal than stealing Jacaranda away and making her so blasted happy.

"Young Sycamore," Kettering said, offering a firm handshake. "To what do I owe the honor?"

Young Sycamore. He would still be *young Sycamore* well into his dotage in this company.

"Kettering. I've come to discuss investments. First, tell me how Jacaranda and the children go on."

Kettering was big, dark-haired, blue-eyed, and not bad looking. The blighter had charm, to hear some tell it—especially some ladies. He also had a genius for turning a profit, and once a man gained that reputation, people with bright ideas and a lack of blunt tended to seek him out. Kettering heard about the best investment opportunities first, and the sovereign himself would interrupt a meal if Kettering had commercial news to pass along.

"My lady wife thrives in my loving care," Kettering said, "as I shall ever thrive in hers. We have reason to hope another delightful addition to the family is in the offing."

Kettering exuded both bashful humility and smug conceit. Probably part of his much-vaunted charm.

"Congratulations. Please convey my best wishes to the expectant mother and to my nieces."

"You might pay a call on them," Kettering said, taking Sycamore's hat and cane. "Surrey isn't that distant, and your club can't demand your presence every night. My office is a disaster. I'm trying to do a fortnight's work in five days so as to more quickly rejoin my adoring womenfolk. It's half day, else my butler would be apologizing for the mess on my behalf. Let's use the family parlor."

The only evening the Coventry was closed was Sunday, meaning the only time Sycamore could jaunt out to Surrey to see his sister was Sunday, with a Monday morning return.

Kettering would know that if he gave Sycamore's situation a moment's thought. "My free time is spoken for lately, what with the club's busiest season approaching. What do you hear from the rest of the family?"

Kettering, married to one of the Dorning clan's better correspondents, rattled off a litany: This little one was teething, that one had taken first steps. Willow and Susannah were awash in spring puppies—they were always awash in puppies—and Oak was finding portrait commissions even in rural Hampshire. Valerian's books were selling quite well, Tabitha's letters were now rendered in creditable French.

"Tabitha writes to you?" *To you too?*

"To us," Kettering corrected gently, opening double doors to an airy, old-fashioned parlor. "She is growing up, doing exactly as young ladies are supposed to do at fancy finishing schools—making friends, gaining confidence, and pretending to a sophistication that in time becomes the genuine article. She'll need it, given her antecedents, and Jacaranda and I will be on hand to lend her our consequence as well."

Tabitha was Casriel's illegitimate daughter, a youthful indiscretion raised at the Hall, and much beloved by the entire family. She had been the only child for years. She was also—or had been—the family member who regarded Uncle Sycamore as great good fun, less stodgy than all those other uncles.

"Do you suppose you could invite her down for a holiday in Town?" he asked, rather than admit he missed her terribly. "One can hardly acquire Town bronze in the schoolroom."

Kettering gestured to a pink tufted sofa. The pale blue wallpaper was flocked with gold fleur-de-lis, and a pianoforte painted with scenes of rural romance stood in the corner. The curtains were lace, the fireplace of pink marble. The room was decorated in the delicate, old-fashioned style of the previous century, and yet, Kettering looked quite at home among its refinements.

The parlor was redolent of the bouquet of lemon blossoms holding pride of place in the center of the mantel, not a typical spring scent, but unless Sycamore was mistaken, one Jacaranda favored in her perfumes.

Lady Tavistock would enjoy this room. She'd like the sense of repose, the light flooding through the tall windows, the books lining the shelves behind the pianoforte. She'd bring her needlepoint to a room like this, because she was a serious-minded woman who'd not bother with cutwork.

Too serious-minded.

"Shall I ring for tea?" Kettering asked. He typically poured out with all the aplomb of a duchess, a skill the successful man of business needed, to hear him tell it.

"No, thank you."

Kettering took a Queen Anne chair that groaned under his weight. "To business, then. What's on your mind?"

Sycamore's mind was full of memories of a woman with a latent skill for wielding a blade. Of the nape of her ladyship's neck, pale, sweet, and tempting above the demure lace of her dress collar. Of red hair bound up in a ruthless knot, begging to be undone and allowed to fall freely to naked hips.

Of a fleeting, just-between-us grin. "Pineapples," Sycamore said. "I had occasion to consume one recently, one of ours."

"Delectable, aren't they?" Kettering said, crossing his legs at the knee like a confirmed dandy. "The French have got hold of a particular variety I'm negotiating to add to our cultivations in the Canaries. Did you save the crown?"

"Already on the way to Dorning Hall." Where the vast conservatory held a dozen maturing plants, which would yield a dozen more crowns, plus shoots, if Casriel's undergardeners could be bothered to tend to them. "Does this project have room for another investor?"

Kettering stared off into the middle distance, while Sycamore imagined the sound of abacus beads sliding and clicking.

"Depends on the investor and the sums involved. Pineapples are not a venture for those in need of a quick profit. The first crop alone takes—"

"A year and a half to mature. I know, Kettering, I read Papa's journals the same as you did." But only Kettering had connected the Dorning hothouses with the rented pineapples crowning the Mayfair hostesses' spectacular epergnes and come up with a profitable scheme. The offsets from pineapples past their prime now found their way into Kettering's keeping, and those not sent to Dorning Hall were gifted to various friends with instructions for their cultivation.

The Dornings had grown up with the occasional pineapple as a treat produced by Papa's botanical "hobby," just as their mother had been presented with an exotic orchid or perfume from time to time.

"Who is this potential investor, Sycamore?"

"What do you know of the late Marquess of Tavistock?"

Kettering wrinkled his aquiline beak. "I turned him down as a client. Too high in the instep, too old-school, too... I simply did not care for him."

"Can you be more specific?"

Kettering rose and strolled the parlor, hands in his pockets. "I don't know as I can. Much of my success has resulted from paying as close attention to my instincts as I do to the gossip on 'Change or from Horse Guards. Tavistock would have expected me to toady, to put his affairs ahead of anybody else's. I am temperamentally incapable of toadying."

"For which," Sycamore replied, "though it pains me to say it, I respect you."

"One is compelled to note that you suffer the same deficit. What brings Tavistock to mind?"

"What do you hear of his widow?"

Kettering paused in his perambulations to sniff the cluster of lemon blossoms in a plain glass vase on the mantel.

"Jacaranda knows her ladyship or knows of her. The former Jeanette Goddard of the Somerset Goddards. Excellent lineage, but the trouble in France affected the family fortunes. The English Goddard sons tended to marry their French second cousins and increase wealth by leaving management of orchards, vineyards, and such in French hands. Jeanette was married off to Tavistock right out of the schoolroom, and her brother's commission was purchased shortly thereafter. Her brother rose to the rank of colonel, but I seem to recall mention of some scandal in the ranks as well."

"Why do you know all of that about a family you declined to do business with?"

Kettering nudged a white blossom closer to the center of the bouquet. "I just do. I research, and the information stays with me. How does Lady Tavistock behave at the tables?"

"She eschews the more complicated games and prefers vingt-et-un, which is prudent, because the house hasn't as much advantage with vingt-et-un. She is a serious player, but not grim, and can keep an entire deck in her head, or nearly so, though she never tries to win a fortune at the tables. She walks away from winning streaks and losing streaks alike, which is the mark of a sensible gambler."

Kettering set the flowers on the windowsill, where they would have more light. "She won a fortune off of Ash at the Wentwhistle house party last autumn."

Kettering would bring that up. "Ancient history, and for the most part, she was simply recouping losses incurred by young Lord Tavistock earlier. Would you consider bringing her into the pineapple scheme?"

Kettering left off fussing with the flowers, or trying to look harmless, long enough to send Sycamore a puzzled glance.

"Why? The more investors, the less profit either of us makes. We don't need her capital, and I rather like keeping money in the family when I can. It's your father's hothouses that gave me the idea, after all."

Sycamore pretended to admire the open lid of the pianoforte, which had been decorated with a scene of some shepherd boy serenading his lady while strumming a lute. An apple tree heavy with fruit arched over the couple, and lambs cavorted at the lady's feet.

What utter twaddle. "Her ladyship enjoys pineapple."

"Those few who've actually consumed the fruit do tend to enjoy it," Kettering said, resuming his lounging posture on the Queen Anne tuffet. "And if she had that opportunity, you gave it to her. What are you about, Sycamore?"

"She is a patron at the club, and I enjoy her company."

"I can be discreet," Kettering said, "even within the confines of the Dorning family. Jacaranda does not want to know every peccadillo and scrape you lot get up to. She trusts me to sort them out if Casriel isn't up to the challenge."

Sycamore rose. "Don't be obnoxious. We are not a pack of schoolboys constantly embroiled with the local constable. Every one of us has found meaningful employment and a way to make some contribution to society, no thanks to you or Casriel."

Kettering's expression shuttered. "I seek to aid a passel of impecunious younger sons, the despair of the sister who loved them—"

Sycamore held up a hand. "Jacaranda had not reached her majority when she ran out on us, and while she had her reasons, her opinion of her brothers was fixed nearly ten years ago, when we were a very different family. I cannot persuade you or her to see us as we are rather than as we were, and neither will I take up any more of your time."

Sycamore reached the door before Kettering spoke. "Wait."

Sycamore lifted the latch.

"Wait, *please*."

He turned. "So that you can cajole and insult me by turns for another quarter hour? I think not. Lady Tavistock, whom I esteem in every particular, asked me about pineapples as an investment. I told her I would inquire of you accordingly, but you don't deserve to invest her money. You can't see the family you've pretended to call your own for the past five years. My love to my sister and my nieces. I'll see myself out."

Kettering prevented him from making a grand exit by physically pushing the door closed. The prospect of fisticuffs loomed temptingly close at hand, but Sycamore would not give Kettering the satisfaction. Sycamore was younger, faster, and fitter than Kettering, and Jacaranda would take it amiss if Sycamore broke Kettering's nose.

"Jacaranda has to occasionally pin my ears back," Kettering said. "I don't enjoy it, and I suspect she doesn't either, but I benefit from her guidance."

Sycamore turned, which put him in very close proximity to his brother-in-law. Close enough that a left uppercut—always lead with the unexpected hand—would have clipped Kettering hard on the jaw.

"Is that an apology, your lordship?"

Kettering grinned—more of his damned charm. "Yes. Yes, that is an apology for insulting you and your forest of brothers. The Dorning family is getting on quite well, and it galls me to be needed so little in that endeavor. Tell me about Lady Tavistock."

Kettering was not needed *at all*, save to keep Jacaranda happy. "This goes no further."

"Now you insult me."

"I mean *no* further, Kettering. Not to Jacaranda, not to your flock of clerks, not to your coded journals."

Kettering eased away. "My word as a gentleman."

"Somebody has taken to following Lady Tavistock of an evening, and I believe she is worried for her safety. She manages the Tavistock accounts, she is the closest thing to a good influence on the young marquess, and the heir and spare—the titleholder's uncle and cousin, respectively—might well find her influence over her step-son inconvenient."

Sycamore had promised to keep the knife lessons private, and they worried him most of all.

"Lady Tavistock's brother has enemies," Kettering said. "Orion Goddard has enemies on both sides of the Channel, and on the Peninsula, and if that man cares for anybody—an open question—he cares for his sister."

"His problems might have become hers?"

Kettering nodded, only the once. "Possibly."

"Then I'd best make Mr. Goddard's acquaintance."

"*Colonel Sir* Orion Goddard, though I don't think he uses his honorific."

In a country that pretended to venerate its aristocracy, why eschew mention of the knighthood? "Then I will make *the colonel's* acquaintance. Thank you for your time, Kettering."

"Will you plant me a facer if I tell you to be careful?"

"Goddard is that difficult?" Sycamore was reminded that her ladyship worried for her brother, mostly from a polite distance.

"He had a rough go of it in the military," Kettering said. "Nobody will quite say what happened. He's known to have a temper, and he and his sister are not friendly. He might not be received, so it's fortunate he doesn't socialize."

A difficult, self-absorbed, unhappy man. The Coventry was full of them on any given night and boasted its share of difficult, self-absorbed, unhappy women too. Even the staff was prone to the occasional tantrum or broken dish.

"Anything else I should know?" Sycamore asked.

Kettering's smile was faint, but genuine. "If her ladyship would like to invest with us, I suggest she buy in by purchasing from each of us a quarter of our shares."

"That results in her having only two-thirds the shares we each hold."

Kettering's smile faded. "You'd bring her in as an equal partner?"

"An equal partner, or not at all. Good day, Kettering, and thank you for your time."

Kettering looked as if he wanted to say more, to resume cajolery as usual, but Sycamore had put up with years of such condescension and was no longer inclined to indulge Kettering's whims.

He slipped through the door, retrieved his hat and cane, and saw himself out.

THE KNIVES, such delightful new acquaintances on first meeting, turned up contrary at the second lesson. Jeanette took a step closer to the target, which was once more sitting on a chair several yards down the corridor, and let fly.

"Blast and perdition." The knife bounced off the wood and clattered to the cobbled floor.

Mr. Dorning, in shirt-sleeves and waistcoat today, cravat still neatly pinned, ambled forward. "You can do better than that."

"I am trying my best, Mr. Dorning." And yet, the occasional throw missed the wood entirely and sailed into the shadows at the end of the corridor.

Mr. Dorning retrieved five blades from various corners of the target and the sixth from the floor. Jeanette liked watching him move, liked the flex of his haunches when he bent to pick up a knife, liked how his fingers wrapped around the hilts. The man was wretchedly distracting even when not half naked.

"I meant," he said, approaching with the knives, "with your

profanity. There's nobody here to judge, nobody to repeat your epithets. I have heard far worse than 'blast and perdition.' You won't shock me, your ladyship."

He passed Jeanette five of the blades and toed the imaginary line, then waited for Jeanette to move behind him.

"Watch how far back I cock my arm, then how far forward it travels. Much of the momentum of the knife comes not from my arm or hand, but from my body. You'll see no flick of the wrist, just an opportune release. The index finger caresses the blade in a lingering farewell. Last week, you were throwing with more of your whole body. This week, you are too tightly laced, or something."

The knife, of course, buried itself dead center in the target. He held out his hand, and Jeanette slapped the hilt of the second blade into his palm. Five more throws resulted in a rosette of blades clustered around the first throw.

"What did you notice?" Mr. Dorning asked, prowling forward to retrieve his knives.

Jeanette noticed his bum, which filled out his breeches with an admirable quantity of tight, rounded muscle. She noticed his wrists, which managed to be elegant, and noticed the frigid focus in his eyes whenever he handled a knife. Would he wear the same expression when handling a woman, or would those marvelous eyes warm with tenderness?

"I noticed that you are accurate, and today, I am utterly incompetent." The disappointment was inordinate.

He passed her a knife. "You are unfocused. What has distracted you?"

What had not distracted her? Trevor hadn't come down to breakfast at all either that morning or the previous Thursday. Jeanette handled the social correspondence, and she doubted he'd been up late swilling brandy at the Lewis musicale. Sopranos were not Trevor's idea of a fine diversion.

"I am a bit fatigued," Jeanette said, stepping forward.

"Fatigue does not necessarily affect aim," Mr. Dorning replied, taking up a lean against the wall behind her and crossing his arms. "Part of the delight of wielding a knife is that it takes very little strength. If you are quick enough, the knife has tremendous force, and you can be quite quick, my lady. What has cost you your sleep?"

She positioned the knife and toed the line. The target wasn't moving—moving targets were on the curriculum after the still targets presented no challenge—and last week, she'd been able to hit the damned thing.

"Trevor is acting like an ass."

"I don't suppose he's very good at it. He's a dear, earnest young man."

Jeanette threw the knife and was rewarded with the *thunk* of metal biting into wood. She'd hit far off center, but a hit was a hit.

"He is a dear, earnest young man, but he is developing bad habits and secretiveness, which most people would refer to as a young man's entitlement to privacy. Knife."

Mr. Dorning passed her the second blade. "Wine, women, and wagering?"

The second knife was more obliging by two inches. "I don't know about the women, but he's over-imbibing and losing at cards. I've had to increase his allowance. Knife."

Number three went wide on the other side of the target, landing only an inch from the edge.

"Focus, my lady. Think of whoever might be leading your lamb astray and let the knife drive them off."

Number four was only a couple inches from the center of the target. "Trevor has one male cousin. Jerome isn't a wastrel, but he's fribbling about Town on an inheritance left to him by an auntie. He hasn't enough coin to marry, he does no useful work, and he sets nothing aside for the funds. Knife."

"And if you dare say something to Jerome about leaving Lord Tavistock alone, Jerome will tattle. You're forgetting to breathe."

Right. Breathe. Jeanette was also forgetting to relax before she threw. Mr. Dorning had explained that all the tension was to go into the throw, not the thrower. Number five benefited from either a good deep breath or relaxation—or luck—for it sank into the center of the wood.

"You're finding your rhythm," Mr. Dorning said, passing her the last knife. "Final throw, so enjoy it. You might ask Jerome for his help."

"His help? He's an idler who befriends other idlers. They think it great entertainment to watch each other dress, which exercise can take all morning and reduce a valet to tears. The Albany ought to change its name to the Dressing Closet by day and the Debauchery by night."

The knife hit with a satisfying *thump* and stuck hard in the center of the target.

"Not debauchery," Mr. Dorning said, once again striding forward to retrieve the blades. "Most young men prefer to do their dallying someplace other than their dwelling. That privacy you mentioned is too tender to be infiltrated by spies in petticoats. Home is where a bachelor-about-Town entertains his friends at cards, nurses a sore head, or takes secret delight in maudlin poetry and a solitary oyster dinner. You are worried for his lordship."

He laid the knives in their velvet-lined case and lifted the target off its chair to set it against the nearest wine rack.

"I am worried," Jeanette said. "I hate admitting that. Worry is pointless."

"I worry a great deal," Mr. Dorning said, passing Jeanette his coat.

She held it for him—was a man ever blessed with a more perfect set of shoulders and a more gracefully masculine back?—and smoothed the fabric before he stepped away.

"What could you possibly worry about, Mr. Dorning? Your club thrives, your family does as well. Your wealth and influence increase by the Season, and as an earl's son, you are received everywhere."

He left his coat unbuttoned and took up a shawl Jeanette had folded over a barrel. She allowed him to drape the wrap over her shoulders, a courtesy her own husband had never offered her.

"I worry about my business," Mr. Dorning said. "The chef leaves, the undercook takes a notion to marry, and my kitchen is no longer up to standards. A rumor is circulated by a competitor that my tables are crooked, and my business fails in a fortnight. Two dozen hardworking people are unemployed, my suppliers lose income, my business associates lose faith in me. My brother Ash, who is my partner and friend..."

He strode off to replace the chair against the wall.

"Your brother Ash?"

"Ash is prone to serious bouts of melancholia. The Dorning family finances are not what they should be, though they are improving gradually. The staff is feuding over wages, and my champagne supplier has realized how much I depend on a volume discount to afford my customers the free drink that flows in such quantity after midnight."

"The Goddards still have vineyards in France. I could make inquiries for you."

He buttoned up his coat and offered his arm. "I would be very appreciative of such inquiries. My supplier was delighted to offer the Coventry a substantial discount when the club opened its doors, but this year he has become greedy. Greed and loyalty are poor bedfellows."

They climbed the steps, and Jeanette realized that even though she'd thrown poorly, her mood had improved.

"Do you throw knives to manage the worry?"

A lit sconce at the top of the steps cast Mr. Dorning's features in shadow, suggesting the serious, mature man he'd eventually become—or perhaps already was, upon closer examination.

"I have a capacity for worry that threatens to overwhelm me at times. I literally quake with dread out of all proportion to the moment, your ladyship, and yes, the knives help. Fencing and riding help. A rousing bout at Jackson's helps, though my brother will no longer spar with me. Good, sensible company helps, which brings us back to your step-son. Why not ask Jerome to keep an eye on him?"

They passed into the hallway that ran between the pantries and on to the next set of steps.

"As Trevor's older male cousin," Jeanette said, "Jerome should already be keeping an eye on him, and from what I can see, the result is increasing inebriation, increasing losses at the tables, and God knows what else."

"Tobacco, certainly," Mr. Dorning said, leading Jeanette out onto the gambling floor. "Hashish is likely, as is an occasional pipe of opium. Opera dancers are nearly a foregone conclusion, but Jerome, being from a titled family without a current heir of the body, will be too fastidious to frequent the truly sorry establishments."

How odd that such blunt speech comforted. "You are attempting to talk sense to me. I appreciate that far more than telling me not to worry."

"Could your brother be of any use?"

The question was posed with a studied casualness, though the suggestion made sense. Marriage created family connections, and in earlier years, Rye and Trevor had developed a passing cordial acquaintance.

"My brother is more in need of help than he is capable of giving it, I'm afraid. The extent to which Rye has kept his distance from me appalls me, but I conclude that he has his reasons."

Mr. Dorning held the dining room door for her and ushered her into a cozy parlor lightly fragranced with lemon blossoms.

"This is lovely," she said, for the table was elegantly set, the lemon blossoms forming a low centerpiece among lit candles and gleaming silver warming dishes.

"Please have a seat," Mr. Dorning said, pulling out the chair closest to the hearth. "And tell me more of your brother. Is he that far sunk into scandal that he's protecting you by keeping his distance?"

Jeanette sat and draped her table napkin across her lap. "The old

Rye would do that, but the man who came home from the war... I hardly know him, and I miss my brother terribly."

Mr. Dorning took a seat at her right hand and patted her arm. "Family is the very devil. I troubled myself to learn of your brother's direction. You could call on him."

He poured Jeanette a glass of white wine, twisting his wrist just so to prevent any drops from running down the side of the bottle.

"I know his direction, but I haven't toured the surrounds lest he catch me at it. I gather the neighborhood is decent?"

Mr. Dorning poured himself half a glass. "Decent, yes, though colorful around the edges. Perfectly acceptable for a bachelor. Perhaps you and Tavistock could call upon him together. My experience of young men is that they need badly to feel useful. My oldest brother saw that and cast his younger siblings out into the world to find the places where we could make a contribution. We have all come out the better for being evicted from the ancestral pile."

Jeanette tasted her wine, a delightful, slightly dry Riesling would be her guess. "But you are homesick, aren't you?"

Mr. Dorning picked up his wineglass, and the picture he made, lounging elegantly, expression slightly wistful, hair not quite perfectly combed, made Jeanette hungry for sustenance other than food.

"I am worse than homesick," he said, sipping his wine. "I am *nostalgic*. I was a miserable boy, always getting into scrapes, spying on my siblings, stealing from them and having my larceny flung in my face at dinner. I was possessed by a mischief demon, probably trying to get myself noticed by my parents, a futile endeavor. My mother referred to me as 'that dreadful imp.' If my father called me by name, he had to first fumble through a litany of wrong guesses—'Valerian, Ash, Oak, I mean, Sycamore, *dammit, boy...*'"

"And you miss those days now?"

"No, but I miss something about them, something about being part of a family that had a place, however awkward, for even a dreadful imp of a boy."

"I can see that boy in you," Jeanette said as Mr. Dorning ladled a creamy hot soup into a bowl. "You are too smart for your own good, and you have a wicked sense of humor."

He set the steaming bowl before her—not too full, but enough to take the edge off an appetite—and ladled himself a similar portion.

"And your sense of humor is not wicked?" he asked.

Jeanette tried a spoonful of soup and found that it went exquisitely with the wine. A *vichyssoise*, whether hot or cold, could be little more than leeks and cream, but in this recipe, the leeks were either absent or too subtle to be detected.

"My sense of humor used to be wicked, and then I was married off at seventeen to Lord Tavistock. The joke was on me."

"Tell me about that," Mr. Dorning said, picking up his spoon.

As the meal progressed, Jeanette did tell him, though the topic did not qualify as polite.

She told Mr. Dorning about Tavistock choosing her from a list, not bothering to court her beyond a few public gestures, and explaining to her on their wedding night that her sole redeeming feature was her womb, which he intended to fill as often as possible with healthy boy babies.

"I was a crashing disappointment as a marchioness," Jeanette concluded, as Mr. Dorning retrieved a tray of brie and fruit from the sideboard. The presentation was a beautiful arrangement of dried apricots, pear slices, and raspberries, all arranged around the cheese and a little white ceramic pot of honey. The finishing touch was a raspberry sauce artfully drizzled over the whole, with more held in another little white ceramic pot. "This is almost too pretty to eat."

Mr. Dorning resumed his seat and took up a cheese knife. "I gather Tavistock was an even worse disappointment as a husband?" He held up the knife, which bore on the end a dried apricot smeared with pale cheese, a skein of honey across both.

Jeanette steadied Mr. Dorning's hand with her own and took the treat with her mouth, suggesting the excellent selection of wines had made her a bit tipsy.

"A wealthy, titled marquess cannot be a disappointing husband," Jeanette said. "The most excellent authority on the subject assured me of that."

"Meaning Tavistock himself," Mr. Dorning replied, smearing brie on a sliced pear. "Did you kill him?"

From Sycamore Dorning, at the end of a good meal and a bad throwing session, the question was merely conversational.

"I was too busy praying for conception to plan murder. Praying for conception and enduring the necessary preliminaries. I ought not to have said that, but I gather you are hard to shock."

"Nearly impossible." He munched his fruit and cheese. "A bore in bed, was he?"

From the back of Jeanette's mind came the voice of caution, warning her to draw the line at such confidences, but her husband was dead, and she'd protected the dignity of his memory to all and sundry without fail. The burden of hypocrisy was heavy and wearying.

Also lonely. "I had no way to know at the time, but Tavistock was less than considerate about his marital duties. 'Perfunctory' might be the polite word." Perfunctory and determined, when he was sober.

"Because," Mr. Dorning said, preparing Jeanette a slice of honeyed pear and cheese, "if he'd been plainly inconsiderate, you would have killed him. How long had he been married to his first wife?"

"Fifteen years."

"Fifteen years with only one child, and those were probably Tavistock's most vigorous fifteen years. The inability to conceive was likely not your fault. I've heard of no Tavistock by-blows, which, for a man of his station and disposition, is hard to believe. Perhaps he was chaste and discreet."

"He was neither."

Mr. Dorning mashed a few raspberries into a portion of cheese, drizzled honey onto the resulting mess and passed Jeanette the knife.

"I'm sorry, my lady. You were barely out of the schoolroom and expected to content yourself with a frustrated, arrogant man twice your age. I can understand why you are concerned that your step-son could end up like his father."

The tart fruit, smooth cheese, and sweet honey all hit Jeanette's tongue at the same moment she realized that Mr. Dorning had articulated the very worry plaguing her of late.

"Trevor is a good young man," Jeanette said. "Kind, considerate, intelligent in a quiet way. I am afraid that as he becomes more worldly, he will turn into his late father. Selfish, sly, demanding, and petulant. Full of his own consequence and heedless of others' suffering, but he's not a boy, and there's little I can do."

"But you worry," Mr. Dorning said, dabbling a pear slice in a few drops of honey, then swirling raspberry sauce and honey together on his plate. "You worry that he's already become good enough at lying to you that he's half corrupted, and you don't even know it. I have a suggestion."

He bit off the end of the pear slice, and Jeanette finished her wine to distract herself from the sight.

"I'm listening, Mr. Dorning."

"Sycamore, or for my familiars, particularly when they are exasperated with me, Cam. You are free to fly into the boughs at what I'm about to say, but hear me out first."

"I never fly into the boughs." Though, why not? Why hadn't she ever?

"His young lordship was here at the club last night. He lost, badly. Do not bail him out. Let him flounder, and when he comes to me, hat in hand—for I bought his markers—don't attempt to interfere."

Interfere? "I am in the habit of interfering where my step-son is concerned, Mr. Dorning. I interfered when his father hired a nasty old drunk to teach Trevor his Latin on the end of a birch rod. I interfered when Trevor had torn his new riding breeches and was terrified his father would find out. That young man is the only good thing to come of my marriage. He's the only proof I have of my own value in anything like a maternal capacity. If he has the airs and graces of a gentleman, I can assure you that is solely a result of my *interference*."

Gracious heavens, she'd just flown into the boughs. Hadn't raised her voice, but she'd delivered a tirade of sorts.

Also parted with a confidence.

Mr. Dorning used the knife to draw the letters S and D in the raspberries sauce on his plate. "I feel the same about this club. I did not build it, but it's mine to protect and take pride in. I detested university, detested being one of a herd of drunken, randy boys pretending to scholarship. At the Coventry, *I am somebody*. I always have something to do that matters to the wellbeing of the club." He drew a line under his initials, which, like the letters, melted back into the sauce. "I took over this place with Ash, and for the first time, I've been in a position to help my family. That is a heady power, to be able to help the people I love."

Whatever Jeanette had expected by way of reply, it hadn't been that. "Precisely. I want to help Trevor. I've endured much on the basis of the hope that I've helped him." And yet, the object of all that aid had been to see Trevor mature into a self-sufficient young man.

Mr. Dorning set the knife aside. "I am asking you, my lady, to give me a chance to help him, too, and to also help myself. I love this club, but by August, I resent it too. I am run ragged by long hours and details that never sort themselves out. I will suggest to Trevor that he work off his debt by assisting me here for the busy weeks of the Season. He can do the pretty with you at Almack's and still trot around at my side several nights a week to see what becomes of young men who can't manage themselves."

For Jeanette, parenting a step-son had largely been a matter of exercising self-restraint. Not laughing when a very young Trevor badly mangled his French. Not scolding, not lecturing, not doing for him what he had to learn to do for himself...

"You won't let me pay off his markers?" she asked, longing to do that and knowing exactly how stupid a plan it was.

"No, my lady. They are his markers. He has turned eighteen, and he aspires to be a man-about-Town. Let him take up the responsibilities of that office. If he's conscientious here at the club, he can work off the debt in a few weeks, and I will start him on the conundrum of finding me a better source of good, affordable champagne."

The urge to argue, to demand to take on Trevor's debts, was strong, also misguided. He was not a nine-year-old boy who needed protection from his martinet of a father. He was the marquess, as he'd said himself, the nominal head of the family.

Jeanette was losing him, though like Mr. Dorning, she could also admit that, at times, Trevor had become a resented burden. A dear, resented burden.

"As you wish, Mr. Dorning, and you have my thanks for taking an interest in his lordship's situation. Others would not be as generous. Does this mean my knife lessons are over?" Jeanette would be relieved if that were the case, and very disappointed.

"Of course not," Mr. Dorning said. "You aren't proficient yet, and as your instructor, I can't turn you loose in your present inept state. Last week was beginner's luck, this week was the daunting reappraisal. We get down to the real business next week. And no, Tavistock will not learn of your lessons, but I do have a question for you."

The last of Jeanette's resentment evaporated, for Trevor had met Mr. Dorning at an autumn house party and seemed to like him. They would rub along well together, and Jeanette could focus again on her own difficulties.

"Ask, Mr. Dorning, but I will not tell you upon whom I exercised my wiles once widowed. I engaged in a few discreet frolics, realized the business was not worth the drama, much less the risk to my reputation, and have been content with a life of decorum ever since."

"You dallied with Lord Forster at the Turners' house party and allowed Mr. Mills Endicott a few turns when you summered in the Lakes six months after Tavistock's death. I consulted with a friend, the Duchess of Quimbey, and because she was concerned for you, she kept an eye on your choices."

Jeanette felt as if all the wine had flooded her mind at once. "I beg your pardon?"

"The Duchess of Quimbey, formerly the Dowager Duchess of Ambrose. She never did care for Tavistock. She said the mumps had probably impaired his fertility and was worried you would choose another dunderhead for your next spouse. More cheese?"

"Tavistock was not a dunderhead, he was a marquess."

"He was both, and those were his better qualities, but your ancient history is entirely your business, my lady. My question has to do with present facts."

"I dread to hear your question." *The mumps. The mumps could affect a man's fertility?*

"Who is following you, and would you care for more wine?"

Who was following...? Jeanette thought back over the exquisite meal, the patient instruction belowstairs, the assistance with her shawl and realized that though the process was more swift, Sycamore Dorning put the same amount of preparation and forethought into every throw of the knife. She would never come close to matching his skill, but she could learn from him.

"More wine, please. What makes you think somebody is following me?"

CHAPTER FOUR

Sycamore had followed the marchioness at several points during the week.

So had somebody else, though only at night and only when she was most likely to travel in the Tavistock town coach, a lumbering conveyance any self-respecting footpad could keep up with easily enough.

"I do not *think* somebody is following you," Sycamore said. "I know it. You are tailed by professionals, street boys dressed up to look like messengers, linkboys whose lanterns are extinguished. You are followed exclusively at night, and the spies abandon you when you return home."

He poured her ladyship half a glass of wine, though he took no more for himself. Drink could unhinge a man's self-restraint, and having spent hours in her ladyship's company, some blunt comment about her fine bosom, her rare smiles, or her bad taste in dallying partners was bound to come out.

Forster and Endicott were good-looking enough, widowed, past the stupid years, and not given to gossip, but if ever habits could proclaim a pair of fellows uninspired in bed, theirs did. No wonder her ladyship had gone no more a-roving after those two timid ventures.

"I have probably attracted the notice of a journalist," she said, sitting up straight and trying for the prim, unwelcoming dignity she usually affected.

"That nonsense won't wash," Sycamore said. "I've seen you smile. I've seen you hurl a knife dead center at a target and watched you rejoice in your accomplishment. Poker up all you please, but you aren't learning to wield a blade out of boredom, my lady."

She sipped at her wine—full glasses this week, for the most part—and regarded him balefully. "The problem with you, Mr. Dorning, is that you listen to me."

"The problem with me," he countered, "is that I talk to you. I blather on about my benighted boyhood, my siblings, my fretful nature, the woes of club ownership, while you turn years of a difficult marriage into a few terse understatements. Not well done of you, my lady. I am to teach you to throw a knife, you are to share a few meals with me, and here you have wrested my secrets from me while barely hinting at your own. Who needs to keep an eye on you, besides Her Grace of Quimbey, that is?"

"Your secrets?"

Sycamore waved a hand. "The feuds among the staff, my reliance on Her Grace of Quimbey for the best gossip. If you haven't made her acquaintance, you must. I think she and Quimbey are very much in each other's confidence, and I envy them that."

Her ladyship speared a fat red raspberry on a two-pronged silver fruit fork. "I cannot. Imagine such a thing, that is. My husband barely spoke to me beyond 'hold still,' 'be quiet,' and 'damnation, woman.' What did you mean about the mumps?"

She slipped the raspberry between her teeth, and Sycamore's brain stalled. He poured himself wine he ought not to drink.

"Tavistock suffered a bad bout at the same time his heir did. The boy would have been seven, according to Her Grace, and the child recovered more quickly than the father did. Were Tavistock's testicles at all shriveled?"

Her ladyship tried to spear another raspberry and missed. "I beg your pardon?"

"His stones, his cods. The little bits you are to kick hard if a man ever menaces you. If Tavistock had a bad bout of the mumps, his stones could have been involved in the inflammation. That occasionally makes it difficult for a man to get children thereafter, though he functions well enough otherwise."

Her ladyship speared her berry on this try. "I did not examine his lordship—had no wish to—though he exercised his marital rights vigorously and often, especially at first."

Sycamore let a silence build, the better to torment himself watching her ladyship consume the second berry. He wanted to consume *her*, to put various parts of her into his mouth and delight in their textures and tastes, and to bring her delight too.

And he wanted to keep her safe, which talk of the late marquess's tiny cods would not do, though as a distraction, the topic had served well enough.

"What business is it of yours if somebody is following me?" she asked, putting down the fruit fork.

She was stalling, and because Sycamore was in no hurry to either part from her or attempt to coerce her, he allowed it.

"Would you believe gentlemanly honor motivates my interest in your safety?"

She made a skeptical face. "Maybe in part, but you allow women to come to grief at your tables night after night. Your gentlemanly honor is bounded by self-interest."

"The rule we apply is, a patron can lose badly once, but they are quietly informed that further adventures at our tables will be ill-advised until all debts are cleared. When the debts are cleared, we will be overjoyed to welcome them back, but not until that day. A woman can come to grief at our tables, she cannot be ruined."

He chose a berry, speared it with the fork, and offered it to her ladyship—because he was an idiot, and she really did have a luscious mouth.

"You apply the same rule to men and women, Mr. Dorning?"

Sycamore, please. "Yes, and the same limits. If you don't believe gentlemanly honor compels me to inquire into your situation, then perhaps I'm motivated by vulgar curiosity."

She took the fork from him, her fingers brushing his hand, and if Sycamore's privy parts had had powers of speech, they would have groaned.

"You have too much self-possession, sir, and you are too busy to indulge in idle curiosity where I am concerned," she said, consuming the berry. "So what does that leave, Mr. Dorning?"

"It leaves me in the novel and slightly uncomfortable position of admitting that I like you, my lady. I am flattered to think there is some modicum of trust between us, and I hope we can be friends. Friends look out for each other."

She chose a berry and held the fork out to him. He took the fruit from the tines with his mouth, as she had.

"Uncomfortable because I am difficult?" she asked.

"I adore that you know your own mind and do not suffer fools. The people who call you difficult would have you keeping silent and holding still. You are done with such as that."

"I am," she said, putting down the fork. "I quite am. The truth is, I do not know who is watching me, but I think it started at last autumn's house parties. I had the sense that my behavior was monitored, sometimes by the guests, sometimes by the staff, but I dismissed my feelings. Trevor attended the house parties with me, and perhaps the gossips were speculating about my relationship with him."

Sycamore's body was clamoring for her ladyship to feed him more fruit, to touch him, to show somehow that desire was wreaking the same havoc with her composure that it was with his. His mind, however, realized that she had not argued with his proffer of friendship, had neither mocked nor rejected it.

And his mind, by the slimmest of margins, was still the ascendant faculty. "Your relationship with the marquess is familial and protective. Anybody can see that."

"Anybody can see what they want to see. I am somewhat well-heeled, and if I could be caught out in a scandal, I could be blackmailed."

"My dear, you are far beyond somewhat well-heeled. You have invested shrewdly, you live frugally for your station, and whatever else was true of old Tavistock, his pride demanded that you have decent settlements."

Her ladyship finished her wine. "Not his pride, my father's solicitors. I was sold to the marquess in exchange for considerable coin, enough to see Papa's debts paid and Rye's commission purchased. I was given the merest pittance of pin money, and Tavistock handled the expenses necessary to keep me. Papa allowed that, but his solicitors demanded a larger widow's portion, and the Tavistock attorneys agreed. They believed his lordship would live to enjoy a vigorous old age, so I would never see a penny of that settlement."

"Because you would have expired after delivering the eighth or eleventh son?"

Hurt flickered in her gaze, quickly replaced by that cool self-possession she could summon at will. "Two or three healthy boys would have sufficed, as his lordship told me on many an occasion. He'd saddled himself with a seventeen-year-old bride precisely so the children could be spaced every eighteen months, the better to ensure I carried and delivered them properly. That timing ensured the first one could be weaned shortly after the second had been conceived. I was to provide sustenance to my children—his lordship did not want strange women of low origins nurturing his babies—and besides, he was paying for the whole damned cow, he might as well have the milk."

"How did you not hate him?" Sycamore hated him, and he'd never met the man.

"I made excuses for him. He was of a different era, he was frustrated. He *was* paying for the whole damned cow... I stopped even wanting children, and now I am glad I was spared, for children would only involve me with solicitors and trustees for years to come. I just wanted him to cease his infernal rutting, and then he began to drink so much... Tavistock was disappointed in me, and that caused him to drink, and drink did largely curb his ability to rut."

She recited this tiredly, all the animation gone from her eyes. She was *glad* to not have children, a degree of bitterness Sycamore could hardly fathom, for she would be a wonderful mother, and who could resist loving a baby?

"You were not responsible for his lordship's drinking, my lady, and his death is cause for rejoicing. Did anybody suggest you had a hand in his demise?" Sycamore mentally scheduled a good, sweaty bout at Angelo's with Ash, because this recitation involving damned cows, a randy middle-aged marquess, and a seventeen-year-old bride was provoking enough anger to mute his arousal.

Which was a lot of anger. Rage, even.

"An inquest was held," she said. "I was told it was a formality. He fell from his horse and was doubtless the worse for drink at the time. Death by misadventure. You are right, though. I rejoiced to be free of him and free of the shame of having failed him. I should be going."

"You are avoiding the topic of who is following you," Sycamore said, rising and coming around to hold her chair. "We can discuss it in the coach."

She stood, and her shawl drooped off to one side. Sycamore tucked the shawl back up, his hand lingering on her shoulder. "You endured your late husband's attentions without complaint. You have no cause for shame, your ladyship. That you kept your dignity throughout the ordeal of your marriage suggests you ought to instead take pride in your self-possession."

She leaned into him, not quite an embrace, but something. "I know that, but pride is little comfort when every time you walk into a room, you see pitying glances and hear whispers. The sympathetic whispers were worse than the mean ones."

Sycamore allowed himself to embrace her, to take her in his arms, though she made no move to reciprocate, other than giving him her weight. No witty remark or flirtatious quip came to mind, but perhaps that was for the best.

He wasn't feeling witty or flirtatious. He was feeling anger on her ladyship's behalf; chronic, leashed desire for her person; and determination to solve the riddle of who was intruding on her privacy.

The combination was unsettling, and also a little wonderful.

"THEY WILL SOON BE in each other's pockets," Lord Beardsley Vincent said, propping an elbow on the parlor mantel. "Jerome took Tavistock to the Coventry last night, and half of Mayfair frequents that establishment."

Viola sat on the blue velvet sofa, winding yarn into a ball, like one of the fates. Beardsley's marriage to her had been a sound match, no excesses of sentiment on either side, but no excesses of animosity either. As a spare, Beardsley had been permitted to marry down, provided the bride had generous settlements. Six children and nearly three decades later, those settlements were a thing of fond and distant memory.

"Jerome cannot afford to frequent the Coventry," Viola muttered, "and you are not to tell him I said that. A young man's dignity must be his sternest teacher."

"You'd see our boy in the sponging house?"

"Debts of honor don't land anybody in the sponging house," Viola replied, the yarn winding into an ever-larger ball. "He'll pay the trades with his competence and lie low until the debts of honor are forgotten or his creditors leave Town."

Beardsley sipped his nightcap, good quality brandy, but inferior to the Tavistock town house offerings.

"Jerome knows his station, my dear, and he will not flee Town just when all the best company is reassembling to enjoy the fine weather. He's a bachelor in demand to make up the numbers, an excellent dancer, and more than willing to avail himself of free food and drink. Particularly if he keeps company with Tavistock—"

"Must you refer to Trevor by the title? He has not attained his majority, and neither has he completed his university studies. Our nephew is little more than an overgrown boy parading around in Bond Street finery. Somebody should send him on a grand tour with a bear leader, rather than pushing Jerome at him."

Viola had aged well, but she had *aged*. With each child, she'd become more outspoken and opinionated, and on matters about which she knew little.

"If Jerome is seen in Trevor's company, Viola, Jerome's consequence increases. Matchmakers will use Jerome to gain access to Trevor. They will invite the pair of them, and the marquess will naturally turn to his older, wiser cousin for guidance."

Viola came to the end of her yarn and tucked the ball into her workbasket. "Why isn't Trevor turning *to you*, my lord? I'll tell you why, because that woman still has him in leading strings. Trevor won't turn to Jerome when he has his step-mama to nanny him over breakfast every day."

Viola had never cared for Jeanette, but then, Viola cared for few people outside her circle of tabbies and godchildren. In Viola's defense, Jeanette was chilly company. She'd been a timid, proper young bride who'd failed spectacularly in the one regard that had mattered to her late husband.

And thank God for her failure, because a nursery full of little spares would have reduced Jerome's standing considerably—and Beardsley's as well.

"Jeanette deserves our pity," he said. "She is incapable of producing children, past her best years, and becoming a tolerated fixture in her step-son's house. For Trevor to send her off to a dower property would be a mercy."

The Vincent family dower property in Derbyshire would do

nicely. An affordable, rustic cottage far from the solicitors' offices in the City.

"Did you tell our son to insinuate himself into Trevor's good graces?" Viola asked. "Somebody needs to ease Trevor away from Jeanette's influence."

Beardsley finished his drink and considered pouring another. But no. That way lay a sore head and an empty cellar.

"I asked *Trevor* to help me keep an eye on our dear *Jerome*," Beardsley replied. "Trevor is the head of the family, our marquess. He was flattered by my view of matters, and if that means he listens to me, to Jerome, or to anybody other than Jeanette regarding family finances, then I consider I've made progress toward a worthy goal."

Viola left off rummaging in her workbasket. "My lord, I'm impressed. Might you also suggest that our Diana would make Trevor a fine wife?"

Diana was about to make a belated come out, and while pretty enough, she was as stubborn as her mother, also several years Trevor's senior. She wasn't keen on marrying anybody until she'd had her Season—young people!—and Trevor would know that about his own cousin. Viola was trying to spare them all the expense of another court presentation and come out, but she was being, as usual, clumsy in her machinations.

Then too, Hera would stage a monumental tragedy if Diana married Trevor, who was closer to Hera in age.

"I have not mentioned marriage to anybody," Beardsley replied. "Jerome will hint to Trevor that the expenses of keeping an ancillary household are worth the rewards."

Beardsley had a mistress in just such an ancillary household. A young widow of good family who was practical enough to take a courtesy lord into her bed if that kept her children fed. She was neither resentful of Beardsley's attentions nor interested in anything more than his coin. He was fond of her, a sentiment he'd felt toward his wife once upon a time.

"If Trevor takes a mistress," Viola said, "he is that much more likely to marry and displace Jerome in the succession."

"Just the opposite," Beardsley said. "If Trevor has a regular source of manly pleasure, then the hunt for a wife becomes merely a business venture, not some tangled-up affair of the heart or impulse driven by his breeding organs."

Viola closed the lid of her workbasket. "Men born to privilege always want more," she said. "A mistress is not enough, a wife is not enough. Such a man will frolic with opera dancers when he has both wife and mistress, and frolic yet more at house parties. The world is his sweet shop, and he will never sicken from consuming to excess. You have hastened Trevor's desire to marry, not put it off."

"He cannot marry without my consent for three more years, madam. You worry for nothing."

Viola sent a pointed glance around the parlor. The appointments were elegant, but in an old-fashioned way. Only the candles on the mantel and a sconce by the door were lit, and the fire was burning down rather than blazing up with a final scoop of coal for the evening.

Economies were subtly in evidence, in other words.

"Jeanette is enjoying the last of her influence with the solicitors," Beardsley said. "I have taken steps to ensure she either flees Town or wishes she had. As Trevor ignores her advice more and more consistently, she's becoming less of a Puritan herself. The stakes at the Wentwhistle house party were quite high, and her success there literally came down to the turn of a card. That is not the behavior of a prudent widow, my dear, and Trevor will soon see that."

Viola rose. "Trevor loves her. I tried to be a mother to him, but she championed the boy's causes to his father, and I could not compete with that."

"You have been in every way an exemplary aunt to him, and I have been a devoted uncle. That is where matters will stand until Jeanette can be persuaded to yield the reins."

Viola studied him, and Beardsley had no idea what she was thinking. How could two people have children, live together for more than a quarter century, and still not know each other all that well? But then, Beardsley did not particularly want to know his wife if that meant she intruded on his privacy too.

"Will Jeanette yield the reins before Diana's come out?" Viola asked. "Town grows only more expensive, and Diana is neither beautiful nor witty."

"All is in hand, my dear. Between Jerome's friendship with Trevor and my own humble efforts, all is in hand."

Viola kissed his cheek and crossed to the door. "Then I will wish you pleasant dreams, my lord, and see you at breakfast."

"Good night, my lady."

Viola had removed to her own bedroom within a year of Jerome's birth, and though Beardsley occasionally visited her of a night, she'd made her wishes known: A single son was all that she had been interested in providing, and now the passage of time had made the question of more children moot.

Besides, one son of marriageable age blessed with an abundance of animal spirits was enough.

SYCAMORE DORNING WAS everything Jeanette could never be: at home with violence and vice, blunt to a fault, and aggressive in pursuit of his objectives. He was charming when it suited him, also alarmingly open about his worries and his family's situation.

With the gossips and tabbies, Jeanette knew to wrap her dignity about her like a velvet cloak. With uncertain young women, she was gracious and kind, but reserved. With the leering bachelors, she was toweringly indifferent. Society was neatly sorted, and with her, Society knew its place.

With Sycamore Dorning, she was all at sea, and had she been asked, she would have said she hated being all at sea, though she did not hate him. Worse—far worse—she was coming to not only like him, but also to trust him.

He handed her up into his town coach, an elegant conveyance with crests turned and footman, groom, and coachy in similarly smart, dark livery devoid of distinguishing flourishes.

"You like your comforts," she said, taking the forward-facing seat. He settled onto the bench beside her, which was bold of him, also considerate. Sitting side by side, Jeanette would not have to face him as he interrogated her about matters she'd dodged at dinner.

"I cherish my comforts," he said, "and all the while, I tell myself that I'm merely keeping up appearances. This coach was the result of a night of cards, with Ash partnering me. He has a talent for keeping numbers in his head that will make him wealthy if he ever decides to use it."

"This is your melancholy brother?" Jeanette knew Ash Dorning, had seen him lending an air of gracious reserve to the Coventry, a subtle contrast to Sycamore's more ebullient hospitality. She had also seen him at cards and knew his skill to be formidable.

"One doesn't bruit Ash's troubles about, but I trust your discretion. Tell me who is following you, because clearly, you trust my discretion as well."

Jeanette would never be that blunt, but from Sycamore Dorning, she found direct speech welcome. "I don't know who has taken an untoward interest in me. Some spy for the print shops or scandal sheets, I suppose. They are ever hungry to catch a wellborn woman in a peccadillo."

Mr. Dorning removed his hat and set it on the opposite seat. "You were followed home from the Coventry last week, my lady. If somebody wanted to make scandal out of that, they could have already done so. We were alone behind locked doors for hours."

Pleasant hours, oddly enough. "Prints take time to create, tattle takes time to write up."

"You do not believe you are being pursued by some scandalmongering journalist, and neither do I. You were followed to the Andersons' card party on Wednesday, where no scandal could possibly attach to you. Who is your heir?"

"What an odd question. Why would you...?" Her mind caught up with his line of inquiry. "You think somebody seeks to find me in a dark alley and put an end to me?"

"Humor me. I have a vivid imagination."

He also had a lovely way of holding a woman that put no demands on her. That half embrace in the cozy parlor, when Jeanette had allowed herself to lean against him, had been luscious and dangerous. He'd taken her weight, wrapped his arms gently around her, and let her rest against him. For Jeanette, the moment had come perilously close to tears, and perhaps he'd sensed that.

The man was damnably perceptive, though what did Jeanette have to cry about? A wealthy, titled widow was in every way to be envied, and Trevor was simply behaving as young men did when new to Town.

"My heir," Jeanette said, pulling her mind from the memory of a sweet embrace. "A few charities, but mostly my brother and his progeny, if any he has. If he should predecease me, more charities and Trevor."

Jeanette had not traveled side by side with a male escort in ages. Trevor did not count, being prone to fidgets and often preferring to ride on the box. Sycamore Dorning had a gentleman's reserve, and more than that, his muscular presence was reassuring.

"And if Trevor should predecease you?"

"The solicitors told me there's a list, by law, and it starts with Rye because he is my only living close relation. We have some cousins scattered around, and Trevor and Lord Beardsley are on the list further down. I have no reason to believe either Orion or Trevor will go to their reward before I do, though. Why do you...?" Again, she made the leap. "You suspect *my brother* means to do me harm?"

"I suspect everybody and nobody. We have no motive for why your privacy is being jeopardized, so we must plan for the worst. Your brother is inured to violence. He has estranged himself from you and bears a grudge against the world, to hear you tell it. If he knows he is your heir, he might plot against you."

The coach was plodding along at the walk, which was fine with Jeanette. She needed to sort her situation out, and Sycamore Dorning was—this still confounded her—a good listener.

"Orion abhors violence. He was an enthusiastic soldier when Papa bought him his colors, but Rye came home from the battlefields a changed man. His body is mostly whole, while his heart and mind... I no longer know him, but I cannot see him murdering his only sister."

"He stays on the list. Pay a call on him, get a sense for who he is now."

"Do not give me orders, Mr. Dorning."

"Do not scold me over trivialities, my lady. I can mince about making suggestions, leaving innuendo in the air for you to consider, or I can speak my mind and trust you will give me the benefit of the doubt."

Perhaps Jeanette had had too much good wine with dinner, perhaps the darkened coach interior and talk of murder had dislodged her wits. She had no other explanation for her reply.

"'Spread your damned legs, woman,'" she said, easily echoing her late husband's annoyance. "'Cease your infernal whimpering. If you can't show any enthusiasm, hold still and let me finish. Clothes off. I'm entitled to inspect my purchase. On the bed, and on your back, where you belong until you can fulfill the most basic of wifely duties.'"

Jeanette's throat abruptly went tight, and the silence in the coach became as painful as a murdered dream.

"He never *asked* me for anything," she said. "Never even asked me to marry him. My father didn't ask if I wanted to be married. Orion never asked what I thought of a military career, because I could have told him he wasn't suited to war. What you regard as a triviality—a demand rather than the courtesy of a suggestion or a request—I regard as a warning sign of impending disrespect. I will never again overlook such warning signs."

The coach rolled along through the darkness, and Jeanette felt the first tear slip down her cheek. What in all creation was wrong with her that putting Sycamore Dorning in his place should upset her so? He said nothing, merely sat beside her in the shadows, his presence no longer reassuring.

"I am not ridiculous," Jeanette said. "The marquess was ridiculous. I knew nothing of marital matters when I spoke my vows. My mother died when I was eleven, and I was kept in ignorance. I hate that I was ignorant, but the marquess made matters ten times worse than they had to be."

"The wedding night was a horror?" Sycamore asked, taking her hand.

"My worst memory. I so wanted to please him, and I was utterly shocked by what he expected of me. I found the whole business uncomfortable on every level. I do not mean to be difficult, but I am what he made me."

Sycamore wrapped his arm around Jeanette's shoulders, which ought to have struck her as a terrible presumption rather than a great comfort.

"You are not a bride ill-used by a cretin of a husband," he said. "You are wonderfully fierce. The old bugger did not make you fierce, you did that yourself. I treasure you for it, and I am sorry for my brusqueness. I should not have presumed."

Ill-used by a cretin of a husband. Jeanette's marriage in a nutshell. "I don't believe a man has ever apologized to me before." Much less so swiftly and sincerely.

"Then I'm your first true gentleman, a signal honor for me and a long overdue pleasure for you." He half hugged her, a friendly squeeze that bewildered Jeanette.

The late marquess had touched her only to exercise his marital rights or, when unavoidable, to observe a public propriety, such as escorting her up the church steps. Her lovers had been uninspired—

she'd suspected as much, and Sycamore had confirmed her hunch—and Rye... Rye's affectionate impulses were distant memories.

Very distant. "I will call on my brother," she said, swiping the back of her glove against her cheek. "The suggestion has merit, and I do worry about him."

Sycamore passed her a handkerchief. "Would you like my escort when you pay that visit?"

She'd just scolded him, blurted out horrid confidences, and behaved like a ninnyhammer, and his response was to apologize, hug her, and pass her his linen.

"I don't know if I should take an escort," she said. "I need time to think. I appreciate the offer." She appreciated the hug more, the arm around her shoulders, the hand holding hers. These overtures disturbed her, but they met a terrible need that all the dignity and self-possession in the world could not quench.

They also blended with the low, insistent hum of desire that had started up when Jeanette had first noticed Sycamore Dorning lounging by the steps at the Coventry months ago. She had ignored the desire—pesky annoyance, desire—but she could not ignore *him.*

"I give a lot of orders at the club," Sycamore said, gaze on the coach lamp. "I make demands rather than requests because I am afraid nobody will listen to me if I'm polite instead of politely overbearing. Do you suppose the marquess was prone to the same insecurity?"

Jeanette let her head rest against Sycamore's shoulder. He could not know how such a capacity for self-examination awed her and unnerved her. To him, his own responses were a puzzle to be understood, not a citadel of masculine dignity to be defended.

"The late marquess," she said, "was an entitled ass, spoiled from birth, and indulged in every regard. Perhaps on some unspoken level, he sensed he had not earned his privileges, and he blustered to distract anybody from noticing that fact. The result was still a miserable staff, a miserable wife, and a son who barely knew him."

"Are you miserable now, my lady?"

She was snuggled against a man who apologized, a man who'd made no unwelcome overtures and who'd offered to take on her troubles out of simple decency. He also threw a lethally accurate knife and admitted to being plagued by worry and nostalgia.

"I am not miserable, Mr. Dorning."

He relaxed against her. "Then neither am I. But, my lady?"

"Hmm?" She was abruptly drowsy, and he made a comfortable pillow.

He shifted again and dimmed the coach lamp. "Never mind. The rest of our discussion will keep. Have a nap, and I will look forward to hearing your decision regarding a call on Orion Goddard."

CHAPTER FIVE

"Lady Tavistock was married off to a rutting martinet who wanted only obedience and sons from her," Sycamore said, pacing around the hazard table as morning sun slanted through the Coventry's windows. The windows were too high to afford a view into the place, but they provided good ventilation. "Now somebody is following her ladyship intermittently, and she can't bring herself to consider motives and malcontents."

Ash Dorning, looking relaxed and a little bored on a dealer's stool, watched Sycamore pace. "So Lady Tavistock asked you to sort out the business for her? What aren't you telling me, Cam?"

Sycamore wasn't telling Ash a great deal. The head waiter had vexed the undercook and nearly caused a kitchen war. Mrs. General Higginbotham had played too deeply and offered ruby earbobs in repayment, but an appraisal revealed the jewels to be paste. The champagne merchant, Monsieur Fournier, was being coy about the date of the next delivery.

So much Sycamore could tell Ash, the point of which would have been to emphasize... what? How necessary and important Sycamore was to the club? To his brother? To avoid admitting how much he missed Ash?

"Not here," Sycamore said, taking the stairs two at a time. The cleaning crew came through at dawn, but the junior kitchen staff would soon arrive, and like the rest of the Coventry's employees, they enjoyed a good gossip among themselves.

Ash followed more slowly, his mood apparently sanguine. His darling wife, the former Lady Della Haddonfield, had hauled Ash by the *ear* off to warmer climes for a winter holiday and honeymoon. Sycamore knew the look of a brother wondering if his wife was already on the nest.

Fast work, even for a Dorning in love. But then, a former Haddonfield had also been involved in the situation, and the Haddonfields were not retiring by nature.

Sycamore closed the office door and remained on his feet. "Lady Tavistock's step-son lost a fair amount here Saturday night. She is agreeable to having his lordship work off his debt to us."

Ash peered at the new print hanging behind the sideboard, a framed version of the late Mr. Gillray's hilarious, satirical, and ever-so-accurate *L'Assemblée Nationale*. Quite a find, that.

"We don't need his lordling-ship flirting with the dealers and swilling our champagne, Cam. He's a nice enough lad, but you might have discussed this with me before you agreed to it."

"I might have, but you barely show the colors here anymore, Ash, and besides, I have not yet put the notion to the marquess. If you object, I will simply hold his lordship's vowels until they are paid off. I am *asking* for your comment, rather than presenting you with a fait accompli."

And yet, even asking for comment was the behavior of a senior partner.

Big Brother was also apparently disinclined to take the seat behind the desk. "Why do this? Why involve yourself in somebody else's troubles when all and sundry know you to be driven entirely by self-interest?"

Lady Tavistock did not believe Sycamore driven entirely by self-interest. "I cannot help that all and sundry *Dornings* insist on seeing me as if I'm eight years old and forced to cause a riot simply to get the jam passed my way. I am drawn to young Tavistock's situation because I had myriad examples of how not to behave as I came of age, while he is on his own."

Ash propped a hip against the desk. In his morning finery, he looked of a piece with the appointments. The beads of the mahogany abacus were marble, the wax jack silver and fashioned to match the pen tray and ink bottle. The room looked like what it was—the administrative epicenter of a thriving enterprise—and also like a gentleman's retreat.

The sofa was long enough to sleep on, the reading chairs both had leather hassocks, and the prints on the walls were among the less bawdy political cartoons.

Ash *belonged* here, but Sycamore had already lost his brother in some material sense. Lost this brother too. Where howling grief should have been, Sycamore felt mostly bewilderment and a little impatience.

"I have been preoccupied," Ash said, a rare smile revealing him for the handsome devil he was. Dark-haired, lean, murderously skilled in a fight, he was also, and more importantly, the apple of Lady Della's eye.

"You have been married and on your honeymoon, but Town is filling up, Ash, and if you don't care to keep your hand in here, we need to find you an understudy." *Argue with me, tell me you're ready to roll up your sleeves and rescue the place from my neglect.*

"Tavistock isn't even of age, Sycamore. You are taking him under your wing solely to curry favor with Lady Tavistock."

Not true, and that Ash would make the accusation was frustrating. "Perhaps I want a younger-brother figure on the premises to regularly insult."

Ash's boot began to swing. "I know I haven't been underfoot much, but what I do—the books, the wages, the inventory, looking after the coal man, and making sure the carpets are beaten—doesn't require that I be here of a night."

For the past four months, Sycamore had managed that list and much else besides. "Precisely. You've left me on my own to sort out the kitchen squabbles, keep an eye on the inebriates trying to fondle the dealers' knees beneath the table, monitor play to see who's losing too much, and remind the waiters that the buffet does not replenish itself. I cannot be everywhere at once, and Tavistock can aid me in that regard."

Ash rose from the desk and settled into a reading chair. "What is afoot with the marchioness, Cam? You were smitten with her at the Wentwhistles' house party, and your passions are as all-consuming as they are fleeting. Not to put too fine a point on it, but I do recall you telling me how much you enjoy a good, hard fuck."

"And you don't? Who knew my enthusiasm for reproductive activity was just another of my endless eccentricities?"

"I have missed you," Ash said, propping his boots on a hassock, "though I'm not exactly sure why."

"Because I am honest to a fault, conscientious, and to those I care about, as loyal as an old dog. The marchioness asked for my help, and I doubt she has other options in terms of practical assistance."

Sycamore took the other chair and was reminded—painfully—of the many nights he and Ash had spent trading ideas, grumbling, and insulting each other before this same hearth.

Now, Sycamore was running the damned club on his own, and Ash was still treating him as if he needed help tying his cravats. Was this same frustration what drove the young marquess to foolishness?

"Lady Tavistock is a well-heeled widow," Ash said. "She can hire bodyguards, put her footmen on alert, and take the knocker off the door."

Sycamore slouched into the cushions, finding the spot that cradled his bum with loving familiarity. "They are the marquess's footmen, and the knocker is on his door. I thought you liked her."

"I do like her, and I respect her, but I like you more—may heaven forgive me such folly—and I don't want to see you either cast aside for attempting misplaced gallantries or entangled in somebody else's stupidity."

"Now you know how I felt when you decided to rescue Lady Della from scandal. 'There he goes,' I thought, 'the finest of men on the most foolish of quests.'"

Ash regarded him in some puzzlement. "My quest was gentlemanly. The tabbies were circling, and Della needed a gallant."

"Am I incapable of gentlemanly sentiments?"

Ash considered that question as if the answer merited some study. "You tend to get consumed by gentlemanly sentiments, one after another. Her ladyship has a brother, if I recall."

"Colonel Sir Orion Goddard, touched by some military scandal nobody seems to know much about. He keeps his distance from her ladyship for no discernible reason. Lady Tavistock's late husband was a petty dictator, her step-son is a self-absorbed bantling, and her father was responsible for marrying her off to the dictator. If she ever had a trusting nature, her menfolk disappointed her out of it."

Ash sat up, his boots hitting the floor with a *thump*. "Thus she turns to you?"

"I served as her banker at the Wentwhistle house party, Ash. She knows I can be discreet and honorable."

She did not yet know Sycamore could be passionate, inventive, and great good fun in bed. When a woman was recounting the horror her marriage had been, for Sycamore to inform her that he desired her madly would have been selfish.

With her ladyship, Sycamore wanted to be very selfish, also very generous, and—this gave him pause—utterly *selfless*. A muddle to end all muddles.

"You can be discreet and honorable," Ash said, rising, "but I've long suspected you show us your gallant side mostly to confuse us as to your true nature. Can Tavistock be any use to you at all, or are you saddling us with a bumbling puppy?"

"A little of both."

"Then let him follow you around for a few nights, and if he survives that ordeal, I'll show him the books and inventories some afternoon next week."

Sycamore rose, his joints protesting. He'd not slept well, and dawn had seen him taking his horse out for a morning gallop in the park nonetheless. Thus did the Season's exhaustion begin, until pleasure and duty blended into a fog of busyness, and grouse season loomed like salvation.

"Do you have any time to spar with me at Angelo's this week?" Sycamore asked.

"Thursday suits. Ten of the clock, and then we can have lunch at the club. Della likes an afternoon outing in the park if the weather is fine."

Della was doubtless scheduling those outings to get Ash into the sunshine and fresh air, part of her prescription for keeping the blue devils at bay—and for showing off her handsome husband.

"Married life is going well?" Sycamore asked as he and Ash descended to the gambling floor. The question was both perfunctory and pressing, for if Ash's mood gave way to melancholia, Della would be coping with a very difficult situation indeed.

"Do you recall when we started here, Cam? We made money from the first day, and both of us were so surprised to succeed that we tiptoed through the weekly ledger balancing. 'Too good to be true,' we thought. 'Any moment, the club will fail, and it will be our fault.'"

"Marriage is too good to be true?"

"Marriage to Della is so lovely, even the rough patches are magic."

Those were the words of a man awash in connubial bliss, and not all of his joy was based in erotic satisfaction. Sycamore knew Della and knew that her regard for Ash was unwavering and reciprocated.

"Tell Della that, Ash. Tell her that even the rough patches with her are magic. And if the weather is fine, *ask* her if she'd like to drive out with you. Don't assume that's what she wants."

Ash paused by the side door to settle his hat on his head and take up his walking stick. "You are giving marital advice now?"

Glass shattered somewhere in the vicinity of the kitchen, followed by fluent French obscenities. Another workday at the Coventry had begun.

"When we ask the ladies what they want, we are obliged to listen to their replies, and who does not appreciate a respectful listener?"

"We will talk further about the situation here," Ash said, "and please give my regards to the marchioness. She struck me as lonely, and loneliness is not a curse I would wish on anybody." He dragged Sycamore into a quick, tight hug, thumped him once on the back, and slipped out the door.

The cursing from the kitchen subsided into the usual yelling, and Sycamore remained by the door, watching Ash stride off to rejoin his bride.

The marchioness might be lonely—Sycamore would ask her about that—but he for damned sure was. Also, worried for her, and randy, and not sure how to resolve any of those dilemmas. That he was more concerned with his club and her ladyship than with Ash's moods and unavailability was cause for some puzzlement—and also a bit of relief.

THE RARE STEAK on Trevor's plate threatened to make the two cups of tea he'd managed earlier in the day reappear.

"You aren't looking quite the thing, old man," Jerome said, pouring them each a glass of claret. "Try a little hair of the dog and see if your afternoon doesn't improve."

Trevor's morning had consisted of rising well past dawn and avoiding Step-mama, solid food, and bright sunshine. He had taken the town coach for the few streets between Tavistock House and Jerome's club and wished he'd sent his regrets to this luncheon instead.

"Tea will do," Trevor said.

Jerome lifted his glass in a silent toast. "Your head is the very devil, I take it?"

"The devil and all his infernal imps singing my doom to the accompaniment of kettle drums." Trevor signaled to a waiter and made a pouring-out gesture.

Monday evening had begun with the clear intention to drop by The Coventry Club and have a word with Mr. Sycamore Dorning about payment of certain debts in a certain little while. Jerome had loyally agreed to accompany Trevor on that awkward mission. A stop at Jerome's club for fortification had become several rounds of fortification and then a few hands of cards.

The direction the cards had taken required more fortification, and at some point, Trevor had been talked into attempting to prove he was equal to a few glasses of Scottish whisky—not a gentleman's drink—and matters thereafter had become very merry.

Also very stupid. Again.

"Town life takes some getting used to," Jerome said. "You'll find your stride in another few weeks. Takes stamina to truly enjoy London. Did her ladyship sermonize at you over your breakfast tea?"

Thoughts of Step-mama were anything but cheering, though a sermon from her might assuage the guilt of being half-seas over yet again.

"I missed her at breakfast, but she doesn't have to sermonize. She looks me up and down, and I feel about eight years old, and as if I've been caught stealing shortbread from the pantry."

Jerome cut into his steak, and Trevor pretended to take visual inventory of the dining room's other patrons. By day, these men were ordinary enough. A baronet's son, an earl's nephew. The grandson of a gun manufacturer who'd grown rich during the unpleasantness with the Americans. By night, they turned into witty, clever, handsome fellows always willing to stand each other to another round.

Or did they?

"Tell your step-mama not to be disrespectful," Jerome said. "I heard your late papa holding forth more than once about what a poor marchioness the most honorable Jeanette made. Uncle chose her, so I suppose we must not blame her for being ill-suited to her role, but you don't have to encourage her presumptions."

Jerome paused in the consumption of his steak to sip his wine. He had mastered the art of lordly dining, of making the meal secondary to the company he offered, while Trevor longed for a dark, quiet room.

"You must not speak ill of her ladyship," Trevor said. "She was a very young bride, and her hopes of motherhood were disappointed. Ah, the tea tray approaches."

Jerome's smile was sympathetic. "You need to put more meat on your bones, my boy. You'd hold your drink more easily, and then Jeanette would have less cause to rip up at you."

The waiter took the steak away—thank God—and Trevor poured himself a cup of salvation. "Where are you off to tonight?" A change of subject seemed in order, lest Jerome wax any more eloquent about Step-mama's nonexistent shortcomings.

And must Jerome look so casually elegant while criticizing his female relation? Whereas Trevor was too tall, too fair, and too skinny —the tailor's word was *slender*—Jerome was an elegant two inches above average height, carried some muscle, and wore his golden hair a la Byron. He knew everybody, was invited everywhere, and was as comfortable at the cockpits as he was mincing through minuets.

He would have made a splendid marquess, though he never once mentioned the title. And yet, the title lay between Trevor and his only male cousin, both bond and barrier.

"Step-mama does not rip up at me," Trevor said, dipping a lemon biscuit into his tea. "She has a care for how I go on because she is loyal to Papa's memory."

Jerome waved a bite of steak around on his fork. "She hated the old rooster. I didn't like him much myself, but he saw to it I was properly educated. Mama is asking when you will visit your lady cousins."

The old rooster. That was blatant disrespect, and Trevor ought not to countenance it, even from Jerome.

"Papa remarried because he did not want the entire burden of the succession to fall on me, and we must respect him for that," Trevor said, though as scolds went, that was a weak effort.

"Your Papa fancied himself a cocksman. Speaking of which, shall we drop around to see the ladies tonight?"

Trevor had so far avoided any visits to the bordellos with Jerome. The whole business of choosing a woman the same way he'd choose a hack at a livery stable struck him as distasteful, also ill-advised from the standpoint of protecting his health.

Temples of Venus were temples of disease, as Step-mama's brother had informed Trevor shortly after Trevor's fifteenth birthday. Goddard's warning had stuck with Trevor as various friends had cheerfully complained of contracting the bachelor's ailment, the Covent Garden ague, or the Corsican's revenge.

So many names for an avoidable misery.

"I will leave the ladies to you, for I must make my obeisance at The Coventry Club," Trevor said. "I want that chore behind me." Thank heavens Step-mama had increased his allowance, and yet, the sum he'd lost would still take some time to repay.

"Come with me," Jerome said. "You can have your chat with Sycamore Dorning after your spirits have been lifted, so to speak."

Trevor poured himself another cup of the tea, the previous three having had a mild restorative effect. "A gentleman pays his debts of honor, Jere." Trevor would also ask Mr. Sycamore Dorning for a few pointers at the tables, in hopes that further losses might be prevented. At last autumn's house party, Mr. Ash Dorning had opined that such lessons would be freely given.

"Perhaps a gentleman has his own bit of muslin secreted away in a pretty little house on a pretty little street in Bloomsbury?" Jerome mused, finishing his wine. "But no, Bloomsbury is too predictable. Knightsbridge. Easy access to the park for a morning ride after your evening ride, not as likely to be frequented by polite society, and—lest we forget the priorities—affordable."

"Until I bring my finances 'round," Trevor replied, "not affordable enough." The increase in his allowance should have made such an arrangement possible. Step-mama was dignified, but she had an ease with the practicalities that Trevor lacked, and she made no inquiries about how he spent his money. Perhaps she had *intended* him to take a mistress, not that he'd ever ask her.

Lack of funds aside, there also remained the conundrum of how to meet a woman willing to occupy such a pretty little house, and on what terms to offer her its use. All complicated, and not a topic Trevor wanted to raise with Jerome—or anybody.

"Until you bring your finances 'round," Jerome said, crossing his knife and fork over his empty plate, "you will be no damned fun. Tell the solicitors to arrange an advance. They send word to the bank, and darling Jeanette is none the wiser."

"Her ladyship is not 'darling Jeanette' to you, Jerome. Have a care." Besides, her ladyship read the bank statements as if they were Wellington's dispatches from the front. She'd notice.

Jerome smiled lazily and helped himself to Trevor's untouched wine. "So protective. Will you call me out, Tav?"

"I will beat you silly for ungentlemanly conduct. Her ladyship has not had an easy time of it, and she is dear to me." Step-mama was family to Trevor in a way nobody else was. She had made certain his tutors were more interested in educating him than intimidating him, and she had prevented him from being sent off to Eton until he'd been twelve years old and eager for the experience.

Jerome left a half inch of wine in the glass. "Jeanette is not bad looking. I've thought of marrying her."

Trevor nearly spluttered his tea all over the table. "I beg your pardon?"

"Jeanette. She's only five years my senior, and that would keep her settlements in the family. When Mama stops nattering on about you marrying Diana or Hera, she lately takes up a refrain about the marchioness being young enough to remarry."

Abruptly, even the tea rebelled. "What on earth can you say to such ridiculous notions?"

"I don't have to say anything. Papa reminds Mama that Jeanette is barren, and Mama subsides into silence. The whole burden of the succession isn't on you, dear boy. A portion of it is reserved for my humble and handsome self."

"Which is more comfort to me than you can possibly know. Stepmama would never have you, though, so you are safe from Auntie's schemes."

Jerome laid his table napkin beside his plate. "You think the marchioness is some sort of paragon of feminine virtue, but she's a woman like any other. She has needs, and she has far too much blunt for one female. I might win her over, given enough time. I can be charming, and I would not put excessive demands on her."

"Hush," Trevor said, more upset than he cared to show. "Hush and don't speak of this again. If her ladyship had any inclination to remarry at all, I would know it, and I can assure you, that citadel will never crumble. Particularly not to suit your notions of keeping money within the family and conveniently within your reach."

Jerome rose. "Never say never, Cousin, but do give the Coventry my regards." He flourished a bow and strode off, a fashion plate on two legs, leaving Trevor upset in body, mind, and belly.

"MY LORD, let's take this discussion upstairs, shall we?" Sycamore gestured in the direction of the Coventry's office. He wore his most genial smile, the better to torment young Tavistock. If the marquess expected a lot of deference and delicacy, he was soon to be disappointed. "I trust you've come to pay off your vowels. I commend you for tending to your debts of honor promptly."

The marquess's fair complexion had a slight greenish cast, poor lad. He went up the steps as enthusiastically as a boy who expects not only a birching from Headmaster, but a lengthy lecture besides.

Sycamore closed the office door and crossed to the sideboard. "May I offer you some brandy? It's a fine vintage, if I do say so myself."

"No brandy for me, thank you."

"You were doing your part to drain my stores of champagne on Saturday night, my lord. Dare I observe that copious drink and wagering are not a wise combination?"

Tavistock took out a pair of spectacles and peered at the Gillray print. "Is that why you serve free champagne, to make people foolish?"

Not exactly the question of a penitent. "I do not *make* people foolish any more than I can make the foolish wise. Shall you have a seat, my lord?"

"I don't want to sit," Tavistock said. "I want to bolt out that door and never set foot in this establishment again."

Sycamore took the chair behind the desk, a minor disrespect given Tavistock's rank. "But here you are."

Tavistock left off pretending to study visual humor that he was too young to truly comprehend. "I need a little time, Mr. Dorning. My allowance is adequate to cover my losses, but not until the next payment. If you would permit me to tend to my vowels in increments, I would appreciate it."

Six months ago, Tavistock had had some boyish charm to go with his inexperience. London, or somebody in London, was not having a good effect on his lordship.

"And if I don't care to wait on your next quarterly installment?" Sycamore said, leaning back. "I run a business, my lord, and if you cannot pay in coin, then you should be looking for a way to pay in kind. A gentleman pays his debts of honor timely."

Tavistock took the chair opposite the desk. "You won't give me even a few weeks? That's a bit harsh, Mr. Dorning."

"Men have been called out for less, my lord. Debts of honor are exactly that. I cannot haul you into court on a gambling marker, and why should I have to? You own several estates, an entire dressing closet of finery, at least three riding horses, any number of matched teams, gold cravat pins, jeweled snuffboxes ... You are more than able to pay. You simply choose not to."

Tavistock's expression was perplexed. "I'm to surrender my goods to you?"

The seraphic chorus might be more innocent than the marquess, but not by much. "I could take a horse in payment, if I needed one, but I don't, and horseflesh is devilish expensive to keep in Town. Have your manservant take some of your uglier jeweled sleeve buttons, rings, or shoe buckles around to the pawnshops, and they'll make an offer. You can redeem the goods at exorbitant rates, but it's not exactly usury, so the authorities turn a blind eye."

"My valet was inherited from my father. He can barely get up the steps to dress me of a morning."

"Put your dilemma to your butler. A good London butler is part magician."

Tavistock crossed his legs at the knee. "Peem is nearly as old as my valet, and to tell him anything, I would have to shout. I'd rather Lady Tavistock remain unaware of my wagering."

I was never this young, was I? "Half the club saw you losing your quarterly allowance along with your common sense and self-restraint. You can't keep this from her, my lord."

Tavistock ran a hand through blond curls. "Her ladyship won't say a word. You have no idea, Mr. Dorning, *no idea* how her silences can rend a fellow's wits. Her disappointment was always worse than my father's, for Papa would bluster and threaten and then settle down to grumbling. Step-mama merely went quiet, and I vowed never to disappoint her again."

"And yet, you made a complete cake of yourself with a half dozen of your very best friends cheering you on. Have any of them offered to make you a loan?"

Tavistock blinked. "Why would they?"

"Because they are your friends?"

Tavistock uncrossed his legs. "I am a year or two behind most of them, but spending more time at university studying Latin that I could translate before I left Eton struck me as silly."

Sycamore was tempted to relent, but this young sprig had no older brothers, and he was to be pitied that poverty. "And losing a small fortune was wise?"

"I was an idiot," Tavistock said, bolting to his feet. "If you'd like me to beg for your forgiveness, I'm not sure I'm capable. Begging is quite *infra dig*."

Infra dignitatem. Beneath one's dignity. "No, actually, it isn't. I would beg for one more walk alone with my father through the Dorsetshire countryside. I'd beg for the lives of my siblings or their spouses and offspring. I'd beg for their happiness and health, and I'd beg for your life, Tavistock, because the marchioness would grieve to lose you. I'll ask something of you far more challenging than simple begging."

"What could possibly make a greater demand on a man's *amour propre* than abasing himself before another?"

"I seek to challenge more than your overdeveloped pride, Tavistock. I will challenge your patience, your ingenuity, your manners, and your mind."

Tavistock's features shuttered into caution. His lordship was entirely too easy to read and very much in need of the sort of education the Coventry—and Sycamore—could provide him.

"I want you to work off your debt to me, Tavistock. Give me your time and your best efforts and assist me to keep this club running smoothly a few nights a week."

Tavistock examined a pocket watch that would have put a noticeable dent in his debt to Sycamore.

"Work for you? You want me to carry a tray of champagne around like a dancing bear?"

Six months ago, Tavistock would not have attempted that haughty arch of his eyebrow. All he needed was a jewel-handled quizzing glass and a flatulent pug to become truly obnoxious.

"I have personally offered champagne to my guests when the

waiters are run off their feet, Tavistock, because I want the people who come to my club to be treated as guests, and I want my staff to know they matter to me as well. I have taken an occasional empty platter back to the kitchen, because it's more important that the tray be refilled than that I impersonate the idle ornaments whiling away their evenings at the table. I *work* at the Coventry, and I earn my way. If honest labor is beneath you, then I can withdraw the offer."

For the first time, a hint of vulnerability showed in Tavistock's blue eyes. "Honest labor is not beneath me, for I have incurred a debt and I mean to pay you. You should know, though, that I tend to make a muddle of everything. Aunt Viola says my dancing is too enthusiastic, by which she means that I have no grace. My valet tells me that I'm not up to my father's standards in terms of fashion, and even when I do shout, Peem still sometimes refers to me by the courtesy title rather than as Tavistock."

The marquess paced the carpet before the desk, clearly not finished with his soliloquy. "Cousin Jerome got all the panache and refinement. I got the extra height and the title. Auntie wants me to marry my cousin Diana, but I like the woman, and the shuddery part that we're cousins aside, she deserves a husband who can manage a waltz without falling on his bum. I want very much to live up to my father's memory, Mr. Dorning, but the job is more complicated than you might think, and I am not suited to it at all."

Tavistock did not resume his seat so much as he collapsed in a brooding heap of fine tailoring and lanky limbs.

Had Casriel felt this overwhelmed and inept when Papa had tossed him the earldom's business and gone botanizing in rural Ireland? From earliest childhood, Casriel had seemed even more adult than Papa, even more forbearing and patient.

Sycamore entertained the possibility—so slight as to be theoretical—that he was not the only Dorning brother to feel invisible among a horde of siblings. That he was not the only brother whose needs and wants had gone unheard beneath the fraternal din and Mama's incessant whining.

"Tavistock, calm yourself. Your duties here at the Coventry would mostly consist of keeping an eye on matters where I cannot. Taking inventory in the wine cellar, monitoring the buffet, and smiling. If anybody asks, tell them you are helping me out a few nights a week."

"I'm not, though," Tavistock said miserably. "I cannot manage my funds. I let Jerome and his cronies goad me into playing too deep, and I can't even sell you my horse. I like him—my horse, that is—so it's as well you won't take him."

Sycamore rose and opened the door. "I'm sure he's a very fine animal, Tavistock. I suggest you have a long talk with him before supper, and for God's sake, take a nap and swill at least a quart of lemonade and chew half a bushel of parsley. Your head will thank you for it. Be back here by about nine, and we'll get started."

"Nine tonight?"

"Yes, nine tonight. Formal attire, as if you were hosting a supper for thirty. Away with you, and let your step-mother know what's afoot so she won't worry. What you say to Jerome Vincent is your business, but if I were you, I'd exercise a bit of discretion." *For once.*

Tavistock rose. He was nearly as tall as Sycamore, but not half so muscular. Time would solve that problem—time and determination.

"Until nine tonight, Mr. Dorning." He marched out the door, probably intent on confessing all to his gallant steed, but he stopped in the corridor. "Thank you. You are being gracious to a titled ninnyhammer. Not everybody would be."

"The title is not your fault," Sycamore said, "and we are all ninnyhammers on occasion."

Tavistock smiled at that, revealing a dimple the ladies would positively swoon over, and slid down the bannister to the landing below. "Until tonight, Mr. Dorning!" He attempted a bow, tripped over the carpet fringe, and nearly upset a tower of drinking glasses stacked on the bar.

"Until tonight," Sycamore said, saluting with two fingers and offering up a prayer for fortitude.

CHAPTER SIX

"How is Tavistock doing?" Jeanette asked, passing Sycamore her cloak. Typical of spring weather, Sunday morning had dawned brisk and sunny, while noon had seen clouds gather, and the afternoon skies had offered a sleety drizzle.

"You should ask him," Sycamore replied, giving her cloak a shake, "and we should hang this in the kitchen." He strode off toward a pair of swinging doors, the sodden cloak leaving a trail of droplets on the bricks of the hallway floor.

Jeanette followed with her umbrella, curious to see the kitchens where so much good food was produced. The space was larger than she'd imagined, being half sunken and high ceilinged.

"Somebody is neat as a pin," she said, admiring gleaming knives, sparkling tiles, and a black behemoth of a range set against the outside wall. Three turnspits inside an enormous open hearth created a forest of cast-iron gears and chains, while no less than four Dutch ovens had been built into the bricks surrounding the hearth.

"I enter here at my peril after sundown," Sycamore said, draping Jeanette's cloak on hooks before the hearth. "Your bonnet could do with drying out."

Jeanette passed over her millinery, among her plainest, and peeled off damp gloves as well. "I don't mind that London is often cold," she said, "but I mind that it's so dirty when it's cold."

"And smelly when it's hot—smellier." He hung her hat on another hook, her gloves draped over the brim. "Shall we to the cellar, my lady?"

Jeanette had hoped that familiarity with Sycamore Dorning would reduce his appeal. She had dreamed of him, as if she were a schoolgirl smitten by one of Sir Walter Scott's brave knights. Dreamed of him walking away, and worse, she had daydreamed of him naked from the waist up, muscles rippling as he let fly with a knife. She was haunted by the memory of his chest, his back, his taut belly, and the roped strength of his arms and shoulders.

Worse yet, she could not get the memory of his smile—naughty and sweet at the same time—from her mind. His mouth was made for smiling, his eyes for flirtation, and his hands...

Jeanette was not smitten, she was merely aware of him as a man. While this occasioned some relief—she was not dead yet, not the Puritan widow she wanted Society to believe she was—she was also at a complete loss for what to *do* about the persistent desire.

"How are you today?" he asked, leading her through the doorway to the cellar steps.

"I am pleased to see my step-son regularly appearing at breakfast, though he then proceeds to bed and does not rise until it's time to rejoin you here."

"Tavistock isn't stupid," Sycamore replied. "He has honestly been helpful to me. His lordship notices when a patron is bothering a dealer beneath the table, for example, and he notices when a lady is imbibing too quickly. His youth means the older women find him harmless and easy to talk to, a role that I, in my advancing years, can no longer fulfill."

"You were never harmless."

He set the knife case on the head of a barrel and undid the locks.

"I am harmless to you, my lady." He opened the case and passed her a knife, his gaze direct and *knowing*.

The target was set on a chair a few yards down the corridor. Jeanette took the knife and held it, the hilt now a familiar shape against her palm.

"You are not harmless," she said, rolling the hilt between her hands. "You disturb my peace by the hour."

Sycamore stepped behind her. "Focus on the target, your ladyship. If you are frustrated, direct that sentiment at the target, not at my hapless self."

Frustrated. Was that the word for burning curiosity about a man's kisses, about the texture of his hair, and the look of him without a stitch of clothing?

"Right," Jeanette said, forcing herself into the routine her instructor had shown her. Focus, relax, breathe, throw. She cycled through the focus-relax-breathe sequence several times, and yet, Sycamore Dorning's presence behind her was a weight on her awareness.

She had virtuosic ability to ignore men, a skill developed of necessity during her marriage. She had learned how to mentally sort linen while her husband rutted, to plan a guest list while he snored atop her, to revise a menu while he fumbled himself into a state of arousal and pawed at her breasts.

She could separate mind and body as effectively as Sycamore's knives sliced through the shadowed cellar to bite into the waiting target.

"Just throw the damned thing, Jeanette. You're thinking it to death."

Jeanette. She hurled the knife and was surprised it hit the target.

"You released too soon," he said, and even that factual statement took on sexual connotations. How often had the late marquess spent only two instants after he'd effected a joining of his body to his wife's?

"Right," Jeanette said. "Knife."

Sycamore slapped the weapon into her hand. "The release is your farewell caress to the blade. Linger a bit."

Thoroughly indecent images came to mind. This throw also hit the target only a few inches off center.

"Better," he said. "Less force this time, more precision. Watch the knife as it sails into the wood. You can build up to both speed and force later in the session. Start with accuracy."

"Knife," Jeanette growled.

He obliged and stepped back.

She wanted to murder not the target, but her preoccupation with Sycamore Dorning. He was so calm, so damned detached, while she was battling an unwanted and completely useless attraction. This was not supposed to happen, and yet, Jeanette was unable to ignore what her mind and body were determined to notice.

She put that vexation into her throw, put the bewilderment—why him, why now?—into the speed and power of her arm.

"That is the smoothest arc you've made so far," he said. "You're finding your rhythm."

Rhythm. Would he be a slow and sweet lover, or sexually relentless? Probably both, damn him. "Knife."

Jeanette allowed herself only one breath, then sent the knife flying. This one also struck close to center, and struck hard.

"Excellent balance between force, speed, and precision, and the release was perfect. Do that again."

Do that again. "Knife." She hit the only side of the target's center not already occupied by a knife, the pattern of the blades cause for dark satisfaction. "Knife."

"Choose where you sink the blade, my lady. High noon, just off ten of the clock, a shade beneath four o'clock. You decide, and the weapon does your bidding."

"High noon," she said, eyeing the top of the target. Her aim was a hair off to the right, but only a hair. "Knife."

"You've finished the set. What is different today from last week?"

I want to kiss you. "I am less worried about Trevor, I suppose." And more fixated on watching Sycamore Dorning's mouth.

"He'll come right. When a man wants to be of use, but he's born to idleness, charting a course can too easily descend into protecting his right to remain idle. I'll retrieve the knives, and we can hope the second set goes as well as the first."

He ambled forward, no coat, just waistcoat and shirt, cuffs turned back, and pulled the knives one by one from the target.

"My lady, you are staring at me," he said, prowling toward her and laying the knives in their velvet case. "I am undone?"

Jeanette focused on the target sitting in the shadows down the corridor. "I was trying to discern whether you are... in a state suggestive of..." Heat flared in her cheeks.

"Whether I'm aroused?" he asked, sounding ever so nonchalant. "I am, moderately, but the experience of desire when I'm around you is apparently my normal condition. Watching you hit that target today tests my usual restraint. I can often think myself into a more genteel frame of mind. I contemplate ledger books and how long the coal in the cellar will last until we need another load delivered into the hole... But today, even that analogy fuels my imagination."

"So why aren't you pawing at me?"

He smiled faintly. "Why aren't *you* pawing at *me*? I am more than willing to be pawed, my lady. Mauled and bitten even, provided you start gently."

He stood two steps away, as luscious and cool as a chocolate ice, and Jeanette felt tears threaten.

"I don't know how, damn you. You aren't like the others. All they wanted was a tame little romp before drifting off to dream about the price of wool. Thank God you are not like my husband either."

Sycamore came half a step closer. "I am not at all like your miserable excuse for a spouse. If you take me as a lover, there will be no holding still, and if anybody gets to whimpering, the cause will be an unbearable excess of pleasure."

The cellar held subterranean quiet, while Jeanette's heart

pounded with both dread and anticipation. *If you take me as a lover…* Sycamore Dorning was offering her something no other man had offered her.

The power to choose. The power to decide, to change her mind, to refine on her options, to come closer or to walk away. At the same time, he was warning her. If she chose him, she'd be flying into the unknown, *with him.*

"I choose to allow you to kiss me," Jeanette said, her voice steadier than her nerves. "So please be about it."

SYCAMORE COULD HEAR a chorus of older brothers all nattering at him in unison: *Do not bungle this one and only opportunity to coax the marchioness into sampling your limited charms.*

"How fortunate," Sycamore replied, "for I choose to allow you to kiss me as well. I am at your service, my lady." The initiative had to be hers. Sycamore was not sure why—he was happy to play the pursuer in the usual course—but instinct told him that with Jeanette, restraint on his part was imperative.

She gave him the sort of look a new footman would earn when he'd buttoned his livery wrong. "You expect me to sashay over there and make free with your person?"

"I long ardently for that very fate. Nobody has made free with me in such a long, lonely time, you see, and until you do, I cannot reciprocate the pleasure."

"But you seem like such a flirt."

She was stalling, bless her. "Flirtation is a skill I hope I can claim," Sycamore said, "a harmless social accomplishment. You inspire *desire*, my lady, and that is a very different and more precious article."

"You called me Jeanette earlier."

"While you have yet to call me Sycamore. I suppose you could call me Mr. Dorning in bed, in that prim, maidenly way you have. I would probably expire of lust on the spot, set the sheets on fire, and singe you in the process."

That earned him a slight, bewildered smile. "Sycamore, I have no idea how to proceed. With Endicott and Forster, I didn't even permit any kissing."

"And they, poor lads, allowed you to deny yourself that pleasure. I will delight in kissing you, Jeanette, in fondling you where and how you wish to be fondled, in encouraging your explorations of my person to the most intimate degree, but you have to give me some encouragement too."

That a man could need encouragement was apparently a new thought for her. She stepped closer, slid a cool hand up Sycamore's chest and around to his nape, and touched her lips to his cheek.

"Like that?"

"Lovely," he said, though damnably, maddeningly chaste. Still, she had made a beginning. "Let's elaborate on that theme, shall we?" He drew her closer, and she came willingly.

"We fit nicely," he said, an understatement. "Let's try a bit more kissing."

He made those inane observations because he sensed Jeanette needed the commentary. She was unsure, and her courage would take her only so far.

Sycamore began by kissing her brow, then her cheeks, then her eyelids, as Jeanette gradually gave him her weight. When she was thoroughly relaxed, he touched his mouth to hers.

"You tease me," she muttered.

"I invite you. Tease me back."

Sycamore's arousal had gone from a pleasant annoyance to a full cockstand in the duration of a few chaste kisses, and Jeanette had to be aware of that. She pressed nearer and sank her fingers into the hair at his nape.

Her kisses were delicate, and when Sycamore seamed her lips with his tongue, she startled, then reciprocated, and he opened his mouth on a groan.

Or perhaps on a whimper. In any case, Jeanette got into the spirit of the expedition, and by the time she was lavishly tasting him, she'd also pressed her breasts to his chest and rubbed against him in a manner designed to pop the buttons from his falls.

"A moment," Sycamore said, his arms wrapped about her. "A moment to breathe, if you please."

"You are breathing," Jeanette replied, her cheek against his chest. "Breathing hard."

"My breathing isn't the only thing that's hard."

She eased back, though she didn't leave his embrace. "Am I to accommodate you now?"

Her wary question gave common sense a small purchase on rampant desire. "You are never to accommodate me. If all I want is to spend, that's simple enough to achieve. I regularly pleasure myself and hope you pleasure yourself too."

Wariness gave way to confusion. "I am not naughty enough to embark on a liaison with you, Sycamore. I don't even understand how to *be* naughty. The naughtiness was married right out of me."

I'm naughty enough for both of us. That reply would have served for a different woman facing different challenges.

"Don't be naughty, Jeanette. Be self-indulgent, curious, brave, and joyous. Play with me as a lady plays with her lover, rejoice in your animal spirits, and to hell with what anybody else thinks."

She studied him as if he'd spoken in a language she barely understood, then she kissed him full on the mouth.

"I like kissing you, Sycamore Dorning. I like it a lot. Is there someplace we might take this discussion? For if I'm to become acquainted with your fiddlestick, I'll want more light."

Sycamore kissed her a swift, hard smacker. "I'll light every candle on the premises and pull back every curtain too. There's a bedroom upstairs off the office. Nothing lavish, but I hope you'll be paying more attention to me than to the accommodations."

"I usually do."

He patted her bum and let her go, lest he back her onto the

nearest barrelhead and introduce her to his fiddlestick in the next thirty seconds.

"Upstairs with us," he said, taking her by the hand and making himself ascend at less than a dash. She had said yes, to next steps at least, if not to consummation, and her yes meant worlds to him. A cautious yes could be fanned into an exuberant certainty, and he was willing to exert himself to the utmost to inspire her to make that leap.

And to restrain himself to the utmost as well.

"This is pleasant," Jeanette said when Sycamore had ushered her into the bedchamber adjoining the office. The room was almost feminine in its appointments, the quilt a lavender blue, the curtains white lace, the rug before the hearth blue, pink, and white.

"Off with your boots," Sycamore said, "and I will light the fire." He ducked into the office to retrieve a lit spill and considered tossing himself off, but discarded the notion. Left to her own devices, Jeanette would fret, and not for anything would he give her cause for worry. He instead took up an extra branch of candles and set them on the bedside table when he rejoined her.

Jeanette sat in the reading chair before the hearth, one boot on, one boot off.

"Shall I assist you?" Sycamore asked, lighting every candle in the room as well as the fire laid on the hearth.

"I can manage. Perhaps you have disrobing of your own to do?"

"I'd rather you disrobe me."

She set her second boot aside. "I see."

Clearly, she did not see, but she rose and approached him, then slipped the pin from his cravat. "I valeted my husband often enough. The job isn't complicated."

"Don't valet me, Jeanette, drive me mad. Torment me with what I might never have." He could not believe those words were coming from his idiot mouth, but he'd made Jeanette smile, and that mattered.

"Like this?" she asked, casually pressing her breasts to his chest as she unknotted his cravat.

"Exactly like that. You might have to unbutton my falls too."

She draped his neckcloth over the back of the chair. "Why?"

"Because my hands are shaking too badly, and I cannot go about in public with half my buttons ripped off."

She slipped his sleeve buttons free of his cuffs. "I don't suppose you can." She undid his waistcoat next, in no hurry what-so-damned-ever. By the time Sycamore was minus his boots and stockings and naked from the waist up, Jeanette was smiling.

"I'd best finish what I started," she said, tugging Sycamore closer to the hearth by his waistband.

"Not so fast, madam. You are overdressed for the occasion."

She looked at the bulge distorting the line of his falls, looked at his face, and her smile became a grin. "What will you do about that, Mr. Dorning? I refuse to miss supper because you were dilatory about your duties."

"Hold still," he said, then caught himself. "If you would please hold still, I will assist you to undress."

"Be quick about it." She followed up with a kiss to his mouth, then turned her back to him. "My hooks, if you please. And thank you, Sycamore." She offered her thanks—for what?—while sweeping her hair away from her nape.

He got her out of her dress, stays, and petticoats without embarrassing himself or falling on her like a ravening beast, but stopped short of removing her chemise.

"You are being considerate of my modesty?" Jeanette asked, taking a seat on the bed.

"No, love." He sank to his knees before her. "I'm trying, futilely I suspect, to preserve my sanity. Might you please spread your legs for me?"

Surely a little ravening to begin the proceedings was permitted, a little ravening and kissing and driving the lady wild? Or more than a little?

~

"SPREAD MY LEGS FOR YOU?" Jeanette did not like the sound of that *at all*. "Why?"

Sycamore grasped her ankles, his thumbs brushing over the bones in a slow caress. "So that I can pleasure you with my mouth, of course. I want you as witless as I'm becoming."

His mouth on her...? She'd heard of such things, or overheard of them, in the women's retiring rooms, though the conversation always ended abruptly when somebody noticed she was on hand.

"Is that really necessary?"

His hands slid higher, to her knees, his touch so very warm and shocking. "Not necessary, but..." Knees were pedestrian joints, bones and sinew fashioned to facilitate locomotion. When Sycamore touched Jeanette's knees, they developed all manner of strange and erotic sensitivities.

He gazed up at her and seemed to come to some sort of conclusion. "Not necessary, no. How would you like to proceed?"

"I thought I would lie on the bed, then you would..." She waved a hand. "And then we cuddle for a bit while you nap."

Sycamore rose and took the place beside her, which meant Jeanette pitched against his side. He wrapped an arm around her waist when she would have risen to pace. The concept of becoming his lover had been alluring. The reality was damnably awkward.

"I'm to climb the Matterhorn while you stare at the ceiling and wonder how much longer I will need to reach the summit?" he asked, taking her hand. "Then we make a mess of the sheets, I become a snoring heap atop your person, and you wish copulation wasn't such an undignified way to earn some cuddling?"

"You make it sound so..." So selfish and tawdry. Jeanette rested her forehead against his shoulder. "Some women are not cut out for frolicking. I am one of them, and I apologize for leading you to believe otherwise."

The perfect man and the perfect moment had finally arrived. She could raise a fist at all the sour memories her husband had left her and take up the mantle of the independent widow at last. She could have some pleasure, maybe gain some insight into why straying wives and friendly widows invariably seemed to be such happy creatures.

And yet, all Jeanette wanted to do was get dressed and forget this day had ever happened.

And maybe cry a little. In private. For no reason.

Sycamore kissed her cheek. "I adore a challenge, and I agree you are not cut out for frolicking. Let's get me out of these damned breeches, shall we?"

He rose and stood before her.

"I don't understand."

"My breeches, Jeanette. That's the next step, and you decide whether to take it."

She did want to *see* him, to lay eyes on the male body part that occasioned such pride in its owners and such mischief in society generally. The marquess would have scolded Jeanette for unladylike curiosity.

She undid the buttons of Sycamore's waistband, then worked her way down both rows of buttons holding the flap of his breeches closed.

He stepped free of the last of his clothing, took a handkerchief from the pocket, and stuffed it under the pillow, then stood idly in the center of the carpet, scratching his chest and resembling an adult male lion rather than a harmless fellow preparing for a nap.

"Let's to bed, shall we, Jeanette?"

He was letting her look at him and trying to be casual about it. Maybe hoping she'd look at him? "Come here, Sycamore." She'd delivered an order, not a request, and that gave her a small, guilty thrill.

He stood directly before her, his hand cradling her cheek. "You are not made for frolicking, but you are made for loving. We do this however you choose, Jeanette."

That he could be coherent while his male member was in such a state... and *such* a member. His arousal put the marquess's endowments to shame and angled straight up along a flat belly crosshatched with muscle.

The idea that copulation could be more than rutting, that it could be *loving*, did something odd to Jeanette's breathing. She traced a single finger up his length, and a muscle in his belly leaped.

"There's a lot of you, Sycamore Dorning."

"And for the next hour, all of me is yours. What do you want, Jeanette? What do you truly, truly want? What have you denied yourself or not known how to ask for?"

She had been denied freedom, independence, privacy, and control of her own body. But that was all behind her now.

"I want..."

He waited, while Jeanette struggled to articulate feelings too raw and intimate for words.

"I want too much. Let's test your climbing skills, shall we?" She scooted under the covers, knowing she had just been either prudent or cowardly, but the day was not going as planned. Her daydreams about Sycamore Dorning had never progressed to well-lit bedrooms and spread knees.

Not quite.

He joined Jeanette on the bed, lying on his back and threading an arm under her neck. "The sheets are chilly. I could use some cuddling."

Sycamore was as warm as a toasted brick and much more interesting. Jeanette curled up against his side, resenting the thin cotton of her chemise. She wanted closeness with him. Maybe that was what she did not know how to ask for.

He wrapped his arms around her and rested his chin against her temple. "Was it awful, being married to the marquess?"

That was not a lover's question. "Yes. He was demanding, bad-tempered, and determined to get a child on me, six children, all of them sons would have been better, and if I'd died delivering the last of the lot, that would have been acceptable too. It took me years to notice that other husbands were at least polite to their wives. Other husbands used endearments as if they meant them. Other husbands… but this is not why you joined me in this bed."

Sycamore kissed her brow. "Right, I dragged you up the steps to have my wicked way with you, but I've changed my mind."

A bolt of real disappointment went through her. "Truly?"

"Yes, truly. I think instead that you should have your wicked way with me. I am eager to be plundered, and you must lead the raiding party."

"I wouldn't know—"

He hoisted her over him, his strength as implacable as it was careful. "The Matterhorn awaits, Jeanette. I promise you the view is worth the climb."

Dear… gracious… glorious… She'd ended up straddling him as he lay beneath her on his back, his arousal only inches from its intended destination.

"I could, for example," he said, brushing aside her chemise to stroke her thighs, "caress your breasts, if you like. I could revel in your kisses. I could join my body to yours while you controlled the depth, speed, and—"

She kissed him to silence him, also because he was filling her body with longing and her head with something other than memories.

"Better," he murmured, his hands trailing up her sides. His kisses were lazy and teasing, also powerfully distracting. Jeanette's braid came loose from its chignon—how had that happened?—and her chemise was soon rucked up about her waist.

While she was marveling over those developments, Sycamore glossed his palms over her breasts.

"Do that again."

He obliged, slowly, then added gentle tugs on her nipples. "Like that?" He curled up and used his lips and teeth through the fabric of her chemise. "Or like that? Say what pleases you, Jeanette."

She liked hearing him use her name, she liked that he knew how to go on. She could barely think for awareness of his arousal, seated along the crease of her sex.

"I like when you use my name."

"I like to use your name," he said, returning to the first breast. "Perhaps the time has arrived to take off this chemise?"

He'd made her ache, and he asked her rather than simply dragged her clothing over her head. But to be naked, utterly naked, intimately exposed… Every instinct Jeanette had shrieked at her to keep the garment, to keep a symbolic barrier if nothing else, a cloak for her dignity should she abruptly leave the bed over some offense or slight.

Sycamore lay beneath her, saying nothing. In his patience, she sensed safety and, more than that, a haven. Keeping her chemise on would protect nothing—he could rip it from her should the whim strike him—but taking it off would be a step in the direction of a trust he deserved and she hoped to give him.

Trust, and something even more complicated. Hope perhaps?

Jeanette untied the bow at her décolletage. "If you would assist me?"

Sycamore drew her chemise over her head and tossed it in the direction of the chair. He frankly stared at her breasts, which were a trifle larger than fashion preferred.

"How you honor me," he said, gathering her in an embrace. "How you delight and honor me."

He delighted her too, with exquisite caresses and an even more inventive use of his mouth on her breasts. Jeanette began to move on him, to glide her sex over the rigid length of his cock, seeking relief of an intimate ache and succeeding only in stirring herself to more frustrated desire.

"Time to climb, Jeanette?" Sycamore asked, smiling crookedly, and pushing her braid back over her shoulder. "Eager doesn't begin to describe my willingness to be climbed."

Jeanette's body clamored for her to accept Sycamore's invitation, and yet, she hesitated, though not out of uncertainty. She paused to marvel at the tenderness assailing her, the gratitude to this man who'd turned rutting into lovemaking.

The view was already breathtaking.

"I will withdraw," he said. "I promise."

And Sycamore Dorning's word was trustworthy. That was what made this encounter possible. Not the liking, the desire, the old ghosts, or even the promise of pleasure, but the *trust*.

She braced herself on one hand and used the other to seat his cock against her body. "Slowly please," she said. "Some pleasures should be savored."

He turned *slowly* into excruciating self-control, allowing Jeanette to remain poised above him while he thrust, feinted, paused, and generally drove her mad.

"Yield, Jeanette," he whispered, gathering her close. "Please, yield."

She was yielding as far as she knew how, riding him with increasing abandon, taking his hand and placing it over her breast.

"I don't... I can't..."

The wanting and heat inside her built, then built some more, then flared yet higher. The frustration was unbearable, enraging, and fascinating all at once.

Sycamore did something, shifted the angle, drove deeper—she hardly knew what—but then she *could* and she *did*.

Cataclysms of pleasure shook her from within. Her passion became an avalanche of tumbling sensation, reverberating shock, and breathless satisfaction. All the while, Sycamore plied her with slow, hard thrusts that became too much and then more than too much, but still she clung to him and endured.

When he at last went still, she collapsed on his chest, and his arms came around her. She was joy and satisfaction and a few unshed tears, while his hand on her hair was gentleness itself.

"You are a revelation," Jeanette said, a thought that had decided on its own to be spoken aloud. She rode the rise and fall of his chest like eiderdown on a summer breeze, her mind a place of peace, warmth, and light.

So that was passion.

That was lovemaking. Finally. At last. That was the uninhibited sharing of pleasure about which so many had rhapsodized so eloquently, and Jeanette could rhapsodize now too, if only in the privacy of her thoughts.

"And you are a treasure," Sycamore replied, stroking her shoulders and back through the covers. His touch was completely relaxed, while inside Jeanette, he was as hard as he'd been when he'd climbed into the bed.

"I should move," she said. "Give you some room."

"I'd like to spend on your belly," he said. "I want you wrapped around me when I die of too much pleasure."

Jeanette raised herself up again to peer at him. "On my back?"

He nodded. "Only if you'd enjoy it."

Sycamore Dorning had showered Jeanette with pleasure so far beyond mere enjoyment... she could tolerate a few moments on her back in the name of reciprocity.

"I'll manage."

Before she could climb off of him, he caught her by the hand. "Don't *manage* with me, Jeanette. Demand, ask, state terms, parlay, listen, as our bodies do when we make love. I am so randy right now, I could close my eyes and finish without moving. You don't owe me a penance because you finally enjoyed yourself in bed for once."

"If you smother me, I will pinch your bum," she said, extricating herself from him and sliding to the mattress at his side.

"I would like for you to pinch my bum," he said, easing his body over hers. "I'd like it a lot."

He braced himself over her on his elbows, while Jeanette waited for a familiar sense of distaste to cloud the moment. When she expected Sycamore to crowd closer, he instead kissed her cheek.

"Get comfy, Jeanette, but you needn't pinch me. 'Sycamore, I need air,' or 'Get off me, you oaf,' will suffice."

Sycamore was a sizable man, much more substantial than the marquess had been, and yet, when he slid his cock over Jeanette's damp sex, she was too fascinated with the resulting sensation to be much bothered by the position they were in.

"That is almost like having you inside me."

"No, it is not. Not nearly." He pressed closer and kept moving. "This is heaven's front terrace, I grant you, but not the celestial hall itself. Don't let me crush you."

Jeanette shifted lower, seeking a better fit, a tighter fit. "Hush. I like this." The sensations were different, but rather than crush her, Sycamore took his own weight while enveloping her in his presence. She lashed her legs around his flanks and began to move with him.

"When you do that..." he muttered, lips near her ear. "God, Jeanette."

She'd sought to arouse him, but the result was greater sensation for her. Without him even inside her, her body was preparing for another flight into pleasure. Such a thing should not be possible, but it most certainly *was*, until Jeanette was clinging to Sycamore, and wet heat spread in the tight seal of their bodies.

"I am..." Sycamore panted, crouched above her. "I am... I don't know what I am. You steal my wits, Jeanette, and please don't ever give them back."

Tucked beneath him, she felt safe and sweet, and utterly baffled. "I'll keep yours if you'll keep mine."

He kissed her nose and rolled with her. "A bargain, dear heart. We will document the agreement if we ever find the strength to leave this bed."

Jeanette lay atop him for another moment, then bestirred herself to fish the handkerchief from beneath the pillow. She sat up and mopped at her belly, then scrubbed him off too. While he watched, she refolded the linen so the soiled portion was inside and set it on the bedside table.

"You are rosy," Sycamore said, brushing a finger over her breasts.

"A good loving leaves a lady rosy. I am rosy too, though in different parts."

She glanced at his softening member. "Isn't that part of you always rosy?"

"Metaphorically speaking, perhaps, and physically, but I referred to my heart, Jeanette. Right now, my heart is very rosy. May I hold you?"

"Yes." She longed to be held, to be cuddled and cosseted, and Sycamore was sparing her that admission.

When she lay down beside him, and he took her in his arms, she was surprised to realize that she also wanted to hold him, to caress him at leisure, to learn the contours of his muscle and bone, and the rhythm of his breathing. This longing was different from sexual hunger, having more of tenderness and loneliness about it.

She would memorize him against the day when he was no longer her lover. Then she would torment herself with recollections of when he had been hers for a magnificent hour here or there.

CHAPTER SEVEN

If Sycamore lived to be a hundred, he'd never forget the sight of Jeanette finding her pleasure in his arms. She'd seized her courage in one hand and Sycamore's heart in the other and surrendered to passion.

For him to hold back should have been difficult, nearly impossible in fact, but he'd been so fascinated with Jeanette's responses, that he'd entered into a sort of meditative state. He had both shared every delight with her and been the awed observer, enthralled with her reactions.

Lovemaking had never gone in that direction before, and he feared it never could again. This encounter had been unprecedented, and the end, when it had come, had obliterated any distance between him and his lover—physical or mental.

Considering that he hadn't even been intimately joined to her at the time, he had much to ponder.

Jeanette, poor lamb, had fallen asleep against his side. Sycamore savored that gift while his mind drifted idly to the rise and fall of her breathing. He felt when she awoke, though she did not open her eyes.

Was she stealing a few more minutes in his arms or plotting an escape? Did she want another round—please, heaven, let him be equal to that challenge—or would she take her clothes behind the privacy screen and leave without sharing a meal with him?

His heart would break if she abandoned him now.

"You are awake," he said, kissing her temple. "What have you to say to your lover, Jeanette?" He would not allow himself the insecure questions new bed partners were prone to: Was I good enough? Did I satisfy you? Or, the easiest dodge of all: One more before we part?

He did not know how another encounter with Jeanette could live up to the initial experience, and that required thought. First times were full of excitement, but usually a little hurried and gauche too. Sycamore spared a regret for all the ladies he'd left after a first time with a cavalier bow and a smile. Had they wanted a few more minutes of conversation? Would it have been asking too much of him to rebraid their hair for them?

Might he have thanked them a little more effusively?

"That I have a lover astounds me," Jeanette said. "I feel all over again as I did the day after my wedding, as if everybody will know I'm different simply by looking at me."

Only Jeanette... "Would it be so bad for others to notice you are no longer that bewildered bride?"

"I have spent every day since my wedding trying not to be that bride. Who knew the solution to my dilemma was hidden in your smile?"

That sounded almost fanciful, and Jeanette was not a fanciful woman. "Or in my breeches?"

She climbed over him and tucked herself against his chest. "No, Sycamore. What's in your breeches is lovely—astoundingly so—but that's not the whole of it. Do not interrogate me on this point, for I lack the wits to understand it myself at present."

That makes two of us. "You are lovely too, Jeanette. Astoundingly so." He left it at that, the bald truth, rather than lapse into flattery or inane analogies. For another few minutes, she rested against him, and he indulged in caresses to her hair, her back, and her shoulders.

Just about the time the loveliness below his waist was waking up to future possibilities, Jeanette extricated herself from the covers and sat on the edge of the bed.

"I am hungry, which suggests you have to be famished."

Even the sight of her back, the untidy braid trailing down to her bum, stirred him. Oh, for brother Oak's ability to paint and sketch, or brother Valerian's talent with a compliment. For Casriel's exquisite manners or Ash's savoir faire. For Hawthorne's earthy humor, or Willow's quiet wisdom.

"We could toss a few more knives first," Sycamore said, "if you'd like that."

A guess, a blind throw, but Jeanette smiled at him over her shoulder. "I would, now that you make the offer. Though the temptation to linger with you here..." Her smile became wistful.

"I am more than willing to linger as well, but I suspect we might do better to treat this intimacy as we do a session with the knives. Limit ourselves to the prescribed pleasure and savor anticipation of the next session. Besides, you might be sore."

She half turned and flipped back the covers to peer at his semi-flaccid cock. "Do men ever get sore?"

"Yes, either from excessive self-gratification, ill-fitting sheaths, or exuberance with the ladies."

She *patted* him. "If I have not already experienced your utmost exuberance, I shudder with a mixture of dread and glee to contemplate the occasion." She curled down to pillow her cheek against his jewels, an odd, intimate, entirely dear gesture. "Thank you, Sycamore. Don't make me say exactly for what, because I cannot, but thank you."

"Thank you too, Jeanette, for more than I can say."

She did not tarry, alas, but was up and shimmying back into her chemise. Sycamore played lady's maid, Jeanette valeted him, and they were soon presentable.

Almost. "I should redo your hair, my lady."

She examined herself in the cheval mirror. "I look tumbled. I have never looked tumbled before."

"You look luscious. Hold still."

Sycamore moved behind her to undo her braid. The actual brushing out and rebraiding took only moments, but he loved the intimacy of the service, loved passing Jeanette one hairpin at a time so she could gather up that whole, shiny abundance into a demure and deceptive chignon.

"I am not fooled," he said, taking her hand and kissing her knuckles. "You appear all tidy and collected, but I've seen you unraveled, and that glorious sight will stay with me for the rest of my life."

She leaned against him for the briefest moment, then preceded him out the door. "Once more to the knives, Mr. Dorning, and you will make no further mention of my unbound hair or other lapses."

He stopped her before she'd made it past the office. "Jeanette, I am not a lapse, and neither are you."

She nodded. "Fair enough, though I don't know exactly what you are—what you have become, rather—and finding my balance will take some time."

He kissed her cheek. "We find our balance together, my lady. I am every bit as undone as you are."

Probably more undone, in fact. Jeanette had quickly reassembled the exterior trappings she wore so convincingly—brisk movements, direct speech, calm self-possession—while Sycamore's soul had been scattered from Land's End to John o' Groats.

Was this how his brothers had felt when they'd become intimate with their prospective wives? Sycamore could ask Ash that question, carefully.

He realized as Jeanette was bustling down the steps at his side exactly what such a query implied. She reached the cellar door first, and Sycamore wanted to tell her to hold still, dammit, so he could propose to her on bended knee.

Instinct kept that foolishness behind his teeth, and yet, offering marriage to Jeanette wasn't entirely foolishness. She wasn't ready to hear a proposal. She was owed a wooing, owed more lovemaking, owed doting and time and much that Sycamore longed to give her.

Did she but know it, the wooing had begun.

"We should have a set of knives made for you," Sycamore said, opening the cellar door for her. "You're working with a set cast for my hand, and the sooner you begin working with your own weapons, the faster you'll become skilled with them."

"My own knives?"

"Of course. Two sets, because you need replacements for any blade that gets lost or damaged, and knives all cast from the same mold and fired in the same flames give you the most uniform performance."

She hugged him, a mere squeeze before descending the steps. "I would adore my own set of knives. I like that idea exceedingly."

Sycamore contented himself with that, but his objective was for her to like *him* exceedingly, one day, perhaps, even to love him as he already loved her.

"BUT, MY DEAR," Viola said, "you must admit that soldiers and sailors are a less controversial direction in which to aim the late marquess's charity. The Magdalen houses have not proven to bring about any beneficial result, not consistently, whereas a soldier fed is plainly improved by the charity shown him."

Jeanette held up a plate stacked with a dozen artfully decorated tea cakes. She made a mental game out of guessing in which order Viola would choose her sweets, and Viola did not disappoint. Lemon cakes had already disappeared, the raspberry would be next, followed by—after at least two demurrals—the lavender tea cakes.

She set the plate down next to Viola's cup and saucer. "Precisely because the soldiers and sailors are the more popular cause, I prefer to devote my money to other struggles." Not the late marquess's charitable funds, which Jeanette was in the process of transferring to Trevor's management. "How are the young ladies?"

Viola went off into a rhapsody about Diana's vocal talent and Hera's skill with a needle. Diana was soon to make her long-awaited come out, and fortunately for her, she was a sensible, pretty, good-humored young lady who knew how to curb her mother's worst fashion suggestions.

Viola had many faults. She was no higher born than Jeanette, but comported herself with the airs and graces of the queen mother. She was a catty gossip, blind to her son's faults, and desperate to see her younger daughters well matched, despite the older three settling for husbands who'd brought more devotion than means to their unions.

But Viola was also a loyal wife and mother, keenly protective of her offspring, and never openly critical of her husband. That last quality was a virtue, one Jeanette resented bitterly.

"Is Diana nervous about making her come out?" Jeanette asked as the first lavender tea cake met its fate.

"Nervous? Of course not. I have spent years ensuring my daughters are the equal of any occasion, most especially a court presentation. Diana will be a credit to the family, as all my children are."

Jeanette wanted to shove the rest of the plate at Viola and summon the Vincent coach, but clearly Viola was working up to one of her grand sermons. She might have been an ally to a much younger Jeanette, might have tried to smooth the way with the marquess.

Viola hadn't, not in the least. She'd waited for Jeanette to commit every possible misstep and then offered muttered platitudes such as *marry in haste, repent at leisure* as Jeanette's consolation. Perhaps Viola had married in haste.

A thought like that would not have occurred to Jeanette a week ago, but a week ago, she had not been Sycamore Dorning's lover—or his something. Twenty-four hours after rising from his bed, Jeanette was still agog at her own daring. Becoming intimate with him had been breathtaking, alarming, delightful, and altogether overwhelming.

Jeanette was counting the seconds until Sunday afternoon and also considering an immediate, extended repairing lease at the Vincent family seat. What had she done, and how soon could she do it again?

"How fares Jerome these days?" Jeanette asked.

Viola set down her tea cup. "Well you should ask, my lady. Well you should ask. Jerome has brought me the most shocking news regarding your step-son."

Trevor was *our marquess* and *his darling lordship* when Viola eyed him as a possible husband for one of her daughters. He was *your step-son* when he'd tripped during the quadrille at the Portmans' ball.

"I try not to pry into his lordship's personal affairs, Viola. I suggest you maintain a cordial distance from them as well."

"You can afford to be indifferent," Viola said, perching on the edge of the sofa cushion like a laying hen about her business. "I must think of the family. What will people say when they learn that your step-son has taken up some sort of apprenticeship in a *gaming hell*?"

"The Coventry Club is a supper club, Viola, and if Tavistock finds the surrounds congenial, then we must look to Jerome for having introduced his lordship to that venue in the first place." Jeanette had offered to take Trevor to the Coventry last autumn, but he'd never indicated a willingness to be seen there with his step-mother.

For which she, of course, did not blame him.

"Jerome is trying to prevent Trevor from stumbling into the worst sorts of mischief that young men get up to, so of course Jerome would accompany Trevor to such a place. His lordship would be a lamb to slaughter without Jerome's guiding influence."

A week ago, Jeanette would have stuffed a tea cake into her mouth and changed the subject to Diana's presentation gown, which apparently boasted more pearls than the North Atlantic.

"According to an eyewitness," Jeanette said, "Jerome has visited the Coventry on at least a half-dozen occasions. He goaded Trevor into playing hazard, made sure the marquess was plied with drink from every direction, and further inspired him to throw good money after bad." Sycamore Dorning had seen the whole drama, and Jeanette was grateful that he had not intervened.

Trevor had lessons to learn that Jeanette could not teach him by wrapping him in cotton wool.

Viola smiled pityingly. "Trevor is becoming mendacious, isn't he? Of course he'd spin you such a Banbury tale, because he is ashamed, but he's too enthralled with a den of vice to simply pay his debts and walk away. I fear for my nephew, your ladyship, and for the influences bearing on him as he approaches his majority."

Those influences included Jeanette, of course. "Speak to him, then," Jeanette said, pouring herself another cup of tea. "He holds you in great affection and will surely abide by your guidance."

Viola clearly wasn't prepared for that salvo. She'd apparently been expecting Jeanette to promise to try to do better, whatever that meant, and to agree that Trevor was behaving abominably, which he was not.

"You are the lady of this house," Viola said, taking the second lavender tea cake. "You should be correcting Trevor's errors and guiding him back to the path of common sense. Jerome cannot bear the whole burden on his own."

"Jerome and his cronies are largely the reason Trevor played too deeply, Viola. Mr. Sycamore Dorning has kindly allowed Trevor to work off the debt of honor by serving as an informal assistant at the Coventry. Trevor earns no coin, but he is learning a great deal about the perils of overindulged impulses."

Sycamore had provided a progress report to Jeanette over yesterday's dinner, and Trevor himself had confirmed that he was "on loan to the club for the nonce." The prospect seemed to cheer him, and Jeanette suspected having an excuse to avoid Jerome and his friends was part of Trevor's improved mood.

"Trevor is learning nothing of value," Viola sniffed. "He is learning to spend his evenings with wagering inebriates who have no sense of decorum."

"Wagering inebriates like Jerome and his friends?"

Had Viola left in high dudgeon or launched into a tirade, Jeanette would not have been surprised, but instead, Viola took out a handkerchief and dabbed at the corners of her eyes.

"I am tired, my lady," Viola said, "of managing a household, managing marriageable daughters, trying to provide you the benefit of my wisdom, and guiding Beardsley in his role as Trevor's guardian. The burden on me has been... But that is neither here nor there. Jerome is a young man of independent means. He may do as he wishes in the company of his fellows and still be quite the gentleman in any respectable drawing room. That is the way of the world, and he understands it. For Trevor to attach himself to a gaming hell, though, is..." Viola dabbed at her eyes again. "You must see that it is unacceptable."

Jeanette did not want to pity Viola, did not want to concede that she had a point. "The situation is temporary, Viola. Trevor badly overspent his allowance, and I do mean badly, and Jerome's influence, for good or ill, did not prevent that. I am unwilling to set a precedent whereby Trevor's entertainments throw him into debt, and no consequences result. Beardsley would doubtless agree with me. Trevor is too young, and too new to Town, also too generously funded, to be allowed to start down that path."

"He needs a wife," Viola said, tucking her handkerchief into her reticule. "A sensible young lady who knows what's expected of her."

Jeanette took a sip of her tea, though it had gone tepid. "Trevor needs to grow up, Viola. He's years away from his majority, and when he does eventually marry, he'll be a better husband for having seen a bit of life first."

Viola rose. "I cannot make you understand the damage he could do to his own consequence by frequenting such an establishment. The occasional sortie with his friends is understandable, but this indentured servitude... Beardsley will have something to say about it."

Having lectured and wept, Viola now descended to threats.

"Beardsley *should* say something about it," Jeanette replied, getting to her feet. "Beardsley should have a strong word with both Jerome and Trevor about debts of honor, about the folly of drunken wagers, about knowing the difference between real friends and the other kind. Perhaps if you and Beardsley add your exhortations to my own, both young men will give us less to worry about."

"But Trevor dwells with you, for now. He respects you. You are a parental figure to him, while I am the aunt he calls on exclusively out of duty. You must take him firmly in hand, Jeanette."

That was the one thing she must not do. "My hope is that he will see at the Coventry the difference between those who can handle recreation responsibly and those who cannot. Trevor is intelligent and well aware of his station. I trust him to make better choices going forward."

Not quite the truth.

Jeanette trusted that Trevor would *eventually* learn to make better choices, but first he'd wake up with many a sore head, make more stupid wagers, have his heart broken several times, and most assuredly have his trust betrayed.

If it hadn't been already.

"You are not a mother," Voila said, firing that broadside as she moved toward the door. "I know you love the boy, but you cannot understand how close to peril he's treading. Beardsley feels as I do, and it's not out of the realm of possibility that Beardsley would ask you to remove to the dower house if matters do not resolve themselves to his satisfaction, Jeanette. Trevor should be at university, but you make it easy for him to neglect his education too."

Good heavens, not the dower house. Viola was truly in good form today. "Beardsley is overdue to have lunch with his nephew, clearly, for I did not invite Trevor to leave school, Viola, and I regularly urge him to return. Perhaps if Jerome added his voice to the chorus, Trevor might see reason."

And Jerome would lose his entrée into the Season's most glittering entertainments, as well as countless rounds of free drinks for him and his friends.

"I will have a word with Beardsley," Viola said, bustling on to the main foyer. "You may be assured of that."

Jeanette saw her guest out, exchanged a long-suffering look with old Peem, and then took herself to her private sitting room, rather than the family sitting room where she'd endured Viola's call. The morning post sat on the blotter, a folded and sealed note—hand delivered—among the correspondence.

Sycamore's handwriting. God save her, she was pleased to see his handwriting, and filled as well with dread. What if he was ending their liaison already, canceling next week's lesson, leaving Town to elude further entanglement?

Later perhaps, Jeanette would ponder why, nearly a decade after accepting the marquess's proposal, she should revert to schoolgirl insecurities and what to do about that dreadful lapse. The present moment demanded that she read Sycamore's epistle.

MY LADY,

The same unfortunate sequence of events transpired as you made your way home last evening as happened the previous week. I am available to discuss this development at your convenience and will call upon you accordingly.

Your obed serv,

SD

SHE'D BEEN FOLLOWED AGAIN, which meant she was not imagining things and that somebody knew she was regularly spending time alone with Sycamore at the Coventry.

~

"HOW DID your call upon the fair Jeanette go?" Beardsley Vincent asked, taking his wife's cloak.

"We should discuss it, sir, if I might have a moment of your time." Viola passed her bonnet and parasol to the waiting butler, who had been with the family long enough to send Beardsley a discreet sympathetic glance.

The staff respected Viola, they did not like her, and for reasons Beardsley could not fathom, she preferred it that way. They did like Beardsley and showed him a thousand courtesies and kindnesses as a result, such as keeping their mouths shut about his personal business.

"I am at your service, my dear. I trust Jeanette is in good health?" The late marquess had often grumbled about Jeanette's good health. If she had to be so damned robust, he'd lamented, why the hell couldn't she produce a son or three?

His late lordship had stopped short of praying for a tragic accident to befall Jeanette, at least in Beardsley's hearing. In a stroke of divine irony, the tragic accident had befallen the marquess instead.

Such a pity.

Viola led Beardsley—did not take his arm, did not walk at his side, did not accompany him, but rather, sailed forth before her own husband—to her personal parlor. Beardsley found the room both amusing and slightly unnerving.

Viola's favorite pastime was collecting dolls, stuffed animals, and dollhouses. In one corner of her private parlor, she'd set up a miniature tea table, the service laid out for two dolls, a bear, and a hedgehog. The glassy-eyed stares of the assemblage, their unchanging postures, and the perfection of the tiny tea service put Beardsley in mind of pharaohs buried with their households.

"Jeanette is in great good health," Viola began as soon as Beardsley had closed the door, "but, my lord, she is utterly indifferent to the dangerous ground upon which the young marquess treads. Jerome tells me Trevor is all but indentured to those dreadful Dornings at the Coventry. Who knows how much he owes them and where this will end?"

The *dreadful Dornings* were brothers to an earl, meaning they could not be all that dreadful in the eyes of Society. The sovereign himself occasionally dropped by the Coventry, as did any number of notables.

Jerome, loyal lad that he was, had warned Beardsley of Trevor's ill-fated sortie to the tables, and Beardsley himself had suggested Jerome also inform Viola. She would take upsetting news better from her son than from her husband.

"Darling wife," Beardsley said, "calm yourself. Trevor's tour at the Coventry will end one of two ways. He will either learn much in a short time and emerge a wiser fellow, or he will be drawn into a world for which he is ill-prepared."

Viola marched up to him, eyes blazing. She had looked after herself over the years and was still a handsome woman. When impassioned like this, Beardsley could almost recall the younger Viola, the one who'd shared a bed with him and hopes for a rosy future.

"And which of those outcomes," Viola demanded, "do you believe the more likely? He is eighteen, my lord. He hasn't even finished university, and his wealth is enormous."

"The family's wealth is enormous," Beardsley said. "Tavistock's access to that wealth is limited until he turns one-and-twenty, and debts of honor are personal. He can gamble himself into dun territory, and beyond a certain point, his only recourse is to take a repairing lease on the Continent."

"I wouldn't like to see that," Viola said. "Though I suppose for a year or two, until he comes of age, some travel might do him good. Diana deserves to enjoy Society with Hera for a bit, after all."

Viola thought of her unmarried daughters, while Beardsley thought of the larger picture. "Here is how I expect matters will be resolved: Trevor will get in over his head. I will point out to the solicitors that Jeanette not only failed to intervene, but has also socialized with the Dornings and in fact introduced Trevor to them at some house party or other."

Viola patted Beardsley's lapel and stepped back. "That is true.

Lady Wentwhistle's gathering caused a fair amount of talk. She held a tournament at the card tables, and Tavistock lost badly, while Jeanette won a significant sum. Both Mr. Ash Dorning and Mr. Sycamore Dorning were present at that house party."

Viola could have doubtless recited the guest list in order of precedence.

"Jeanette is getting above herself, but, Viola, I tell you honestly that anything that coaxes Tavistock out from under her watchful eye is a good thing. She exercises far too much influence over his lordship, and she is not even a blood relation to him."

Viola moved to her tea tableau, adjusting one doll's braid, straightening the other's pinafore. "We are in agreement in that regard, Husband. Jeanette ought by rights to content herself with a placid existence at the dower house. It's nobody's fault but hers that she has no children to occupy her, and yet, here she is, hanging on to Tavistock's coattails like a governess with a toddler."

Beardsley had suggested Jerome court the woman. Jeanette was wealthy, and much of that wealth had been provided by the Vincent family, after all.

"Exactly as you say," Beardsley replied. "Jeanette is *de trop* and hasn't the grace to quit the scene. I am confident that she will shortly be forced to heed my direction to take herself off to Tavistock Hall, leaving Trevor free of her meddling."

Viola sat the bear up higher on his little chair and stroked the hedgehog's quills. "Forced how?"

"Lady Tavistock's brother is a man with an unfortunate past. The talk about him never really stops for long. Should he meet with renewed accusations of dishonorable conduct, he would be ruined past all recall. He might not care for his good name, but Goddard is Jeanette's only family. To preserve what's left of Orion Goddard's reputation, Jeanette will do exactly as I say."

Viola smiled at him, a warm, admiring smile he hadn't seen from her in ages. "My lord, you astound me. That plan is elegantly simple and likely to work as all of my lectures and threats have not."

"You had to try, my dear, and I do thank you for your efforts. Do you truly have Trevor in mind for Diana, or would you prefer to see him wed to Hera? Diana is only a few years Trevor's senior, and older sisters generally marry first."

Viola's smile became wistful. "If I knew Tavistock was engaged to one of our girls—a real engagement, not one of these harum-scarum overnight courtships—I could turn my energies to seeing Jerome wed. He is older than Trevor and still in line for the succession. He really ought to be taking a bride."

Exactly what I've told him over and over. "Let's not build castles in Spain, my dear. First, we will free Trevor from his step-mother's meddling, then we will see what develops for him in terms of marriage to a cousin. Tell me more about this house party of Lady Wentwhistle's."

Viola took a place on her tufted sofa and prattled on about trysts, tournaments, and tattle until Beardsley felt like the glassy-eyed bear, sitting perpetually before a tea tray he would never enjoy. When Viola eventually wound down, Beardsley patted her shoulder, kissed her forehead, and bid her good day.

An impromptu call on his mistress was in order. A plan years in the making was smoothly under way, and that was cause for celebration.

"MR. DOORKNOB?" The Tavistock butler peered at Sycamore's card. "I will see if the marchioness is in, sir. Please do make yourself comfortable." He toddled off down the corridor, Sycamore's card in his hand.

Leaving Sycamore to doff his greatcoat and hat, hanging each on a hook opposite the porter's nook. He laid his walking stick across the hooks, lest he forget it. This was his first venture into Jeanette's home territory, and he would be damned if he'd linger in the hallway like a penitent outside the confessional.

He made a circuit of the spotless grand foyer, early afternoon light pouring onto the parquet marble floor from a skylight overhead. Romanesque busts occupied opposing alcoves, overgrown ferns billowing at the foot of the plinths. A portrait of what had to be the late marquess hung in the space between the alcoves.

His lordship was a severe-looking fellow depicted in formal attire, a painting of some ancestor or other tucked into the background of his own portrait. The composition was designed to make his lordship look imposing—the perspective slightly low relative to the subject, the somber colors, the coat of arms over the mantel.

Cold eyes, a grim mouth, pale hands... This was the lover Jeanette had cuddled up to as a seventeen-year-old bride.

"My late husband," said the lady herself, the butler hovering at her elbow. "That was done two years before his death. His hair wasn't so uniformly dark then, but the artist had a commission to earn."

A riding crop, roweled spurs, dueling pistols, fowling piece, crossbow, and huntsman's coiled whip were discreetly included in the marquess's portrait, each probably intended to subtly reinforce his masculinity and vigor. A globe, presenting Britain at the center of the Northern Hemisphere, occupied the desk behind him.

Not a knife to be seen, though, and nothing of learning, beauty, or grace. "A thoroughly jovial fellow, wasn't he?" Sycamore said.

Jeanette glanced at the butler. "Peem, a tea tray in the blue parlor."

"Very good, my lady." He bowed and withdrew at a funereal pace.

"I was hoping to drive out with you," Sycamore said. "The day is lovely." *And so are you.* She wore a soft green velvet afternoon dress, a hint of lace across a modest décolletage, pink embroidery adding a graceful touch on the bodice and cuffs.

"I would have to change into a carriage dress," she replied. "Let's find somewhere comfortable to chat."

Jeanette appeared composed and calm, and she did not look

particularly happy to see Sycamore. She showed him to a small parlor across the corridor from a yawning library. Sycamore paused to examine the library, which smelled of books and coal and boasted more dull portraiture presiding over perfectly symmetric groupings of perfectly matched furniture.

"I've never met anybody who lived in a mausoleum before," Sycamore said, joining Jeanette by the parlor door. "I can almost hear the angel choirs singing their panegyrics to the late marquess. How do you stand it?"

Jeanette left the parlor door open, which was not a good sign. "This is the home of the present marquess, who doubtless finds respect for tradition comforting. I make sure the staff is content and the house well run. It's not my place to comment on the decorations."

"Something has upset you," Sycamore said, considering the slight tension around her mouth, the anxiety in her gaze. "Please tell me."

She gestured to a sofa in the same blue as the flocked wallpaper. The carpet, curtains, and the rest of the upholstery were all embroidered in the blue and gold theme, with hints of pink the only nod to variety. Gilt-framed landscapes were a marginal improvement over the disapproving stares of the dead, and an arrangement of pink silk roses on the low table before the sofa suggested this parlor was for entertaining ladies.

"I am not upset," Jeanette said, settling on the sofa. "Please do sit."

Rather than sit beside her like the hopeful, presuming bachelor he was, Sycamore chose a wing chair angled at the end of the sofa.

"What exactly has you not upset?" he asked. "Was it the note I sent?"

"Partly."

Was it the passionate lovemaking? In her present mood, she would pitch him out a window if he asked that. He wasn't sure how he drew that conclusion, but he trusted its accuracy.

"Your butler referred to me as Mr. Doorknob. This suggests both his hearing and his eyesight have suffered the ravages of time."

"Mr. Doorknob?"

"In all seriousness, while peering at my handsome little calling card."

Jeanette's lip twitched. "Mr. Doorknob. Peem is the soul of dignity. He wasn't being insulting on purpose."

"Of course not, but given the contents of my latest note, you might want to consider replacing him with somebody a little more..."

"Peem has been with the family for ages," Jeanette said, "and it's not for me to suggest he retire."

"Yes, it is. Tavistock doesn't think it's his place, so that leaves you, and don't tell me that a gentleman doesn't argue with a lady. Where your safety is concerned, I am prepared to impersonate a barbarian."

"You are a barbarian," she said, smiling at the silk roses.

Finally, a smile. "Your barbarian."

Her expression became complicated, a little exasperated, a little bewildered. "I have missed you."

"Thank God. I'd hate to think I'm the only one staring off into space at odd moments, wondering what day it is, and forgetting where I put the spectacles perched on my nose."

Before Sycamore could embarrass himself with further confessions, a footman who might have gone to sea on the Ark pushed a tea trolley into the parlor.

"Shall I pour, your ladyship?" he asked.

"No need, Elliott. Thank you."

"Will there be anything else?"

"No, thank you."

Elliott perused Sycamore with the gravity of a disapproving bishop, offered a stately bow, and withdrew at a similarly unhurried pace.

"Please tell me," Sycamore said, "that you have at least one footman under the age of thirty who could be dispatched hotfoot to rouse the watch should the household catch fire."

"You aren't worried about the household catching fire."

"When I behold you, my lady, I worry about my privities catching fire, for my imagination is already ablaze."

He'd hoped to make her smile again with that riposte, but her expression was, if anything, nonplussed.

"Forgive me," Sycamore said. "I am not flirting, I am stating the truth. I will put aside further disclosures regarding how utterly smitten I am with you and focus on the business I came to discuss."

"Please do." Jeanette made no move to pour the tea, suggesting her calm was manufactured at the cost of considerable self-control. "I do not care for the notion that I'm being followed."

"I loathe it. Did you suspect somebody was keeping an eye on you before you sought to learn the use of the knife?"

Jeanette toyed with the fringe of a blue velvet pillow. "I had a feeling, a vague sense of unease. I went out to the stables one morning to check on my mare—she'd shown a little soreness the day before, though she'd not been lame—and a stable boy I'd never seen before was raking an aisle that was already perfectly raked. I haven't come across him since."

This was bad, and yet, this was information Sycamore should have asked for two knife lessons and one passionate coupling ago.

"Go on."

"I was shopping for a memento to remark my niece Diana's come out and picked up several other items for her sisters. A set of beaded gloves, an embroidered silk reticule, a silver bookmarker with the Tavistock coat of arms etched upon it. The same young ticket porter was on hand at each shop to take my purchases home for me."

"He followed you rather than take the first item home when your maid passed it to him."

"Or he knew how ladies go from shop to shop and was being sensible, but I've never known a ticket porter to carry three items when he can earn his coin carrying one."

Neither had Sycamore. "Is there anything else I should know?"

"I told myself I sought to learn to use knives mostly out of boredom, but I have been uneasy too. As you note, the staff here is aging and not exactly loyal to me. I wanted a project of my own, and you… you tempted me. Since the Wentwhistle house party, I tried to put you from my mind, but you refused to be banished."

Sycamore was torn between pleasure that he'd attracted her ladyship's notice months ago and the need to look more closely at the unease she'd referred to.

"You are uneasy, you decide to learn to use a knife, and then you find out you're being followed from the Coventry and elsewhere. Now other incidents that caused you little concern at the time are appearing in a less sanguine light. Do I have that right?"

Not a cheering recitation.

"You do," she replied. "My mare is recovered from whatever ailed her—a stone bruise, apparently—and Trevor and I went for a rare hack together this morning. I was so pleased to be doing something enjoyable with him again, and yet, I suspect we were followed."

"Did you get a look at your pursuer?"

She shook her head. "I heard hoof beats on the path behind us. My mare whinnied, and another horse responded. When Trevor and I picked up the pace, so did whoever pursued us. The only place for a truly good gallop is along Rotten Row, but we were not followed there. Please tell me I am being fanciful."

"You are the least fanciful woman I know. If your instincts are telling you to be wary, my lady, be wary. Is there more?"

She wore no jewelry, and her hair was done up in a simple chignon. How Sycamore would have loved to have started his day watching her rise and dress, to have brushed out her hair for her and tied the slippers on her feet.

The intensity of his feelings should have been alarming. Instead of alarm, what he felt was fascination—with her, with the deep sense of yearning and protectiveness she inspired.

"I can be fanciful," Jeanette said. "I said nothing to Trevor this morning because of course somebody else might simply have been taking the same bridle path we were, and maintaining a polite distance. I used to be fanciful, when I was a girl."

"Then you married the Marquess of Marital Duty and learned to hide your dreams from even yourself. Is something else troubling you, my lady?"

Jeanette set aside the pillow she'd been toying with. "Viola called on me yesterday. She is married to Lord Beardsley, my late husband's younger brother. Trevor's only male cousin is their son, Jerome."

"Whom I have had the pleasure of meeting. They could be brothers, so closely do the cousins resemble each other." Though Trevor was taller and not as much of a dandy as Jerome, nor did Trevor curl his locks à la Byron. Trevor had no need to be the center of attention, while Jerome always had a pack of fawning cronies with him when he came to the Coventry.

"They are friends, which is a mixed blessing."

"Family can be like that." Sycamore's siblings doubtless considered their connection to him a mixed blessing.

"Jerome isn't awful, but he's a typical ornament. His means are too modest to allow him to marry, and why should he? He's kicking his heels from quarterly allowance to quarterly allowance, and now that Trevor is on hand, he can ride Trevor's social and financial coattails."

Jerome was nearly awful, in Sycamore's expert opinion. He was vain, idle, and jealous of his cousin's title. Sycamore had seen that in the first half hour of play, and Ash had confirmed his impressions.

"Go on, and perhaps a spot of tea would be in order?" Sycamore did not care for any tea, but he suspected Jeanette would be soothed by a familiar activity.

"The tea. Of course, and please do forgive me. With a drop of honey?"

"I am flattered that you'd recall my preferences. What about Viola's visit bothered you?"

Jeanette unswaddled the teapot from its linen wrap. She poured with a steady hand and served herself a cup as well.

"Viola threatened me," Jeanette said. "I was feeling quite on my mettle for a change, unwilling to meekly accept her scolds. When she told me Trevor will come to a bad end by spending time at the Coventry, I replied that Beardsley, who is Trevor's legal guardian, ought to have a talk with his nephew if Trevor's doom is so close at hand. Moreover, Jerome was in a better position than I to influence Trevor's behavior. Viola suggested if I were unwilling or unable to intercede, I would soon find myself consigned to the dower house."

"Where is the dower house?"

"Derbyshire, at the edge of the Peak."

Nearly two hundred damned miles from London. Sycamore sipped his tea, an unremarkable and surprisingly weak blend. If Jeanette removed to Derbyshire, he'd... buy an adjoining property?

"How can that threat be carried out?" he asked. "You are a widow, and this house belongs to Trevor. He isn't about to order you off the premises."

Jeanette had not tasted her tea, which was probably a surer sign of agitation than if she'd paced and ranted.

"Trevor might send me off—politely, but he has the authority. Why keep me around when he and Jerome could share this house? Viola has never liked me, nor I her, but something about her air was more confident, more dire. She still has two daughters to fire off, and that weighs upon her. She'd like Trevor to marry one of his cousins, and with me out of the way, that scheme would have a better chance of succeeding."

"For the nonce, Trevor should not be marrying anybody." Not until he'd met a woman who made him think of leaving all he'd worked for to move to benighted Derbyshire.

"Something is changing, Sycamore. For the past two years, I've been the widow out of mourning. I occupy myself with my charities. I socialize enough that I can be a competent hostess for Trevor when the time comes. Until recently, I would have said the dower house was a lovely property, and I could be content there."

"But?"

"But I have the sense of forces in motion, perhaps because Trevor refused to serve his full sentence at Oxford, or Viola is having trouble launching the younger girls, or Beardsley is tired of my meddling with the solicitors, but something is afoot."

Sycamore moved to sit beside her. "It's worse than that. Your staff is behindhand, Jeanette. The tea leaves have been reused, the ferns in the foyer are choking to death in those pretty pots, and somebody is spying on you. You aren't willing to even close a door in your own home for fear that your behavior will be reported to Viola. Come driving with me."

"I would have to change my dress."

"No, you wouldn't. Find a shawl, don your half boots, and meet me in the foyer in five minutes."

"You are ordering me about, Mr. Dorning."

"Pleading with you."

A hint of her usual self-possession returned. "Very well. Ten minutes." She kissed his cheek and left him with the tea tray, in which he had no interest. Instead, he used the time to snoop about the residence of the current Marquess of Tavistock.

What he found pleased him not one bit. Boring art, lax housekeeping, lumpy chairs, and no place where a lady might secret herself with a gent bent on stealing so much as a kiss.

CHAPTER EIGHT

Driving out with Sycamore Dorning had been a revelation.

He'd called early enough that the park was not yet thronged, and yet, the hour was sufficiently advanced that Jeanette's excursion had been noticed. To each passing carriage or equestrian, Sycamore had offered a tip of his hat, a nod, a smile.

And he'd received many smiles in return, not only from the ladies.

For Jeanette, there had been other smiles—not exactly friendly, but rather, appraising, assessing, envious. *Why is a glorious specimen like him driving out with a Puritan like her?*

Jeanette wasn't a Puritan. She gambled, for pity's sake, mostly for the mental exercise of working through probabilities and also to get out of the blighted house. She did not, however, engender envious glances from matchmakers, or curious smiles from the eligibles. Not unless Sycamore Dorning was at her side.

Simply driving out with him had changed how Society saw her.

"My lady, you have a caller." Peem took her bonnet and cloak.

"Did this caller have a card?"

The old fellow looked momentarily confused, then patted his

pockets. He passed over a little rectangle of cream linen. *Lady Della Dorning*.

Well. Lady Della had attended the Wentwhistles' house party, but Jeanette did not consider her ladyship a close acquaintance. Jeanette didn't consider anybody a close acquaintance, not even Sycamore.

He was a lover, possibly a friend, and even more likely a problem. Two weeks hence, turning him into a fond memory would be no mean feat.

"Where is her ladyship?" Jeanette asked.

"The blue parlor, madam."

Jeanette took herself down the corridor, Lady Della's card tucked into a pocket. She hadn't had real callers since the previous Season, when one at-home every fortnight had been sufficient to allow the gawkers to look Trevor over and measure him as a groom for their daughters and nieces.

"Lady Della." Jeanette curtseyed. "A pleasure. I hope married life is agreeing with you."

Her ladyship was petite. Her hair was an in-between brown, neither auburn nor blond, and her features, while pretty, were unremarkable. What distinguished Lady Della was a sense of leashed energy, a quality of focus and purpose that gave her a larger and more memorable presence.

"Lady Tavistock, good day. Married life is the fulfillment of all my cherished dreams and not a few of my girlish fantasies. How fare you?"

"Well, thank you. Shall we be seated? Oh, dear." Jeanette was mortified to see that nobody had removed the tea tray, much less provided a fresh one. "I do apologize. Shall I ring for a fresh pot?"

"No need," Lady Della said, removing her gloves and taking a seat in a wing chair. "I gather Sycamore called on you before he took you driving?"

Jeanette hadn't been home five minutes, and already she was being interrogated. "Would Mr. Dorning appreciate your curiosity about his socializing, my lady?" Jeanette took a seat on the sofa, not as affronted as she wanted to sound. To be noticed, to have one's companion remarked, was a little flattering, wasn't it?

On the heels of that thought came another: If Lady Della already knew that Jeanette had spent an hour in the park with Sycamore Dorning, who else knew? Jeanette hadn't been followed that she'd noticed—Sycamore would have said something, wouldn't he?—but she'd been *seen*.

"Sycamore told his brother his plans for the afternoon. I am married to that brother, ergo, I knew Sycamore's plans. May I help myself to the shortbread? I realize the request is quite forward, but my digestion has become unreliable, and right now, the thought of a buttery nibble of shortbread..." Lady Della smiled, and Jeanette knew why Ash Dorning had lost his heart to this woman.

"Help yourself, of course."

Her ladyship selected two pieces and put them on a plate. "Sycamore says Lord Tavistock is actually of some use at the club. That is high praise, but what do you think of the marquess attaching himself to the Dorning brothers at this juncture?"

How different Lady Della's call was from Viola's. No lectures here, no sermons. "I was under the impression Lord Tavistock is mostly at Mr. Sycamore Dorning's beck and call. The marquess is working off a debt of honor and gaining a rapid education in how not to waste his inheritance, I hope."

"Ash is going over the books with the marquess later this week. Tavistock seems like a bright young fellow, though I should warn you, the Coventry can be seductive."

Her ladyship was doing justice to the shortbread, though she stopped at two pieces.

"The Coventry can be seductive? I would say rather that Sycamore Dorning is seductive."

Lady Della dusted her hands, and Jeanette realized what exactly she'd revealed with her observation.

"Like that, is it?" Lady Della said. "I thought so. I hoped so.

Sycamore was quite taken with you at the Wentwhistles' house party, and not his usual infatuation either."

"Mr. Dorning kindly advanced me needed sums for a short time at the house party."

"But he didn't charm his way into your bed, did he? That is very curious."

He had expressed a willingness to join her in bed, and Jeanette had been so shocked, she'd brushed him off and spent the whole winter regretting it.

"Your question is quite bold, my lady. Might I ask you to come to the point?" Jeanette would have asked her ladyship to leave, except that Lady Della's gaze was both puzzled and benign. She was not trolling for gossip or making any sort of threat.

Jeanette did not know what Lady Della was about, but then, her ladyship had married a Dorning, and Dornings apparently did not adhere to Society's usual expectations.

"That Sycamore exercised some restraint where you are concerned is a vast compliment," Lady Della said. "He is quite,"—she waved a hand—"frolicsome in the ordinary course. He plays by the rules, never mixes business and pleasure, and does the pretty when the occasion requires proper manners, but with you, Cam is all at sea."

Cam. Sycamore had a nickname, a family name, one he'd mentioned but never directly invited Jeanette to use. To Jeanette's brother, she had once upon a time been Nettie, a name that had always carried a hint of endearment because only Rye referred to her as such. Nobody had called her Nettie for years.

"Mr. Dorning seems very self-possessed to me." Under all circumstances, particularly the intimate ones.

Lady Della rose to study the landscape hanging over the sideboard, though even in that image, a troop of soldiers emerged from dark woods into rolling countryside. Billowing clouds dotted the sky above, and an eagle flew at the head of the military column.

A stupid composition, all symbolism and no story, no beauty. The blue sky qualified it for admission to this insipid little parlor, and abruptly, Jeanette wanted to toss the damned thing out the window.

Toss her insipid life out the window.

"Mr. Dorning has you all at sea too, doesn't he?" Lady Della asked, sending a sympathetic glance over her shoulder. "Cam is like that. He sets everybody on their ears then looks innocently about as if to wonder who could have possibly caused all the commotion. I love him dearly."

One did not say such things, not about a brother-by-marriage, but perhaps one did say them about Sycamore Dorning. "He loves you too, Lady Della. You are family to him, and thus he loves you."

"It's the other way around," Lady Della said, resuming her place in the wing chair. "If Sycamore loves you, you become part of his family. I did not realize that as quickly as I ought. I thought he was meddling between Ash and me, but he was looking out for us. What are you about with him, my lady?"

"Is every Dorning this direct?"

"No, some of them are deviously polite, others overwhelm with charm, others listen with the sort of inordinate attentiveness that soon has all your secrets spilling onto the floor. I haven't the subtlety for those approaches, so here I am, managing as best I can. What you tell me stays between us, my lady. You were kind to me at the Wentwhistle debacle when I very much needed kindness. I will countenance no disrespect toward Sycamore, but I thought you could use a friend."

A friend. What a novel concept, and one disconcertingly lacking in Jeanette's life. The marquess had told her upon whom to call and whom to ignore. The young ladies she'd gone to finishing school with were to be politely excised from her life, while wives of powerful MPs or high-ranking lords were acceptable connections.

Jeanette rose to close the door, though the servants would remark it.

Too bad. "I like Sycamore," she said. "But I suspect everybody likes him. He charms all and sundry, and he knows every small courtesy to make a lady feel cherished. He passed me the reins when he hopped down from the curricle, he held my hand only one instant too long when I alighted. He pats my glove when I put my hand on his arm. He is a gentleman and a rascal. He would turn any woman's head."

"Has he turned yours?"

That question was easy to answer. "He has, which is lovely and awful at the same time. I have fashioned a persona—confident, content, rational. Sycamore Dorning upends everything I've spent years telling myself I value, and at the worst possible time. I could not forget him after the Wentwhistle house party, and I have forgotten everybody. The brother I used to know and love, my well-intended parents. My governess who warned me that marriage is an adjustment. I've forgotten them all, then along struts Sycamore Dorning, and my imagination refuses to eject him."

And that, oddly, was exactly the status the late marquess had sought: all-consuming focus of Jeanette's thoughts, the origin of her every conjecture, fear, and hope.

"My husband would have hated Sycamore," Jeanette added, a realization that gave her pause. "The late marquess would have feared Sycamore, feared his courage, his boldness, his unwillingness to endure pretenses or stupid conventions for the sake of approval."

"A lot of people fear Sycamore, and he likes it that way. His own siblings aren't always sure how to deal with him, though Ash has developed the knack. I hope you do not fear him."

Jeanette did, or she feared the power Sycamore could have over her if she surrendered her heart to him. Fortunately, she'd promised him only two more encounters, and even against his formidable campaign, she could guard her heart that long.

"Mr. Dorning would never intentionally harm those less powerful than he," Jeanette said. "Have I answered your question to your satisfaction, my lady?"

"No, but I don't think you have the answers to give. Sycamore does that—he confuses people. He's not easy company, but he's fierce, loyal, funny, sweet, and roaringly masculine. I suspect you confuse him too."

"*I* confuse *him*?"

"For Sycamore to allow himself a love of his own, not another addition to his vast collection of friends, neighbors, and family, but a love loyal firstly unto him, likely scares him witless. Be kind to him, my lady, or he will haunt you far more than your dead husband has."

Good heavens, this woman was blunt—also perceptive. "How can you tell the marquess haunts me?"

"You said you forgot everybody, but you did not mention him on the list, and from what my sisters tell me, the marquess was a pathetic, prancing martinet desperate for a spare."

A dutiful widow would have defended her husband's memory. Jeanette's dutiful widow tiara was apparently slipping, because the image of her late husband prancing around the bedroom in his silk dressing gowns made her smile.

Or smirk perhaps. "You give me much to think about, my lady," Jeanette said. "Am I correct that you and Mr. Ash Dorning are in anticipation of a precious event?"

"How can you tell?"

"I simply can. I spent years praying nightly for conception and have developed an eye for those who are now praying for a safe delivery. I hope you will call again, my lady. Your direct speech is as bracing as it is refreshing."

Lady Della rose. "You need not be polite with me, madam. I will report to Sycamore that you are as lovely upon further acquaintance as I had imagined and that he'd best marry you at the first opportunity."

Jeanette had risen, intent on seeing her guest out. Lady Della's casual observation nearly had her toppling back to the sofa. "*Marry me*?"

"Of course, marry you. He is smitten, thoroughly, absolutely, and Sycamore-ly smitten. Yes, he's a handful, but if you accept the true heart that he offers, you acquire not only a loyal and dare we say *manly* spouse, but an entire family of Dornings who will never let one of their own suffer alone. Think about that."

Lady Della took a last look around the parlor, while Jeanette heard an echo of figurative cannon fire.

"Have a word with your cook too," Lady Della said, marching for the door. "The shortbread is a bit stale."

"DORNING HALL IS a little worn around the edges," Sycamore said, "but worn in a comforting way. We decorate the place with Papa's botanical prints because he loved them, and we loved him."

Ash glanced up from whatever catalog of wines he was reading. Increasingly, he was to be found in the Coventry's office only during daylight hours.

"Botanical prints are pretty," Ash said, "and Oak drew a lot of them, so we had to pay nothing for them."

"That's not the point," Sycamore said, pacing before the office's desk. He'd slept in the adjoining bedroom last night—again—and dreamed of Jeanette. "The point is, those prints mean something to us. We know where Papa found many of the specimens, we've actually read the plant properties he listed in the margins for this weed or that blossom, and we like seeing his handwriting framed on our walls."

"They are Casriel's walls. I gather champagne is becoming more popular. These prices are ridiculous."

"You are ridiculous," Sycamore said, turning a straight-backed chair away from the desk and planting himself on it astraddle. "I am trying to pour out my heart to you, and you babble about the price of wine."

Ash closed the catalog. "The price of wine matters when we're giving the stuff away by the barrel. Tavistock suggested we serve our champagne in slightly smaller glasses to achieve an economy."

"A brilliant idea, except we'd need to order special glasses, which would not be an economy. Have you ever been to Tavistock House?"

"I sent a reconnaissance officer," Ash said, smiling slightly.

Sycamore knew that smile. "Della paid a call on the marchioness?"

"Earlier in the week. Della claimed the house reflects dull taste two decades out of fashion, the staff is antediluvian, and the whole place is quiet as a tomb."

"A portrait of the late marquess hangs in the foyer," Sycamore said. "Another two in the library—boyhood and young manhood. I suspect we'd find the baby portrait in the nursery and the marquess as a new husband in the bedroom. He haunts that house like a grumpy Scottish ghost."

Ash watched as Sycamore rose and resumed his pacing. "This bothers you."

"Of course it bothers me. What wall space the marquess doesn't occupy, his sainted antecedents take up, each one more dour than the last. The lot of them look like they suffer a serious case of the wind, and the staff wouldn't hear the French army marching past trumpeting *La Marseillaise* as they approached. Her ladyship can be neither safe nor happy in such an abode."

Ash leaned back and propped his boots on a corner of the desk. "Why would you, who have driven out with the woman exactly once, have a care for her safety?"

"Because I am a gentleman, and somebody should."

Ash crossed his arms and stared at the ceiling. "Sycamore."

"Because she is being followed, because she is concerned for her safety. Because her late husband made her life a genteel hell when she did not conceive his blighted spares."

"She struck me as a sensible woman. Why does she fear for her safety?"

Sycamore closed the door to the bedroom. "Her in-laws resent her, her brother keeps his distance, the young marquess is becoming an unreliable ally, and she has no idea why anybody would watch her comings and goings. She is worried, Ash, and I cannot abide to see a lady made to fret for no reason."

"You are worried," Ash said. "Not simply your usual fretful, grumbling self. You are worried."

Sycamore was spared further statements of the obvious by a rap on the office door.

"Enter," Ash called, removing his boots from the desk and sitting up.

Trevor, Marquess of Tavistock, joined them, though not the natty version of his lordship Sycamore usually saw.

"My lord," Ash said, getting to his feet, "if you are the worse for drink, I suggest you go home and sleep it off."

Tavistock's coat was missing two buttons, his cravat was ripped and dangling askew, his sleeve was muddy, and his knuckles were scraped. One cheek sported a rising bruise, and he was bleeding from the lip. The scent of brandy hung thickly in the air.

Sycamore stuck his head into the corridor. "Ice, now! Bandages, arnica, and I do mean instantaneously!" He closed the door and considered the marquess. "Either you've been scrapping, or you've consorted at close range with the wrong sort of pickpockets."

"I'd just left Angelo's," Tavistock said, panting slightly. "A fine session with épées. I popped around to the alley to have a nip—one doesn't want to drink in the actual street, does one?—and three unsavory-looking fellows blocked my egress."

"You can form complete Etonian sentences," Sycamore said, drawing the marquess's coat gently from his shoulders. "The unsavory fellows must not have done too much damage."

"They probably didn't expect me to give any account of myself," Tavistock said as Sycamore unknotted what was left of a once-fine cravat. "I dashed my brandy in their faces—good brandy, it was, and now I'm wearing some of it—and did that business where you hook your boot behind a fellow's knees and drop him. The largest of the three wasn't having any of my cleverness, though."

"How did you best him?" Ash asked, accepting a basin and box of medicinals from a waiter at the door.

Tavistock blushed. "Knee to the cods, a move you showed me months ago. Not sporting, but neither is three against one. I would rather not go home looking like this, so I came here. Step-mama will worry, though London's street gangs are hardly worth panicking over."

"Sit," Sycamore said, exchanging a look with Ash. "Shirt off. If your ribs are injured, for the next six weeks at least, you do nothing more strenuous than lift a tankard of ale or escort a lady at the promenade. Breathe deeply as often as you can to ward off lung fevers, even though it hurts like your best profanity." *And stay out of deserted London alleys, for God's sake.*

Getting Tavistock's shirt off necessitated cutting the fabric to spare his lordship the pain of raising his arms above his head.

"You're putting on muscle," Sycamore said when a tactile inspection revealed no broken ribs. "Pugilism?"

Ash passed his lordship a towel folded around chipped ice. "You will hurt less if you limit the swelling now."

"Pugilism," Tavistock said, sinking into the chair behind the desk and applying the ice to his cheek. "Fencing, riding out. I asked around at Jackson's for a few defensive maneuvers not covered in the usual prize ring rules. I never expected to use that knowledge, but a fellow wants to be prepared for every eventuality."

Ash disappeared into the bedroom and emerged with a fresh shirt and cravat. "These will be loose on you, though not by much. Have we buttons, Sycamore?"

Sycamore took the knife from his boot and sliced off two buttons from his morning coat. "We have buttons." He opened the desk's bottom drawer and produced a small sewing kit. "A fellow wants to be prepared for every eventuality."

Tavistock looked at him as if he'd conjured a pot of gold sovereigns from a bowl of marbles. "I knew a stop here was well advised, but what on earth do I tell Step-mama? She will say I am associating with the wrong sorts, and she might not be far from the mark."

Ash gathered up the clean shirt to ease down over Tavistock's head. "Your waistcoat can wait until we've fed you and refilled your flask. Coffee or ale with luncheon?"

"Tea, if you have it. The old breadbasket is feeling a bit tentative."

"Tea it is." Ash sent Sycamore a look and decamped in the direction of the kitchen.

"If the old breadbasket is tentative," Sycamore said as he tucked gold sleeve buttons into the marquess's cuffs, "does that mean somebody kneed you in the gut?"

"I avoided the blow, but one can only twist so far when being held by the arms. Do you know what went through my mind when I was being pummeled?"

"You did some pummeling too, my lord." Sycamore fashioned a second towel full of ice. "For your lip."

"I did, didn't I? I had the oddest thought: These louts didn't smell as louts ought. The last time I was set upon by toughs, the stench was almost worse than the blows. This lot was by no means a trio of dandies, but they had some acquaintance with soap and water. I shall hurt tomorrow, won't I?"

"Wonderfully, and worse the day after, but breathe deeply anyway. Aches like hell, but keeps the lungs clear. I'd avoid laudanum, because you took a few blows to the head, but willow bark tea can't hurt, and further applications of arnica to the cuts and bruises won't either."

"May I tell you something, Mr. Dorning?"

"You may."

"I wasn't frightened when I realized what was afoot. Jackson says I have good science, decent reach, and some speed for a pampered puppy. That's high praise from such as he. I was eager to show those fellows what I knew, and in broad daylight, all they could do was rob me and leave me in that alley."

Sycamore wrapped an arm around the marquess's shoulders, kissed his crown, then scrubbed his knuckles over blond curls. Courage was giving way to sense, and that was always a bad moment.

"But you're feeling a touch of the collywobbles now, is that it?" Sycamore certainly was. "What if one of them had had a knife, or they'd thought to bring a fourth? You could be lying with your throat slit and nobody the wiser."

"One of them did have a knife. I kicked it out of his hand, but still... not very sporting of them. Three against one *and* a knife. What is London coming to, and in St. James's itself? Bad form, Mr. Dorning."

Sycamore dumped the last of the ice onto the soil of the nearest potted fern. "Will you be sick? No shame in it if you are. I'm feeling tentative myself." He set the empty basin on the desk. *One of them had had a knife...*

"No, but neither will I frequent that alley again anytime soon."

Ash returned bearing a tray of beef barley soup, buttered bread with the crusts cut off, and a pot of tea. "Soft food for a sore jaw," he said. "A week from now, you'll be back to regular rations."

Tavistock set aside his ice compresses long enough to eat, while Sycamore sewed the replacement buttons onto the marquess's coat. Tavistock was, all things considered, recovering well—the blessings of youth—while Sycamore was growing more upset.

London streets were not safe, hence the ongoing clamor for a regular city police force. Tavistock had already made the point, however, that if anywhere ought to be safe, it was the hallowed streets of St. James's. London's dandies, gents, and Corinthians congregated there and would mete out swift retribution to any violating the peace and safety of the neighborhood.

And yet, somebody had. Three somebodies.

"I'll send you home in the coach," Sycamore said, "and we won't expect to see you here until next week."

"But I'm fine," Tavistock said, rising so that Ash could help him into his waistcoat. "A bit bashed up, but truly none the worse for a little scrapping."

"What will you tell her ladyship?" Sycamore asked, passing Ash the fresh cravat.

"That I had a few good rounds at Jackson's? That my sparring partner was too enthusiastic?"

Ash was the only married man in the room, so Sycamore let him reply. "Tell her the truth, Tavistock. You were set upon by toughs, you fended them off. Do you still have your purse?"

"I don't often carry anything more than a few coins."

Typical lordling, his credit was good everywhere. Sycamore pushed Ash aside and tied the marquess's cravat. His lordship preferred some style to his appointments, as Sycamore did.

"Tell her ladyship the truth," Sycamore said. "She can sense when you lie, and I suspect you don't lie well. You fended off some street thieves and stopped by here for lunch."

"I lie quite convincingly," Tavistock said as Sycamore affixed a gold cravat pin among the folds of linen and lace. "Nobody expects me to because I resemble such a dratted choirboy on stilts."

"You resemble a marquess," Sycamore retorted, threading his lordship's watch chain through a buttonhole. "Who knew where you'd be this morning?"

"Step-mama. We tell each other our general plans for the day. Jerome met me at Angelo's to watch. He and I were supposed to have lunch at his club afterward, but he was inclined to stay for the next match, and I was hungry. I'm always hungry. Will I do?"

Ash held up the repaired coat, from which Sycamore had also brushed the dried mud. "Did anybody say anything during your encounter with your assailants?"

Tavistock buttoned the coat closed. "I might have used some foul language. 'Damn the lot of you,' 'what the devil,' that sort of thing."

"Such a wicked fellow," Sycamore muttered. "Did the others say anything? Did they address each other, call any warnings to each other?"

Tavistock, looking only slightly the worse for wear, stared off at nothing. "The beating was singularly quiet, though one of them did say, 'You've traded on your expectations for the last time.' I haven't any expectations. I'm past the expectation part and now wearing a title that sits upon my head like an oversized crown. I suppose he meant my general expectations as a young man-about-Town?"

"Did they say anything else?" Ash asked. "Anything that would hint at a regional accent, a station in life, a calling? Did they address you directly?"

"One of them said something like 'bloody fop' when I kicked the knife from his hand, but they were mostly intent on giving me a drubbing rather than chatting. Why am I suddenly in need of a nap?"

"You've had an adventure," Sycamore said. "Napping is part of it. You can nap in the coach—tell the coachy to wake you upon arrival—and avoid going anywhere alone for a while, please."

"You gave a brilliant account of yourself," Ash said, "but if these men want to get back a bit of their own, they know you are not at your best right now. Let your friends take them on next time, though we must hope there is no next time."

Tavistock picked up the last slice of buttered bread from the tray. "You lot know how to go on. I suspected you would, and I am in your debt. My thanks, and if there's ever anything I can do, and all that."

"Be off with you," Sycamore said, shoving him—gently—toward the door. "You did well, Tavistock, both in defending yourself and in stopping by here on your way home. That you could not rely on your valet to deal with this situation tells you the man needs to be replaced, and that is not a task your step-mother can see to for you."

Tavistock made a face. "Truer words... I'll just be going, and again, my thanks." He sauntered out, the picture of elegant young manhood, though his gait was a trifle conservative.

"Jeanette won't like this," Sycamore said.

"I don't like it," Ash replied. "He still had his watch, cravat pin, and sleeve buttons. This was not an attempted robbery. This was a warning of some sort."

"I suspect it was, but perhaps for Jerome, not for the marquess. The two of them are peas in a pod, but for the difference in height, and Jerome, as the current spare, has expectations to trade on. I believe I should pay a call on young Mr. Vincent."

"Be nice," Ash said, gathering up the discarded shirt and cravat. "Our ladies frown on gratuitous displays of violence."

"I haven't a lady." *Yet.*

"Yes," Ash said gently, "you do. The question is, will she have you?"

~

JEANETTE KNEW, by the relative haste with which Peem brought her the card, that Sycamore Dorning intended to be difficult.

"The gentleman insisted, my lady, and on the Sabbath. I do apologize." Peem was not apologizing so much as he was disapproving.

"I will see Mr. Dorning in my sitting room, Peem." Jeanette's personal parlor was one floor above street level and thus safe from prying eyes. Or less unsafe.

"Shall I have the kitchen send up a tray?" Peem asked.

"A tray will not be necessary." Mr. Dorning's visit would be brief.

Jeanette had barely perched on her favorite sofa before Peem showed Sycamore into the room. "Mr. Sycamore Dorning of the Dorset Dornings," Peem said, managing to make even that announcement chiding.

"My lady." Sycamore bowed correctly. "Thank you for receiving me."

"That will be all, Peem."

The butler departed, leaving the door wide open.

"Mr. Dorning, have a seat."

He flipped out his tails and took the wing chair angled beside the sofa. Too late she realized the error of having allowed him into the one room where her own taste had been given free rein.

"You like flowers," Sycamore said, "and very bright colors."

"My grandmother's family holds land in Provence. Most of the paintings are of that region. The light is warmer in the South of France."

"Land in Provence, vineyards in Champagne. How much of those holdings survived the wars?"

"You would have to ask my brother, who inherited from our French relatives. I have not ordered a tray because I trust you will not be staying long." She added a pointed glance at the open door. "Today is Sunday, Mr. Dorning. While I might have invited you to join me for Sunday dinner, the marquess and I seldom bother with a weekly feast. The staff works hard enough without adding a large Sunday dinner to their duties."

Sycamore touched a finger to the bouquet of red, white, and pink roses on the low table before the sofa. "Real," he said. "Thorns and all. Are you truly indisposed?"

The diffident quality of his question surprised her. "Why would I have written you a note claiming indisposition if I was not truly unwell?"

"You don't look unwell. Women sometimes resort to polite fictions when they are trying to be diplomatic, and with me, sooner or later the ladies are either diplomatic or exasperated. I've missed you."

That last admission was grudging, maybe even a touch bewildered. Also another surprise. "Missed me?"

He snapped off a white rose and added it to the boutonnière of violets on his lapel. "Lately, I look forward to Sundays with inordinate pleasure, my lady. If you are unwell, I am concerned. If you are not unwell, I am alarmed. Are you unwell?"

Violets were an exquisite complement to Sycamore's eyes, but they also had symbolic meanings: modesty, which did not strike Jeanette as apropos to Sycamore Dorning in any mood, also faithfulness and humility. The white rose carried sentiments of new love, grace, and again, humility.

"Sycamore, I am *indisposed.*"

His expression became puzzled. "As ladies are indisposed?"

Heat rose across Jeanette's cheeks. "Exactly thus."

"Truly?"

"We are not discussing this."

"Does this indisposition that we are not discussing cause you discomfort?"

Jeanette resisted the urge to bury her face in a pillow, but Sycamore was nothing if not persistent, so she dispensed with futile gestures. She instead focused on the painting of Grandmother's lavender fields in full bloom under a spectacular azure sky.

"There is some discomfort."

"You hurt. Does the ginger tea help?"

"What ginger tea?"

"Ginger-ginger tea. Works best if you start drinking it before the pains start. Among the kitchen staff at the club, fennel also has a following, and the pot girl's granny swears by some pine bark infusion from the South of France. If all else fails, there's always the poppy. Where's your hot water bottle?"

"I am receiving a caller," Jeanette said. "I do not typically receive callers while clutching a hot water bottle to my... my middle." And yet, she was glad to see him. Mortified, but glad. Sycamore's gaze held concern, and he was making helpful suggestions—or trying to.

He rose, and if he'd been intent on closing the door, Jeanette would have scolded him severely. He instead cracked a window.

"The roses will last longer if the air isn't so stuffy," he said. "You don't order a hot water bottle because you don't want the staff to know of your indisposition, which is silly. They know everything anyway. I brought you a peace offering."

"Are we at war?"

"I thought we might be. I adore you, and my adoration sometimes provokes... Well, that is to say..." He regarded her with a brooding sort of frown. "Never mind that now." He bent to withdraw something from his boot and presented Jeanette with a flat, dark curve of metal, sharpened to a lethal point at one end. "For you."

"A knife?" Not like any knife Jeanette had seen before. The darkness of the metal, the elegance of the curve, and the wicked point all announced that this was a deadly weapon rather than a serviceable tool.

"A trial design. We could give it a toss in the mews, see if it fits your hand."

"You brought me a present." The metal was smooth and cool, the weight exquisitely balanced. This knife was sleeker than the ones Jeanette had thrown previously and not quite as long.

"I know calling on the Sabbath isn't the done thing, my lady, but somebody is following you, then Tavistock is set upon in an alley, and now you tell me you are indisposed. I leaped to fearful conclusions. I often do, which is not entirely a bad thing, because if one anticipates fearful outcomes, then one can—I am babbling."

He took the place beside Jeanette—very presuming of him—and Jeanette lost a piece of her heart to him. A passionate Sycamore was arousing and impressive. A babbling Sycamore, bearing gifts and spouting off about tisanes, was a dear man, indeed.

"Every month," Jeanette said, passing him back the knife, "I am reminded of my unfitness for the title I bear. In years of incessant attempts to conceive, I could not produce a single child, Sycamore. Not *even* a daughter, as my husband reminded me month after month. I was interrogated and examined by physicians, accoucheurs, and midwives. I drank vile concoctions, I took the waters at half the spa towns in the realm, and I prayed without ceasing to an indifferent God. I hate this time of the month, and it's as if my body hates it too."

"Did the late marquess ever impose his attentions on you at this time of the month?"

Where had the knife gone? Probably back into Sycamore's boot, though Jeanette hadn't seen him put it away. "Of course not."

Sycamore put a large hand low on her belly and kneaded gently. "If the mumps wasn't the problem, that might be why you didn't conceive. My sister-in-law Margaret is a genius with herbs, and between her, the countess, and my sister Daisy, I've overhead more about lady's ailments than you can imagine. Gives a fellow pause."

"You should not be sitting next to me, Sycamore."

"You should not be suffering, Jeanette. Does this help?" He used firmer pressure.

"Yes, damn you. Nobody conceives while the womb is bleeding."

"Says who? The late Marquess of Mopery? He got all of one woman pregnant that we know of, and that doubtless took heroic forbearance on the part of his wives, mistresses, and casual romps. Perhaps you would conceive right as the bleeding ends, and the business wants a few days head start."

As Sycamore's shocking familiarities continued, Jeanette resisted the urge to rest her head against his shoulder. He was contradicting medical science, and also making sense.

"Peem will be up here with a tray," she said. "I told him we were not to be disturbed, but he's set in his ways."

"He's softening toward me," Sycamore said, working his way across Jeanette's belly. "Witness, I am no longer Mr. Doorknob. Let's see how your new favorite toy fits your hand."

"You are flirting with me."

"No, I am not. If I invited you to fit your hand to *my* favorite toy, then I would be flirting. Shall we sneak off to the mews and engage in a little diversion, my lady?"

She wanted to see how the knife behaved, and she wanted to sneak off with Sycamore. Not in that order.

"A few throws only, and that assumes the mews are deserted."

"Of course." He rose with his usual energy and offered her his hand.

Jeanette got to her feet more slowly and realized the horrendous cramping, which made her ache from the arches of her feet to her ribs, was somewhat abated. Not gone, but better.

She took up a shawl rather than bother with a cloak and saw her guest out through the back garden and across the alley.

"Tavistock was not set upon in an alley," she said as Sycamore's earlier comment came back to her. "He was right on the street, and some of his friends weren't far behind him."

Sycamore led her around to the back of the stable, to the dusty yard where horses were often groomed, the farrier did his work, and barn cats lounged in the sun.

"Tavistock was very clear that he'd ducked into an alley to have a nip from his flask. While I know the use most gents will put an alley to—the uses—I believe the lad because the fragrance of brandy was strong on his person in the middle of the day."

Sycamore walked off a distance from the side of the carriage house. No windows broke up that wall, and he used a penknife to scratch three concentric circles at chest height on the wooden siding. From the stable across the yard from the carriage house, curious horses munched hay and watched over their half doors.

"Sycamore, what are you going on about? Tavistock's mishap occurred late at night, on the street, and the only brandy involved had been consumed over cards at Jerome's club."

Sycamore used the heel of his boot to draw a line in the dirt. "Tavistock told you he'd sparred a little too enthusiastically at Jackson's?"

The cramps in Jeanette's belly were joined by a feeling of general unease. "He did, and knowing young men, I believed him. He lied to me, didn't he?"

Sycamore passed her the knife and moved behind her. "He apparently did, though with the best of intentions. Focus on the throw, Jeanette, and aim for the center of the target. We will discuss Tavistock's little mishap later, but for now, focus on the throw."

She toed the line and tried to relax and breathe, but when the knife left her hand, it ended up a yard above the ground, buried in a post six feet away from the damned target.

CHAPTER NINE

Sycamore had in fact brought three knives, all of the same design. Jeanette's first throw was a predictable disaster, but a dozen more attempts, and she was wielding the blades with reliable accuracy—and no little temper.

"I believe we've established that the design works for you," Sycamore said as another set of three throws clustered toward the middle of the makeshift bull's-eye. "Do you like it?"

Jeanette glowered at the blades embedded in the carriage house wall. "I suppose I must if I hit the target so consistently."

"Not so," Sycamore said, retrieving the knives. "Just as you accommodated the old marquess in every wifely sense, hating the whole ordeal, you can competently throw a knife you don't care for, or throw well at one distance and fail at every other. Did you *enjoy* wielding these knives, my lady?"

He slipped one blade into each boot and passed the third to her.

"They fit my hand," she said, running a finger over the elegant curve of the metal. "The other knives were too big and heavy for me, though I would never have known that without throwing these."

Sycamore busied himself scratching the ears of a muscular bay gelding rather than watch Jeanette caress the blade.

"Just as this design is an improvement for you over my own knives," he said, "another design, even lighter, or finished to a smoother grip, might be better still."

"I like these," Jeanette said. "May I keep this one?"

"Of course, and I'll have a case made for the set. Are you calm enough to discuss Tavistock's lying yet?" He offered the slight to her self-control deliberately as a test of that calm.

She retrieved her shawl from the half door of a pretty chestnut mare. "You throw knives to calm your temper?"

"And my worry." Sycamore took the shawl from her and draped it over her shoulders, because he needed the excuse to touch her. "Also to help me think. My father would go on long walks to help him solve problems, though his practice was to note all the flora and fauna, the state of the crops, and the condition of the tenant cottages. By the time he came home, the walking had often jostled a solution loose in his brain box."

"One cannot safely go for long walks in London. Hence, you play with knives." Jeanette gestured to a bench in the shade of the stable's overhang. The location was outdoors yet private, a good place to have a difficult conversation. "You are about to present a case for the defense of his lordship, to put a gentlemanly gloss on Trevor's dishonesty."

She sank onto the bench a little gingerly, and Sycamore's wayward imaginings were pushed aside by a reminder that the lady was uncomfortable.

"I hate that you hurt," he said, taking the place beside her. "I hate even more that you've nobody on hand to commiserate with you and cosset you. I want to hold you and pet you and bring you hot water bottles and tisanes while I rub your feet and read you Byron's poems."

"Instead, you bring me a sharp blade and a thorny dilemma. I understand why Trevor would keep a fight in an alley to himself. He does not want me to worry, and that is a kind impulse. I have not wanted him to worry, and thus I haven't been entirely forthcoming either."

A sparrow lighted on the cobbled walkway ten feet away. Sycamore produced a butter biscuit pilfered from his morning tea tray, broke it in half, and offered one portion to Jeanette.

"Thank you," she said, taking the treat and popping it into her mouth.

The rest he crumbled up and tossed at the sparrow, who moved from crumb to crumb according to some map known only to the bird.

"Do you refer to general reticence, my lady, or have you, too, been set upon by brigands in broad daylight?"

"Not brigands. I sought your instruction with knives because I was uneasy. Then Trevor had that brawl, now you tell me he's been attacked again." She watched the little bird hopping from crumb to crumb. "I have received two notes, Sycamore. One came some time ago, telling me a widow riding a step-son's coattails was a pathetic creature who'd be well advised to rusticate out of Society's view. That was merely insulting, and I have learned to ignore insults."

"And then somebody started following you."

"Then I *noticed* somebody following me, and now Tavistock has had not one but two encounters with London's purveyors of street violence. And just yesterday I received a second note, telling me I'm not safe in London. I could dismiss the first as the infantile dramatics certain members of society are prone to. The second is more threatening than insulting. I was going to tell you about it, but then I became indisposed. One wants to be on one's mettle when one broaches such a topic."

Sycamore battled the impulse to gather Jeanette in his arms and spirit her away to some safe place—Dorning Hall came to mind, a very hard two days' journey from London if the roads were dry. Oak, out in Hampshire, could provide sanctuary, as could Jacaranda at Trysting.

"This is why Viola's threat to consign you to the dower house upset you so," he said. "Because you had been threatened before. May I see the notes, Jeanette?"

"I keep them with me," she said, fishing in a pocket. "If the notes are real, then my fear is justified. I hate even saying those words."

Sycamore took two folded pieces of foolscap from her. "How did these arrive?"

"With the morning post on both occasions. The mail sits on the sideboard in the foyer for half the day. Any of Trevor's friends who come and go with him could have added those notes—the young men put locusts to shame when they join us at breakfast. A servant could have found the notes on the floor and included them with the stack of letters on the sideboard."

Sycamore unfolded the first note.

A widow past her prime trading on a step-son's consequence is a blight upon Society. Get thee to a dower property, where you belong, and stay there.

The second was more to the point: *London is no longer safe for you. To the country, my lady, posthaste!*

"Nasty," Sycamore said, holding the paper up to the light. "No watermark, suggesting we are not dealing with a complete fool. Educated handwriting, proper spelling, a vague allusion to Hamlet's insults."

Jeanette balanced the knife horizontally on her fingertip. "'Get thee to a nunnery'?" she quoted.

"Meaning Ophelia was to go to either a convent or a brothel, but either way, a low insult to one's intended."

"Unless Hamlet was trying to keep her safe."

"Hamlet broke her damned heart and drove her mad, but an uneducated person isn't likely to have alluded to Shakespeare. Why haven't you left London, Jeanette?" Sycamore wished the answer could be that she hadn't wanted to leave him, but that was foolish. The first note had arrived before he and Jeanette had become lovers.

"I refuse to be cowed," she said, watching the sparrow fly away with a crumb held in its beak. "For the first twenty-four years of my life, I did what I was told to do. I am no threat to anybody, and these notes could be from some matchmaker who thinks I'm preventing Trevor from standing up with her niece. I was afraid of my husband. He never raised a hand to me, but I disgusted him, and he took infinite, intimate pains to make sure I knew that. I retreated and retreated and retreated in the face of his disapproval. Recovering the ground I yielded has taken me years."

Jeanette gripped the knife firmly now, and it fit her hand exactly.

"Tell me what you know of Trevor's first encounter with street roughs."

She angled a glare at him.

"Please," Sycamore amended. "Won't you please tell me what you know of that incident?"

"He was coming home from supper and a late-night round of cards at Jerome's club. Jerome stayed behind, though several other fellows left when Trevor did. Trevor had lost, he was half-seas over, and he hadn't bothered to hire a linkboy. A pair of ruffians set upon him, and his friends apparently came around the corner in the next instant. Trevor hasn't exactly boasted of the occasion, but I gather he gave a good account of himself."

"And the whole business in our great and elegant metropolis is entirely unremarkable. Not so this week's incident." Sycamore took Jeanette's free hand. A pale measure compared to spiriting her off to Dorning Hall, but he hoped his touch reassured her.

As hers reassured him.

"As best I can tell," Sycamore said, "Friday morning, Tavistock apparently had an appointment to fence with a chum at Angelo's. Jerome and the usual gang of foplings came to watch. The agenda had been for Jerome and Trevor to share lunch at the club following Trevor's session. Jerome became engrossed in observing the next match, so Trevor left on his own. He wanted a nip from his flask, but was too much of a gentleman to drink on the street and popped around to an alley. Three professional bullyboys met him there, one with a knife."

Jeanette shifted her grip on Sycamore's hand to lace her fingers with his. "He could have been killed."

"Not likely. I suspect both attacks were a case of mistaken identity. If three men wanted to kill one unsuspecting marquess in an alley, they would all come armed, they would wait for cover of darkness, and they would finish the job."

Jeanette watched the sparrow return to snatch up the last of the crumbs. "You think Jerome was the target?"

How Sycamore loved her mind, as quick and sharp as a Damascus blade. "The facts line up with that hypothesis, and Jerome and Trevor look very much alike."

"Trevor is taller and leaner, not half such a dandy as Jerome." Said with no little disdain for dandies.

"But to those who don't know them, or to whom every gent in St. James's is a peacock, that's a distinction without a difference. I can think of many reasons why somebody might want to beat some humility into young Mr. Vincent."

The little bird came back, or another very like it, while Jeanette appeared to consider Sycamore's theories. "Jerome has debts. Trevor has let that much slip."

"Jerome might well have taken liberties with somebody's sister or companion, led somebody else's brother into the River Tick, or offered an insult to someone's mother. He is an only son, from a titled family, and of an age to be quite stupid."

"Quite arrogant," Jeanette said. "Of all Trevor's fine qualities, what I love in him most is his decency. He's not consumed with his own consequence. If I seek to safeguard any aspect of his character, it's that reservoir of humility. Do you think Jerome is trying to banish me to the country, the better to gain influence over Trevor?"

Not a theory Sycamore would have come up with, though it fit. "Somebody is determined to beat Jerome silly. If he's deeply in debt or has committed some serious breach of honor, then sending you two hundred miles away allows Jerome to move in with Trevor and shelter under the marquess's consequence."

"And get his cousinly fingers into the marquess's purse." Jeanette rose to pace the cobbled walkway beneath the overhang. "How does Jerome's situation connect with somebody following me?"

"Perhaps," Sycamore said slowly, "the next beating is intended for you. Somebody is trying to scare you clear back to Derbyshire."

Jeanette half turned away from him, her hand rubbing absently over her belly. "I hate this. I want to scoff, stick my nose in the air, and conduct myself with complete indifference toward a lot of foolish dramatics."

Sycamore rose. "Instead, you sought to arm yourself and kept the whole business from the marquess lest you trouble his handsome head. Jeanette, there is another course between ignoring the problem and taking the whole matter on in solo combat."

"I can retreat to Derbyshire. It's not even near the family seat, just some property acquired in an advantageous marriage a couple of centuries ago. Rye would never see me, Trevor would correspond with me out of duty, and I would receive an annual invitation from Viola to come to Kent in the autumn when the men were off shooting, but she'd hope I'd decline—and I would."

"That's not the option I refer to and not one I'd suggest. Until you know who is trying to bully you and why, leaving Town doesn't necessarily keep you safe. In Derbyshire, you would be quite easy to dispose of."

She paced back to him and kept coming, slipping her arms around his waist. "You do not try to hide the truth from me. I treasure your honesty, but I am afraid, Sycamore. I hate being afraid. I was afraid for too long, of never having my husband's respect, of every overheard whisper in the ladies' retiring room. I became sick with dread and began to fear I'd be set aside—or worse—so the late marquess could try for his spares with a third and fertile wife."

She leaned on Sycamore, the sweetest, most precious gesture of trust in the world, also alarming. Men from kings to paupers had *set aside* troublesome wives for affronts less serious than barrenness, and Jeanette had lived with that fear for several years.

"Nobody would care if I suffered a tragic accident, Sycamore, but I would care. Rye might shed a few tears, the charities I support would miss my coin, but a week on, nobody would care."

I would care profoundly. "Tavistock would be devastated."

"What if Trevor sent the notes? What if he's too polite to tell me to leave him a clear field here in Town?"

Jeanette's marriage had taught her to fret like this. "An odd sort of manners, that threatens a woman's peace of mind with vile notes." And yet, the theory had merit. Sycamore was reminded that Tavistock had claimed to be a skilled liar, an odd but credible boast.

"Please hear me out," Sycamore said, guiding Jeanette back to the bench and keeping an arm around her shoulders. "You trusted me enough to ask me for instructions on how to use a knife. You trusted me enough to take me to bed. Can you trust me enough to enlist me as an ally in the effort to keep you safe?"

She sat beside him, her hand on her belly, her gaze on the bull's-eye scored into the carriage house planks across the yard.

"I already have enlisted you as an ally, though nobody is more surprised to find it so than I am."

Surprised, and not exactly pleased, apparently. Sycamore charged on nonetheless. "Let me pay you my addresses, Jeanette. As a regular caller, as a devoted suitor, I can keep a closer eye on everybody around you and do a better job of investigating the beatings, the notes, and whoever is following you."

She pulled away and sat up very straight. "Don't be ridiculous. I have no wish to marry ever again, Sycamore. You must know that. Marriage to Lord Tavistock was hell. Lapdogs are treated better than I was, and I will never again become a man's property, to be used intimately and insulted at his whim."

Well, damn. Sycamore had not seen that knife whistling toward him in the dark, but he should have.

"I hadn't meant to propose actual marriage, Jeanette." Sycamore had. He absolutely had. Marriage, a home of their own, safety for her, pleasure for them both. The whole bit, including—maybe, eventually

—a few fat, chortling babies to put paid to the late marquess's worst insults to Jeanette. "I meant to propose a pleasant fiction that allows you to better direct me in aid of your safety."

"You are trying to cozen me."

"I am trying to keep you safe. We might not be the best of friends, but I am a gentleman, and you are in a difficult situation." They were also *lovers*, not simply passing romps. Sycamore had had enough of the latter to know the difference.

"You are truly a gentleman," Jeanette said, a brooding admission accompanied by a perusal of his person.

"I am also a Dorning. I have family coming out my ears. Willow can provide you a watch dog. Ash will teach Trevor the finer points of pugilism. Kettering is merely an in-law, but he can acquaint us with the details of young Jerome's finances, and darling Margaret will brew you up a potion to banish the worst of your monthly pains. Casriel is an earl—earls come in handy at odd moments—and his beloved Beatitude corresponds with every literate gossip in England.

"I remain attached to my family," he went on, "because they are all the safety I have, Jeanette, and I offer them to you for the same purpose."

Not quite what he'd wanted to say, but then, *Please, for the love of God, marry me* wouldn't serve either.

Jeanette braced her hands on the bench and leaned forward, brushing her slippers against the cobbles. "I want to keep you safe too, Sycamore. I haven't finished my knife lessons, after all, and you wield a blade very competently."

Had any other woman made that observation, Sycamore would have known she was flirting. "I do, and we have a bargain, and I will make a very biddable suitor, I promise you."

"No," she said, "you won't, and you are not to court me, Sycamore. You are to attempt to court me. To consider courting me. To try to interest me in a passing liaison. Pay me enough attention to help me solve the puzzles currently vexing me, but don't start too much talk."

Progress indeed, over the status of clandestine dining partner. "I am the soul of discretion," he said, "and I never start talk." His entire family, including Willow's dogs, would be overcome with hilarity at that pronouncement, but his family wasn't sitting on a bench with Jeanette, longing to hold her hand again and mentally vowing to punish whoever had disturbed her peace.

Jeanette sat back and rested her forehead against his shoulder. "Be patient with me, Sycamore. I don't want to draw you into my troubles, and against all good sense, I like you, very much. That leaves me in a badly timed muddle."

"I like you too, Jeanette." He liked her *passionately*. "I'll have the blacksmith cast you a full set of knives, shall I?"

"Please."

They remained on the bench for another few moments, the sound of horses munching hay an accompaniment to an odd fluttering of both joy and anxiety in Sycamore's heart. Threatening notes were bad, but liking him very much was good. He bowed over Jeanette's hand at her garden gate and agreed to call on her the following day, possible-suitor fashion.

Or trustworthy-gentleman fashion. Both roles were lovely to contemplate, though becoming Jeanette's intended would be lovelier still. Her marriage truly had been a horror, the damage worse than Sycamore had first suspected.

He was rambling along in the alley, his thoughts swirling from Jerome's possible debts to picnicking with Jeanette at Richmond Park, to Trevor's apparent gift for dishonesty, when out of nowhere, a fist like iron clipped him hard across the jaw.

"TAKING THE GARDEN AIR?" Trevor asked as Jeanette let herself into the house through the library's French doors.

The afternoon light and the way he cocked his head combined to create a strong resemblance to his father. To the casual observer, the late marquess had been a handsome man making an elegant transition into distinguished maturity. Trevor would age well, too, and just now the boy was far less evident than the emerging young man. The faint bruise on his jaw did that, as did the fine tailoring and the indolence with which he occupied the chair at the desk.

"I have been throwing knives," Jeanette said, "with Mr. Sycamore Dorning."

Trevor put down his quill pen and came around the desk to brace his hips against it. "Step-mama, did I hear you aright? You were *throwing knives* with Mr. *Sycamore Dorning*?"

His tone was faintly disbelieving and put Jeanette in mind of all the times his father had mocked her.

You do not seriously intend to wear that in public, do you?

You thought to plan a menu all by yourself, without even consulting Viola. I applaud your initiative, but you will understand if I avoid consuming the results.

Oh, gracious. Her ladyship is endeavoring to read a book. Such a lofty ambition in one of her limited capabilities.

"Mr. Dorning and I practice weekly," Jeanette said, "and he is having a set of knives made for my personal use."

Trevor crossed his arms. "He's said nothing about this to me, and I have been practically in his pocket of late."

Jeanette wanted to order herself a hot water bottle and some ginger tea and spend the rest of her Sabbath reading in bed, but she and Trevor had business to discuss first.

More lost ground to recover. "Mr. Dorning has said nothing about my lessons to anybody, because I asked for his discretion. When did you plan to tell me that you were set upon by three brigands in an alley, Trevor?"

Trevor stalked across the library to the sideboard and poured himself a drink. "You asked Dorning for discretion? Perhaps I should have insisted on it from him as well. What sort of gentleman tattles on another fellow?"

When had Trevor lost the quality of a gangly youth and instead become a tall and increasingly muscular young man?

"What sort of gentleman lies to a lady, Trevor? Your safety matters to me very much, and if those men had been intent on robbery, you'd have left the alley without your watch, sleeve buttons, rings, coat, and boots."

"Did Dorning pass that along?" The question was nearly sneered.

"I saw you on Friday when you tried to sneak in from the mews, Trevor. Saw you dressed more or less as you'd left the breakfast table, before your round of fisticuffs *at Jackson's* got a bit out of hand. I am worried about you, and I do not care for deceptions between family members."

Trevor sipped his brandy, he didn't gulp it. Jeanette took some consolation from that.

"Deception is required of a gentleman," Trevor said, sounding slightly exasperated. "If I told you of the vulgarities that pass for humor at the club, the low talk that passes for gossip, or the nocturnal strolls through the park my friends delight in, you would box my ears."

After dark, most of London's public parks turned into open-air sex markets, a situation that the newspapers delicately decried at least once a quarter. The streets around the theater were similarly thronged with those intent on risqué pleasures, which only added to the popularity of the theater as an evening entertainment.

"I expect decent manners from you, Trevor, but I also expect honesty regarding something as important as a violent crime committed against your person. This is the second time you've been accosted on the street, and you do not frequent bad neighborhoods."

"All of London is a bad neighborhood, to hear the preachers tell it."

She marched up to him, unwilling to indulge his masculine pouts. "You could have been killed, Trevor, and I would mourn your passing deeply. I have watched you grow from boy to man, and I dearly want to see the man take his proper place in Society. I will never have children. You are the only person I have left to love in this world, and when you lie to me, it hurts."

That he would lie was also *frightening*, proof that the darling boy was gone forever, replaced by a dear but increasingly distant young man whom Jeanette didn't know as well as she'd thought she did.

"Don't cry," he said, sounding genuinely horrified. "I have never seen you cry, and if I give you occasion to cry now, I will have to call myself out." He passed her a handkerchief and patted her shoulder awkwardly. "You are upset, the very thing I sought to avoid. I have made you cry, and this is all Mr. Dorning's fault."

"Your mendacity has upset me, and I am not crying, Trevor. I am disappointed that you would not trust me with the truth."

Trevor offered her his drink. She shook her head.

"Both Dorning brothers told me to be honest with you," he said. "I thought them daft. Why burden my step-mama with a recounting of such villainy? And here you've been nipping out to the mews to throw knives. Why, my lady?"

My lady, not *Step-mama*. "Somebody has followed me, Trevor, on many occasions."

He set his glass down rather too hard. "I beg your pardon? Followed you?"

"Somebody followed my coach when I borrowed my brother's less conspicuous conveyance and followed our town coach when I took it out midweek."

Trevor gazed across the library at nothing in particular. "You borrowed Orion Goddard's coach? Whatever for?"

"Privacy. I got in the habit when your father was alive. If his lordship took the town coach, and I did not want to travel in an open vehicle, I borrowed Orion's. Rye seldom goes out, at least not to society's usual entertainments, and I have never cared for ostentation anyway."

Then too, sending along a note asking to borrow the carriage was one way to ensure Orion still drew breath. He never scrawled more than a word or two in reply, but that was better than the long silence that had followed his return from France.

"So I take the town coach," Trevor said, "and you get up to God knows what, God knows where, without a word to me? Throwing knives, for example? Being followed? Having Mr. Dorning procure a whole set of knives for you?"

Jeanette produced the blade she'd carried in from the mews. "You are attempting to distract me from your own dishonesty, Trevor. It won't wash."

He peered at the knife lying across her palm as if it would writhe to life before his eyes. "That is a formidable accessory you have there. Perhaps I ought to carry a knife myself."

"Ask Sycamore Dorning for advice. He'll probably show you the rudiments of throwing if you want him to. Tell me about the men who accosted you behind Angelo's."

Trevor took a wing chair before the empty hearth and recited the facts more or less as Sycamore had relayed them.

"I wasn't afraid at the time. I was annoyed," he concluded. "Then I arrived at the Coventry, and it occurred to me that I'd had a narrow escape. As Sycamore said, if there had been a fourth man, or a second knife, perhaps a cudgel or two... Those fellows were expecting to thrash a fop, and if they come after me again, I won't have the element of surprise on my side."

Jeanette sat opposite him, her knife wrapped in a handkerchief and slipped it into her pocket. "Are your debts paid?"

"Of course. The increase in my allowance was more than sufficient to bring everything up to date, and you apparently know my arrangement with the Coventry."

"Have you offended anybody?"

Trevor stared at the ceiling. "What do you take me for, my lady?"

"A young man new to Town, who is the dearest person in my world. Answer the question."

"Not that I know of."

"Are Jerome's bills up to date?"

Trevor swiveled a puzzled gaze to her. "Cousin's affairs are quite in hand, I'm sure."

"You look like him, Trevor, and both times you were accosted, he might well have been accompanying you, but he sent you out alone instead."

Trevor shot to his feet. "Madam, that is the outside of too much. Jerome has earned more respect from you than that—he's considered offering for you, if you must know—and I will not hear a word against him."

Jeanette knew she'd blundered badly, but the conversation wasn't over, and Jerome had never earned her respect. He wasn't considering offering for her, he was considering a cockeyed scheme by which to get his hands on her wealth—or his mother was.

"I'm not saying Jerome sent you out to be set upon by ruffians, Trevor, but might the ruffians have mistaken you for him? You and Jerome look very much alike, and you both frequent the same venues. He uses the family crest when it suits him, and you aren't that much taller than he is."

Trevor stalked toward the door. "You are being fanciful, my lady. You ask why I did not burden you with the details of a small misadventure, and this is exactly why. You are overreacting and flinging wild fancies about, heedless of whom you insult. I will leave you to regain your... your... to collect yourself."

He had about half the library yet to cross, and Jeanette was not overreacting. She took out her knife, rose, and threw it such that it bit into the door at shoulder height.

His lordship stopped short.

"Insult me like this again, Trevor, and we will have words such as you cannot imagine. You are upset to think that Jerome might have involved you in an intolerable situation, and you thought to protect me from fretting over his difficulties. You are also protecting *him*, a grown man nearly three years your senior, resplendent in his town bronze."

Trevor's gaze went from the knife to Jeanette, something cool and appraising in his eyes. "I have not even discussed this situation with Jerome. The idea that I have been the target of malice meant for him never occurred to me."

"But you must admit that theory makes sense. Sycamore Dorning saw the connections immediately, and if you can't respect my opinion, you should respect his."

Trevor pulled the knife from the door and examined the blade. "He said nothing to me about Jerome being the intended victim. This is a peculiar sort of knife."

"The design is specifically for throwing, not for hand-to-hand combat, or for any kind of practical use. This blade is smaller and lighter than other knives, fashioned to suit my hand."

Trevor palmed the knife. "Fashioned by Sycamore Dorning?"

"Yes."

He passed the blade back to her. "I do not want to argue with you, my lady—Jeanette. But allow me to point out that regarding a matter involving your personal safety, you went to Dorning rather than to me, and I am both the head of this family, despite my lamentable youth, and somebody who would be devastated should harm befall you. You have not been forthcoming with me, and yet, you castigate me for exercising some gentlemanly discretion. There is reason here for more than one party to be hurt."

Good heavens. Trevor had delivered that set-down in perfectly measured, calm tones. He'd been honest with her, not the condescending aristocrat and not the whiny adolescent.

Jeanette wrapped the knife in her handkerchief and returned it to her pocket. "You are correct. I kept my own counsel about being followed because I did not want to be told I was overreacting and behaving like a hysterical female. For all I knew, some journalist was doing a piece on titled widows and nosing around in hopes I'd create a great scandal in my spare time. When Sycamore told me what had happened to you—told me in the last hour—I put aside my doubts and confronted you with the situation."

Trevor regarded her for a long moment, his blue eyes giving away little. "What is it you want from me, Jeanette?"

"The truth. I will keep you informed should I sense any threats to my wellbeing, and I hope you will do likewise for me. I cannot battle a foe who hides behind your gentlemanly sensibilities, Trevor, and you cannot protect me from an enemy I refuse to discuss with you."

He ambled toward the door this time, no sweeping off the stage in high dudgeon. Surely that was cause for encouragement?

"Do you ever consider leaving London?" he asked. "Just bowing out of the whole social whirl for a few months?"

"The spring Season is the whole social whirl," Jeanette said, "and I would not abandon you here to the matchmakers and Aunt Viola's schemes."

Trevor scrubbed a hand over his face. "Auntie is quite determined. If you should take a notion to rusticate, I would be happy to escort you from Town. I have no wish to return to university, but spending my mornings lounging from one print shop window to the next, lunch at the club, fencing in the afternoon... I could put it aside to see you safely to Tavistock Hall."

"And Viola would descend with your cousins within an hour of our arrival."

He paused at the door, his hand on the latch. "I've thought about getting rooms at the Albany. That address is the height of fashion for bachelors of means, and Jerome would keep me company."

Jerome would whizzle free room and board for himself and half his loutish friends. "You must do as you see fit, though I cannot endorse a move to the Albany."

Trevor tossed her a smile over his shoulder. "I can't very well abandon you here if somebody is skulking through the bushes making you fretful. The Albany isn't going anywhere, and Jerome would probably never come up with his half of the rent anyway."

"And I would miss you."

Trevor slipped out the door without offering Jeanette any reciprocal assurances.

CHAPTER TEN

Sycamore had a knife in his hand before he found his balance. The blow to his chin had been stout and completely unexpected, but the follow-up fist to the gut never happened.

He faced a man—a gentleman down on his luck, based on the fellow's attire—of substantial height and even more substantial bad humor. Ill-will rolled off the fellow in a palpable wave, as did the crisp scent of lavender.

Sycamore's assailant was a tower of contradictions. Lavender was a clean scent, while this man's boots were dusty and worn. The second button on his morning coat was coming loose, and his hat needed a good brushing. He wore a patch over one eye, as if his demeanor generally wasn't piratical enough. His hair was dark and badly in need of a trim, while his eye was the blue of bachelor buttons and summer skies.

His cravat was a lacy old-fashioned jabot, and yet, like any conscientious London street tough, he wore no gloves.

"Put your little toy away," Sycamore's assailant growled. "Continue to disport with my sister as if she's a common doxy—and on the

Sabbath, no less—and a blow to the face is the least you'll have coming to you. Consider yourself warned."

Even the voice was a contradiction, a dark baritone that yet managed to convey public school elocution. He got a half-dozen steps down the alley before the puzzle pieces formed a pattern in Sycamore's mind.

"Orion Goddard?"

"*Sir* Orion to you, Dorning." He kept walking, his gait uneven and less than brisk.

"Good day to you too," Sycamore said, catching up to him easily. "You have a peculiar way of skipping the introductions, *Sir Orion*." Also a formidable uppercut.

"You have a peculiar sense of decorum, imposing yourself on a lady whose hems you are not fit to touch."

"Lady Tavistock likes me," Sycamore replied. "I more than like her. Because she apparently has a care for you as well, I will allow your little tap to my chin to go unreciprocated—for now."

"I'm a-tremble with dread." Goddard turned at the intersection of two alleys, confident of his direction. "Jeanette has been through too much already at the hands of a randy arsewipe from a titled family. Leave her alone."

"My brother Willow has dogs like you," Sycamore said, beginning to enjoy himself. "They growl, they show their teeth, they are quite menacing, until some child tosses a ball for them in the back garden."

Goddard shoved Sycamore hard against a stone wall, and abruptly, there was a knife at Sycamore's throat.

"Bother Jeanette again, you randy pestilence, and I will leave you for the crows to feast upon."

"If my English serves adequately," Sycamore replied, "what you meant to say is that you love your sister dearly and wish to know if my intentions are honorable. And by the by, that slight pressure you feel at your crotch is the knife I had in my left boot—always carry two, you know. You are welcome to slit my throat—my affairs are in order, after all—but be assured that your cods will be parted from your irascible person ere I take my last breath."

Sycamore moved the blade a quarter inch. A throwing knife was not made for slicing, but Goddard would get the point, as it were.

Goddard smiled, an incomprehensibly charming flash of teeth and humor. That smile turned a saturnine countenance sunny and revealed either hidden warmth of heart or a criminal's black-souled ability to regard violence as entertainment.

He stepped back and bowed. "Well done, Dorning. A bit slow, but an adequate performance. You are teaching Jeanette to wield a knife?"

"To throw a knife," Sycamore said, slipping the blade back into its sheath. "Hand-to-hand combat for a lady wielding a knife is not well advised." Goddard's question, though, revealed that he'd been lurking in the alley for the better part of an hour. "Why are you spying on your sister?"

Goddard approached a stout, roman-nosed bay gelding dozing in the shade of a plane tree.

"Because if I demanded to escort Jeanette openly, she would fillet me more effectively than you threatened to. I am *not good ton*, and she has worked endlessly to keep a place in Society she has earned twenty times over. I could ruin that for her in a single evening and without even trying to."

The horse was no longer young, with gray around the muzzle, and the wizened eye of an old campaigner. He'd been well cared for, though, and was in good weight and good condition.

"I can escort her openly," Sycamore said. "She has in fact given me leave to..." Not pay his addresses, but what, exactly?

"Yes?"

"To escort her. To respectfully show my esteem and liking."

"But not to pay her your addresses," Goddard said, taking up the girth a hole. "How much has she told you about her marriage?"

"Enough. Tavistock was fixated on having more sons."

"Many a man is fixated on having sons, but he doesn't have to be mean about it. Jeanette could have popped out a baby boy annually, and Tavistock would still have made her life hell. He wanted a dog to kick as well as a wife to pester. Why did you offer to show Jeanette how to use a knife?"

"We are to air your sister's business in an alley? You could instead come to the Coventry and share a meal with me. The club is closed, but the kitchen has made a Sunday feast nonetheless. And lest you think your scurrilous company will redound to my discredit, my staff is discreet."

"And is your cook competent?"

"The undercook is on duty at present. Quite competent, does not suffer fools, well compensated."

"You never answered my question," Goddard said, untying the horse's reins from the oak tree. "Why teach Jeanette to use a knife?" He ambled off down the alley, a man who clearly held a map in his head of London's lesser byways, for he was making directly for the Coventry.

"Her ladyship asked me to show her the rudiments, and natural talent and determination are doing the rest. Did Tavistock abuse her physically?"

Goddard was silent for a good dozen yards, the only sound his horse's hooves clip-clopping against old cobbles.

"I don't know, but Jeanette came to loathe his marital attentions. When I left for Spain, she was a shy bride with a brusque new husband twice her age. By the time I came home on my first winter leave, the light in her eyes was all but gone. By then, it was too late. Tavistock had bought my commission as part of Jeanette's marriage settlements, and Jeanette was the one taken captive by hostile forces."

They reached the mouth of the alley, and Goddard crossed the thoroughfare, tossed the crossing sweeper a coin, and took the next alley rather than travel on the main street.

"How did the late Marquess of Tavistock die?" Sycamore asked.

"I didn't kill him, more's the pity. I was traveling in France at the time, becoming *bad ton*. The public cause of death was a fall from one of his crazy colts, but I suspect the marquess choked on a fish bone at his new mistress's house."

"For a fellow who was larking about France, you are prodigiously well informed."

Goddard slanted a glance in Sycamore's direction. "Had you bothered to ask your great friend Her Grace of Quimbey, you could have gathered the same information. Is the Coventry doing as well as the gossips claim?"

"Better, probably, and yes, the tables are honest."

"So why is Trevor frequenting your establishment? Jeanette keeps him on a tight financial rein, and he has no business consorting with that crowd."

"Trevor slipped the leash, abetted by his cousin, Jerome Vincent, and a half-dozen simian cronies. I agreed to let his lordship work off an indenture rather than beggar himself with the pawnbrokers."

"Because you are trying to get under Jeanette's skirts?"

"Because Tavistock has no father or brothers to show him how to go on, and his step-uncle is too busy collecting gossip to pay the boy any mind. I don't care for Jerome Vincent, or for idle ornaments in general—except the ones dropping fortunes at my tables, of course."

"So out of the goodness of your solid-gold heart, you took Trevor under your wing?"

"I am working his skinny arse to flinders, and he is loving the challenge. I like having a loyal minion, truth be told, and my brother Ash, who is also my partner, is recently wed and of no use whatsoever to anybody save his wife."

Goddard paused at another thoroughfare. "You jealous?"

"Pathetically."

"Jeanette won't marry you, Dorning. Resign yourself to worshipping her from afar, or a-near. She won't be your consolation prize in the Dorning family's marital sweepstakes."

"That is for Jeanette to decide. Take the next turning to the right, and we can use an entrance to the club that opens onto the carriage house."

"Why skulk about like that?" Goddard said, nonetheless turning his steps to the right.

"Because we are being followed."

"WHAT ON EARTH brings you to my doorstep during daylight hours on the Sabbath, old boy?" Jerome Vincent made a production out of peering up at the sky outside his door. He was attired in a dressing gown and pajama trousers, with slippers on his otherwise bare feet. "Do come in, Tav, and tell Cousin Jere what's amiss."

"How can you tell something's amiss?" Trevor replied, stepping over the threshold. Even Jerome's foyer bore a taint of tobacco—with worse yet lurking beneath the smoke stench—and the lone fern in the window wasn't long for this world. Cobwebs wafted from the chandelier, and a stack of correspondence—bills, most likely—was about to teeter from the edge of the deal table.

"I'm making an educated guess," Jerome said, closing the door. "I base my conjecture on your downcast phiz, the strange hour, and logic."

Trevor took off his hat and set it beside the letters. "What sort of logic?"

"The sort of logic that says if you don't want to get leg-shackled to Hera or Diana, then you'd best get yourself leg-shackled to somebody else, and Auntie Jeanette, being a shrewd and female-ish sort of person, has doubtless started presenting you with lists of those somebody elses. The situation calls for a drink."

Nearly every situation with Jerome called for a drink, and today Trevor wasn't in the mood to argue. He was in the mood to be cheered up, though he wasn't sure exactly why that should be.

"Jeanette has never breathed a word to me of the matchmaking variety," Trevor said, except to commiserate with him regarding Viola's schemes and to counsel forethought regarding his eventual choice of bride.

"The best matchmakers never do." Jerome led the way down the corridor to his parlor-cum-study-cum-smoking-room. Newspapers were strewn about, along with two discarded cravats, one slipper, a hat with a crushed crown, a pair of spurs and a riding crop, a smoking jacket, and more correspondence. No less than three trays of cigar ashes needed emptying, and a pipe with a small bowl lay on the stones beside a hearth much in need of tidying.

"Where is Timmons?" Trevor asked, moving a stack of papers from a chair and taking a seat.

"Gave him the sack," Jerome said, crossing to the sideboard to hold up a bottle to the sunlight slanting through a dingy window. "He was impertinent."

The poor fellow had probably requested his delinquent wages. "You'll hire another valet?"

"The agencies have already sent me three candidates. The first will start on a fortnight's trial tomorrow. Tell me what troubles you." Jerome found two glasses on the mantel and poured a slosh into each one. "A health to the ladies."

Trevor drank to that, though Jerome offered a very indifferent brandy. "I had a spat with Jeanette."

"About damned time. You treat her as if she's your governess, not a dependent relation."

"She's not a dependent relation. Her settlements are generous, and she manages her funds exceedingly well."

"She's dependent," Jerome retorted, tossing back his drink. "She's dependent on you for a roof over her head, dependent on you for her consequence. Without you, she'd be just another slightly used widow trying to attach followers and generally failing. Why did she harangue you this time?"

Coming here had been an impulse, and now that the moment to discuss particulars was at hand, Trevor was afraid it had been a foolish impulse.

"Jeanette wasn't haranguing me, Jerome. She is concerned for me."

Jerome refilled his glass. "You are in good health, only passingly ugly, possessed of a lofty title, not all that stupid, and deucedly plump in the pocket. What manner of worry could Jeanette find to plague you about if not holy matrimony?"

"You recall I had a bit of a dustup in the alley behind Angelo's on Friday?"

"Was it Friday? Of this year?"

"The day before yesterday. I mentioned this yesterday."

"If you mentioned it over cards, I was too busy watching Fremont lose his curricle to Westerly, though my money says Westerly will have to give it back within a month. Neither of 'em can hold their liquor."

While Jerome was able to consume prodigious quantities and at least seem sober. "Three men accosted me at high noon. They scampered off when I repulsed their overtures, but one of them had a knife."

"Knives." Jerome made a face and sank into a reading chair. "Nasty business, knives. Not gentlemanly. Give me pistols or swords on a foggy morning, and let God decide the outcome."

"Jerome, could that attack have been meant for you?"

Jerome set his glass on the floor. "For me?"

"They called me a bloody fop, and you are more of a dandy than I am. I told only Step-mama of my morning appointments. You, on the other hand, arranged with a half-dozen fellows to spend the morning at Angelo's. Those three men were waiting for me, or for someone."

Jerome ran a pale hand through hair that was for once not artfully styled. "Everybody nips around to the alley to take a piss or enjoy a quick tup, Tavistock. Of course ruffians would lurk there."

"Ruffians don't lurk in St. James's. Fine gents and Corinthians do. To accost me there was very bold, even desperate."

"Foolish, too, I gather, if you ran them off."

"Prize ring rules were not observed." And Jerome was not answering the question.

"Do tell. Did you resort to schoolyard tactics? Toss dirt in their faces?"

"Brandy, and I kicked the knife from one fellow's hand and delivered a blow to another fellow's tallywags. Hated to do it, but needs must."

"And where was I while you were having such fun?" Jerome reached for the drink at his feet and knocked it over. "Damnation, that is the last of the everyday. We'll have to break out the good stuff now."

Trevor passed over his flask, which he'd taken to keeping full since Friday. "Not quite yet. In any case, Jeanette was alarmed at my mishap and more alarmed that I failed to mention it to her before she heard of it through a third party."

Jerome took a good, long pull from the flask. "The Tavistock cellars do not disappoint. Don't suppose you could send over a couple bottles of this?"

"Of course. You must have a birthday coming up one of these months."

"Or you do," Jerome replied, passing back the flask. "Maybe Fremont does. If all else fails, we can celebrate old King George's natal day early, eh? Did Dorning peach on you?"

"He didn't know he was peaching on me. I'd told Jeanette that I'd gone a few rounds at Jackson's, which I sometimes do, but this time... I glossed over the truth." And despite all posturing to the contrary, Trevor felt bloody awful about lying to Jeanette.

He felt bloody awful-er that she was being harassed by some snooping journalist and hadn't seen fit to tell him. The conviction with which she'd hurled her knife suggested worse yet was afoot, but she either could not or would not confide the particulars to her mendacious step-son.

And that felt the bloody awful-est of all.

"I was a perishing prig to her," Trevor said. "Tried to excuse a lie as gentlemanly consideration."

"You meant well." Jerome picked up the overturned glass from the carpet and shook the brandy dregs into his mouth. "Jeanette is too arrogant by half, Tav. You really need to remind her of her place. She'll thank you for it."

The last person to hand Trevor that advice had been a bullying house party cheat by the name of Chastain. He had decamped for Tuscany, last Trevor had heard, a horde of creditors on his heels, and not even his new wife was sorry to see him go.

"Jeanette was right," Trevor said, "and I did not apologize."

"Did *she* apologize?" Jerome asked, rising to return the glass to the mantel.

"I am a gentleman, and I was in the wrong."

"So you'll crawl home, stopping only to steal a placatory bouquet of daffodils from the garden? Promise to be a good boy, cross your heart, and never ever keep a few little things to yourself in the name of dignity and privacy? Will Jeanette interview your mistresses for you? Or will you remain as pure as Yorkshire snow, lest you disappoint Saint Jeanette?"

Coming here had most assuredly been a mistake. "You are drinking on an empty stomach, aren't you?"

"P'raps I am. There's a loaf of bread around here somewhere. I haven't been down to the kitchen to check. I sacked Timmons, you know."

"You did mention that. Wait here." Trevor found bread and butter in the downstairs kitchen, put together a tea tray, and brought it up to Jerome's study.

Jerome was nodding off in his chair, his dressing gown gaping open to reveal a pale chest. A trick of the afternoon sun turned him into an aging roué, rather than a scion from a titled house, but he snapped awake, grinned, and the illusion was dispelled.

"You found buried treasure. Bless you, my child."

Trevor used his foot to push a hassock before Jerome's chair. "Manna from heaven and all that. When does Uncle Beardsley send out your next payment?"

"Soon, though it's never enough. God, I hate tea." He slurped from a steaming cup nonetheless. "You will think me quite daft, but I really am considering taking a wife."

Trevor paused between emptying the second and the third trays of ashes into the dustbin. "I can't imagine why. You'd give up all this for companionship, cleanliness, regular meals, and wifely comforts. Perhaps you suffered a blow to the head."

"The place is a bit squalid on purpose, Tav. I want to see if the new valet is up to my weight, so to speak."

"The place is a disgrace. Timmons has been gone for at least a week, your larder is empty, and you are reduced to drinking the desperation rations. Timmons left because you could not afford to pay him, and your next allowance isn't due for at least a fortnight."

"Forgive me," Jerome said, setting down his tea cup. "I wasn't aware that I'd been assigned a nanny. How do you prefer to be addressed, Miss... Miss Vincent?"

Trevor put the stack of papers he'd gathered up beside the dustbin. "You'll never attach a wife with that attitude. Jaunt down to Tavistock Hall for a repairing lease if you're pockets to let. I'll come with you, and we can enjoy the fresh country air."

"Mama will jaunt down on our coattails, hauling Hera and Diana with her. You will be engaged within a fortnight. I believe I shall court Jeanette."

This again. "That is drink talking." Trevor found the second slipper peeking out from under the sofa, rolled up the wrinkled cravats, and draped the smoking jacket over the back of the wing chair. He cracked open a window and set his own half-full brandy glass on the mantel, where Jerome would doubtless find it.

Jerome scrubbed a hand over his face and eyed the glass. "One of us has to marry, Tav. And Jeanette isn't that hard to look on. I could doubtless succeed with her where the old marquess failed, too. I'd certainly give it a good go anyway."

"Generous of you, though I suspect Jeanette would laugh any proposal from you to scorn. She did not have an easy time of it with my father, and there's no earthly reason why she should remarry."

"Of course there's an earthly reason." Jerome wiggled his eyebrows, clearly unaware of the distasteful picture he made, disheveled, unbathed, unshaven, and not quite sober.

Trevor cracked a second window to get some cross ventilation. "Keep further thoughts of that nature to yourself, please. I have said my piece, and you deserve whatever fate Jeanette chooses for you."

"She might have me," Jerome said, his gaze going again to the brandy glass. "I can be persuasive. She's not as impervious to argument as you think, Tav. She has vulnerabilities. Papa has intimated as much."

As if threats to a lady were the basis for lasting connubial bliss? "She's also not an idiot. I will see myself out. Let me know how you fare with the new valet."

"Will do, but I don't suppose before you go, you could spare a fellow a coin or two? Desperation rations and all that."

Perhaps coming here had not been such a bad idea after all. This was what shared quarters at the Albany would mean, and Trevor would become a nanny in truth.

"All I have with me," he said, putting half a dozen coins on the tea tray. "I'll have Cook send over a basket, and you will share dinner with me at the club tomorrow."

"Don't mind if I do," Jerome said, pouring himself another cup of tea. "Until then."

No thanks, no veiled acknowledgment of kindness, no apology for poor hospitality... And Jerome thought Jeanette would willingly marry herself to such as he?

Though Jeanette enjoyed a challenge, and given that Jerome had taken to pilfering glasses from the Coventry, he would provide her at least that. Trevor stopped in the foyer to put the potted fern outside on the steps, where the poor thing would at least have some sunlight and regular rainfall.

Then too, sitting in the out of doors rather than sitting in Jerome's foyer, the struggling plant was less likely to be misused as a chamber pot.

Trevor was halfway home when he realized that in nearly thirty minutes of conversation, Jerome had never answered the question regarding whether the incident in the alley could have been meant for him.

Given the state of his finances, the answer was all but obvious.

"OF COURSE WE'RE BEING FOLLOWED," Goddard said. "The streets are unsafe, and many would still put period to my existence, as miserable as it is. I am considered a traitor by half the officers in my former regiment. Just when I think they've found somebody else to gossip about, their aspersion circles back to me again."

Even Sycamore, in the rarefied atmosphere of the club, had heard the occasional insulting snippet regarding Orion Goddard, but then, half-pay officers and former military were prodigiously accomplished grumblers.

"What harm can talk do you?"

Goddard slanted him a look. "Your beautiful club could be closed overnight if the right word were whispered in the ear of the right magistrate."

A nightmare possibility Sycamore managed to ignore most of the time. "You are not running a questionable enterprise, that your fortunes can be destroyed by tattlers." Sycamore hoped that was true, but many merchants relied on the coastal trade to import their goods from the Continent, thus putting money directly into the hands of smugglers and their families rather than tithing to the exciseman.

"My business is entirely legal," Goddard replied, "but I earn my coin by selling my family's champagne here in London. This, among other failings, apparently makes my loyalties suspect."

Sycamore surveyed the shady alley behind them. The boy who'd been shuffling along in their wake was nowhere to be seen.

"A half-grown boy in unmatched boots isn't a likely assassin,

Goddard, and ending your life while I stroll along at your side on a Sunday afternoon hardly demonstrates the sort of discretion such a task calls for."

Goddard gave two short, shrill whistles. "A half-grown boy can be a more effective assassin for being unexpected. Theodoric has turned over a new leaf, though. He is a purveyor of safety rather than mayhem these days, or so he claims."

A rustling in the branches above was Sycamore's warning to step back. An instant later, the boy dropped to the ground before him, as silently as a cat.

"Everything all right, guv?" the lad asked, eyeing Sycamore as a stern nanny regards a habitually naughty charge who has yet to begin the day's round of offenses.

The lad was not quite the genuine article. His boots were unmatched, true, but they fit, they were neatly laced, and they were sturdy enough. His clothing was wrinkled past all hope, though clean. His hands were also clean—a sure sign of some security in life, for soap and water to wash with were in short supply on the street. Then too, the lad was skinny but not gaunt.

Somebody fed him regularly, and that somebody was apparently Colonel Sir Orion Goddard.

"Greetings, Otter," Goddard said. "My thanks for the escort. I will have dinner with Mr. Dorning and see myself home. You may take my horse if you'd prefer to ride back to the house."

Otter shook his head. "Benny takes over from me at half past. I'll mind the beast until then." He swiveled a flint-hard gaze on Sycamore. "Benny takes any disrespect to the colonel hard."

"I would be a poor host if I disrespected my guests," Sycamore replied.

This earned him a snort. Otter took a few steps' running start and was hidden within the oak's branches in the time it took Sycamore to offer the lad a bow. Goddard tied the horse in the shade of the oak and once again loosened the girth.

"You have an honor guard," Sycamore said, leading Goddard not to the carriage house—why give away a secret entrance when the likes of Otter and Benny would enjoy ferreting it out for themselves?—but through a stout gate into the little patch of potted plants and uneven flagstones that served as the Coventry's back garden. The space was walled and had two benches, one each to catch morning and afternoon sunlight.

"Be still my lonely heart," Goddard said, stopping to close his eyes and sniff the air. "That is roasting beef, with a touch of tarragon, basil, and black pepper."

"All I smell is supper, and for once I do not hear my undercook cursing unreliable ovens."

"All you smell is supper," Goddard replied, "because you never spent weeks with your eyes bandaged, fretting that the senses of smell, hearing, and touch would have to replace eyesight as your means of navigating life safely."

"Do those without sight have a more acute sense of taste?" Sycamore asked, opening the doorway to the Coventry's back hallway.

"Yes, so I hope the flavor lives up to the scents, Dorning."

That was probably supposed to be some sort of subtle warning, which Sycamore was too hungry to parse. He showed Goddard to the private dining room, let his guest use the washstand first, and poured them each a glass of claret.

"Does Jeanette know you were injured?" Sycamore asked after serving his guest a bowl of potato leek soup. He held out the plate of crumbled Stilton, and Goddard garnished his soup generously.

"Jeanette knows I was injured, she does not know the details. That's our bargain. I know she was sacrificed on the marital altar to Tavistock's ambitions, I do not know the particulars. Her suffering was doubtless greater than mine."

"Why do you say that?" The soup was good—hot, flavorful, and rich—and Goddard's expression upon taking a taste suggested he'd lucked into a bowl of ambrosia.

"You have to have known Nettie before Tavistock got his paws on her. She was everything good and sweet and dear, while our Papa's finances were everything hopeless and rapidly worsening." Goddard tore off a chunk of bread and dipped it into his soup. "If your cook ever goes missing, look for him in my kitchen."

"This is the undercook's effort, prepared at my particular request, and you make off with *her* at your peril. She wields a knife almost as enthusiastically as I do, and her sauces are the glory of the kitchen. Jeanette is still everything that is good and sweet and dear, but I gather you are saying Tavistock essentially bought her."

Jeanette certainly saw it that way. Not that unusual an arrangement, if the lady had a title and the gentleman's family had means, but Jeanette had had nothing but youth and apparent good health on her side of the ledger. Tavistock had doubtless held that against her.

That too.

"She was seventeen," Goddard said. "As innocent as a dove. She knew only that Papa very much wanted the match, and the marquess was considered an exceptionally fine catch. Papa was a commoner, and debtors' prison was a real possibility. We depended on income from our French holdings, and that money had disappeared. Revolution and war are ever so expensive, and the revenue owed an English family by its French cousins honestly became difficult to transfer."

"While the Empress Josephine's roses were guaranteed safe passage."

"As were, thanks to the emperor's decree, vessels of a scientific nature," Goddard retorted. "But this brings us to Jeanette's hard-earned state of freedom. You are not to trifle with her, Dorning."

Sycamore dipped his bread into his soup and considered tactics. "Is she permitted to trifle with me?"

Goddard wrinkled an aquiline beak. "I want to say no, but who am I to tell my sister anything? She was sold into marital bondage so Papa could avoid prison and I could buy a commission. I did not care for how Tavistock looked at Jeanette, and yet I bought my colors with a shameful sense of relief."

"And then what happened?"

Goddard put aside his empty bowl. With that casual gesture, his fiction of a jovial dinner guest was similarly set aside, revealing the same flint-hard, cold-as-the-grave gaze Otter had treated Sycamore to earlier.

"None of your damned business, Dorning. I am prepared to protect my privacy with my dueling pistols, if necessary."

Sycamore lifted the lid over the roast and let the steam waft upward. Thanks to Goddard's earlier effusions, he could detect the tarragon and basil in the roast's scent.

"Spare me your histrionics. I have six brothers, all older than I, and they are bookended with a pair of sisters. You may breathe the flames of doom upon me all evening, but even I know that if you posit the challenge, I choose the weapons. When it comes to knives, you are unlikely to best me. Make yourself useful and pour us each another glass of that splendid wine."

Sycamore carved off several slices of perfectly turned roast, set the dish of mashed potatoes by Goddard's plate, and served himself a smaller portion of meat.

"Besides," he went on, "Jeanette would take a dim view of us both if we descended into brawling. She loves you dearly."

Goddard paused, a mound of mashed potatoes on a serving spoon over his plate. "She said that?"

"She makes it apparent. She worries for you, she misses you terribly, and she would do anything to see you happy, but she has concluded that all you want of her is respect for your much vaunted privacy. I believe she borrows your coach on occasion in part to ensure you yet dwell among the living."

Goddard slapped the potatoes onto his plate. "I want her to be happy, and if she and I associate, that isn't possible."

"I marvel at how two siblings—only two—can so badly bollix up being a family. I thought a half dozen was the necessary complement for such crossed purposes, but perhaps the Goddards have a talent in this regard."

"Shall you wear that glass of wine, Dorning? Seems a shame to waste such a fine vintage."

That was standard sibling blather. "Jeanette is content by force of will, she is not happy. She is lonely, a condition with which I am acquainted, and no, I do not refer to those longings afflicting all in a state of randy bachelorhood. I mean loneliness, nobody to sit by the fire with on a cold night, nobody to bemoan an overly long sermon with, or recall how silly the old dog was in his puppyhood. Nobody to grow sentimental with on certain anniversaries."

Goddard stared at him as if he'd burst into a soprano aria. "You are smitten with her. This cannot end well, Dorning. Not for you, anyway."

"Your sister is widowed after years of hard combat on the marital battlefield. She is weary of heart. When she thought she faced a renewed threat, she did not turn to the one man who ought to be looking out for her. She instead turned to me. That preempts all duels, arguments, fisticuffs, and snide repartee from you, sir. Jeanette asked me to teach her how to throw a knife, because your damned gang of rogues frightened her into thinking she was being followed."

Goddard frowned, then cut into his steak. "My young friends are too skilled to be so obvious in their surveillance."

Sycamore had suspected as much, which was no reassurance whatsoever. "But you admit setting them to the task?"

"I admit that my authority over the lads is dubious and fleeting. They might have taken some initiative of their own or—if they *are* involved—they might have noticed somebody else pursuing my coach when Jeanette borrowed it, and assigned themselves to further reconnaissance."

"You don't know what your feral boys have got up to?"

"Gentlemen at large do not take kindly to inquisitions." Goddard chewed his steak. "This undercook of yours, is she yet unmarried?"

The question was a prevarication, or possibly an attempt at humor. "Talk to your minions, Goddard, and shake the truth from them if you must. Somebody is trying to hound Jeanette from Town just as the social whirl is resuming, and somebody is definitely having her followed, or they were. If you are not behind this mischief, who is?"

Goddard stared at the ceiling, then at the little pot of violets in the center of the table. "Tell me what you know, and withhold nothing."

Sycamore's steak grew cold while he reported *almost* everything that he knew to Goddard.

"PAPA, I AM NOT MANAGING WELL," Jerome said. "I am ashamed of myself, but particularly since Cousin Trevor has come to Town, my expenses have been significant."

Beardsley regarded his only son and considered what the late marquess would have done with the boy. This audience was taking place in Beardsley's private office, and Jerome had not sent word ahead to warn his mother he'd be staying for a meal.

This was to be a confidential chat, apparently. "Why should Tavistock's company increase your expenses?" Beardsley asked. "He's the titleholder, and it's his place to be beneficent toward his relations." Not how the late marquess had regarded the patriarchal role, but dear Trevor was built of more malleable and tenderhearted stuff.

"Trevor is generous," Jerome retorted, tossing himself onto the sofa and crossing a boot over a knee. "He's been feeding me from the Tavistock larders since Monday, and he told the club to put my meals on his bill for the rest of the month. He's not the problem."

"But his lordship is new to Town," Beardsley said, "so you're showing off. Taking him around to the fancier hells, making wagers to impress him. Your behavior is understandable."

Jerome was a handsome young man in the usual Vincent tradition, all golden locks, aristocratic features, and exquisite tailoring. To Beardsley's eye, the boy was nonetheless looking a bit ragged. His boots had been merely dusted rather than polished. His cravat was tied in a simple mathematical rather than the elegant knots Jerome preferred. His eyes held an air of the dissipation that signaled the end of youth and the beginning of wisdom—or folly.

"I told Trevor I'm considering offering for Jeanette." Jerome stared at the carpet as he made this announcement, his air that of a martyr offering a last prayer.

Beardsley would rather Jerome had not approached Trevor with this plan. Trevor was the nominal head of the family, and the more he was shown the deference due a patriarch, the more he'd step into the role.

"Trevor disapproves?"

"He all but laughs every time I bring it up. Says Jeanette won't have me."

Beardsley poured a drink for his guest, but refrained from indulging. Viola took a dim view of a husband who came to luncheon with spirits on his breath.

"Trevor's opinion is not the one that matters," Beardsley said, passing Jerome the glass. "Have you tried charming Jeanette?"

"That puts me in mind of charming a wolf. Not well advised for the charmer and both nutritious and entertaining for the wolf." Jerome tossed back half his drink, confirming Beardsley's suspicion that his heir was going through more than a passing rough patch.

Which was a stroke of good fortune for Beardsley, actually. "Offer her a white marriage, then. All the independence of widowhood, none of the bother of marriage."

"I don't want a white marriage, Papa. Nobody sane wants a white marriage, and lest you forget, securing the succession might fall to me if Trevor has no sons."

Not something Beardsley—or Viola—ever forgot, but that problem was years in the future. "You offer Jeanette a white marriage, but who's to say what transpires once the vows are spoken? Nobody sane wants to go to debtors' prison, my boy, and I honestly cannot bail you out. Your mother has commandeered every spare groat for your sisters, and I am lucky to be able to afford my own necessities." That was overstating the case somewhat, but if a well-placed family began selling off its teams or culling its art collection, tongues wagged, and credit disappeared.

Worse yet, daughters became spinsters, wives became shrews, and mistresses became strangers.

"Then what am I to do, Papa? Some of my debts are the honorable kind, and the fellows are too decent to dun me, but others... The agencies are no longer sending me the best for the exalted post of valet, and I don't blame them."

Beardsley took the chair at the desk rather than sit beside Jerome. "A mere valet won't take you to court for wages owed. A servant who gets above himself in that regard will never work again."

"You haven't met Timmons."

"I know his type. They are humble and helpful for about two weeks, then they start ignoring orders, telling you how to go on, and taking far too long to fetch the next day's beer of an evening. You're better off without him."

Jerome finished his drink. "I can renege on wages owed and forget my debts of honor, fine gentleman that I am, but what of the tailor, Papa? A gentleman cannot remain in arrears with his tailor or the chop shop. The trades don't extend credit to young fellows the way they do to a settled man of means."

"What Jeanette needs is an incentive to marry you," Beardsley says. "As I see it, you have two possible strategies for inspiring her to look with favor upon your suit."

"Even if she marries me, she won't necessarily turn over her fortune to me. She's not stupid."

"She's also not plagued with a lot of needy relatives, Jerome. Who else is to get that fortune if not her husband's family, which is where much of the money came from in the first place? Her brother, scoundrel though he is, has income from the Goddard family holdings, and the only other person she cares for is Trevor."

Jerome peered at the dregs in his glass. "What are my two options, then?"

"You can charm her to the altar and offer her whatever she wants in the way of independence, companionship, and everything in between, or you can threaten her."

"She lived with the late marquess for seven years, Papa. Never spent a night away from him, to hear Trevor tell it. She won't threaten easily."

"She will understand when somebody with superior influence brings his consequence to bear upon her. A few rumors about Orion Goddard's dastardly behavior during the war, idle speculation in the right venues about why nobody has called him out, musings on his generous French income... The man is already held in near-disgrace for reasons nobody ever mentions. Jeanette will do anything to protect her brother."

She might also do anything to protect Sycamore Dorning. Beardsley set that intriguing notion aside for further contemplation.

"She must care for Goddard very much if she'd marry to keep him safe."

"Women can be fierce, Jerome. Witness your dear mother and her crusade to see your sisters launched. Jeanette married once for the sake of her menfolk, and spared to her father an ignominious death."

Jerome rose to refill his drink. "Trevor ain't keen to marry a cousin."

"Trevor's wishes might not come into it. You have another option where Jeanette is concerned."

Jerome's expression was bleak, not in a self-pitying, youthful sense, but as a man disappointed in life and in himself was bleak.

"Right, threaten her brother, except I don't know exactly what Goddard got up to in France, and for all I know, his vineyards have simply enjoyed good harvests. Then too, Trevor might take a dim view of my slandering Goddard's reputation, particularly when Trevor is perched on my elbow most of the time when I go out socializing these days and would hear every word of the calumny I directed at his... his step-uncle."

Another glass of decent libation met a summary fate.

"Papa, can't you simply find me a minor diplomatic post? My French is excellent, my German and Italian passable, and I can read Spanish. Even a few years in America might be tolerable."

The suggestion had merit on its face, because it would solve Jerome's immediate problems, while leaving his family without any solution whatsoever. Besides, Jerome apparently did not want to see more of the greater world. He wanted to continue to strut about London, patronizing the finest tailors and staying out until all hours with his friends.

"Sending you abroad for a few years wastes time this family cannot afford, Jerome. The immediate problem is how to retrieve the money Jeanette appropriated from us. Once Trevor attains his majority, matters in that regard become more complicated. You could encourage Jeanette to acquaint herself with what you have to offer. To be fair, she might not be the reason Trevor has no siblings."

Jerome made a face. "You're saying if I could get her with child, then she'd have to marry me?"

"It's been done. It has definitely been done. Your mother wasn't always the prim matron she began presenting to the world twenty years ago. To a marquess's spare, she was quite friendly well before the vows were spoken. The man is every bit as ensnared as the woman when a child is conceived, if he's a gentleman."

"And if she's a lady." Jerome frowned at the painting over the mantel of Beardsley's own dear papa and his wife. They had never known want or worry, unlike their younger son. "I don't fancy rape."

"Of course you don't, so set your mind on enthusiastic seduction. The staff at Tavistock House lurks in the servants' hall as much as they can, and half of them are too venerable to hear a riot in progress. Work with that, drop a few hints about Goddard's good name, and use a delicate but firm hand. Jeanette put up with my older brother for seven years. She'll find marriage to you no imposition at all by comparison. You aren't a hopeless clodpate, and as you say, she's not stupid."

More's the pity.

Jerome finished his drink and left the glass on an end table. "I'll consider it, but meanwhile, I could use a little blunt, Papa, and some inquiries about a diplomatic post wouldn't go amiss."

Beardsley mentally gave Jerome credit for tenacity. He wrote out a bank draft for a few pounds and passed it over.

"Don't tell your mother."

Jerome folded the paper into an inner pocket. "How is Mama?"

"Quietly desperate to get Diana launched. She will throw your sister at Tavistock and keep Hera in reserve. Beautiful needlepoint and a good soprano are about all Diana has to recommend her."

"I'll put in a word for Di at my clubs. She's pretty, sensible, and wellborn. She and Fremont share a love of books, and Westerly has an ear for music."

"You might pass that along to your mother when next you join us for a meal."

"Sunday," Jerome said, pulling on his gloves. "I can most definitely be on hand for the Sunday roast. And thank you, Papa, for the blunt and for the advice. I will consider all you've said."

Having been given a few pounds, Jerome was doubtless considering which bills to pay off first, or if he had to pay any of them in the immediate term.

Ah, youth. "My regards to Tavistock—and to Jeanette."

Jerome bowed his farewell, while Beardsley wondered if perhaps he himself ought to call on Jeanette. He was roused from his musings by the luncheon bell, and not for anything would Lord Beardsley Vincent insult his wife by coming late to her table.

CHAPTER ELEVEN

"Mr. Sycamore Dorning, my lady." Peem stepped aside to permit Jeanette's guest entry into the breakfast parlor.

Sycamore, resplendent in riding attire, sauntered into the room. "My lady, the beauty of the dawn pales beside the wonder of thy fair countenance. Are those apple tarts?"

"Yes," Jeanette said, "and if you're to enjoy them, you'd best be about it. If Trevor brings any of his fellow locusts home with him from their morning hack, those tarts will be but a memory. Peem, that will be all."

Peem withdrew after casting Sycamore a dubious glance.

Sycamore filled a plate at the sideboard, helping himself to toast, ham, and two apple tarts. "How does this day find you?" he asked, taking the place at Jeanette's right hand. "Are you well?"

He was asking about her bodily functions, though not as Jeanette's husband had asked. The late marquess had interrogated rather than inquired: *Why haven't you conceived? Don't you want to conceive, Jeanette? You have a brother, and you have male cousins. Is there some breeding defect in the Goddard line that your father failed to disclose? Be honest with me, or it will go hard for you.*

"I am quite well," Jeanette said, setting the teapot by his plate. "My indisposition is painful, but generally brief. To what do I owe the pleasure of your company?"

Sycamore poured himself a cup of tea. "I missed you, and I would be a sorry sort of swain if I allowed you to languish for more than three days without offering you the pleasure of my company."

Why must he look so lovely, all hale and masculine, exuding vitality and smiling so devilishly? "I cannot tell if you are teasing or in earnest. You aren't having any eggs?"

He sipped his tea, managing to make even that an exercise in elegance. "I am in complete earnest. If I had my way... Well, we can discuss that later. The omelet savors of mushrooms, which do not agree with me, and there looks to be hardly enough for a decent serving for one."

"That omelet is just for me. Trevor feels as you do about mushrooms. The French half of me says you are both ridiculous. When his lordship returns from the park, the kitchen will send up a horse-trough-sized dish of eggs, cheese, cream, chives, and I know not what else. Trevor and his friends do unto the omelet as they do to the apple tarts."

"And the ham, toast, currant buns, and any other comestibles left in plain sight. Will you drive out to Richmond with me today? Please say you will."

Jeanette was torn between the part of her that distrusted all spontaneity and the part of her that hadn't been on a picnic in far too long.

"This is more of your swaining?"

"This is an excuse to spend hours in the company of a woman I esteem greatly. If the prospect of my exclusive company is not inducement enough for you to accompany me, then please join me so I can share with you some information relating to your brother."

Jeanette pushed aside half of her serving of eggs. "Is Rye well?"

"Obnoxiously so. We enjoyed a companionable meal on Sunday, and I have much to tell you, none of it bad. He is concerned for you, but keeping his distance lest his past reflect poorly on you."

"I know. The war is over, but I gather some affronted fellow officer could challenge him over any imagined slight simply for a chance to blow Rye's brains out."

That Rye had dined with Sycamore was curious indeed, and even a little encouraging.

"What exactly did Sir Orion do to put himself beyond the pale? I did not inquire in the interests of living to see my next sunrise."

"Spied for the French, supposedly. All Rye will say is that things were not what they seemed, and his conscience is clear. I love my brother, and I don't particularly care if he did warn a village that Wellington's troops approached. The army was happy to use his language skills and knowledge of French culture. They had to know making war on Mama's homeland was hard on him."

Sycamore patted her wrist—more of a caress, really—and because nobody wore gloves at breakfast, Jeanette felt that fleeting touch clear to her... middle.

"You are so fierce," he said. "Sir Orion worries for you, and you worry for him, and all the while, you tiptoe in a circle around each other like cats of new acquaintance. This is exactly the sort of ridiculousness families indulge in, but who would look askance if you and he enjoyed a quiet cup of tea from time to time?"

"Half the tabbies in polite society."

"I doubt you need worry about the tabbies, my lady." Sycamore rose without warning and stalked silently to the door. "Peem, if her ladyship has need of you, she will use the bell-pull." In the space of a single sentence, Sycamore had gone from an affable gentleman caller to a man seriously affronted on behalf of his hostess.

He returned to the table and sat for a moment, staring at his apple tarts. "You are deciding whether to castigate me for presuming or thank me for interceding. Peem is your butler, Jeanette, and his place is by the front door, not lurking outside the breakfast parlor after you've dismissed him. Besides, I wanted his ire directed toward the disgracefully presuming Mr. Dorning, rather than at you."

"I am too upset with Peem to be angry with you. How did you know he was out there?"

Sycamore tapped his nose. "Peem wears bay rum. My father was particularly critical of it as a scent, and Papa knew of what he sniffed. Dare I suggest once again that you sack the old fellow?"

"You dare." Jeanette finished her tea, which had gone tepid. "You dare much. Peem doesn't hear well enough to eavesdrop well."

"Are you sure of that?"

Jeanette rose and went to the window that looked out over the garden. "I am not sure of much, Sycamore. Trevor and I had a blazing row after you left me on Sunday. We've been cordial but distant since then. He now either misses breakfast or brings at least three friends with him and has luncheon and supper at his club. Then he spends his evenings with you."

Sycamore bit into an apple tart. "What was your row about?"

"I confronted him about lying to me regarding the attack in the alley, and I told him I'd been followed. He was peevish because I had kept that to myself, and I was disappointed that he'd dissemble regarding a potentially fatal encounter. I asked him not to lie to me again and assured him he would have honesty from me."

"And he swore eternal honesty to you?"

"He threatened to move into the Albany with Jerome."

Sycamore took the place at Jeanette's elbow, and his mere presence was a comfort. "Tavistock has been preoccupied all week at the club. Staring off into space, marching out smartly smack into a faro table, missing the dealers' attempts to flirt with him. He's doubtless upset with himself and fretting on your behalf."

The door to the breakfast parlor was still open, and yet, Jeanette let herself lean, just a little, against Sycamore.

"There's more," she said. "Trevor asked if I ever considered leaving Town, abandoning the social whirl. He volunteered to escort me down to Tavistock Hall, though I pointed out to him that he would be accosted by marriageable cousins if we rusticated at the family seat."

Sycamore slipped an arm around her waist, and Jeanette rested her head against his shoulder.

"You worry that you should have told Trevor about the notes, but wonder if he sent them. My lady, you should not be afflicted with all this intrigue and drama."

"Is the solution to marry you?"

Sycamore's posture subtly changed so their situation became more of a cuddle. "Marrying me would solve any number of dilemmas, but I sense you'd be unreceptive to such an overture at the moment. You are sad to think Tavistock will go out into the world as young men do, leaving you here with aging retainers of dubious loyalty.

"You are worried," he went on, "about your brother and perhaps resentful that he would dine with me and not with you. He was swayed by my endless charm, so you cannot be too wroth with him, my lady. And you are vexed to think somebody wishes you or Tavistock ill, when neither one of you wishes harm to anybody."

Jeanette closed her eyes and turned to wrap her arms around Sycamore's waist, feeling all out of sorts and unaccountably sentimental. Sycamore obliged with a gentle embrace, and that made things both better and worse.

"You are telling me what I feel," she said.

"And you are not berating me for my presumption, because I have put into words what you had not wanted to admit. Admit this too, Jeanette. A day of fresh air and spring sunshine will do wonders to restore your spirits, and mine too." He leaned near enough to nuzzle her ear. "I brought your new knives, my lady. Wickedly hard and sharp and eager for your touch."

Jeanette remained in his embrace for the length of three heartbeats, the better to hide her smile. "You are being naughty." And that was a wonder, that Sycamore Dorning—handsome, outspoken, funny, passionate, and protective—would be naughty with her.

"Between adults who know what they want, naughtiness doesn't signify. Come with me, Jeanette, try out your new toys, and forget your cares for a few hours. Your troubles will all patiently await your return, I assure you."

Of that, Jeanette was certain. "You will tell me what Rye had to say?"

"I will, and I will tell you what he did not say. Siblings really ought not to be estranged, Jeanette. I feel quite strongly about that."

She stepped back, though that took an effort. "You feel strongly about everything."

"Bear that in mind when you assess my regard for you." He kissed her cheek—the wretch—and winged his arm.

Jeanette let him escort her from the parlor, collected a hat, shawl, reticule, and cloak, and did not tell Peem where she was going or when she'd return.

A CURIOUS METAMORPHOSIS of Sycamore's erotic appetites was under way, one that ought to alarm him, but did not.

He desired Jeanette madly, particularly when he was alone late at night after another long evening at the Coventry. He wanted to take her in his arms and exhaust himself in shared pleasure, then hold her and indulge in the quiet, mundane talk that was another kind of delectable intimacy.

And yet, his desire was responsive to Jeanette's moods and needs. On Sunday, when she'd been ailing, Sycamore's need had been to offer comfort. Now, in the roomy confines of a traveling coach, he needed to listen to her and offer affection, while desire receded to a humming undercurrent.

The depth of his feelings for her surprised him, though the intensity felt good too. He would propose marriage when the time was right for Jeanette to hear that offer.

"Trevor really is at the club most nights?" Jeanette asked as they clattered across the Vauxhall Bridge and onto the Surrey side of the Thames.

"Young Lord Tavistock is at my side three nights a week, and he's increasingly comfortable in the role of my supernumerary. He has a particular gift for settling the feathers of the kitchen staff. His French is flawless—your influence, I trust—and his sense of humor is quick without being cutting. I have not, however, seen hide nor hair of Mr. Jerome Vincent."

"Dodging his creditors?" Jeanette asked, resting her head against the squabs.

"Or avoiding a venue where the play is more than Jerome can handle. Your brother has little good to say about the Vincent family in general."

Jeanette closed her eyes. "I have little good to say about the military. We're even."

"Goddard will not admit that he had you followed, Jeanette, but he might have caused you to be followed."

"Explain yourself."

At some point, Sycamore had taken Jeanette's hand, or she had taken his. Holding hands was at once prosaic—elderly couples held hands—and precious, because the hand Sycamore held was Jeanette's.

"Goddard's existence is precarious, given the past nobody will describe in any detail." If Goddard had spied for the French, why hadn't he been tried for treason, stripped of his knighthood, and sent to the gallows? That fate would have been kinder than consigning him to wait years for a bullet through the heart—or through the back.

"I don't know Rye's past in any detail, and you are not to ask him, Sycamore."

"One sensed a need to tread lightly. In any case, despite having a certain number of detractors, Goddard apparently also has some loyal associates, gentlemen at large, to use his parlance."

"*Highwaymen?*"

"Maybe reformed youthful highwaymen—slightly reformed. He has their loyalty, and they look after him, as he looks after them. I gather on their own initiative, some of his young friends might have kept an eye on you."

Jeanette half turned so she rested against Sycamore's side. "I prefer this explanation to others. Jerome Vincent joined Trevor and me for breakfast yesterday. He ate an unseemly amount and sent me brooding looks over his coffee cup."

"Is he in love with you?"

"If he's in love with anything, I suspect it's my exchequer. From one or two comments Viola has made over the years, I gather she and Lord Beardsley nurture a sense of injury over my settlements."

"And you," Sycamore said, "being a gudgeon, tolerate their pique because you failed to produce the entirely unnecessary spare. I long to get you with child, not only because babies are wonderful and I adore you and please marry me and all that other whatnot, but because I want it established beyond doubt that the only party in your first union suffering reproductive impairment was the marquess. Of course, if we had children, I'd have to share you with them, and I do like having you to myself."

Jeanette kissed his cheek. "You say the most idiotic things."

Sycamore used that opportunity to lift Jeanette into his lap and to expand a peck on the cheek into mutual petting, which passed more than few miles very agreeably. By the time he handed Jeanette down from the coach, his breeding organs were in a pleasant state of anticipation, and he hoped Jeanette had forgotten all about volunteer escorts of the surreptitious variety, a moody step-son, and meddling relations.

Also about nasty notes urging her to quit Town.

"I've been thinking about the notes," Jeanette said as the footman set down a large wicker hamper, and the coachman turned the team in the direction of the nearest posting inn. The footman hopped onto the boot as the coach clattered past, and Sycamore was at last alone with his lady.

"I was hoping you were thinking of enjoying a secluded picnic *à deux* followed by shocking liberties taken with my willing and eager person."

"What is gained by sending me north, Sycamore?" Jeanette replied while opening her parasol. "I can communicate with the solicitors easily enough by mail, Trevor's funds remain mostly tied up in trusts for another three years, and it's not as if I host lavish entertainments. We are not at Richmond."

"We have arrived at Richmond's purlieus. This property borders the royal estate."

Jeanette peered about at a wide, rolling park ringed by hedgerows of maple and oak. Across the open expanse, a two-story white manor house sat on a rise, and the roof of a cottage peaked over the hilltop in the direction of the river.

"Do you know the owner?"

"He is in Paris on business, and I am in negotiations with him," Sycamore said. "The land hereabouts is not blessed with rich soil, so the ideal owner will mostly want pasture acreage and a retreat from Town. Market gardens or hothouse plants are another option. I had hoped you could tour the house with me after we enjoy our picnic."

Jeanette turned in a slow circle, her skirts belling gently around her ankles. "Did you bring me here to seduce me, Sycamore?"

Was that hope in her voice? "Seduce you?" Sycamore studied puffy white clouds in a blue sky rather than ogle Jeanette's ankles. "Of course not. What do you take me for? I might exhaust my powers pleasuring you witless, but I would never stoop to seduction. Mutual ravishing, shared raptures, ecstatic communion, most assuredly, but not seduction."

"Good," she said, taking his arm. "For I did not finish my breakfast, and your efforts would be doomed to fail, at least until we empty that hamper."

"The top of this rise affords a pleasant view of the river, also plenty of privacy in the form of a summer cottage. We will not be disturbed."

He picked up the hamper and soon had Jeanette ensconced on a padded bench overlooking the Thames. The porch of the summer cottage had been kitted out as a folly, open to the spring breezes, but sheltered from the midday sun.

"This is lovely," Jeanette said as Sycamore pulled up a low table before the bench. "I think of you as a Town man, haunting your club at all hours, but I am much more comfortable in the country."

"I was raised in Dorsetshire, which is as rural as England gets. I had a mostly happy boyhood, riding hell-bent with my brothers, learning a prodigious amount of useless botany from my father, and vexing my mother with all the mud I left on her carpets. I miss it, but I am no longer a boy who can take my welcome at the family seat for granted. Champagne?"

The bottle was still cold thanks to the Coventry kitchen staff's care and skill packing a hamper.

"Champagne would be lovely. What do you mean, you no longer take your welcome in Dorsetshire for granted?"

Sycamore poured two servings of wine, passed one to Jeanette and touched his glass to hers. "To pleasant memories."

The champagne was from the better stock at the Coventry, a touch sweet with enough effervescence to tickle the nose. More than the wine, the image of Jeanette, relaxed and smiling for once, gave Sycamore pleasure—and hope.

"Where did you grow up?" he asked as he made up plates of cold chicken, buttered bread, sliced cheese, and forced strawberries. Explaining how Dorning Hall had changed—from Sycamore's home, to the family seat, to Grey Dorning's personal household—was complicated.

Encouraged by Sycamore's occasional questions, Jeanette painted a picture for him of a quiet girl raised in the shadow of a favored older brother, a girl who'd lost her mother early and become increasingly invisible as war with France had decimated the family fortunes.

The Goddards had been among the wealthier gentry—very wealthy indeed—when Jeanette's parents had wed. Commercial and familial ties with France had been a tremendous advantage until they'd become a tremendous liability.

"Whatever I expected of marriage," Jeanette said, considering her last strawberry, "it wasn't what the marquess had in mind for me, but Papa said the match was a triumph for the Goddards and the answer to his every prayer. What girl doesn't want to be the answer to her Papa's every prayer? He did not live to see my first anniversary. A mercy, that."

She popped the strawberry into her mouth, while Sycamore hurt for her. "Had the late Lord Tavistock shown you the least bit of affection, you would have found a way to adore him." She adored her brother, who showed her no affection whatsoever, and her step-son, whose devotion was marred by youthful dunderheadedness.

"Perhaps I would have merely esteemed his lordship, but I did want to respect and like my husband." She eyed Sycamore's plate. "Will you finish those strawberries, sir?"

He held the largest berry up to her mouth. She nibbled it from his fingers, and the moment became something more.

"Through that door is a parlor, my lady, and beyond the parlor, a bedroom." Sycamore fed Jeanette another strawberry. "I'd like very much to take you to bed, but only if you are inclined to take me to bed too."

She leaned over to give Sycamore a strawberry-flavored kiss. "I wondered what you'd brought along for dessert. Your suggestion will make a lovely next course."

Sycamore kissed her back, gently and sweetly, for once savoring desire that rose on a slow tide. With Jeanette, he would not be satisfied as he'd so often been, by a merely pleasurable interlude. He wanted the childhood stories, the past disappointments, the intimate joys, and the hopes too.

As he led his lover to the bed tucked into a sunny corner of the little cottage, Sycamore silently apologized to every sibling whose marriage he'd resented. Those brothers and sisters had been in the grip of something larger than family loyalty, something wonderful and precious that family loyalty was built upon.

He aspired to share that something wonderful with Jeanette, and for the next few hours, meddling relatives, nasty notes, estranged siblings, and any plagues yet to come could all go to blazes while he made wild, passionate love to the woman he adored.

THE MORNING SHOULD HAVE BEEN nothing remarkable, Jeanette reflected as Sycamore undid her dress hooks. Londoners who had the leisure and means frequently enjoyed Richmond Park, and picnics figured on that agenda. Meals al fresco allowed couples to spend time together without violating the many, many dictates of propriety.

Every wellborn young lady expected to enjoy the regular occasion of picnics with attentive gentlemen.

Such a lady also expected to dance with those same witty, pleasant fellows.

To drive out with them in the park.

To have their escort at musicales or other social gatherings.

To enjoy the occasional bouquet sent by such gentlemen after those outings.

And Jeanette had had none of that. She removed Sycamore's cravat pin and watch, her emotions a mixture of sexual anticipation and an odd sort of sorrow. Recounting the circumstances of her engagement to the marquess, she'd seen for the first time how ignorant she'd been.

How her own father had taken advantage of that ignorance and moved her about like a chess piece in a game she'd never consented to play.

A picnic was a small thing. Could Papa not have married her off to a wealthy widower who was yet capable of sharing a picnic with her? Waltzing with her? Driving her in the park? The marquess had spared her none of those courtesies and had instead subjected her to ceaseless rutting and even more relentless criticism.

The act of coupling, the simplest and most profound privilege of the committed couple, had become resounding proof of her inadequacy, a punishment rather than a pleasure.

And thus did her sadness acquire an edge of anger.

"You're sure?" Sycamore asked, shrugging out of his riding jacket and draping it over the back of a chair. "Just because we have time and privacy doesn't mean you must take me to bed, Jeanette. I would be happy to cuddle with you and indulge in a discussion of your family's French vineyards or the latest fashion in lady's bonnets."

She unbuttoned his waistcoat and laid it over his jacket. "You mean that. You would snuggle up with me and make idle conversation if I wished it."

He passed her his cravat, undid his shirt buttons, and pulled the shirt over his head. "I would. Mind you, I might have to see to myself before leaving the bed, lest I go blind with frustrated desire, but that's the work of a moment and hardly work at all. Ask any male over the age of fourteen."

He tossed the shirt onto the chair and stood naked from the waist up, his hair slightly disheveled. "Shall I take off your boots?"

Her first inclination was to wave him away and finish undressing unassisted, as she had many times before. Her corset laces tied in front for that purpose, because she did not like being fussed at as she disrobed at the end of the day.

But Sycamore had *asked,* his touch was exquisite, and the right to enjoy such intimate consideration was also something the marquess had stolen from her.

Jeanette sat on the bed and hiked her skirts a few inches. Sycamore knelt before her, and soon her boots were off. He sent her a questioning glance—still asking her permission, though more subtly—and she nodded.

He made removing her garters and peeling down her stockings into a worshipful act, and why, oh why, had Jeanette never known that a man's touch on her feet, ankles, and calves could inspire erotic sensations?

"You have the prettiest knees," Sycamore said. "If I could draw as well as my brother Oak does, I'd immortalize your knees." He kissed each one, left then right, and rested his cheek against her bare thigh.

Jeanette stroked his hair, feeling awash in regret—why had she ever, ever agreed to marry an arrogant fool twice her age? The regret was edged aside by tenderness for the man kneeling before her.

"I am overdressed for the occasion," she said, rubbing Sycamore's earlobe between her thumb and forefinger. "So are you."

He eased back and to his feet in one motion and held out a hand to Jeanette. She expected him to whisk her dress over her head, yank off his boots and breeches, and toss her onto the bed.

Instead, he kissed her, first on the cheek, then lightly on the mouth, until Jeanette stepped close, got a firm grip of his hair, and showed him how she longed to be kissed. She paused a few breathless moments later to remove both her dress and her chemise, and the sensation of being skin to skin with Sycamore's heat had her nearly pushing him onto the mattress.

"My boots, Jeanette," he muttered as she plastered herself against his chest. "Must not..." He stepped back, panting, his eyes dancing. "Country air agrees with you, my lady."

"It does. I had forgotten that. Get out of those clothes, Sycamore, lest I rend them from your person."

He closed his eyes for one moment, as if praying for fortitude—or for his clothes to be rent from his person—then toed off his boots and peeled out of his breeches and stockings.

"Does my lady approve of this ensemble?" he asked, turning in a slow circle. "Perhaps she'd like to inspect the adornments I've chosen for this delightful occasion?"

He was thoroughly aroused and thoroughly unconstrained by self-consciousness. Sycamore was, in fact, smiling at her, his expression conveying buccaneering high spirits, a challenge, and also deep affection.

"You are showing off your great good looks," Jeanette said, folding back the covers and settling onto the bed. "Do you know what my favorite part of you is?"

He closed his hand around his rampant shaft and stroked himself idly. "You can have more than one favorite part of me, Jeanette. A lady should not have to choose."

"Come to bed, Sycamore. My favorite parts of you are your eyes. You have honest eyes."

"I have girlish eyes, all periwinkle and lavender and unmanly. Do you know what my favorite part of you is?"

He climbed onto the bed and kept coming until he was crouched over Jeanette like a lion guarding his next meal.

"I am not inclined to be reduced to my female parts," Jeanette said, "though a general sort of appreciation for them is permissible under the circumstances."

Sycamore nuzzled her breasts, took a nipple in his mouth, and suckled just long enough for Jeanette to begin undulating her hips, not quite long enough to make her groan.

"I love your heart," Sycamore said, crouching closer. "I love that fiercely guarded citadel you call your heart. You will never give up on your brother, no matter how clodpated he is. You will still be looking out for Tavistock when he's a grandpapa, and when you ought by rights to be bitter and shallow and vain, you are dear and lovely and brave."

"Sycamore, I'm not." And yet, had Jeanette been given those words of flattery as a new bride, as a girl of seventeen... Had somebody looked upon her with that much respect and liking before her engagement, she might have been the woman Sycamore spoke of.

"You are all of that," he said, levering himself up to kiss her brow. "And my every most passionate longing come true. Please don't argue with me, for I will win by cheating."

He nudged at her with his cock, the merest, most maddening tease.

"I might let you win, Sycamore, this time."

"Right," he said, getting a hand around a breast, "lull me into anticipation of an easy victory. Lull away, Jeanette, and then thoroughly trounce me."

He began the joining in slow, sensual earnest. He could not know how his teasing banter, his determination to see her aroused and unraveled, met a need not only of the body but also of the heart. This was not merely rutting, but mutual adoration and joy.

Jeanette's desire and emotions blended into one yearning and then into one great conflagration of satisfaction. Sycamore trounced her, thoroughly, with more pleasure than she could endure, until she was a moaning, heaving beast beneath him and then a quietly shaken, tenderly kissed lover in his arms.

"It's too much," Jeanette said as Sycamore rested his cheek against hers. "With you, it's too much, Sycamore."

"Good," he whispered. "And next time, we're using some damned sponges, so it can be beyond too much for all concerned. Hold me, Jeanette."

He eased out of her heat and finished on her belly, and when Jeanette ought to have fussed him about making a mess and giving her room to breathe, she instead held him close and endured a few tears.

For whom or why she cried, she could not have said, but Sycamore had not cheated, and she knew that, with her, he never would.

DID JEANETTE CRY FOR JOY, sorrow, or something of both? Sycamore wanted to ask her, but that would invite her to question him about his own emotions, which were new, tender, and powerful.

She changed him for the better, with her stubbornness and self-possession. When she came all undone in his arms, surrendered to what he could give her and to her own pleasure, he was suffused with joy and awe, and with a towering need to both be close to her and be what she needed him to be.

All quite... quite... befuddling, in a lovely sort of way. He had been infatuated regularly, and what he felt for Jeanette made those enthusiasms so much frolic by comparison.

Jeanette slept on her side, Sycamore curved around her. A cool breeze off the river came stealing through the open window, and Sycamore resisted the urge to join Jeanette in slumber—to rejoin her in slumber, for he'd already stolen a nap. He instead tucked the covers up around her shoulder and considered what he knew of her situation.

She might well have been followed by Goddard's minions.

Trevor's misadventures could have befallen anybody who strolled London's streets, and they could have been aimed at Jerome, if they'd been aimed at anybody.

A matchmaker bent on chasing Jeanette away from guard duty where Trevor was concerned might have sent along the nasty notes.

Sycamore wanted to cobble together a string of unfortunate, unrelated mishaps, but that took a great deal of cobbling, and thus other explanations wanted examination.

"You're awake," Jeanette said, taking his hand and kissing his knuckles. "I slept like I'd been out dancing until dawn."

"You slept like a well-pleasured lady." A well-*loved* lady. Sycamore tried on the word in his mind and was pleased that it fit. This welter of concern and desire and affection, the thinking of Jeanette when they were apart, the pleasure he took in her company, no matter the occasion...

He did not simply love her, he had fallen *in love* with her.

His first thought was that his brothers would laugh themselves silly if he announced this state of affairs, but his second was that, no, they would not. He'd not be announcing anything so important to that lot of buffoons anyway, but if he did, they wouldn't laugh.

Not this time.

"I am worried," Jeanette said, shifting to curl against Sycamore's side. "About Trevor, about the staff at Tavistock House, about nasty notes, and ruffians in alleys."

"I am worried about you," Sycamore replied, wrapping an arm around her shoulders. "I want to excuse all that has occurred as happenstance. Each incident on its own can be reasoned away, but the pattern is unsettling." To say nothing of supposedly hard-of-hearing butlers lurking in corridors or Jerome Vincent's brooding looks and mounting debts.

"Precisely, and there's something else, Sycamore. Why, when I borrow Rye's coach, do his young friends pursue me? If they want to know what I get up to of an evening, they can simply ask the coachman. He's been with Rye for years and would protect me with his life."

As delightful as drowsing naked in bed with Jeanette was, as temptingly as renewed lovemaking beckoned from the merrier part of Sycamore's imagination, Jeanette was raising a troublesome point.

"And why spontaneously decide to start following you now?" Sycamore murmured. "Why follow you when you're off to a mere musicale and Goddard's coach is nowhere to be seen?"

Jeanette sighed, kissed his chest, and rolled away. "I should practice with my knives, Sycamore. I've been getting acquainted with the blade you gave me, and it's amazing what the right weapon will do for a lady's aim."

She wasn't flirting, alas, but rather, sitting on the edge of the mattress and looking about like a woman who'd had enough frolicking for the nonce. She paused to rub her temples when Sycamore expected her to hop off the bed and begin dressing.

"A touch of hay fever?" he asked, taking the place beside her. "Too much champagne?" Though Jeanette had had only two modest glasses with a full meal, and she'd sipped rather than guzzled her wine.

"I'm sure all I need is some fresh air. You brought me more knives?"

"The whole set. Shall I rebraid your hair?" He wanted to, wanted to linger and bill and coo, which was surely a symptom of excessive country air.

Jeanette rose and pulled her chemise over her head. "A touch-up with a comb and a few well-placed pins ought to suffice. You'd like to tour the manor house, too, wouldn't you?"

Something was wrong. This abrupt change of mood, complete with brisk good cheer, was not how lovers who'd just swived each other to exhaustion behaved.

"Jeanette, are you sorry you went to bed with me?"

She wiggled into her stays and gave him her back. "Why would I be?"

"Because," he said, slipping his arms around her middle, "the feelings refuse to be put into tidily labeled crocks with lids sized to match."

She had no reply for that, so he gently tugged her laces into submission. "Tighter?"

"That will do. The feelings are complicated, Sycamore, and I don't know what to do with them."

He passed the laces forward and tied them off loosely. "You need not *do* anything, Jeanette. Enjoy having a devoted admirer, for I do admire you."

Don't leave me. The lament was old, aimed by a small boy at a mother overwhelmed by too many rambunctious children. She'd frequently decamped for Bath in an effort to gain the notice of a husband preoccupied with his botany, and then she'd gone to Bath and never come home.

Don't leave me had been silently flung at two sisters, one lost to matrimony, the other to service and then, again, to matrimony.

Older brothers had disappeared to public school, and—worst hurt of all—Papa, after disappearing on endless botanical excursions, had died. They all left, all of them, and that Jeanette might cast Sycamore aside caused him something approaching hysteria.

"I worry," she said, turning into his embrace. "If something seems too good to be true..."

He held her gently, knowing her pessimism was justified. "I am not a swaggering marquess twice your age and bent on securing my dynasty at the expense of your happiness. I am not a father who appears to dote on you—when I recall you exist—while I in truth burden you with making my hopes and dreams come true. I am not your brother, gone to war and come home to you an unhappy and guilt-ridden stranger."

She pressed her forehead to his chest. "But you are dear, and I did not intend that you become dear. You were to be annoying and possibly charming, though mostly useful."

From anybody else, that would be an almost humorous lament, but from Jeanette...

Sycamore kissed her temple. "Let me be dear to you, Jeanette. You are very dear to me."

She sighed and, for a luscious moment, yielded to his embrace. "I am daft. You make me daft, and I like that, but now is not the time to be daft. Where is my dress?"

He aided her to don the costume of a proper lady. She tucked and tidied him into a gentleman's riding attire. Her touch was impersonal and unloverlike, from which Sycamore took a backhanded satisfaction. Jeanette would ruthlessly suppress only those emotions that threatened to swamp her self-possession.

"Will I do?" he asked, draping his riding jacket over his arm.

"You more than do. You are a fashion plate of masculine pulchritude. Do you know why I first graced the Coventry with my presence?"

"You were curious, and the Coventry is fashionable?"

"I was bored, that's true, and I like the challenge of a fresh deck, but I'd passed you riding in the park of a morning. You tipped your hat to me, and I saw your extraordinary eyes."

"My extraordinary eyes earned me a number of schoolyard thrashings," Sycamore said. "They are *pretty*, in the opinion of more than one youthful pugilist. Until Ash showed me how to defend myself, I suffered regular beatings. The beatings were nothing compared to the work it took to hide their effects from my family."

"And that was the last time anybody laid a fist on you, I trust." Jeanette began straightening up the bed. "You were tired when I passed you on that bridle path, had probably been up all night at the club. I saw the weariness in your eyes and the complete lack of flirtation. 'There,' I thought to myself, 'is a man of depth and substance. A man thinking about more than his last tumble or his next pint. He would never be obsessed over something as shallow as a spare of the body.'"

"A man of substance and depth?" Had anybody ever paid him such a high compliment?

"Yes," she said, sitting once again on the made bed. "Would it be possible to return directly to Town, Sycamore?"

"You don't want to practice with the full set of knives?"

She put a hand over her tummy. "Perhaps tomorrow. Something I ate did not agree with me, and a return home posthaste appeals strongly."

Sycamore assayed the state of his own digestion, for he'd partaken of the same food at lunch that Jeanette had. Jeanette was asking politely, but for her to even mention feeling unwell she was doubtless in distress.

"The coach will have returned by now, and I'll tell John Coachman to spring 'em. Can you walk, Jeanette?"

She managed, but before climbing into the coach, she was sick in the grass. They had to stop halfway to London for her to be unwell again, and by the time Sycamore carried her into his house, she was pale, clammy, complaining of a serious headache, and in immediate need of a chamber pot.

Sycamore sent for a physician he trusted, but he did not need a doctor to tell him that Jeanette was suffering a serious, possibly fatal, case of food poisoning.

CHAPTER TWELVE

"You are no longer begging for death, but rather, simply longing for it. That is progress."

Jeanette rolled over to face a petite, dark-haired woman whose observation carried a hint of a Northern accent. The lady had the inherent reserve of the denizens of the Northern counties as well, though her eyes, a startling green, were kind.

"I am..." Jeanette looked around at the room and saw a fan of knives arranged on the opposite wall. The bed was enormous, the sheets softest flannel, the quilts even softer. "I am not at my best. You are Ann."

"Miss Ann Pearson, and you are going to live." She pulled draperies closed over two windows and poured half a glass of water. "Drink, please. A bout of the flux necessitates fluids."

The flux, a raging headache, body aches worthy of an eighty-year-old granny in winter, and a belly that had rejected Jeanette's entire lunch hours ago and still felt tentative. She recalled watering eyes and cold sweats as well.

"What time is it?" The water felt good in Jeanette's mouth, though Ann permitted her only a few sips.

"Going on eight in the evening. Mr. Dorning sent a note to Lord Tavistock not to wait supper on you. You will feel much better by tomorrow morning."

This woman had an air of competence, suggesting she was no maid. A housekeeper perhaps?

"I am the undercook at the Coventry," she said. "Sycamore Dorning is my employer and my frequent cross to bear. He intrudes into the kitchen, claiming he is trying to help. Monsieur Delacourt takes a dim view of infidels who attempt to offer aid to his culinary art. Men must have their little dramas."

"Mr. Dorning brought me to his home."

Ann set the water glass on the bedside table and helped Jeanette sit up. "Mr. Dorning brought you here, refused to leave your side even when the physician made his examination of you, tended to you until I reminded him that his club does not run itself, and will doubtless be back at regular intervals, once again claiming he is trying to help."

Even changing positions caused a crescendo in the throbbing at Jeanette's temples. She nonetheless made the effort, hounded by a nagging sense that a puzzle needed urgently to be solved.

"Mr. Dorning did help." Jeanette had mortifying memories of Sycamore assisting her to her feet after she'd cast up her accounts into the grass, carrying her up a flight of steps, and summoning a physician.

"I am wearing one of his shirts, am I not?"

Ann passed her the water glass. "Your clothing needed the attention of the laundress, though your things are dry now. Mr. Dorning will doubtless object to you going anywhere for at least the next year."

The water was an exquisite pleasure. Jeanette permitted herself three small sips. "Is Sycamore—Mr. Dorning—well?"

"As obnoxiously hale as ever. He suspects you ate some bad mushrooms at breakfast. Lord Fairly and I concur with that theory."

"I barely had any breakfast." A few bites of omelet, because she had been eager to leave the house on Sycamore's arm. "Is Fairly the physician?" A soft-spoken man with a light, competent touch.

"He is, and he came quickly. Mr. Dorning was quite insistent."

"He often is." But Sycamore hadn't insisted on throwing knives, hadn't insisted on tarrying out in Surrey.

"As is Monsieur Delacourt, and there I am, surrounded by open flames, sharp objects, and stubborn fellows. The life of an undercook is never easy. I would put Sir Orion in the same category of stubbornness, but he at least keeps his mouth shut."

Unease that had nothing to do with bad mushrooms joined Jeanette's general malaise. She took one more sip of water and set the glass on the bedside table.

"Sir Orion was here?"

"Pacing the corridor like a man awaiting judgment. Mr. Dorning sent for him as well. Do you think you could keep dry toast down?"

"Must I?"

"Your body needs nourishment, fluids, and rest, but of the three, nourishment is the least pressing. Many a child goes all day without eating in this great metropolis."

"Is Sir Orion still in the corridor?"

Ann busied herself refolding the quilt draped across the foot of the bed. "Lord Fairly assured your brother that the worst was behind you, and Sir Orion decamped amid many threats to Mr. Dorning's wellbeing if anything more should happen to you."

"A worried man is not at his best." Though Sycamore had been the soul of calm all the way back from Richmond. Jeanette recalled that much and had vague memories of him easing her out of her clothing. He'd jollied her along, like a nanny with a fractious toddler, and roused the watch all without revealing his worry to her.

The beatings were nothing compared to the work it took to hide their effects from my family. When had he said that?

"I should get dressed," Jeanette said.

"You should rest." Ann regarded her with the sort of dispassion Jeanette associated with artists and scientists. "But stubbornness apparently runs in your family. You will need it, if my reading of Mr. Dorning's intentions is accurate. I must look in on the kitchen. I have had your clothes brought up, but you are not to get out of that bed without somebody to assist you. Lightheadedness can follow a bout of food poisoning."

Ann set the water pitcher on the bedside table, gave Jeanette a final perusal, and opened the door.

Sycamore stood on the other side, his expression as serious as Jeanette had ever seen it.

"You are awake," he said, sidling past Ann. "Ann, Monsieur is threatening to give notice if you don't return to your post. I was about to sack him to stop his whining. In my present mood, that is not an idle threat."

"Neither is Monsieur's threat idle." Ann sent Jeanette a you-see-what-I-have-to-contend-with smile, a little tired, a little resigned. "My lady, you should know that your brother was very worried about you. I heard him praying, importuning the Almighty to spare you, in French no less. I was"—she frowned at Sycamore—"touched."

She sketched a curtsey and left, pulling the door closed in her wake.

Sycamore took the place on the bed at Jeanette's hip. "You are still pale. How do you feel?"

"Like I have been trampled by a coach and four. Even my eyes ache."

"You shed many tears, which is an effect of the poison. You might also recall sweating, salivating, and panting as well as loose bowels and stomach upheaval. Your head doubtless feels as if you consumed half a barrel of bad ale."

"I would rather not recall any of it," Jeanette said, though Sycamore's words provoked nasty memories. "You saw all of that?"

Sycamore wore formal evening attire. That contrast, between the symptoms he recited and the elegance of his dress, reminded Jeanette of her first impression of him. Sycamore Dorning had depths. He had perspectives and experiences that made him as competent at the fast-paced game of hazard as he was at patiently coaxing confidences from a dowager duchess.

He was *formidable* in a way the late Marquess of Tavistock, for all his wealth and standing, never had been, but did Sycamore see himself in that light?

"I have observed all of those miseries before," he said, taking Jeanette's hand. "My father was a botanist, and because mushrooms can be deadly, he took a passing interest in them. Your symptoms were typical of those caused by a dose of *Clitocybe rivulosa,* Fool's Funnel in the vernacular, which in moderation is an effective purge. The species has the audacity to grow among edible varieties, and thus Papa made sure we knew how to identify it."

Holding Sycamore's hand was good medicine. The unease in Jeanette's belly receded and the pounding in her temples diminished, even as a different ache started up in her heart.

"Where does your household acquire its mushrooms this time of year, Jeanette?"

Of course, Sycamore would ask that. "Mushrooms are not yet in season, so I assume Cook had them sent up from the glass houses at the family seat. We get a weekly delivery of produce from Kent, as does Lord Beardsley's household. The same wagon brings provisions for both Viola's kitchen and my own. I am the only person at the town house who will eat a mushroom omelet, so we don't need many."

Sycamore kissed her knuckles. "The likelihood of a poisonous mushroom growing among a glass house crop is small, Jeanette, and the omelet I saw on your sideboard was barely more than one person would consume."

"You are trying to make a point, or leaping to a conclusion." A conclusion all but obvious to the casual observer, unfortunately.

"You ate little more than half of your omelet before I whisked you off to Richmond. Do you normally eat the whole thing?"

"Yes."

Sycamore enfolded her hand in both of his. "The indications are you were poisoned. The question is, were you intended to consume a fatal dose, or was this a warning?"

Oh, it was a warning. Of that Jeanette was certain. Jerome's brooding looks had been another warning, as had Viola's call, as had the notes, and possibly even the beatings Tavistock had endured. If Jeanette ignored this warning, Orion's business would be targeted next—perhaps it already had been—and even the Coventry was not safe.

That last thought made Jeannette ill all over again. Sycamore had worked so hard to build the club into the impressive venue it was, and he was so rightly proud of what he'd accomplished.

He kissed her knuckles and smoothed a hand over her brow. "The thought of you returning to Tavistock House is unbearable. Say you will marry me, Jeanette, and I'll have a preacher and special license here by noon tomorrow."

SYCAMORE HAD REMAINED OUTWARDLY calm when Jeanette had asked to be taken straight back to Town. He'd remained calm as her body had done its best to reject the poison she'd ingested. He'd remained calm as the doctor had peered into Jeanette's eyes and measured her pulse, and he'd maintained a façade of manners as preparations for an evening's business had begun at the club.

But inside, where a growing boy had watched his enormous family come unraveled year by year, where an adult male knew the metallic taste of terror, and where a fellow in love was nigh insane with the need to keep his beloved safe, Sycamore had panicked.

And he had planned.

The application for a special license had been lodged before sunset. Goddard's minions had already set a watch at Sycamore's expense on the Tavistock town house. Ash had been summoned to arrive at the Coventry in the next hour, and a quick note had been dashed off to the Duchess of Quimbey.

Jeanette's hand in Sycamore's was cool, her face pale. He had just proposed marriage to her, and she showed no reaction at all.

"You think the solution to my situation is marriage?" she asked, gaze on their joined hands. "I don't see how that fixes anything."

"Marriage *to me* gets you out of the Tavistock town house and away from the Vincent family. Marriage to me will keep you safe, Jeanette. We can be in a fast coach headed for Dorsetshire within the hour."

"I don't want to go to Dorsetshire." She spoke slowly, and Sycamore realized he was blundering. The situation called for reason, for sweet reassurances, and more blasted calm.

"Your safety must be of paramount importance, Jeanette, and at Dorning Hall, the loyalty of everybody from the earl himself to the goose girl is beyond doubt."

Jeanette withdrew her hand, and Sycamore's panic escalated to blind determination.

"I have been safe enough at Tavistock House for nearly ten years, Sycamore. You are overreacting to what could easily have been a mistake. You said yourself that the bad mushrooms often grow in proximity to the good."

"Jeanette, please do not turn up stubborn now." Sycamore resisted the urge to go down on his knees beside the bed, lest he be dismissed as histrionic. "Bad mushrooms do not spring up beside the good in a hothouse or conservatory. You were poisoned, and you must marry me."

She sent him a brooding look. "Must?"

Do not tell her what to do. Do not order this woman about. Every brother who'd ever taken up residence in Sycamore's mental Greek chorus of critics and judges warned him to back away from the discussion and leave a reasonable woman to come to a reasonable conclusion.

And he mentally shouted them down. "What if you'd finished that omelet, Jeanette? The omelet prepared exclusively for you. I cannot allow you to totter out of here without any sort of plan to ensure you are safe."

Still, she merely gazed at him, her vast reserves of self-possession apparently none the worse for her ordeal.

"We don't know that an omelet had anything to do with it. I might have simply suffered a passing stomach ailment. Eggs go bad even without the addition of questionable mushrooms."

"Not eggs brought in fresh from your own country estate, Jeanette. Please apply a scintilla of logic to the situation and realize that somebody has tried to harm you. The symptoms you suffered exactly describe the results of ingesting Fool's Funnel. By your own admission, the Vincent family is after your money, and all I seek to do is *keep you safe*."

She flipped back the covers and swung her feet over the side of the bed. Pale, slender, lovely feet, and the sight of them sent the last pretension to manners from Sycamore's grasp.

"Jeanette, don't be foolish. You aren't in any fit state to go anywhere, much less—"

She stood and put a hand on his chest, a gentle touch that filled Sycamore with a sense of implacable doom.

"You have no right, Sycamore, to keep me here. You are not in a position to *allow* anything where I am concerned. If you want a plan, then I will make it a point to eat nothing that Trevor hasn't also partaken of. I should be going."

"You cannot leave." He managed, barely, not to seize her by the shoulders. "Jeanette, you are not safe."

She eased around him and went behind the privacy screen. "I will be careful. I will hire some new footmen, loyal to me. I will pension off Peem and suggest Trevor do the same with his valet. I will, if necessary, retire to Tavistock Hall, and Jerome and Trevor can have the town house for their youthful bacchanals, and—"

"I cannot permit you to remove to Tavistock Hall." Sycamore had nearly shouted. "If you remove to the Hall, then you can't use young Tavistock as your personal taster, and besides, he's out most evenings, and you can be poisoned at supper as easily as at breakfast. For the love of God, Jeanette, why won't you marry me?"

She emerged from the privacy screen wearing her dress, and Sycamore wanted to tear it off her, the better to hold her hostage. The Marchioness of Tavistock would not be seen on London's streets in her chemise.

"I like you," Jeanette said. "I like you exceedingly, Sycamore, and I believe your motivation is honorable, but you cannot know—you cannot have any idea—how it chills me to hear you telling me what to do, accusing me of a want of logic, speaking to me in terms of *allowing* and *permitting*. I never wanted to remarry, and I have been honest about that."

She was probably making a sort of female sense. All Sycamore knew was that the woman he loved was preparing to resume a life where she'd be vulnerable to harm.

"I married once to safeguard my father's fortunes," she said, taking the seat at the vanity, "and to give my brother a start in the military. I married because it was a spectacular match for a mere Goddard. I married because I hadn't been *allowed* or *permitted* to dream of any other future. Now you demand that I marry again, because of some bad eggs."

"Bad eggs, beatings in alleys, threatening notes, family desperate for money... How can you not see a pattern in those events, Jeanette?"

She coiled her braid at the nape of her neck and began shoving pins into the resulting bun. "I do see a pattern, and I will take steps to ensure that pattern doesn't escalate, or affect innocent parties, but how can you fail to see a pattern in your dealings with me, Sycamore?"

He was losing her, possibly forever, and that was the only pattern he saw. "I care for you. I am protective of you. The two go hand in hand."

"The marquess married me to secure his dynasty. He did not need a young wife—he had an heir and spare, of sorts—but he desired more security than that. Jerome wants to marry me, of all the daft notions, because he, too, has a need to safeguard the Vincent family fortunes. You seek to safeguard my person, a commendable goal compared to the others."

More female logic, and all of it beyond Sycamore's comprehension. "And my commendable goal makes me like your bleating, rutting marquess?"

Jeanette rose from the vanity, looking damnably tidy and serene. "What do *I* want, Sycamore?"

"To never again spend a day as you did today, sweating on the banks of the River Styx and so far gone in bodily misery that you didn't particularly care if Charon invited you into his boat."

Don't leave me. Please, just don't leave me.

"What an ambitious creature I must be that the sum of my longings is to avoid future occasions of food poisoning. I have desires and needs beyond that, for your information."

Sycamore wanted to stand before the door and physically prevent her departure. "You admit you were poisoned."

"I admit I probably ate the wrong kind of mushroom. Will you lend me your coach to see me home?"

She wasn't asking him to see her home in person. "I do not understand why you are willing to return to a household where you are not safe, Jeanette. Please explain that to me."

"If I was deliberately poisoned, then the malefactor won't make another attempt using that means. I will send to the agencies for more footmen and maids tomorrow, Sycamore. I have the means. You must not worry."

She kissed him on the cheek, and he caught her up in a hug. "*All* I will do is worry, Jeanette. Every waking and sleeping moment, I will worry. I will do nothing but worry."

"Then throw your knives and know that I will be practicing with mine as well."

In the part of Sycamore's mind that always stood a little apart and kept vigil, he saw the irony: Jeanette was telling him what to do. He must not worry, he must throw his knives, he must pretend she had not become the most precious person in the world to him.

She was telling him what he could and could not do, how to feel and what to think, and he despised it.

JEANETTE SLEPT, as the expression went, like the dead, though she forced herself to put in an appearance at the breakfast table. Trevor was already seated at the head of the table, still in his evening attire.

He read the paper, a cup of tea at his elbow. Whether the difference was a few weeks of boxing at Jackson's and fencing at Angelo's, or a few nights at Sycamore's side at the Coventry, Jeanette's step-son was growing into his consequence.

On his smallest finger, he wore a signet ring that Jeanette had last seen on her late husband.

"Good morning," she said, looking over the offerings on the sideboard. "Will you go for a hack after breakfast?" No small omelet in the blue-flowered dish, just the larger variety prepared for his lordship.

"I think not," Trevor said, putting the paper aside and rising. "How are you?"

Trevor's plate held the detritus of ham, bacon, eggs, and toast, but Jeanette's belly wasn't up to such adventures. She set an empty plate at her place on the table.

"I am well, and you?" She was not well, but she was determined, which was nearly the same thing.

Trevor held her chair, not a courtesy he typically showed her. "Your digestion still troubles you."

"Mr. Dorning has been telling tales." Jeanette spread her table napkin on her lap and wondered if toast and butter could be poisoned. She'd left the Coventry barely able to walk unassisted, thinking only to find some peace and quiet in which to think.

In the light of a new day, her list was revealed to be inadequate. Peace and quiet were all well and good, but peace, quiet, and safety would have been better. Sycamore had been quite right about that.

But safety for her alone would not suffice.

"Mr. Dorning refused to leave your side," Trevor said, "to hear the undercook tell it. He sent for a physician who was as knowledgeable as he was discreet, and no effort was spared to keep you comfortable."

"Are you scolding me for eating some bad eggs, Trevor?"

Trevor set the teapot by her elbow. "No, Jeanette, I am not scolding you. I am simply curious as to what in blazes you think you're doing here, at the self-same table where you consumed those bad eggs? Dorning knew precisely how you were poisoned, and a larger dose of the same plant has occasionally been fatal."

"Do not take that tone with me, Trevor."

"Do not engage in the sort of stubborn display of bravado that results in young men expiring in their beds from drinking too many bottles of spirits on a bet."

Jeanette put two pieces of toast on her plate and made no move to add butter or jam. "You sound exactly like your father, and that is not a compliment. I merely ate breakfast, Trevor. That is not a stubborn display of bravado."

"You threw Sycamore Dorning's proposal back in his face."

Abruptly, Jeanette felt miserable in a whole different way. Her head still hurt, and her belly was tentative, but now her heart joined in the sense of leaden doom.

"He wasn't proposing for the right reasons, Trevor. He was upset and flailing around for a means to bring the situation under control. Though I like Mr. Dorning, his behavior wasn't that different from your papa's, marrying solely to address a lack of heirs."

She had tried that reasoning out on Sycamore, and he hadn't been much impressed by it. Neither was Jeanette, but then, that was hardly her whole argument for leaving the Coventry—and him.

"Mr. Dorning deserves to marry a woman who can reciprocate his affections," Jeanette said, pouring herself a cup of tea.

"You reciprocate his affections," Trevor said, watching the teapot tremble in Jeanette's hand. "He is wild for you."

"Mr. Dorning is wild for a different woman every fortnight. That's part of his charm." *Forgive me, Sycamore.*

Trevor took the toast from her plate and applied butter, as a nanny might do for a charge in the nursery. "Either the poison affected your reasoning powers, or you are hatching up some machination which I cannot fathom. Dorning *loves you.* He would die for you, he would kill for you. He'd take a torch to the club he depends on for his livelihood and turn his back on all of Society for you."

Precisely what Jeanette did not want. She stared at the cold, buttered toast on her plate. "You used to be such a sweet boy."

Trevor sat back, his gaze holding nothing of that sweet boy. "Did you reject Dorning's overture because you sought to guard me, Jeanette?"

The sweet boy had become a shrewd young man. "You are alone here, surrounded by aging staff of questionable loyalty. You can use an ally."

Trevor rose—when had his height become so imposing?—and aimed at Jeanette the first contemptuous look she could recall him turning on anybody.

"Don't protect me, Jeanette. I'm not yet of age, but neither am I the motherless child you took up for so many times with Papa. I heard you arguing with him, and I told myself I would never be like him—shouting and insulting a woman I was supposed to esteem. So I won't shout and insult you, but neither will I stand idly by while you put your life at risk, supposedly for my sake. If you have any sense, you will send Dorning a note of apology and marry him by special license."

He stalked out of the breakfast parlor, the silence all the louder because he'd not raised his voice.

Jeanette managed one slice of toast and two cups of plain tea before Peem brought her the morning mail. No note lurked among the usual invitations and correspondence, though Peem dithered for a good five minutes while Jeanette sipped tea and read through the solicitor's latest report.

She was debating whether to attempt another discussion with Trevor when Jerome came sauntering into the parlor, his hair windblown, his riding boots less than pristine.

"Have I missed Tav already? I thought the day too nice to remain abed and hoped to join him for a hack."

"Tavistock has broken his fast and has likely gone up to catch a nap," Jeanette said, assaying a cordial smile. "Feel free to help yourself to the buffet, Jerome, and tell me how your dear sisters are getting on."

Jerome took up a plate. "It's as well Tavistock has sought his bed, my lady. I've been meaning to broach a topic with you that should not have an audience. Might I close the door?"

He certainly wasn't wasting any time, but then, perhaps that was for the best. "Close the door if you must," she said, "but please be brief. I am expected elsewhere this morning."

Jerome closed the door and took the place at her left. "I will get straight to the point."

"WHAT THE HELL are you doing here?" Orion Goddard had asked that rude question quietly, probably in deference to the small child searching through the grass a few yards away in what passed for a back garden.

"That is a female of very tender years," Sycamore said, tipping his hat to the girl, who peered up at him with the solemn curiosity of an owlet. "She has your chin, Goddard, though on her the feature is piquant rather than stubborn." And she had Jeanette's inherent sense of self-possession, a painful thing to see in one so young.

Goddard took Sycamore by the elbow and tried to steer him down the walkway. Sycamore was not in the mood to be steered.

"I do not receive visitors, Dorning. Take yourself off and don't come back."

By virtue of a move that was part twist, part jerk, and all annoyance, Sycamore removed Goddard's hand from his person.

"You are a bad brother," he said. "I know of few insults that ought to rouse a man's ire more effectively, but the shoe fits, Goddard. Do you know what today is?"

Goddard gave him a peevish look that also put Sycamore in mind of Jeanette. "The day I am plagued with an unwelcome intruder."

"Jerome Vincent has called on Jeanette twice since she nearly died of food poisoning five days ago. He's calling when he knows Tavistock isn't likely to be underfoot. What does that tell you?"

Goddard walked away this time, and it occurred to Sycamore that the point of the evasion was to avoid troubling the child with an adult discussion. The girl went back to her search, though Sycamore knew better than to trust that display. He'd eavesdropped on many a grown-up discussion while pretending to peruse some storybook or other. Toy soldiers were also useful for duping adults into believing a child was distracted by play.

"If Jerome is helping himself to breakfast," Goddard said, "that tells me Beardsley's darling boy has overspent his allowance again and is scrounging meals from one end of Mayfair to the other."

"Tavistock says Jerome has plans to marry Jeanette." About which possibility, the young marquess was properly alarmed.

Goddard watched the girl searching through the grass. "Jeanette's choices regarding remarriage are none of my affair, provided they are choices freely made. Her ladyship does not take kindly to meddling, in case you haven't noticed."

"What I have noticed is that it's not meddling if you're family, and you are the only person to claim that honor in a meaningful sense where Jeanette is concerned. For God's sake, rescue her from Jerome's schemes."

Goddard took a seat on a wooden bench. "I haven't the means to aid her, Dorning. She's better off if I keep my distance."

Of all the twaddling nonsense. "*You are her brother*. Either fulfill the honors of that office, or get to your feet so I can draw your cork."

Goddard remained sitting on his rosy arse. "Cease your histrionics, Dorning. There's a child present. I am Jeanette's only family, true, but others have the more pressing claim on my resources. Jeanette is an adult. This offer from Jerome is not a scheme of recent provenance, and viewed from a certain perspective, it makes sense."

Sycamore hauled Goddard to his feet by virtue of a secure grip on the man's neckcloth. "You bloody liar. You knew what Jerome was about, and that's why you had Jeanette followed. You didn't want him making off with her and heading to Scotland."

"Language, Dorning. I didn't lie, I dissembled in the interests of taking your measure. There was also the possibility Jerome might have attempted to force his attentions on Jeanette and chivvy her to the altar that way. He wouldn't pull a stunt like that in Trevor's house, but in the mews, or in the carriage itself, I did not trust him. Now you have equipped Jeanette with knives, and we must conclude she can take care of herself."

Because there *was* a child present, and because Sycamore did not have time to administer a proper thrashing to Goddard, he instead made his words count.

"I do not take you for a coward, Goddard. What the hell stays your hand from more obvious measures?"

Goddard's smile was bitter. "Do you know the power of gossip, Dorning?"

"Of course. My club rises and falls on that very tide." A problem Sycamore had been pondering lately with increasing focus.

"Your club..." Goddard nearly sneered the words. "A profitable venture all but handed to you, the maintenance of which consists of idling away your evenings, while Mayfair's finest toss money at one another for their own amusement. The Vincent family's propensity for talk can add enough fuel to the flames of army gossip to see me destroyed."

Goddard's town house was modest but well maintained, his garden a small luxury. The child was healthy and well fed, and Goddard's attire was that of a man of means.

"Destroyed, how?"

"We have already discussed this. All it takes is whispers, Dorning. A snide comment here, a little innuendo over dinner at the club, and the fellows at Horse Guards aren't so keen to include you in their card games. You become a pariah, and then your business begins to sour. I have weathered the storm several times and the last gale nearly ruined me. Then, I thought the talk had finally stopped for good but now I'm hearing rumors again. For the sake of my dependents, I must keep to myself and hope the worst is behind me. Jeanette will manage. She always has."

An odd calm settled over Sycamore, because in Goddard's situation, he could see a familiar pattern.

"This isn't how it's supposed to be, Goddard, where you don't speak to your only sibling, keep a niece hidden from her, and try to manage all on your own. We have family for good reasons. We make more family as we go on, and that's for good reasons too. Jeanette might have helped you weather that storm, but you didn't give her the chance."

The child rose and scampered to a different patch of grass, flopping to the ground without a care for her snow-white pinafore. Her hair had reddish highlights, and something about her bony little knees struck Sycamore as another family trait.

"The child is not my niece," Goddard said. "Dornings might grow family like topsy, but Jeanette and I... Jeanette knows how to take care of herself. It's what she does best. I had no business having her followed, but I do not trust Jerome."

Sycamore clasped his hands behind his back, so great was the urge to plant Goddard a facer. "Jeanette has been taking care of everybody else since she was a girl. She married to see that you had your commission and to keep your father out of debtors' prison. She took on the raising of the present marquess lest he turn into the same sort of monster as his father. She endured her husband's pawing and disrespect because she sensed he was a fragile and shallow man. She tacitly manages young Tavistock's funds because Uncle Beardsley hasn't the knack."

Sycamore stepped closer, lest Goddard think to saunter off again. "*Of course Jeanette takes care of herself, because she can't trust her worthless menfolk to help her with the perishing job.*"

And when Sycamore had tried to appoint himself to the role of protector…? She'd collected her things and told him to go play with his knives.

A great weight lifted from his shoulders as insight took its place. He was still worried nearly witless about Jeanette's situation, but he was no longer worried that she cared nothing for him. She cared for him, cared for him *a very great deal.*

Enough to protect him, enough to put herself in harm's way for his sake.

Sycamore strode down the walk until he came to the patch of grass. He sank onto his knees beside the child and waited for her to stop searching long enough to treat him to another serious inspection.

"Cousin Rye doesn't like you, sir."

"Cousin Rye is having a bad day, as grouchy old fellows sometimes do. I'm Sycamore." *Cousin Sycamore* would have been an improvement, but with children, only the literal truth would do.

"I'm Nettie. I'm looking for a lucky clover to give to Cousin Rye."

"You are very intent on your mission. I need to borrow your cousin for a couple of hours, but I promise I'll return him in one piece."

Goddard watched this exchange with the banked wariness of a wild beast, ready to pounce at the least hint of harm to his cub.

Nettie sprang to her feet, nimble as a baby goat, and hugged Goddard about the waist. "*Au revoir*, Cousin. I will find you a lucky clover the next time I visit."

Goddard caught her up in a hug. "Be good for *Tante Lucille*, Nettie. If the weather holds, nurse will take you for an ice on your way home."

"I will be perfect," Nettie said, squeezing Goddard about the neck. "Better than perfect. You will see, Cousin!" She skipped away and disappeared into the house, while Sycamore kept to himself entire lectures about perfect little girls who felt it incumbent to find their menfolk some luck.

"Why this urgency, Dorning?" Goddard asked as Sycamore led him through the garden gate and into the alley. "Why intrude into Jeanette's affairs when she obviously gave you your congé?"

"Jeanette has not given me my congé. Just the opposite." This visit with Goddard had clarified that much, which was an enormous relief. "She put a challenge before me, though she won't see it like that."

"What the hell does that mean?"

"Jeanette has added me to the collection of men whom she feels she must protect. I am honored to have her devotion, but I must take issue with how she expresses her regard for me. Come along, Goddard. We are off to pay a call on the estimable and insufferable Worth Kettering."

CHAPTER THIRTEEN

The note came one week after Jeanette had recovered from her bout of food poisoning.

Now will you leave?

Four words that created something of a puzzle, considering that Jeanette had agreed to marry Jerome. The prospect was distasteful, though Jerome was amenable to a platonic union. Why would Viola, or Beardsley, or the pair of them still try to drive her off when she'd expressed a willingness to capitulate to their schemes?

"Will there be anything else, my lady?" Peem asked, hesitating by the sideboard.

"No, thank you, Peem."

He bowed and withdrew from the breakfast parlor, his gait stately. Jeanette had hired two more footmen and a lady's companion, but that staff would not take up their duties until the end of the week. She was safe until she married Jerome, and then she would, by arrangement with her intended, withdraw to the dower house.

Far from Beardsley, Viola, petty gossips... and the terrible temptation Sycamore Dorning presented.

Then too, Jerome lacked the old marquess's bitterness, but he had enough of his late lordship's mannerisms and appearance that Jeanette could never dwell comfortably under the same roof with him.

So she would flee to the shires and hope that her fortune was the only price she was made to pay for dwelling in obscurity. Her fortune, and her heart.

Jeanette no longer ate eggs when she broke her fast. She locked her sitting room and bedroom doors every night before retiring. She refused all invitations. The excuse of record was a spring cold, but she'd also taken to practicing with her knives when the alley was deserted. Until the settlements were signed, she wasn't safe.

And thus Sycamore Dorning was not safe.

"Pardon me, my lady," Peem said, returning to the breakfast parlor. "You have visitors. Lord and Lady Beardsley await you in the family parlor with Mr. Jerome Vincent."

Beardsley had worked quickly, but then, he was motivated by money. "I'll be along in a moment. Thank you, Peem."

Jeanette waited until Peem had withdrawn to examine her appearance in the window's reflection. She was no longer the timid bride she'd been, no longer the retiring widow.

She was also no longer Sycamore Dorning's lover, her signal regret. She brushed her hand over the pocket where she'd sheathed her knife, spared a final sigh for a man who deserved better, and made her way to the family parlor.

"My lord, my lady, welcome. Jerome, good day." She curtseyed to her guests, though as soon as she officially accepted Jerome's suit, they would not be her guests. She would become the interloper at Tavistock House, and Trevor would assume the last of her authority here.

Somewhere beneath duty, expedience, common sense, and the other imperatives of responsible adulthood, a part of Jeanette quietly grieved.

I do not want to leave a home I've made comfortable, if not exactly welcoming.

I do not want to dwell so far from my only brother, even if he never wants to see me.

I do not want to marry a strutting fopling—Sycamore's word—whose promise to leave me in peace is entirely unenforceable.

Most of all, she did not want to leave Sycamore, who must think very badly of her indeed.

"The tray will be here in a moment," she said, gesturing to the sofa. "Please do have a seat. Viola, how is Diana managing?"

"Diana is quite well," Voila said, taking Jeanette's favorite wing chair, "and serenely awaiting the honor of her presentation. Jerome, stop pacing."

Jerome sank into the second wing chair, leaving Jeanette to take a love seat rather than share the sofa with Beardsley, though his lordship was apparently inclined to remain on his feet.

"We can dispense with the tray," Beardsley said. "When Jerome told me you'd agreed to his suit, I directed the solicitors to draw up the settlements posthaste. I have the final documents with me, and Jerome has applied for the special license. This whole business can be resolved within the next week. You, my lady, will remove your effects from the marchioness's suite so that Viola can take over the duties of hostess here, and—"

"Papa," Jerome said, "that is not what we discussed."

"Don't interrupt your father," Viola chided. "And we most certainly will not dispense with the tea tray, my lord. The trip into Town was dusty, and I am parched."

A portrait of the late marquess scowled down from over the mantel, and he seemed to be sneering directly at Jeanette. The role of passive victim was hers for the taking once more.

As Jerome and his parents fell to bickering—Jerome had expected to move into Tavistock House with Trevor, no parents allowed—Jeanette gained a new appreciation for Sycamore's familial exasperations. His family would fill the parlor and the adjoining music room to overflowing, with a few left over to wander the library.

And he cared for them all, as they must inevitably care for him.

Peem wheeled in a trolley, which occasioned a ceasefire among the verbal skirmishers. He set the tea tray before Viola rather than Jeanette, then seemed to realize that Jeanette was not in her usual chair.

"I do beg your pardon, my lady," he said, returning the tray to the cart. "Shall I pour?"

"We've no need for any damned tea," Beardsley snapped. "Be off with you, Peem, and close the door behind you."

Peem straightened slowly, glanced pointedly at the portrait over the mantel and then at Jeanette.

"You may be excused," she said, somewhat surprised at the show of deference. Peem underscored his display of loyalty by leaving the door open.

"Mama and the girls should certainly bide here from time to time," Jerome said, "but it's Tav's house, not ours, and we can't just move in like a lot of beggars descending on a wealthy uncle."

"Jerome, mind your tongue," Viola muttered.

"Lord Tavistock remains my legal ward for the next three years," Beardsley retorted. "He has nothing to say to it, and he should enjoy having his family about him. Jeanette has been lady of the manor quite long enough."

"I am the Marchioness of Tavistock," Jeanette said, wanting these people out of her house, "and until such time as I become Mrs. Jerome Vincent, Society will expect me to be treated as such."

Viola sent her a brooding look. "A valid point, and for that matter, a special license has an aroma of unseemly haste about it. Nothing must be allowed to detract from the notice that Diana is due in her debut Season, perhaps her only Season."

And they were off again, debating the special license, to which Jerome, oddly, was also opposed.

Jeanette let them bicker, because this was surely nothing more than a foretaste of what she'd endure on those occasions when they trotted her out for the sake of appearances. Every other year at

Christmas, perhaps, or when the granddaughters made their come outs.

Resignation to that fate ought to have been a matter of long habit. The respite of widowhood could not last forever. Nothing sweet, comforting, or dear lasted forever, after all.

"Jeanette will sign the damned documents and be married to Jerome by this time next week." Beardsley hadn't raised his voice, but in the very coldness of his tone, he'd sounded exactly like his deceased older brother.

The effect on Viola and Jerome was interesting. They looked to each other, mother and son united in rare commiseration.

"I will read the settlements," Jeanette said. "Jerome and I discussed precise terms, and I want to ensure that those terms are reflected accurately." Even the old marquess had cautioned her never to sign a document she hadn't read, his caution taking the form of tiresomely repetitious sermons.

"You will sign the documents," Beardsley said. "They say what I want them to say, and that is all that matters."

Jerome, the traitor, was absorbed with a study of the gleaming andirons, while Viola had decided to plumb her reticule for heaven knew what.

"I will read the documents," Jeanette said, "lest I enter a bargain in ignorance of its terms and thus render the agreement unenforceable."

"Papa, I told you she would never—" Jerome began, only to be cut off by his father slashing a hand through the air.

Beardsley produced a sheaf of papers bound up with a red ribbon and waved them at Jeanette.

"You will take these to the library and sign them now. You will threaten me with no lawsuits, my lady. No consultations with the solicitors, no marginalia or hasty amendments. Your brother has been teetering on the brink of ruin for years. The rumors regarding his treasonous misdeeds never go entirely silent, and I can ensure they never do. If that doesn't motivate you to see reason, I will set about destroying the Coventry for good measure."

And there it was, the loaded gun pointed directly at Sycamore Dorning's happiness, and ultimately at the social standing and financial security of the whole Dorning family.

Jeanette rose and took the rolled-up documents from Beardsley, though her knees had gone weak, and she felt again as if she'd eaten bad mushrooms. Peem had at some point slipped back into the room and stood near the door, looking pained and elderly.

"You *slandered* Orion?" Jeanette asked, pacing away from Beardsley. She had known that Sycamore's enterprise was in jeopardy, but that Orion had already become a target for her in-laws ambushed her resolve.

Beardsley's smile was smug. "Viola gave me the idea. She was grumbling about his lack of consequence, about him being in trade, about his departure from the military being under a cloud, else he might have been among the escorts standing up with his nieces by marriage. He's not bad looking, in Viola's opinion, but he was very nearly bad *ton*. For me to nudge him a few steps farther along the path to disgrace was the work of a moment and only reignited the glowing embers of old scandal. Nobody would ever attribute to jovial Lord Beardsley anything approaching a nefarious motive."

Jerome was on his feet. "Papa, that's not something a fellow ought to—"

"Hush," Viola said. "Goddard weathers periodic talk adequately."

Had Viola helped Orion weather that talk? Put in a quiet good word for him despite Beardsley's campaign? Or had she fanned the flames?

"My lady," Peem began.

"Not now." Ire gave Jeanette's voice an uncharacteristic edge as she rounded on Beardsley. "You have defamed my brother, or as good as. You are clearly much of the reason he and I have remained estranged. He is my only brother, and you..." She fell silent as Beardsley regarded her with patient bemusement. "Why? Why do that to a man who hasn't harmed you in any way?"

Though if his lordship would attack Orion, he'd not hesitate to ruin the Coventry.

Beardsley waved a hand in another gesture the late marquess had favored. "You are easier to manage without a meddlesome brother to encourage your headstrong tendencies. Goddard's own fellow officers don't speak well of him, and haven't for years. Then too, dashing Uncle Rye was the war hero in Trevor's eyes. I didn't care for that."

Jeanette crossed the room to stand toe-to-toe with Beardsley. "Now you think you can get your hands on my fortune, run tame in Trevor's house, and steer him to the bride of your choice by threatening my brother all over again?"

"No," Beardsley said, his gaze running over her in a manner that made her flesh crawl. "Goddard has learned his lesson, tending to his vineyards and keeping to the social shadows. I'll remind you of your place by destroying the Coventry. The Dornings are notably impecunious, with that club as their sole means of avoiding cash shortages and other emergencies. If I can wreck that one venture, I imperil the whole family. And a rumor of crooked tables is enough to close the Coventry's doors."

Jeanette felt again the sense of the late marquess sneering at her, while Jerome would not meet her gaze, and Viola's expression was unreadable. Beardsley's scheming was precisely what she'd predicted, but the arrogance with which he owned his plans took her aback.

"My lady," Peem said, "you have callers."

"Send them away," Beardsley retorted. "Her ladyship is not receiving and will be indisposed until such time as she speaks her vows."

Jeanette wanted to shred the damned settlement agreements to bits. She wanted to lay about with the fireplace poker. She had accepted that the Vincent family meant to get their hands on her money, accepted that she had become a liability to Sycamore and might well have to tolerate Jerome as a husband.

But she had sorely underestimated Beardsley's capacity for sheer evil, and that blunder frightened her badly. *Sycamore, I was wrong. I was so very wrong.*

"Her ladyship has documents to sign," Beardsley said, leaning closer. "Fetch her pen and ink, Peem."

Peem slipped out the door as Jeanette realized that Beardsley even wore the same cloying, bay-and-clove scent his late brother had. That scent brought with it memories of staring at the floor while being lectured, staring at the bed canopy while praying for dawn, staring at a mirror that reflected a frightened young girl where a new marchioness ought to have been.

Jeanette pushed the memories aside and tried desperately to think. She'd miscalculated. She was without allies and signing the documents could well be the same as signing her own death warrant.

"Beardsley, I am barren," Jeanette said. "You cannot think to marry your only son to me."

Beardsley grabbed her wrist. "Sign the damned documents, Jeanette. I have had quite enough of your meddling with the solicitors, keeping Trevor in leading strings, and hoarding wealth you never earned."

Jeanette tried to wrest free, which sent the papers careening from her grasp, and gave Beardsley the leverage he needed to jerk her arm over her head.

"Behave," he snarled, "or you will wish you had."

"Papa," Jerome began, "a gentleman doesn't… That is to say—"

A whisper as soft as a night breeze was Jeanette's only warning, and then her hand was free.

"Bad manners," Sycamore said, pausing in the doorway. "Very bad manners to treat a lady thus, Lord Beardsley, for shame. Marchioness, good day. Sorry about the portrait, but the frame can be repaired."

A knife protruded from the frame of the portrait over the mantel, Beardsley's sleeve held fast until he jerked the blade loose and tossed the knife to the floor.

"What manner of barbarian throws a knife at an unarmed man?" Beardsley shot back. "Peem, summon the footmen to eject this scoundrel."

Trevor slipped into the room, followed by *Orion*. "Uncle," Trevor said, "this is not your house. God willing, it never will be. Peem, you may leave us. Mr. Dorning has matters in hand."

Peem melted away without so much as a bow.

Sycamore snatched his knife from the floor and slipped it into his boot. "If you were intent on a family gathering, Vincent, you should have at least included Lord Tavistock and Sir Orion. I am here at the lady's sufferance, but I doubt she will object to my call."

"I do not object," Jeanette said, sinking onto the sofa. "I do not object in the slightest."

SYCAMORE HAD NOT SEEN this parlor previously, and he took a moment to study the portrait over the mantel. The marquess had been a good-looking devil, sharing with both Trevor and Jerome flowing blond locks, a somewhat prominent nose, and a certain cast to his brow. Trevor was taller and leaner than his father had been, while Jerome had a rounder chin, though the family resemblance was strong.

Beardsley had inherited the blond hair and the nose, but the resemblance between Trevor and Jerome was closer than that between Beardsley and his late older brother. Another rendering of the marquess hung between the windows, this time with a brace of hounds at his feet and an open blunderbuss cradled over his arm.

What a bloody perishing bore he'd been, even when pictured at his recreations.

"My lady, you really must redecorate," Sycamore said. "The sight of your oppressor glaring down from two walls shades into martyrdom. You have paid a high enough price for your marital heroics."

Jeanette rubbed her wrist and looked at a coil of papers on the carpet as if it were the pantry mouser's latest accident.

"Beardsley set out to destroy the remains of Orion's reputation," she said. "I married into this family thinking to solve my brother's problems, and all I did was make them worse."

"Don't say that," Goddard retorted. "I was desperate to buy my colors, and the family business will come right eventually. Then too, since mustering out, my reputation has never been what I'd wish it was. Beardsley, name your seconds."

"And don't," Sycamore said, "think to involve the lads. Their loyalties are divided, and besides, Jeanette wouldn't allow them to indulge in such nonsense."

Trevor stood next to Jerome before the hearth. While Jerome was clearly aquiver to involve himself in his first affair of honor, Trevor's distaste was plain on his handsome face. Had Sycamore not known better, he would have said that Trevor was the elder of the two, for he was certainly the wiser.

But then, younger siblings seldom enjoyed the respect they were due.

"No duels," Viola Vincent said. "Please, no duels. Diana and Hera cannot in any way be associated—"

"Madam," Sycamore interjected, taking the place beside Jeanette on the sofa, "putting aside the issue of Sir Orion's social standing, Lord Beardsley was also just now on the point of extorting Jeanette's widow's portion from her as well as her personal freedom. Unless I miss my guess, Diana's come out is part of the reason Beardsley felt justified in his larceny."

Trevor propped an elbow on the mantel. "We cannot have my uncles dueling, Mr. Dorning. These things never stay quiet for long. Moreover, Uncle Beardsley would lose, and he might be a scoundrel and a halfwit, but he's still my uncle."

Beside Sycamore, Jeanette was as still and quiet as a garden saint. "My lady," Sycamore said, covering her hand with his, "what say you? Will you *permit* your brother to seek satisfaction? Will you *allow* him to put a bullet between Beardsley's eyes? A quick end would be kinder than transportation or the gallows, if you want my opinion."

Jeanette's fingers were as cold as her composure, though Sycamore knew her calm for the well-rehearsed act it was. The words *permit* and *allow* earned him her regard. She gazed at him steadily, her thoughts unfathomable.

The old marquess had taught her that trick, how to hide in plain sight, how to become a sphinx in marchioness's clothing, but what had been learned could be unlearned.

"No duels," Jeanette said. "No duels, no transportation, no gallows."

"Of course not," Beardsley retorted, "because all I've done is repeat a little ancient gossip where Goddard is concerned and try to effectuate a marriage between family members when Jeanette has nobody to speak for her."

Oh, the fool. The hopeless, yammering fool.

"I can speak for myself," Jeanette said, "and Mr. Dorning doubtless has the right of it. You are approaching dun territory, Beardsley, with two more daughters to launch, a son headed for the sponging house, a wife determined to maintain appearances, and not one whit of financial self-discipline to your name. You launched your campaign against me rather than moderate your lifestyle, and now you have dragged your loved ones to the brink of real scandal."

"If intimidating a widow, setting ruffians on a nephew, and lying about an in-law isn't scandalous," Sycamore said, "I don't know what is."

"Jerome must marry," Beardsley said, "and Jeanette never provided the sons Tavistock was due. Why should she keep every penny of those settlements for herself when she hardly entertains, has no intention of remarrying, and has no daughters to support?"

"Papa," Jerome said, "I don't want to marry Jeanette. Jeanette is a fine lady and all, but she's... I would make her a miserable husband.

She already put up with the old martinet for years, and why didn't you tell me we were in trouble?"

"Why not tell me?" Jeanette retorted. "Why not give me the chance to take more of a role in the girls' situation? I am still the rubbishing marchioness. I've made more than one match, and I know well the perils of a poor choice."

"You?" Beardsley's dismay was palpable in a single syllable. "Involve yourself with my finances? You're a woman."

Viola had aged a decade in the course of this conversation. She gathered up her reticule and scooted to the edge of her seat. "We should be going. I trust all and sundry will forget this unfortunate meeting ever occurred. Jerome, your hand, please."

Sycamore rose and scooped up the papers from the floor. "Nobody is going anywhere until we resolve the little matter of felony attempts to kidnap his lordship—two attempts, if I'm not mistaken."

"Kidnap me?" Trevor straightened. "*Kidnap* me?"

"For ransom, I gather?" Jeanette's gaze on Beardsley narrowed. "The street toughs who set upon you when you were alone or in your cups. Jerome knew your schedule, and Beardsley apparently was in Jerome's confidence."

"Papa," Jerome expostulated, "is this true? You had your own nephew set upon by rogues? Are you out of your mind?"

"He's out of money," Sycamore said. "For some younger sons, that does equate to a loss of wits."

"You can't prove anything," Beardsley said. "London's streets aren't safe, and Tavistock was in the wrong place at the wrong time."

"There," Goddard said, "you would be wrong. I keep some interesting company, Beardsley, as does Mr. Dorning's brother-in-law Worth Kettering. Between our various minions and their friends, we know exactly how much you paid to see Tavistock spirited away. The criminals you hired were smart enough not to take anything from Tavistock's person and not to forcibly make off with a peer, though they did keep *your* money, didn't they?"

Jeanette was on her feet. "You couldn't content yourself with menacing my brother and Mr. Dorning's sole livelihood, you had to go after my step-son? That young man,"—she waved a hand at Trevor —"is among the most decent and honorable people I know, and you thought to steal from him and me both. I should let Mr. Dorning and each of his brothers go ten rounds with you at Jackson's."

Ah, there was the glimmer of the true Jeanette that gave a man hope. "Tavistock deserves first crack," Sycamore said. "Head of the family and all that. I suspect Goddard might want to teach the old man a few lessons as well, and I wouldn't mind having a go at him."

Lady Viola should probably have been invited to join the queue as well.

"*I* want a go at him," Jeanette said. "What I don't understand are the notes. Were you just trying to frighten me, Beardsley? Were you planning to have me kidnapped on the Great North Road and held for ransom?"

Viola shrank back into her wing chair. "I sent the notes. I wanted you away from Town because I knew Beardsley was up to something. The modistes were humoring me, pretending to take an order for Diana's carriage dress, then never delivering it. I knew the situation was growing dire. Beardsley has a temper, though he usually guards it well. I did not want that temper turning in your direction, Jeanette."

Jeanette resumed her seat beside Sycamore. "You don't even like me. Why protect me like that?"

Trevor and Jerome both turned at the same moment to regard Viola. Whether it was the angle of their heads, the shared look of expectation, or the resemblance to the nincompoop in the portrait, an explanation for Viola's behavior popped into Sycamore's head.

"Viola's conscience is guilty," he said. "She had the one thing you, Jeanette, could not produce. She had the old marquess's son."

A silence stretched, broken by the jingle of the harness on a passing gig.

"I do not understand," Jeanette said as Trevor and Jerome turned speculative gazes on each other. "Somebody explain this to me."

Beardsley dropped onto the love seat, while Viola clutched her reticule in her lap and said nothing.

"It's all right, Viola," Beardsley said tiredly. "I've known all along, and when Dorning is underfoot, there is apparently no keeping secrets in this family. You have nothing to be ashamed of. It was my idea."

Sycamore's aim in confronting Beardsley had been to win Jeanette free of a coerced marriage and stop the plundering of her financial security. Honor demanded that much of him, and love demanded that he then leave Jeanette free to enjoy her life as she saw fit.

That she chose that moment to reach for his hand was thus a fierce and dear consolation. "Explain yourselves," Sycamore said, closing his fingers around Jeanette's. "Her ladyship and the young men are due the truth. You are family, after all, and you owe each other that much."

Jeanette shifted closer. "You heard Mr. Dorning. Somebody start talking, and don't think to dissemble, or there will be consequences that make ten rounds at Jackson's seem like a toddle in the park."

JEANETTE KNEW TWO THINGS.

First, she had had a very narrow escape. Her signature on a lot of legal papers would have created a tangled web of binding obligations that even Sycamore's ferocious determination would have been hard put to cut through.

Second, she should have married Sycamore when she'd had the chance. He'd sensed the complications swirling around her, when all she'd seen was Beardsley's need for coin and *one* of his plans to extract it from her. Attempted kidnappings, Viola's notes, legitimate bastards... Jeanette had had no clue how complicated the tangled web had grown and still did not entirely grasp the details.

"The late marquess had a certain gruff charm," Viola said. "Or he did twenty-odd years ago. He'd been married for years by that point. His wife was in good health, and they'd had no children. I was fertile. If the Vincent family knew nothing else about me by then, they knew I was fertile."

"You were also lonely," Beardsley said, "and your consequence married to me was far less than you'd envisioned. My brother put the scheme to me, and I told him that as long as no force was involved, I was amenable. He was willing to persist with the affair until a boy child resulted."

Sycamore's hand was warm in Jeanette's grasp, his voice was arctic. "How much did the marquess offer you for the privilege of seducing your wife?"

Beardsley gazed at Jerome. "Ten thousand pounds, which pulled me from the River Tick for a few years. Tavistock never once offered to take on the burden of my debts himself. I suspect he allowed my problems to mount precisely to facilitate his scheme with Viola."

"The scheme," Viola said dryly, "was obvious to me only in hindsight. Tavistock's marriage was a disappointment to him. He confided in me, he praised my daughters, he praised *me* for my maternal devotion. He lamented that the one thing he sought in life had been denied him, but hinted broadly that I, as the lovely wife of the Vincent family spare, could grant him that boon."

"You were manipulated by a pair of schemers," Sycamore said, sparing Jeanette the admission.

Pity for Viola was as unwelcome as it was inevitable. She'd been young, a neglected wife, an overburdened mother, and the late marquess had offered her the means to revenge every slight and indignity while calling her actions a noble sacrifice.

"Tavistock would not relent," Viola said, "and I well knew Beardsley was playing me false by then—had been from the first year of our marriage. I was angry, lonely, and not getting any younger. I did care for Tavistock, and I hope in some regard, he cared for me."

Jeanette doubted that, but kept her peace. Viola had been used, and then she'd had to watch as Tavistock later fathered the boy who'd depose Viola's son as heir to the title. Used, cast aside, and left to believe that she'd betrayed the husband who'd set her up to be seduced.

"Tavistock established a trust for Jerome," Viola said. "Modest, but something. That trust gave my son a gentleman's education and has been his sole support in recent years."

"I thought I had a great-auntie," Jerome said, sinking into a wing chair. "I thought... I don't know what I thought."

"I thought you were my cousin," Trevor said, looking bemused. "Appears that's not the whole story."

"I thought the Vincents were my family," Jeanette said. "I thought my own brother had willingly turned his back on me, that my husband had no spare of the body, that Beardsley was a benign if negligent guardian to my step-son. I believed a parcel of lies, and if there are any more untruths to be aired, please air them now."

Jeanette could make that demand because Sycamore sat beside her, holding her hand and exuding a brisk pragmatism in the face of family upheaval.

"Well, I certainly don't want to marry you," Jerome said. "Another one of Papa's—I mean, Lord Beardsley's—schemes. Meaning no offense, such a marriage would be distasteful in light of present disclosures."

"Orion?" Jeanette said, regarding her brother. "What do you want? Beardsley wronged you, and you have suffered much as a result."

"The deepest hurt," Rye said, his smile a ghost of his old ebullience, "was that you thought I had shunned you willingly. I honestly don't know why my fellow officers hold me in such contempt, but they do, and Beardsley's whispering campaign ensures they will for some time to come. My objective, Jeanette, has been to preserve the family legacy in France, so I can bequeath that to you as some sort of reparation for all the sacrifices you made for me."

Sycamore passed Jeanette a handkerchief, though he remained

silent. That wasn't like him, to sit back and watch, but even a silent Sycamore fortified her.

"I don't want a lot of perishing grapes, Rye. I want my only sibling." Had Jeanette not had an audience, she would have presumed so far as to hug her brother. "You will call upon me next week, please."

Sycamore sent Rye a look that glance held daring and reassurance both. Equal parts *don't let me down* and *I won't abandon you.* Jeanette had let Sycamore down *and* abandoned him, which had her dabbing at her eyes and tucking his handkerchief away.

"I will call upon you tomorrow," Rye said. "What shall we do with Beardsley?"

Jeanette did not care what became of Beardsley, provided he never troubled her again.

"We could send him to the dower house," Trevor said, "except I intend to sign that over to you, Jeanette. If you don't want to spend your dotage in Derbyshire, you can sell the damned place. The estate is self-supporting and would bring you considerable coin."

Jeanette regarded the tall young man lounging by the mantel. "You have been paying attention."

He shot his cuffs. "I read the reports. Can't allow you to have all the fun."

"You've been hanging back regarding the finances?" she asked. "Allowing me free rein and pretending you had no interest?"

Trevor pushed away from the mantel and went to the sideboard. "When I bungled so badly at last year's house party, I had a talk with myself. What the hell sort of marquess won't turn his hand to either university studies or his own affairs? I saw the Dornings, sons of an earl, taking on the Coventry and making no apologies for it. They have another brother who writes books, one who raises fancy dogs. They figure out how to go on and then sally forth. I was disappointing you. Papa disappointed you. Your brother disappointed you. The trend was lowering. Would anybody care for a drink?"

This little speech both hurt—Trevor had grown up when Jeanette wasn't looking—and comforted. He was already the marquess and a compliment to the peerage.

"A bracer for my nerves," Viola said. "Jeanette, I am sorry. Had I known how far Beardsley was blundering from decency, I would have done more than have Peem slip you a few notes."

Sycamore accepted a drink from Trevor and passed it to Jeanette. "What of the food poisoning?" Sycamore asked. "Was that your doing?"

Orion accepted a drink as well, and seemed content to hold his peace—for now.

"The mushrooms were a mistake," Viola said. "A very serious mistake, for which I abjectly apologize. I wanted Jeanette to leave London and grew too desperate in my schemes, though the worst she would suffer as a profound bellyache. If Trevor could be talked into marrying one of his cousins, then Beardsley's schemes for Jerome and Jeanette would become unnecessary. Trevor would never allow his wife's family—his own cousins, aunt, and uncle—to come to financial grief."

Jeanette sipped her brandy, finding it nearly as good as what Sycamore served at the club. "You could have simply asked me for help, or asked Trevor. You did not need to skulk about, either one of you."

They could have done as Sycamore had—as Jeanette had never done—and confronted family difficulties with equal parts goodwill and blunt courage.

"And you," Beardsley said, "would have put me on an allowance, would have seen two of my daughters wearing the same presentation gown, would have seen Viola shamed by economies."

Sycamore shook his head when offered a drink. "Pimping your wife to your brother rather appropriated the lion's share of the shame, Vincent. How do you intend to make amends to the multitude of parties you've wronged?"

And that was why Jeanette loved Sycamore Dorning. Because he was honest with himself and others, because he faced life squarely and took the path of truth when others wilted at such a prospect. Because he worried about those he cared for. He loved passionately, and wasn't afraid to be seen holding hands with a woman who desperately needed his hand to hold.

"If it's money," Beardsley began, "I would remind you all that my wife and daughters are blameless."

"Viola is far from blameless." Trevor made that statement as he passed Jerome a drink. "And she would have foisted me off on a cousin and considered that a triumph. I will cheerfully dower both of them, Auntie. You had only to ask."

"You could have offered," Viola said, chin coming up.

"His lordship is not even of age," Jeanette retorted. "I could have helped with their dowries too. I could have helped with their presentations, but you, Viola, had to hoard those honors for yourself."

"I can also assist with dowering the young ladies," Sycamore said, "and even dear Uncle Rye might contribute to the family project, but what of Beardsley? He has betrayed his family, from wife and daughters, to nephews—note the plural—to widowed sister-in-law."

Jeanette considered Beardsley, who had no son of his own, no fortune, no real friends, and a marriage that imprisoned the parties far more than it sheltered them. Then too, in a sense, Beardsley had been betrayed by his own brother.

"We could do nothing," she said. "Simply put him on remittance at the family seat."

Trevor wrinkled his nose. "Unacceptable. That is the *family* seat, the staff would show him undue loyalty, and the rest of us would avoid Tavistock Hall to avoid his company."

"The dower house appeals to me," Viola said. "It's remote, but still a family holding. I could retire there once the girls are launched."

Sycamore held his peace, and Jeanette realized why. He was allowing the Vincent-Goddard family to muddle through a problem to its solution. Showing them the way without saying a word.

"What about France?" Trevor said quietly. "I've a mind to learn the vintner's trade. There's money to be made purveying fine wines, and if the colonel could point me in the right direction, I'd happily apply myself to it."

Jerome studied his drink. "Don't suppose you could use company in that endeavor? I'm not stupid, and my French is almost as good as yours, but Papa—Lord Beardsley—was never one for encouraging me into a trade or profession. If you're planning to buy up some vineyards, you could use a fellow to manage them."

"Jeanette?" Orion cocked his head. "Shall we banish Beardsley to France until the last of his flotilla of daughters is launched? I can show the lads the basics of winemaking, though it's an art not learned in a few months. They can keep an eye on Beardsley, and he can live inexpensively while keeping a proper distance from those who don't care to see him."

"And I can do something besides kick up my heels while I'm waiting to come of age," Trevor muttered.

Trevor wanted to go to France, that was clear. Jerome needed to go, and Orion was anxious to make amends by shepherding the young men about the Goddard family vineyards. Viola looked hopeful, and Sycamore would speak up if he objected.

And clearly, he did not object.

What Beardsley wanted... *did not signify*. Jeanette tried to feel some guilt about the conclusion, some compassion, some pity even, but Beardsley hadn't spared anybody else any pity, and neither had his damned brother.

They'd thought only of themselves and their wants, and all around them—Jeanette included—had colluded to allow them their monstrous selfishness.

"France is a solution," Jeanette said slowly. "If Beardsley is accompanied by the colonel, Lord Tavistock, and Jerome, the journey will have the appearance of a family excursion. Nobody should depart until after Diana's presentation."

"Thank you," Viola said, rising. "If that's settled, I will return to Surrey and explain this situation to the girls."

Trevor collected her glass. "You will inform my cousins that their brother is also my brother. Either you tell them, Auntie, or I will. Jerome shouldn't have to have that discussion with them, and we cannot trust Beardsley to handle it."

Viola nodded and spared her husband a glance. "I'll send a trunk to your club, my lord. The girls and I will see you off when you depart for France."

Beardsley rose. "I'll escort you to the coach."

Viola gave him a long, complicated look, then took his arm. They left the parlor in silence, though Jeanette predicted that at some point, a blazing row would take place.

Or maybe not. The Vincents were new to the habit of honesty and, with the exception of Trevor, not a very courageous bunch.

Orion set his empty glass on the sideboard. "If I'm to plan a trip to France, I'd best be on my way. Tavistock, Vincent, expect to travel light, because the Goddard family holdings are scattered in both the north and south of the country, and we will visit them all."

"Should we develop an itinerary?" Trevor asked, brows knitting. "Jeanette will want to know where we bide, and we must find a suitably obscure village in which to deposit Beardsley."

"I know just the village," Orion said. "Run by an order of nuns and abetted by a phalanx of grannies. Let's repair to your club, and we can sketch out our route."

Too late, Jeanette realized that her darling brother and her doting step-son were conspiring to leave her alone with Sycamore. She rose, and Sycamore stood as well.

"I will want that itinerary," she said. "And I will see you off as well."

"Of course," Trevor said, patting her shoulder. "We will not leave without giving you a full accounting of our plans first." He bowed and pulled Jerome by the arm from the room.

"I can't speak for Jerome," Sycamore said, "but heed me on this, Goddard. Tavistock is one of those people who never says much, and thus you assume he's not thinking much. Then he opens his mouth, and you realize he's not only noticed every single detail, he's pondered and parsed the connections you never made. I had hopes for him at the Coventry, but alas, he's off to France."

"A bright lad," Orion said. "He's had the benefit of good examples. Nettie, I will call on you tomorrow."

Do you promise? Jeanette could not quite put that question into words, so she instead hugged her brother for the first time in years.

"We'll talk," he murmured. "I have much to tell you, and we'll talk."

"Come early," Jeanette said. "Please come early." She stepped back, though she never wanted to let him out of her sight again. She did not realize she'd taken Sycamore's hand until he linked arms with her, and they walked Orion to the front door.

When Orion had gone jaunting on his way, Sycamore bowed over Jeanette's hand, kissed her cheek, and followed the others out the door.

CHAPTER FOURTEEN

"You've been invited to supper," Ash said, passing Sycamore a single folded sheet of vellum. "Looks like her ladyship penned it herself."

Sycamore snatched the paper from Ash's grasp. "You *opened* my mail?"

Ash made his way between the club's tables, which were deserted at this midmorning hour. "If she was tossing you over with one of those dreadful letters about fond memories and eternal friendship, you would need somebody to get you drunk."

Sycamore perused the invitation, which had, indeed, been written in Jeanette's tidy hand. "You've received many such letters?" Sycamore sniffed the page, though he knew Ash watched him do it. So bloody what? He was rewarded with a faint whiff of jasmine—and hope.

"I've written a few myself," Ash said, using a hooked device to open a window on the alley side of the club. "Della thinks you should call on her ladyship privately."

"Why?" Sycamore reread the invitation, looking for some clue that it was anything more than a polite gesture to scotch talk.

Ash opened another window. "Because what you have to say to the marchioness requires privacy."

"How can Della know what I have to say to Jeanette—to her ladyship—when I've hardly sorted that out for myself?" A week ago, Sycamore had kissed Jeanette's cheek and left her alone in her foyer. She had been buffeted by multiple betrayals and intrigues. Piling a renewed marriage proposal onto her plate would have seemed... opportunistic, impetuous, ungentlemanly.

Rash and selfish, and those were not attributes Sycamore aspired to.

"You love her," Ash said. "Tell her that."

"I already did. Told her I wanted to marry her, keep her safe, and spend the rest of my life with her, more or less. She wasn't impressed." He'd told her that he cared for her too.

Ash set aside the hook and ambled behind the bar. He poured two glasses of lemonade and brought Sycamore one of them.

"But did you tell her you *love* her? Did you say the words, Sycamore? You are among the bravest men I know, but those three little words, when sincerely offered, make even the stoutest knight quake in his armor."

"I'm brave?" Sycamore did not feel very brave. "I am frustrated, uncertain, and lonely in ways that... If Jeanette refuses me this time, Ash, I can't tell myself she's again protecting me as she protected every dunderheaded male in her family."

"If she turns you down," Ash said, touching his glass to Sycamore's, "she's the dunderhead, and I do not take her ladyship for a dunderhead. Neither does Della."

The lemonade was both tart and sweet, as Jeanette could be. "Della said that?"

"She says you're perfect for each other, and no less authority than our own Lady Casriel concurs. Jacaranda has also been consulted and agrees you and the marchioness would make a fine match."

Three formidable Dorning women had rendered judgment. Not long ago, Sycamore would have brushed aside their pronouncements as so much casual matchmaking. He knew better now. If a woman deigned to offer her considered judgment on a delicate matter, a man of sense listened to her.

"Wish me luck," Sycamore said, setting aside his drink. "I'm off to woo a damsel who has professed an abiding desire to remain independent."

Ash cuffed him on the shoulder. "Which is precisely why you and she are perfect for each other. Give her the words, Sycamore. You are magnificently honest even when those around you wish you'd keep your mouth shut. Don't turn up reticent and retiring on us now, and if the lady accepts, you and I will have a long talk about where I fit into the future of this club."

"You're scarpering on me?" The idea ought to engender panic and bluster, possibly even outrage. The past months had proved that Ash did not need the Coventry, though, and—apparently—the Coventry did not precisely need Ash.

As a brother, Sycamore would always need Ash. As a business partner, he could accept that priorities changed, and sometimes that was a good thing.

Ash affected a severe expression, though his eyes were dancing. "I do not scarper on my siblings."

"We'll talk," Sycamore said. "And please give Della my regards." He went up to the office to retrieve a box, checked his appearance in the cheval mirror, then gathered up hat, gloves, and walking stick and prepared to make a cake of himself.

The fellow who admitted him to the Tavistock town house was young and spry. "Where's Peem?" Sycamore asked.

"Off to Derbyshire, sir. He's taking the dower house in hand. Has family in the Peak and was happy to quit London."

Sycamore passed over his hat and cane and peered past the butler. "I'll announce myself." For there was Jeanette across the foyer, amid big copper pots, a liberal sprinkling of dirt, and several large ferns removed from their pottery containers.

"My lady, good day."

Jeanette popped to her feet and brushed at her skirts. "Mr. Dorning. The hour is early for a social call."

One knee of her long white apron was damp, and dirt streaked both her hem and her cheek. Her hair was in its tidy chignon, but her hands were gloriously dirty.

To Sycamore, she had seldom looked more wonderful. "You're repotting the old guard," he said, stripping off his gloves. "I can help with that. They want room to breathe and grow, but not so much room that they're lonely."

"You did not come here to repot ferns, Mr. Dorning."

Proposing marriage while the butler remained ever so attentively by the front door did struck Sycamore as imprudent.

"I came here to give you the rest of your knives," Sycamore said, "and to see how you're getting on. You want to tell me that you are perfectly capable of managing this job on your own, and you are, of course. How about if we send that helpful fellow for a tray, and I simply keep you company while you muck about?"

"Do you want a tray?"

Sycamore stepped closer. "I want to be private with you on any terms I can finagle, even if that means enduring the pretense of the tea tray. I've missed you abominably."

Finally, a smile. A mere seedling of a smile, but all Jeanette. "Feeney, please excuse us."

The butler bowed and withdrew, bless the fellow.

"Where shall I set these?" Sycamore asked, hefting the knife case.

"May I see them?"

He put the box down on a windowsill. "If you see them, you will want to throw them, and you can't leave these poor fellows lying about with roots exposed for all the world to see. How are you, my lady?"

She surveyed the foyer, which bore the fecund scents of dirt and greenery. "I felt guilty every time I came in my own door. I imagined the ferns chiding me for my neglect of them, and nobody calls at such an early hour."

"Friends call at such an early hour," Sycamore said, unbuttoning his coat. "Friends who need not stand on ceremony. I have your dinner invitation. Is that how we're to go forward now, Jeanette? An occasional quadrille, all smiles when we encounter each other in the park, and nothing more?"

He draped his coat over the bannister of the curved stairway, slipped his sleeve buttons into a pocket, and turned back his cuffs. Jeanette hadn't made much progress with her project, but she'd nearly left it too late. Each of the plants showed yellowing foliage, and an abundance of tangled roots conformed to the shape of the old pots.

"I will happily offer you an occasional quadrille or a smile in the park," Jeanette said, "but I had hoped to offer you a proposition. That invitation was for a private dinner, Mr. Dorning."

Sycamore did not want another perishing proposition from her. He knelt among the ferns and chose the largest of the lot.

"You got to this fellow just in time," he said, gently brushing dirt away from the roots. "When the roots in the center go weak, you know the plant's in distress. He's still managing, but it's a near thing. Were you thinking to divide your ferns or simply repot them?"

"I was thinking to offer you one slightly used marchioness," Jeanette said, coming down beside him. "I was wrong, Sycamore. I should not have tried to manage Beardsley, Jerome, and Viola on my own. I wanted to protect you, Orion, and Tavistock, but I was not thinking clearly."

Sycamore pried patiently at tightly bound roots, an operation that took all of his focus when Jeanette was kneeling at his side. He detected her jasmine fragrance blending with the earthy scent of the ferns, his new favorite perfume.

"The business wants patience," he said, untangling roots, "or you do more harm than good. My father claimed the plants preferred to be transplanted at night under a new moon, but how is one to see in such limited light?"

He fell silent lest he descend into outright babbling. The collective fraternal chorus in his head was shouting at him to tell Jeanette he loved her, but listening to what she had to say mattered more.

"I did not want you involved in my messes," Jeanette said. "I did not want Beardsley to have an excuse to go after you and your club. He threatened to, before you arrived."

"We should have sent him to darkest Peru," Sycamore muttered, gently peeling the fern into two halves. Dirt showered the marble floor, and not a little of it got onto Sycamore's breeches. "When does the great French exodus take place?"

"A fortnight hence. About my proposition?"

He set aside the two halves of the plant and sat back on his heels. "I don't care to be propositioned, Jeanette." Not a statement he could have made before he'd started courting her.

"You offered me marriage once." Jeanette made the observation quietly, very much on her dignity.

"I realize you don't want to be married, that the old marquess was a horror, the Vincents an embarrassment to the concept of family, and Goddard a less than exemplary brother, but, Jeanette..."

"Yes?"

Tell her you love her. "I have been wrestling with a question of logic," Sycamore said, dusting the dirt from his hands. "Though my family does not account me a very logical fellow."

"You are logical," Jeanette said, arranging her skirts to sit tailor-fashion on the floor. "You are frightfully good at seeing logic that eludes others."

"I'm not feeling very logical at present, but here is my conundrum. You sent me on my way because you sought to protect me from Beardsley. I understand that and thank you for it, but why was I not permitted to protect you as well? All I wanted—all I needed and asked for—was the chance to keep safe the woman I love to distraction, to have the right to face your battles with you, and yet, you banished me. I was left to make shift with half measures taken from the periphery."

He moved to sit beside her, resting his back against the wall and his wrists on his bent knees, when he wanted desperately to take Jeanette's hand. More half measures.

"You can protect me," he went on, "but I cannot protect you. If that is your proposition, then I ought not to take up more of your time. Friends don't behave like that, as if one is some noble martyr and the other a bumbling incompetent. Family certainly doesn't behave that way—my family doesn't—and I cannot imagine a marriage on such terms."

The plants lay about them in dirty disarray, roots exposed, pots half full of soil, a general mess. This was not the genteel drawing-room proposal Sycamore had aspired to, but that performance would have been wrong for the conversation he needed to have with Jeanette.

This was the discussion he and Jeanette needed to have, or at least begin. A discussion of trust and expectations, rather than hearts, flowers, and empty poetry.

JEANETTE HAD PLANNED CANDLELIGHT, excellent vintages, superb cuisine, and an intimate dining parlor for her next encounter with Sycamore. Instead, she was sitting on the floor in the foyer, where any footman might come upon them, dismembered plants creating a spectacular mess.

And Sycamore wanted to talk about... Jeanette could barely fathom the question he was asking.

"Of course I sought to protect you," she said. "The Coventry is all you have, and Beardsley could have wrecked its reputation as surely as if you'd turned up drunk at Almack's. At the time I refused your proposal, I thought Beardsley—or Viola—was willing to nearly kill me to bring me to heel."

Though Beardsley hadn't been the sum of Rye's troubles apparently, merely a badly timed makeweight.

Sycamore leaned his head back against the wall and closed his eyes. He was a strikingly attractive man, and also toweringly unhappy—with her. His posture was one of weary defeat, and that was Jeanette's fault.

"As the threat to you increased," he said, "your determination to bear your troubles alone also increased. Do I have that right?"

"I could not risk that you..." Jeanette stopped, marshaled her courage, and tried again. "What if you abandoned me too? What if you decided that a woman you married in well-intended haste—a difficult, barren widow with a pack of lying, impecunious in-laws—was a mistake? I was the girl child my father never needed, the sister Rye considered a pest, the wife who'd failed her lordly husband, the step-mother of no particular use... I am good for little more than making up numbers at house parties and managing charities. What if you rode to my rescue and then cast me off, Sycamore?"

Jeanette drew her legs up to wrap her arms around her knees. "I could not bear your polite tolerance, could not bear to become another woman wishing you hadn't tired of her. To know I had become a burden to you would break my heart."

The floor of the foyer was cold and hard, like the floor of a prison cell, nothing of softness or comfort to be had. The silence stretched as Jeanette's heart did break. She had betrayed Sycamore's trust, and still he had come uninvited to avert disaster.

"Say something," Jeanette muttered. "Get up and leave, tear up my invitation, but don't simply sit there wishing you hadn't paid this call."

"Say something." Sycamore scrubbed a hand over his face. "Right. Very well. Here is what I have to say: In what strange and forbidding world are women only lovable if they are perfect? Am I perfect, Jeanette?"

"You very nearly are, to me."

"You are being polite and I am far from perfect. And yet, you sent me a dinner invitation, suggesting that even with my myriad flaws—my big mouth, my horde of siblings, my flair for blunt speech, my vanity, and on and on—I am somehow desirable company. Do you expect perfection of me?"

"No. I expect you to be yourself."

"How fortunate for me, because I can be none other than who I am. You, however, expect yourself to be..." He flung a hand toward the ceiling. "A pattern card of self-sufficiency, feminine perfection, never cross or ill-spoken. You are to be an automaton whose knives never bounce off the target. Why, Jeanette? Why put such unreasonable demands on yourself?"

Sycamore hunched forward, drawing his finger through a sprinkling of dirt across the marble squares. "Don't answer that, because I know what you're thinking. If you are perfect enough, mannerly enough, smart enough, charming enough, maybe somebody will love you, or at least stick by you for a time. Well, I'm not perfect either, Jeanette. I badly bungled my first offer of marriage to you, and I am probably bungling this one too."

Jeanette wiped her fingers across her cheek. "You're not bungling, Sycamore." He wasn't leaving, and at that moment, not leaving counted for everything.

"Yes, I am, because what matters is that I love you. I love you, *I love you*. I worry for you, I desire you. I want to know what you think of every stupid article I read in the paper. I want to consult you on all the petty annoyances that come up at the club. I quote you to my brother, and his wife likes you already. All the wives do. They vote by letter. I will soon descend into spouting gibberish, but I want you to grasp one thing before I do."

Jeanette wiped away another tear. "You love me."

"I absolutely do, and I should have told you that. I should have been honest about my sentiments and begged you to humor me enough that we could sort through Beardsley's foolishness together. I am proud, though, and I worry too much, so instead I flung a proposal at you like I hurl my knives. Badly done of me, but here's the thing: We will disappoint each other, Jeanette. We already have disappointed each other. Perhaps to love is to be disappointed. God knows

I've disappointed my family, and they regularly vex me, but that's not what matters."

Jeanette took his hand, though both of them had dirt in the creases of their palms. "What matters, Sycamore?"

"To love anyway. I will get it wrong again, Jeanette. I will speak intemperately or say something ill-advised about your favorite bonnet. You will criticize a play I adore, and we will bicker and make up, and feud and stumble. But I know this about myself: I will love you madly through it all and count it my greatest blessing if you can love me too."

Jeanette tried to think, to find logic in what Sycamore said, to make his words fit a new definition of herself—as a woman who was loved, flaws and all—but her mind was not up to the challenge.

"You want me to trust you, to trust *us*."

"I am begging you for the chance to deserve your trust, and I am freely offering you mine."

She cuddled close, and Sycamore looped an arm around her shoulders. "You unnerve me, Sycamore Dorning. You utterly unnerve me."

He sighed and something soft brushed Jeanette's temple. "Well, thank God for that. I wouldn't want to be the only person in this foyer feeling witless and muddled."

"You are witless and muddled, and perfect, Sycamore."

He bent near. "Say that again."

A deep, quiet joy came over Jeanette, a letting-go of old sorrows and a welcoming of new challenges. "I said I love you, Sycamore Dorning. I love you, *I love you*."

He scooped her into his lap and gathered her close, and then nobody said anything—with words—for the next little while.

EPILOGUE

"I cannot understand her French," Tavistock said, sounding slightly dazed, "but she is so earnest about it, I feel I must try."

"Have another glass of champagne," Sycamore said. "Tabitha is equally voluble in English, Latin, and German. We are hoping as my niece matures, her verbal engines acquire some lower gears." Though not just yet.

Casriel had decreed there was to be a massing of his troops in London for Sycamore and Jeanette's wedding, and thus Tabitha had been hailed from school, the infants rounded up, and the countess given field marshal responsibilities.

Valerian and Emily had arrived a week ago, claiming Valerian needed to meet with his publisher, and Emily needed to do some shopping. In that regard, she was abetted by Jacaranda and Della, while Margaret—wife to Hawthorne—was making an inspection tour of London's apothecaries and herbals.

Penweather and Daisy had also come up to Town, in separate coaches from separate abodes, but they had already acquired the look of a settled couple, and Penweather certainly exhibited paternal patience with Daisy's brood. Oak and Verity, Penweather's neighbors in Hampshire, had journeyed with him to Town as well.

Even Willow and Susannah had torn themselves away from their rural pursuits, the requisite wedding mastiff trotting at Will's heels. Susannah had disappeared with Della and Verity to make a circuit of their favorite bookshops, and they'd dragooned Jeanette into joining them.

The wedding, a quiet ceremony at the Dorning town house, had been attended by every Dorning to which Sycamore could claim a near relation. Tavistock and Goddard had stood up with the bride, and—in a gesture of goodwill Sycamore would not have thought to offer—Jeanette's nieces and nephew had also been invited.

The wedding breakfast was held at the Coventry, which showed to good advantage when full of loud, happy Dornings. The staff looked happy too—extra wages were always cause for joy—and Sycamore had given orders that Goddard's excellent champagne was to flow freely in the kitchen too.

"She's quite lovely," Casriel said, taking the place on Sycamore's right. "Your marchioness, that is. Has an air of friendly dignity about her."

"She has a head for numbers," Ash added from the right. "Always a fine quality in a woman."

Hawthorne, who had made the supreme sacrifice of pulling himself away from his acres in springtime, peered over Sycamore's right shoulder.

"She's good with children," he rumbled. "Margaret noticed that right away."

"Well-spoken," Valerian added from Ash's right. "Likes books and doesn't babble. I could listen to her speak French all day."

Willow, holding a flute of champagne, gazed over Sycamore's left shoulder. "The pup likes her. No more need be said, though Susannah also claims Jeanette has excellent literary tastes."

A double endorsement, coming from dear Willow.

"I will come back to Town to do your wedding portrait," Oak offered, passing around a plate of sandwiches. "Or we might stay for a time. The children enjoy London, and they should get to know their cousins."

"They should get to know Uncle Sycamore and Aunt Jeanette," Sycamore countered. "We intend to bide in Town for much of the year, so you will all send us your offspring from time to time. Jeanette will insist upon it. She thinks having a huge family is wonderful."

Casriel munched a sandwich and surveyed the chattering, laughing, happy throng who had long since abandoned mealtime decorum to move about, talk across the table, and otherwise turn a breakfast into a celebration.

"You don't think a huge family is a blessing?" he asked.

Jeanette was across the room, one of Casriel's infants perched on her hip. Daisy and the countess were in discussion with her, but as if she'd known her husband—*her husband*—gazed upon her, Jeanette looked up, smiled, and blew Sycamore a kiss.

"Smitten," Hawthorne muttered.

"Besotted," Valerian added.

"Top over tail," Oak said, and thus the roll call went.

"Of course I love my wife," Sycamore said. "I love even saying that: I love my wife. She loves me too, and I love saying that as well."

"We meant," Hawthorne said, taking a tray of glasses from a waiter and passing the drinks out, "she is smitten with you."

Casriel held his glass up. "Papa always said when it came to his children, practice made perfect, and the best was saved for last. Jeanette is apparently of the same opinion. To the best, truest gentleman, and to many years of happiness with your lady."

Sycamore took a sip of champagne before his brothers thumping him on the back could cause him to spill his drink. "Papa said that?"

"I wanted to hit him for it," Casriel replied. "He was doubtless only saying it to goad me, but his ploy worked. I became the best gentleman I could be, and thus Beatitude holds the same opinion about me that Jeanette holds about you. Dornings aren't wealthy by the world's standards, we can't command a great deal of consequence, and we will never be a motivating force in government, but we are a happy family and I defy you to name me a greater blessing."

Being Jeanette's husband qualified, though that was probably the sine qua non of a happy family.

"Uncle Sycamore." Daisy's youngest, little Chloe, tugged on Sycamore's hand. "You have to come. Auntie Jeanette says you must."

This provoked much hooting and laughter from Sycamore's brothers, also many understanding smiles.

"Then I must away to my lady's side," Sycamore said, passing Casriel his glass. He let Chloe lead him by the hand to Jeanette, plucked the baby from her grasp, and passed the child back to her mother. "My lady, you summoned me?"

Jeanette took his hand. "I did. Oak is asking when we will sit for our portrait, and her ladyship suggested we make a wedding journey to Dorsetshire by way of Hampshire."

"A royal progress?" Sycamore replied.

Casriel's wife tucked the baby against her shoulder. "We can't get to know your bride if she doesn't spend time with us, Sycamore. Ash can look after the Coventry for a few weeks—he owes you that—and you and Jeanette can make your calls on family. Susannah would love to have some company too."

Beatitude went on speaking, extolling the virtues of touring the English countryside in spring, while Sycamore looked to Jeanette.

He still had to pinch himself every time he realized that he beheld not simply the magnificent, passionate female who had stolen his heart, but *his wife*. His to love and cosset and build a future with, his to strut and stumble through life with.

Jeanette squeezed his hand, all the while appearing to attend to the countess's diatribe. Across the room, the brothers were watching, silent for once, and smiling at him as if they'd always known he would do them proud. They raised their glasses again to Sycamore, and while he did not feel as if he were the last true gentleman to bear the Dorning name, he certainly knew himself to be the happiest.

Then Jeanette kissed him, in front of his whole, whooping, cheering, laughing family, and he was happier still.

Made in the USA
Columbia, SC
22 December 2021

52601699R00154